FORESEEN

Mary R.B. Greco

*To Marie
with Love
Mary Greco

Sept 30 - 2023*

 FriesenPress

One Printers Way
Altona, MB R0G 0B0
Canada

www.friesenpress.com

Copyright © 2023 by Mary R.B.Greco
First Edition — 2023

All rights reserved.

No part of this publication may be reproduced in any form, or by any means, electronic or mechanical, including photocopying, recording, or any information browsing, storage, or retrieval system, without permission in writing from FriesenPress.

ISBN
978-1-03-915605-0 (Hardcover)
978-1-03-915604-3 (Paperback)
978-1-03-915606-7 (eBook)

1. FICTION, HISTORICAL

Distributed to the trade by The Ingram Book Company

This story is dedicated to my beloved husband, Greg.
Your sustainable love, devotion, and constant encouragement
inspired me to write this story.
My eternal thanks, Greg, for all we shared,
and mostly for loving me so completely unconditionally.

PROLOGUE

To my readers, I ask you two questions that are at the core of this story: Do you believe life is predestined for us? Or do our choices and actions determine our future? For Violet, a poor fifteen-year-old girl living in a small remote town in the South of Italy in 1951, the first option seemed true for her. Life seemed inevitable and definitely laid out for her.

As we are not omnipotent, Violet's worse day turned out to be the beginning of her new life.

CHAPTER 1

HUMILIATION

Rising before first light every morning was Violet's harsh reality. Since the age of twelve her father, Ornesto, had demanded she get up at five a.m. and go with him. Together they walked to their small parcel of land at the edge of town. There, the unfortunate child was made to do most of the chores. Her father decided what she needed to get done—usually jobs he'd rather not do himself.

In only two short months, Violet would turn fifteen. On this particular morning, the girl had an overwhelming feeling of dread about her upcoming birthday and future.

"You must get everything done before we leave for Olivera," her father commanded.

His cheerfulness made Violet's spirit sink even lower. It was Ornesto, her own father, who had conjured up and arranged this fateful trip to the neighboring town. The time had come to "seal the deal" with the Torantino family.

Violet's mother, Maria, had pleaded with her husband. "Please don't go through with this, look at our Violet, she is just a child." Sadly, it was to no avail.

Ornesto insisted his word was gold. "I will not dishonor myself or my family."

It did not matter he was in a sleazy tavern, leaning drunk over a soiled table, when he pledged to the agreement. His eldest daughter, Violet, would be the wife of one of Lorenzo Torantino's six sons.

"We shook hands," he spat, trying to sound honorable. But there was no honor in what he was doing, just greed. Ornesto believed having a son-in-law from a wealthy family would lend him physical and financial help. The sooner he married off his daughters to prime prospects, the better for him.

Today was the day. Violet's father promised the elder Torantino he would bring his daughter to their house. There his sons could inspect and decide which one of them would pick her as his bride.

Maria tried to reassure Violet by saying, "Sometimes, things happen for a reason." But it was hard to be convincing when holding back tears. Her husband's greedy demands had overpowered Maria's giving nature. She loved and cared for all her seven daughters and was expecting another child in three months.

Ornesto grumbled indignantly to all in the village. "It too will be a girl because my wife hates me." This was one demand he could not control and achieve from her. His misplaced pride left him disappointed, blaming Maria every time she gave birth to another daughter instead of a son. This was heart-wrenching and humiliating to a loving mother. His ranting abuse, for a lack of a son, infested every aspect of their family life. The villagers pitied Maria, which was the last thing she wanted.

Ever since Violet had been old enough to pray, she had asked God to give her father a son, believing it would put an end to the family's problems. She could not understand why her father was cruel to them, since they all tried so hard to please him.

Maria would constantly tell her daughters they were her blessings, her "precious flowers." Her passion for nature's beauty inspired Maria to name her seven daughters after her favorite flowers. While tucking them in bed at night, Maria would tell her girls of the garden she left behind when she married their father. "I am the luckiest mother in the world to have such a perfect garden right here," she would boast, collecting them all in her arms.

Maria's loving reassurance sustained her daughters. Violet, in particular, nurtured herself with her mother's encouraging words when she needed them most.

Ornesto had manipulated Maria into marrying him. His deceitful true character was exposed shortly after he was told Maria would not be inheriting her family's ocean-view house. His warped sense of entitlement and self-absorption contributed to his laziness.

Maria, devastated by her failed marriage, had but one recourse. She promised her husband, "I will be an obedient wife, as God would want me to be, but the first time you lay a hand on any of us, I will leave and never return."

She had confided all this to her daughters, assuring she would protect them. "If ever your father strikes any one of you," she warned, "let me know." She feared his uncontrollable temper would lead to serious damage to her delicate flowers. This a loving mother would never allow.

Unfortunately, they had to tolerate his verbal abuse. The marriage vows, "till death do us part," had to be honored. Ornesto had no doubt Maria meant every word and gave his promise, fully aware he had gotten the better deal.

"There is no time for nonsense, let's go," Ornesto growled at the mother and daughter, displeased with their show of affection.

Maria immediately hugged Violet, whispering, "Be strong my child." Both were sadly aware this battle had been lost. "We'll speak more tonight; I will make his favorite meal," she promised, winking.

CHAPTER 2

THE FATEFUL DAY DAWNS

It was very humid. The early morning dew made it seem as though it had rained all night, however! the storm had still to come. Tending to the pig was always Violet's first chore. While it fed, she would shovel the manure and lay new straw in the pigsty. Alone, the child was made to plant all the tomatoes and bean seeds her father gave her. All the while, Ornesto slept under his favorite tree. This ancient decaying tree had been his place of repose for years. He did as little as possible, ordering his family to do most of the work. This was the reason Violet was forced to get up at five a.m. Ornesto deviously and cleverly wanted the townspeople to think he did the work and to never suspect the extent of his laziness. Maria tried to minimize her daughters' workload when she could. Being pregnant most of the time made it very difficult. Meanwhile, Ornesto did only what he wanted. He demanded respect and blind servitude from his family.

By eight a.m., a well-rested Ornesto hollered at his soiled daughter to wash with the cold water from the bucket. He ordered the child to put on the dress her mother had made and tossed a pair of second-hand shoes at her to wear. Ornesto abusively made clear his motive for purchasing the broken-down shoes. "I don't want to be embarrassed by your appearance," he snarled at her.

Violet's small body had not yet developed. Completely flat chested, without an ounce of fat, she looked more like a twelve-year-old child than a potential bride. Her black, wavy hair, inherited from her mother, framed her pretty porcelain face, highlighted by big, almond-shaped, emerald eyes.

Ornesto looked annoyed, almost disgusted with her, which was nothing new. Violet had been barely five the first time he looked at her that way. Her mama had walked in, lamenting about a rose thorn stuck in her finger. Violet had innocently asked, "Is a rose thorn bigger than the 'Ornesto-thorn' Aunt Margaret complains Mama has in her side?" It was then her father had called her a stupid girl and stared at the child in disgust. This belittling was now a permanent look, directed not only towards Violet but also her sisters.

This morning the unreasonably crude demands on Violet were even more severe. "Take off your new shoes and start walking," he shouted down at her while sitting comfortably on the donkey.

Ornesto had perfected his deceptive ways over the years. He never exposed the extent of his abuse around witnesses. The moment they entered the Town of Olivera, he jumped off the animal. He then ordered Violet to put on her shoes and sat the child on the donkey. Regrettably, the indignant man would not stop his verbal attack. His words were always bitter and insulting. "I'm sacrificing myself so you worthless girl will look well rested." The daughter was so exhausted despite her father's ranting, she dozed off. Her slightly bent little body loosely swayed in rhythm with the donkey's stride.

A short time had elapsed when the child was awakened by Ornesto's loud voice ordering her to get down. They were now in view of the Torantinos' old, grey farmhouse. As they approached, the child became intimidated by the huge, weird-looking stone structure. In Violet's vivid imagination, the strange angles of the house resembled a big, hungry monster with extended arms ready to grab her. Horrified, the girl hesitated, reluctant to continue. Considering her two choices, the frightened child bravely forged ahead. The monster walking behind her was definitely more terrifying.

CHAPTER 3

INNER STRENGTH

The woman who opened the front door caused Violet to stumble backwards. Her enormous size was intimidating, but it was her manly moustache that shocked Violet. Instantly the girl cast her wide eyes downward to keep from staring at her potential mother-in-law.

"Welcome," the woman said, moving from the door, allowing them space to enter.

The two guests stepped into a warm room saturated with the smell of herbs and spices. Violet sniffed in the aroma with puppy-like pleasure. In the center of the room was a large rectangular table overflowing with food. The hungry child's mouth began salivating. The display was so inviting she temporarily forgot the reason for their visit.

"Lunch!" yelled out the huge woman. The abrupt roar startled the child and caused the father to jump. Ornesto clumsily bumped into Mrs. Torantino, barely nudging the woman but almost knocking himself down.

In a matter of seconds, the table was surrounded by monstrous men. Their appearance brought to Violet's mind the Bible story of David and Goliath. She decided that, like David, she would also stand her ground.

Despite her father's constant belittlement, Violet was a tough, courageous young girl. There were times she could've let the high waves of insult drown her, but her strong sense of self-preservation kept her afloat. In this awkward situation, she knew she had to dig deeper into her determination for additional confidence. She decided to sit up straight and ignore all the rude stares.

Not one word was spoken until Mr. Torantino commanded, "Let's eat."

The food disappeared so fast; Violet was glad Mrs. Torantino had filled her plate. *"Mangia! mangia!"* the huge woman encouraged the runty child, with empathy in her voice and eyes.

After the meal had been devoured by the famished men, a dead silence filled the room. With a quick roughness, the two older brothers emptied their wine glass, grunted, and left. Of the four remaining brothers, two showed their signs of frustration, while the younger two men seemed amused. They were rudely pretending unsuccessfully to contain their laughter.

Suddenly, a verbal explosion erupted as everyone started speaking at once. Words of disappointment and displeasure were all directed towards the bride-to-be. Violet wondered if all men were mean spirited as her father.

Mrs. Torantino stood up, and in a determined tone, yelled out just one command. *"Basta!"* Instantly, the room went silent. No doubt she had given this order many times before. With the same loud voice, she added, "I will handle this."

Mrs. Torantino's index finger summoned Violet to stand in front of her. She shook her head as she studied the slim child. Stroking her chin in judgement, she pondered over this obviously hopeless situation. With little conviction and a softer tone, she said, "Let's see what the girl can do." Pointing at a crate full of wood next to the stone fireplace, the matriarch commanded, "Go! Bring that crate to me!" Violet quickly obeyed, walking towards the fireplace, and bending over to pick it up. With all her strength, she was unable to budge it, not even an inch. The crate of wood felt as if it were cemented to the floor. It might as well have been a mountain for poor Violet. Mortified, her face blushed, revealing the obvious to Mrs. Torantino and the men in the room. She had failed her first task.

The robust woman again directed the child to come stand before her. She balanced a basket on the girl's head and proceeded to fill it with potatoes. "Let's see how much weight you can actually carry."

In preparation, Violet tried with all her might to stiffen her legs and upper body. As the weight increased, she staggered and seconds later fell to the floor in a seated position.

An avalanche of potatoes bounced on her shoulders, then on her lap, and rolled onto the floor. Not one person moved an inch to help. They seemed to be mere spectators, watching a show. With condescending laughter, all four brothers in the room rudely mocked her.

Humiliated but not defeated, Violet quickly stood as tall as she could, almost on her toes. Disastrously, the defiant attitude from the child amused the rude men. They pointed their fingers at her and laughed even louder.

Mrs. Torantino's eyes speared Ornesto. "Take this child home to her mother."

Violet lowered her head, not wanting to look at anyone, especially her heartless father. Her shame and embarrassment were his fault. His thoughtlessness and greed had done this, but it would be her failure, and the entire family would suffer.

Mr. Torantino harshly reprimanded the girl's father. "You are delusional, Ornesto, if you believe this little creature would be a fitting wife to any one of my sons! How dare you even suggest such a possible union? Look at my Emily!" he boasted, wrapping his muscular arms around half his wife's thick middle. "This is the kind of woman my sons deserve, strong and healthy".

Ornesto, unflinching, was still determined to seal the deal. "Give her a few months; she will get bigger and stronger."

His arrogance sparked a groan of disapproval among the men in the room.

Mrs. Torantino remained silent, shaking her head, and closely studying Violet. In a hasty manner, the woman advanced towards the child, grabbed her sleeve, and marched her towards a separate room. Everyone was bewildered, but no one dared question Emily.

In the privacy of what seemed to be a storage room, the big woman exposed a slight smile, softening her whole demeanor. She sat on a low wooden chest to get the face-to-face intimacy she wanted with the girl.

"My dear child." Emily spoke softly, looking directly into Violet's big, green eyes. "If inner strength and beauty were what my sons needed, you would be a Torantino bride tomorrow." Before saying more, she paused to take Violet's hands. There is a courageous spirit inside you, don't let anyone ever take that away from you. Especially that brute of a man that should have never been a father!"

Astonished by the woman's candid words, Violet stared at her, not knowing how to react.

"I can see." Emily's serious expression confirmed her intuitiveness of Ornesto's cruelty. "You, my child, have been bruised many times, but! You must hold on and stay steadfast." Emily's message was precise and given with sympathy.

Violet reacted by lowering her head, partly in shame, mostly in disbelief. These kind words of encouragement from a stranger surprised her, nicking at her tender heart. Looking at Mrs. Torantino's face now, Violet dismissed her moustache and was drawn to the gentleness in Emily's eyes.

Sensing an understanding between them, the large woman hugged the child. "I'll prepare some supplies for you to take home."

Violet accepted Mrs. Torantino's act of kindness. These gifts were intended to calm Ornesto, lessening his disappointment, and hopefully his abuse.

"*Grazie, grazie.*" The child whispered, meekly demonstrating she was undeserving. To further show her gratitude for all the support and generosity, Violet hugged Emily even tighter.

CHAPTER 4

A LONG WAY HOME

By mid-afternoon, the reprimanded man and the humiliated child were ready to leave the Torantino's home. The lady of the house had been more than generous. She had her sons load the donkey as much as possible.

"All this is for your daughter's courage," Emily made sure to point it out to the callous father. She added, "I'd like to smack some sense into that stupid head of yours."

Ornesto held his tongue, aware the woman could easily knock him down with one slight blow. He didn't give any sign of remorse, simply nodded grudging. Taking the reins of the over-loaded donkey, Ornesto's stride demonstrated he'd never admit doing anything wrong. Violet didn't miss her cue as he started the trek home. Quickly, she scurried to his side.

At the outset, they traveled in silence. Violet was engulfed, with the unmistakable calm before the inevitable storm. She anticipated rain would soon pour down in more ways than one. Once out of the Torantino's sight, Ornesto would heap abuse on her.

He stopped the donkey, lifted a heavy bundle, and threw it at her. "Useless, useless girl! You didn't even try!"

"Yes, father, I really did try." she pleaded, grabbing the huge potato sack, knowing this was her punishment.

Ornesto's angry expression revealed to Violet he believed she alone was responsible for ruining his plan. Squeezing himself onto the donkey, he kicked the beast hard, deliberately putting distance between them. Violet was left to trudge further behind.

Unable to contain themselves any longer, the blackish clouds burst with a vengeance. Violet's thin dress wasn't much protection from the stinging downpour. Chilled and shivering, she ran to her father, grateful the donkey had slowed considerably.

"Father," she pleaded, "may I have my shawl? My new dress might get ruined." She purposely mentioned caring for the dress, hoping at least that would matter to him.

Ornesto looked up from under his protected rain cover to throw the child her shawl. To the right side of the road, he noticed the most magnificent automobile he had ever seen. "Those people are visitors and appear in trouble." He stated the obvious aloud. "I'll ask if they need my help."

Violet knew what attracted her father was the allure of the automobile, not real concern for the strangers' well-being. Besides, what knowledge did he have of auto repair? The only vehicle he had ever ridden in and been close to was his cousin's Lambreta. Nevertheless, she was grateful for the distraction. It meant she could rest before the climb up the steep hill leading home.

She had conflicting feelings about the homecoming. On one hand, she could not wait to run into her mother's comforting arms. On the other hand, she knew her father would be impossible to live with. She felt remorse for bringing even more hardship on her family. Her only recourse was to work even harder for them.

Relieved the rain was temporarily taking a break, Violet decided to do the same. Unaware how long her father would be, she decided to use the potato sack as a stool. Her weary body was not yet positioned when she spotted a loaded, two-wheel vegetable wagon speeding down the hill. She had heard of mischievous boys enjoying pulling pranks like this. They would remove the well-placed brake-stone from behind the wheels of a parked wagon, just for some excitement. Carts hurtling uncontrollably down a steep hill rendered them deadly. Violet knew to stay clear and wanted to move even further from the potential danger.

CHAPTER 5

SELFLESS AND HEROIC

As she bent to grab her potato sack, Violet noticed a small boy running aimlessly. He was literally heading into the mortal wagon's path. Instantly, she dropped the sack, and with sheer determination conjured her last ounce of strength and ran. Without a thought to her own safety, she dashed and grabbed the boy from harm's way. The impact caused both bodies to fall backwards, mere seconds before the wagon sped by them. It continued with increasing speed until it smashed into a barrier. Regrettably, the barrier happened to be the tail end of the luxurious automobile. The collision overturned the wagon, quickly dispersing its load. An array of vegetables bombarded the once shiny vehicle. This unexpected infraction happened so quickly, Ornesto and the tourist stood stunned. They were oblivious to the real tragedy that had been averted seconds earlier.

In the rescue, Violet had banged her elbow, but she immediately shook off the pain. Her concern was for the child. She patted him gently, hoping none of his bones were broken from her aggressive tackle.

The boy was small in stature, with blond hair and blue eyes. He was dressed like a cute boy doll Violet had once seen in a magazine photograph. He wore short pants and matching tweed coat and cap. Violet presumed he was about six years old.

An elegantly dressed woman, breathing heavily, knelt and clutched the boy to her bosom. She had obviously witnessed the rolling cart and had run to save the child herself.

"I'm good, Mommy." The boy would not be contained; he was energized and enthusiastic. "Did you see? This girl saved my life!" He pulled away from his mother and hugged Violet tightly.

The woman grabbed both children in her arms and let out a sigh that came from the depths of her soul. In a trembling whisper she repeated, *"Grazie, grazie."* She then slowly collected herself and checked each child to ensure neither one was injured.

Satisfied both children were fine, she spontaneously reached for her purse. Opening its latch, the lady grabbed a hand full of money and handed it to the girl.

Violet placed her hands behind her. "NO! *Signora.*" She firmly refused the money; happy her father was not in hearing distance.

"Please, you deserve a reward, my dear," the lady insisted, speaking in broken Italian.

Again, Violet was adamant. *"Grazie,* but no." She shrugged. Her action to save the boy had been nothing more than the right thing to do.

The owner of the runaway wagon was screaming in his native dialect. "All the saints in heaven help me." The vendor was also unaware of how much more tragic his day might have been.

Violet heard her father angrily yelling out her name. She stiffened but then relaxed to smile at the boy. He grabbed her hand as she started to leave.

"What is your name?" he asked, which his mother repeated in Italian.

"Violet Conti," she said and kissed him on his head.

"Grazie, Violet," he said, staring into her eyes, then hugged her again even more tightly.

Violet then found the misplaced potato sack and ran with it to her father.

Ornesto was still in a foul mood. "Where were you hiding? I almost got killed!" he exaggerated. "I am wet and exhausted. We must hurry home before the downpour starts again. I don't want to be around in case the *polizia* starts asking questions." His last statement revealed the real reason for his quick departure.

"Father." Violet wanted to tell him what had happened, hoping he might be tempered, just a bit. The child's hopes were short-lived. The father, as unusual, demonstrated a total disinterest in anything she had to say.

He began chastising her. "You don't listen, you never listen. Keep your mouth shut when I am speaking. I don't want to get involved in other people's problems." He stomped off towards the donkey and mounted it. Ornesto kicked the poor animal so hard its cry could be heard from the house.

CHAPTER 6

THE HERO REWARDED

Maria anxiously awaited their return. She had promised Violet she would prepare Ornesto's favorite meal, hoping to persuade him to rethink the Torantinos' arrangement.

Standing on their front door watching their arrival, Maria was not surprised. Ornesto, on the donkey, looked refreshed, while her poor child staggered behind totally exhausted. What she didn't expect was the furious look on her husband's face. She allowed only her eyes to question Violet. The daughter's expression told the mother things didn't go as he had planned. Maria never asked her husband what happened or why he was angry. Ornesto would always scream out all his disappointment and frustration to his family.

The dinner table was his yelling arena. No matter how the day went, he'd complain about someone or something. Ensuring his family enjoyed a quiet meal was never a consideration for the man. On the other hand, his complaints apparently gave him a big appetite. Between his ranting, Ornesto always ate more than his share of the meal.

This particular evening Ornesto criticized more than usual. He accused Violet of deliberately sabotaging a match with any one of the Torantino brothers. "She brought shame on me and all my ancestors," he kept repeating, banging his fist on the table.

Everyone was so preoccupied with his abusive reprimand, the knock on the door was ignored. It took Rosa, the second-oldest daughter, a few minutes before she dared to whisper, "There's someone at the door, Father. Should I answer it?"

"Of course! You stupid girl!" he barked.

A tall man in a dark blue suit stood on the other side. He respectfully held his cap in hand, revealing his light brown hair. *"Buona sera,"* he said, then introduced himself in perfect Italian. "My name is Albert. I am Mr. Suttons' chauffeur."

"Come in," Maria invited, motioning for her daughter, Delia, to move and give the man her chair.

Violet noticed her father tensing up. They both remembered this man from the auto accident earlier that day. Ornesto intentionally looked away not wanting to show any signs of recognition.

"I am here on a delicate matter. My employer—"

Before he could continue, Ornesto interrupted. "I do not want to get involved. I am a very busy man."

"I have no doubt." The chauffeur's strong yet calming voice politely continued. "I am sure you are, sir, but this matter concerns your daughter, Violet Conti. I have been asking around town and was directed here." Albert obviously had no recognition of the intended girl. He gave a curious smile towards the several young girls intensely watching him.

Ornesto yelled directly at the one sitting next to him. "What did you do now?"

Instantly, Albert gave Violet a warm, appreciative smile. "Your daughter saved my young master from being crushed by that runaway vegetable wagon today. She, sir, saved my master Edward's life!"

The room fell oddly silent. Even Ornesto was confused, and for the first time ever, speechless.

"I have come here on behalf of my employer," Albert continued in a professional tone. "Mr. and Mrs. Sutton have been considering hiring a companion for their only son. Following the events of today, they would like to hire your daughter to accompany and watch over their young son." Albert spoke slowly, wanting to be clear, hoping the parents understood what he was proposing.

Mama and sisters immediately responded by taking turns proudly hugging Violet, admiring her heroic deed. Ornesto was unusually silent but nervously tapping one foot.

He then gave an arrogant grunt before responding to Albert. "I must think about this, after all, Violet is my oldest and dearest daughter." He looked as though calculating what this arrangement potentially would bring to him financially.

Albert's responds seemed as calculating as the other man in the room. He looked straight at Ornesto as he answered. "Sir, I respect and totally understand how difficult it is to allow your daughter to be employed in a different country. The Suttons have already left; they are on their way to Naples. Tomorrow evening, they travel back to England. Although they have interviewed a few other, frankly more-qualified candidates, they chose your daughter, Violet, on the merits of what happened today. They feel they can trust her."

"Absolutely!" Ornesto jumped in, stopping Albert from saying another word. "My daughter is the best choice!" His voice was now determined. He was afraid that by acting reluctant with this man he might lose this financial opportunity. "Come sit by the fire. Maria, get the man some wine. Alfred, is it? We have a lot to discuss, especially the wages."

Ornesto's last statement insinuated he was willing to let his daughter go work for this rich family. It was evident all that mattered to this father was the sum of money they would now negotiate. The particulars of Violet's employment would be discussed, but she was obviously not a priority or concern.

Violet met her mother's agonized eyes and shared an unspoken recognition of fear. Could this be happening? A distant separation was more than mother and child could bear. Ornesto had made it clear Maria was not included in this decision.

"Come, girls! It is getting late." Maria made an effort to disguise her devastation in front of the stranger. "We must get ready for bed." She was at the brink of screaming out. Violet knew her mama held back; fully aware she would never avert the outcome. Not once in their marriage had Ornesto respected anything she had requested. Both mother and daughter resigned to their fate, as they had earlier that morning. Maria, heavy hearted, was unable to say another word; she simply gestured for all her girls to come.

The family's hesitant march up the stairs resembled a climb to the guillotine. Each one of them were consumed with sadness, knowing their family unit was about to be broken. After tonight, one link would be gone, severed probably forever. Tomorrow, Violet would be on her way to England and her new life.

CHAPTER 7

UNKNOWN JOURNEY

The next morning, the family's routine had changed. Violet was allowed, for the first time in three years, to sleep in. Ornesto was uncharacteristically calm, almost cheerful. He did not concern himself with his family's heartbreak over the imminent departure of the eldest daughter and sister.

"Violet!" (His scolding manner when speaking to her hadn't changed.) "You must do everything you're told. Work hard without complaints. Do not get sent back! Do you hear me? This is a great opportunity for us and you. I have arranged for ALL the money to be wired directly back to me. You will have free room and board from these people. I am your father, and I know what is best."

A nod was all Violet could manage, determined not to let him see her cry. After his self-indulgent goodbye speech, Ornesto left for his stroll around the town *piazza*. No doubt his new financial status now made him feel satisfied and somewhat superior.

In mournful silence, Violet's sisters helped pack her minimal belongings.

Rosa cried out first, "I do not want you to leave. I don't want to be the oldest sister."

All Violet's sisters had benefited from her overprotective nature. There had been many times when she had put herself in the front line and taken their father's abuse on their behalf. "We need you, Violet!" they all cried, clinging to her.

Maria knew she had to put a stop to her children's despair and give them hope. "We must all try to be brave. Violet will still be helping us. The monthly salary will lessen our burden in more ways than one." The children understood their mother's brutal honesty, especially Violet. "She will write every day and tell us about her new life in England," the mother said, wanting to sound encouraging as well as hopeful, to give them all peace, "and about the nice people that have taken her in . . . " Maria almost choked on those unsure words.

Gardenia and Giglia smiled at their mama and skipped around, excited. "We agree, Mama," the girls spoke together, "it is best for our sister to go to England because it's better than having a husband—right, Violet?"

Out of the mouths of babes reality was spoken. The other sisters quickly agreed; having a husband was definitely worse. From what they had witnessed all their lives, no woman with a husband was happy, especially not their mama. Of the two options, going to England now fared best indeed for their big sister.

Violet, always in her mature role, saw the chance to create a cheerful, lasting memory. "Let's make it unanimous!" she said, extending her left arm, palm down. One by one each added their hand on top of the other, with Maria's at the very top. "On the count of three, together," Violet yelled. "We choose England!" The explosion of hands waving upwards helped clear some of their sadness. Laughter filled the room. They all celebrated the moment, wanting to believe they had some control over the sad send-off.

Deep down, they knew their father would not stop with his new quest. It was just a matter of time until Violet would forcefully be married off. Awareness of this fact aided them in their slow acceptance of Violet's fate. If nothing else, it meant no cruel husband!

Violet kissed and hugged each of them, then opened her arms for a big group hug. "Don't forget me," she whispered.

Maria took Violet aside and spoke softly. "Remember you are my child, no matter where you are or what happens. I love you unconditionally. You might not have money, but you are rich in here." Maria put her hand on her daughter's heart. "You love purely and care deeply. You are courageous, my child, and your capabilities are endless. You might feel lonely, but do not ever feel alone. Distance does not erase family. If you ever need me, just send this back." Maria then put in her daughter's hand a medallion of the Madonna. This gift, from Maria's mother on her sixteenth birthday, was now passed on. "I will come and get you, even if I have to stop the world from turning. Violeta, I will be there."

Violet knew if anyone could stop the world, it would be her mother.

CHAPTER 8

HER WORLD CHANGES

Albert, as pre-arranged, drove Violet the five hours to Naples' train station. The Suttons, as he mentioned, had left her small hometown the night before. They wanted to spend a day enjoying Naples' beauty before returning to England. The arrangements were specific: Violet was to meet with the Suttons on board the train, half an hour before its departure time.

The atmosphere at the rail station mimicked Violet's emotions—the heavy rain, chaotic bustle of anxious travelers, and the sad beacon whistle from the train. Understanding her sacrifice would benefit her family financially was the only sustainable reason for this departure. Violet needed to believe this money would stop some of Ornesto's cruelty towards her mother and sisters.

Before leaving her at the station, Albert gave Violet simple instructions: "Make sure you tell the porter you are to meet the Suttons." Both were unaware this was easier said than done.

The train was jammed with aggressive passengers. Violet's inexperience plus her small stature made it difficult to get where she needed to be. Tossed about by rushing crowds, she unwillingly got squeezed onto a bench and seated between two older men.

The one nearest the window had a chicken hidden under his coat. Occasionally it stuck out its head and aggressively pecked Violet's arm.

She was forced to squeeze further to her left. The man she leaned towards, held a basket of smelly cheeses and salami. The combined potent odour caused her to feel nauseous. Before attempting to escape and find the elusive porter, she needed to get relief. She covered her nose and shut her eyes, hoping to settle her stomach.

A loud male voice startled her. "There you are!" yelled an angry porter. He grabbed at her crocheted shawl, crumbling her name tag. "Come with me," he ordered.

Violet obeyed, not caring where he took her. She was happy to get as far as possible from the foul smell.

Extremely agitated, the Italian porter dragged her with him, complaining he had been looking for her for hours. He continued with his exaggeration, adding his frustration with Mr. Sutton, who had given him the specific task of finding her. "Am I supposed to be a mind reader?" he yelled at her while wrestling through the swarm of passengers. He shut his mouth just as he knocked on the Suttons' compartment door. He proceeded to open the door and shove the child inside.

The wide-eyed little boy rushed over and gently took her hand. Violet recognized the lady and assumed the gentleman was her husband. She noticed the compartment was spacious; it had a bed, and the boy's parents were seated comfortably on the window bench. Mr. Sutton stood and greeted her in perfect Italian, "It's my honor to meet such a courageous young lady." He took her hand and gently shook it.

Mrs. Sutton smiled, putting her hand on Violet's shoulder. "*Mia cara*, we appreciate you accepting this unexpected request more than we can say. Edward has not stopped talking about you. He keeps saying your presence will make him feel safe and wants you to be with him at all times." There was a hint of concern in the boy's mother's words. Mrs. Sutton hastened to add, "We hope this arrangement is agreeable to you."

"*Si, si!*" Violet promptly responded, "Edward is *molto carino*." She had to reassure her employers and try sounding mature.

Both parents gave her an approving smile. Mr. Sutton glanced at his watch and announced, "It's getting late." He then turned his gaze towards Violet and assured her, "We will speak more in the morning. Our quarters are beyond this door. If you need anything, knock! Good night precious boy."

Edward kissed his parents goodnight and was quick to close the door behind them.

Giving Violet a big smile, he jumped into bed and motioned for her to join him. She tucked the child in and lay beside him over the covers. The small boy shifted closer to her, making Violet feel warm inside. His cuddling reminded her of her sisters. This needy child was actually fulfilling her needs, giving her back the role of big sister. *How ironic,* Violet thought to herself, *I have a little brother before my father has a son.*

The fifteen-year-old was comfortable in her abilities to be a big sister. She stroked Edward's forehead and sang him a lullaby. Violet was in her element. The two would share this ritual for a long time.

CHAPTER 9

INFORMED AND ACCEPTED

In the morning, voices coming from the Suttons' adjoining compartment awakened Violet. Edward's animated voice radiated through the slightly open door. His parents sounded amused yet calm.

Violet quietly straightened herself up but decided not to interrupt. She sat at the edge of the bed waiting to be summoned. Her mind drifted to the long conversation Albert had had with her. He had been genuinely concerned and showed empathy towards the frightened girl. During the five-hour drive to Naples, he shared information about their mutual employers. He'd tried to reassure her, speaking sincere and honestly. "I know how difficult this sudden change must be for you. I was also a young boy when my father took the position as chauffeur to the Suttons." Albert spoke in his perfect Italian. Sutton Manor, as it was called today, could be traced back five generations. Before that it was owned by a duke. Edward's grandfather, Matthew Sutton, initially built his fortune on supplying goods and services for the military. His great-grandfather, William Lloyd Sutton, had been an admiral in the Royal Navy. The cargo fleet now owned by William Sutton and son operated globally in commodity trades. Eric, the oldest son, was from William's first wife. Sadly, she'd died two years after Eric's birth. William had taken her death extremely hard, pouring himself into his work. He'd traveled extensively, adding enormous wealth to his estate.

He had convinced himself it was all for his son's future. Unfortunately, time spent with the boy was limited. Five years later, after the loss of both his elderly parents, Mr. Sutton reduced some of his traveling. Shortly after, at one of the many business dinner parties, he met Catherine. She had the same caring disposition as his first wife. Mr. Sutton decided to spend even more time at home and with her. Their relationship soon amplified, and the two married a few months later.

As he spoke, Albert observed that his little passenger was appreciative and notably listening. Since they were only halfway to Naples, it prompted him to continue sharing. This, he made clear, was not gossip, but rather Violet's right to feel connected with the Sutton family.

Catherine was the only daughter of a gun manufacturer from America. Her parents had indulged her with the best their money could buy. She was highly educated and a sensible young lady. Her belief in the common good had earned her high esteem. Her caring and giving nature was reflected by the many charities she supported and her countless friends. Her father's numerous business ventures had brought them to England. His motto was: "'Never stand with your arms down! Reach out and grab what you can!"

"It took Catherine seven years to conceive and give William another son. That would be your Edward," said Albert. "Mrs. Sutton," he spoke amiably, "is and always has been a loving stepmother to Eric. She insisted and made sure William spent quality time with them as a family."

Shortly after Edward was born, Eric, then fourteen, had left home to enter private boarding school. He would visit on holidays and spent his summers at the manor. As he got older and had other interests, he returned home less often. Mr. Sutton made time to visit Eric at his school when away on his business trips. At Eric's elaborate twenty-first birthday party, William had announced he was handing over control of their Asian operations to his eldest son.

Violet was so deep in thought recalling all Albert had shared, she was unaware Edward had walked in. The unexpected one-finger poke he gave her shoulder made her jump. They both laughed at her startled reaction. Immediately, Violet composed herself and followed Edward through the adjoining door.

In the larger-than-expected compartment, a table was set with breakfast. As Mr. Suttons' Italian was proficient, he now acted as spokesperson and translator. "Edward is insisting I first tell you how happy he is that he finally found you."

This made no sense to Violet. She presumed it meant Albert was made to look around town to find her. It was understandable at times that words got lost in translation.

"As for us," William said, including his wife by affectionately placing his hand on her shoulder, "words fail us. Our debt to you is unmeasurable. It's impossible to express our profound gratitude to you for saving our son's life. We can only hope to demonstrate it all in time. Sit and eat your breakfast. We have already had ours."

As Violet indulged, Mr. Sutton continued. "Your main purpose is to be Edward's companion and keep him occupied."

"In other words," Catherine said softly, as a loving mother, "care for him and be a good friend."

"We have made a unanimous decision," Mr. Sutton continued. "Since you are merely fifteen, it will be best we introduce you as a distant cousin to our household. Our Edward insisted, and we adamantly agreed you be regarded and treated as one of the family." The father paused and gave Violet a confirming smile. Her selflessness and commitment to their son had integrated her into the family.

Violet stopped indulging on the food and looked in astonishment at the three people who would now be her relatives. Lost for words, her eyes turned to look tenderly at this sweet boy, then she whispered, "*Grazie, carissimo.*"

Edward smiled at her, indicating he understood her meaning.

"My wife will arrange for all your needs. You will not want for anything while living with us. Your father, Mr. Conti, told Albert he wants half of your salary sent to him and the other half put away in your name."

Violet did not speak but knew this arrangement did not come from her father. He'd specifically told her he asked for all the money to be sent to him. She credited Albert for cleverly dealing with Ornesto. This news had her intensely overjoyed. She considered how this extra money, concealed from Ornesto's greedy hands, would actually benefit her mama and sisters.

"Violet." Mr. Sutton enunciated her name slowly, ensuring her full attention. "We need you to be aware of some particularities. Our eight-year-old son is very shy and does not want to play with other children."

This surprised Violet since Edward had been overly affectionate and friendly with her. She noted a bit of hesitation from Mr. Sutton but sensed he had more to reveal. She remained silent, waiting on his readiness. One of the many things her father had pounded into her was to never ask questions. She realized she had been wrong in assuming Edward was only six. It struck her as somewhat amusing that an English boy and an Italian girl had one thing in common: both looked much younger than their actual age.

"Before I divulge more," Mr. Sutton spoke hurriedly, "I want to make it clear I'm now speaking on my son's request. Edward expressed his complete trust in you. He insisted we inform you, without delay, of his difficulties. For the last two years, our son has been tormented by nightmares. As you can well imagine, this has caused us all a great deal of worry. We want you to be aware of this impairment and ask for your understanding when Edward turns to you for help." The father paused, looking at the child he was confiding in, and slowed his speech. "We of course have commissioned many physicians throughout the years, regrettably without success. Some suggested he needs psychiatric help, and his treatment would be better in their clinics. We dismissed those incompetent individuals, threatening to challenge their professional ethics if any of their idiotic diagnoses were publicly repeated. Sadly, my wife and I have not been successful in alleviating Edward's fears." Mr. Sutton sat down next to his wife. He looked drained, as though he had gone through intense labor getting it all said.

Mrs. Sutton had her own comments to add. "You are the first person Edward has shown any interest in years. Imagine our relief!" She sounded exalted. "We now have hope."

Catherine caressed Violet's hands, showing her gratitude. "You saved our son's life, and for that we will be forever indebted to you. Our son's happiness means everything to us. He seems excited and happy with you. Please, Violet, help him!"

Violet understood Mrs. Suttons' plea for help; her own mama would have done the same. However, she had never seen a father show loving emotions before. Mr. Suttons' respecting and listening to his son's request actually exposed his own vulnerability. The constantly abused child was enthralled with the dynamics of this family.

Looking at their little boy, Violet felt an instant tug in her heart. She had experienced some of her own nightmares, but two whole years. How terrifying! She was not sure how she would be able to help, but she was sure she wanted to at least try.

Violet understood the parents' devotion to their son was immense, and they needed reassurance. She had to convince them of her total commitment. "I promise to be Edward's faithful companion and support him completely, at all times. I vow to watch and care for him as long as he needs me." The young girl's words showed a high level of maturity. Her sincerity was absorbed by the parents. Although Edward did not understand what she'd said, he reacted with a smile, cheering and giving them all hope.

CHAPTER 10

VIOLET'S NEW HOME

April's weather did not disappoint. Its duty was to rain, and rain it did. As they entered the London station, the downpour was steady. A dutiful man with a big, black umbrella met them as they stepped down from the train. One by one, he accompanied them into a silver-grey automobile. Except for the colour, Violet thought it looked identical to the one smashed at the side of the road near her hometown.

Edward squeezed next to Violet. She responded by putting her arm around him. Mr. and Mrs. Sutton were amazed with their son's affectionate and uninhibited behaviour.

"Edward, my pet, give Violet some room," Catherine tried to modestly gear her son.

"She's cold, Mommy, I need to keep her warm."

His mother translated her son's concern. Violet gave the boy a grateful smile, wondering how he'd known, if she had shivered. If not, was Edward a mind reader? She was feeling cold in her unseasonably thin clothing.

In less than two hours, they reached the Sutton Estate. Violet had never known anyone could possibly own so much land. The manicured grounds continued for miles up a wide drive. When the manor came into sight, she gasped in astonishment. *"E un castello!"*

Edward was pleased at her reaction and pressed his face next to hers by the window.

Mr. Sutton proudly announced, "Welcome, Violet, to your new home!"

As they approached the manor, Violet continued to praise the family estate with many colourful Italian expressions. The others joined her enthusiasm, appreciating their home anew through her eyes. They pointed to architectural features they had ignored or taken for granted over the years.

The household staff were gathered on the steps to the main entrance waiting to greet and assist the family. Violet was not sure if some were family members, since not all wore uniforms. A distinguished older man promptly opened the automobile door. He welcomed the Suttons home and uttered distinct orders to the others. Immediately, the enthused stuff dashed to their specific duties.

Turning his attention to the young newcomer, the impeccably dressed man greeted her in Italian, "Miss Violet, we are all pleased you have come to stay."

Violet was stunned he knew her name. She was so out of her element; the poor girl did not know how to behave or what to say. It was obvious the Suttons had called in advance to inform him of their permanent new family member.

She desperately wanted to make a good first impression with this very important man. Her mother's words came to mind. "Remember, you will never go wrong by being polite and courteous." Instinctively, she smiled, extended her hand, and asked, "What may I call you?"

"Simon," he said, taking her small hand with a friendly shake, adding, "Betty will assist you, Miss Violet."

In a flash, Betty was at Violet's side, giving her a slight curtsy. *"Vieni,"* she said, smiling. Violet was hesitant to follow Betty. She looked towards Mr. and Mrs. Sutton for permission. They both gave her an agreeable nod, while Edward waved his hand, encouraging her to go.

Foreseen

The young assistant led Violet up the stairs to her room. Betty desperately tried to communicate with her young charge. Unfortunately, her limited Italian vocabulary consisted mostly of verbs: *dorme tu stanco*—"sleep you tired." Violet was pleased with Betty's attempt and understood her meaning; she agreed responding, *"Grazie,* Betty."

CHAPTER 11

EMBRACING HER NEW LIFE

Immediately after Betty left, Violet began gazing at the room and all its beauty. The poor child was bewildered. She twirled in delight, barely holding back her squeals of joy. The soft, turquoise-blue walls with gold, curved trims gave the spacious room elegance she had never known, or even dreamed of. French doors adorned with floor-to-ceiling ivory lace curtains led to a Juliet balcony. The canopy bed was draped with ivory satin fabric, floating down loosely. Its panels gathered and tied at the four posts with matching turquoise and gold tassels. The silk turquoise duvet, framed with a half-dozen silk pillows edged with golden rope, completed the soft, heavenly bed.

In the center of the twenty-foot ceiling was a carved golden medallion vitrine, a Murano chandelier. Its delicate blown glass was also tinged with turquoise. The wall-to-wall armoire had gold leaf carvings that matched the other furniture. On the far right, a large unpolished marble stone fireplace was surrounded by a divan with a velveteen throw and two armchairs, conveying a cozy lounge feeling. Three well-placed multi-coloured Persian rugs crowned the white, veiny marble floor. Violet hesitated to jump on the bed, still in disbelief this magnificent room was actually all for her. In the last few days, her life had turned upside-down. From a poor existence, she had now traveled by train and luxurious automobile to live in a castle.

Never far from her thoughts resonated her mother and sisters. Now more than ever the ache of missing them was even stronger. Her big, broken heart wished desperately they could also share in all this glamour. *How dare I be happy without them.* Violet's guilt ate at her. She found it hard to accept all this luxury and comfort, knowing her family was struggling. She had always been the first to do without, for their sakes. She would pretend she was full and take smaller portions and convince her sisters she really did not like sweets.

The monthly salary they were to receive because of her new position now became more worrisome. Her father's command, "Don't get sent back! Do what you must with no complaints!" echoed in her head.

Violet felt unworthy as well as extra pressure. *What right do I have to be in a place like this? I really don't belong here. I don't deserve all this,* she repeated to herself, over and over. All the insecurities caused by her father's disparagement now haunted her. "I will be obedient and do whatever they ask of me," she vowed. Looking around, Violet took a deep breath and embraced her future. She shamelessly admitted, *It's all so beautiful. I want to stay.* The downside of all this was the longing in her heart for her mama and sisters. From her dismal life's experience, she had learned never to share her sadness. This was her personal burden, and she would bear it alone.

"Violet!" Edward's voice came from one of the doors. He rushed in and grabbed her arm dragging her with him into an adjacent room, which was a magical place full of amazing toys. Undoubtedly, this was Edward's haven.

"Mamma mia!" Violet gasped in astonishment. Her jaw dropped as Edward dashed around showing her his treasures. She was most impressed with the electric train set. It had flashing lights, tunnels, and a model station full of miniature people. She concluded his parents could not decide what to get, so they bought him the entire toy store.

Violet was very cautious, reluctant to touch anything. But Edward insisted she play with all his toys. Eagerly, he put several in her hands. His big smiles and hugs gave her the sense he wanted and appreciated her being in his life. Violet remembered his parents saying he didn't play with other children. *How sad,* she thought, *having all this and no one to share it with.* However, the moment the two jumped on his bed, the exhaustion brought on by the last few days took hold, and both fell sound asleep.

After supper, Mrs. Sutton took Violet to the library to speak with her private. "I have made several phone calls and arranged for some items to be delivered in the morning. You will also be measured for a wardrobe." Violet observed Edward's mother was very efficient and precise in everything she did. She had wasted no time in strategizing and categorizing what needed to get done. Violet's dismal appearance was obviously an embarrassment and a priority.

"I believe preparing schedules is the key to organization and a happy, productive household. I've spent many hours of my time categorizing what needs to be accomplished, and Simon makes sure it all gets done." Mrs. Sutton smiled as she spoke openly to Violet. "Simon is our head butler, and he is indispensable; I depend on him explicitly to manage the staff efficiently. His accuracy has always exceeded my expectations. By seven-thirty tomorrow morning, Simons will have the new schedules. He will promptly rework the staff's duties to ensure whatever is necessary to accommodate my specific time changes."

Mrs. Sutton seemed adamant Violet be aware, understand, and be prepared. "I will introduce you to Miss Kerr; she will be yours and Edward's tutor. She came highly recommended and speaks several languages, including Italian. I can see you are a clever girl. I'm sure you'll have no problem, learning to speak the English language."

"*Si signora,*" Violet promptly answered, hoping to prove her right.

"Miss Kerr has recently joined our staff, replacing Edward's previous governess." A disappointed tone entered Catherine's voice as she added, "We had to discharge her from her position. The governess showed terrible judgement, giving Edward sleeping herbs. They weren't harmful but did cause him to walk around dazed most of the day." With a hint of ambivalence she continued, "She lost our trust; therefore, we couldn't keep her. Our staff is very loyal. Most of them, including Simon, are third generation here at the manor. Even the delusional governess believed she was helping Edward get much-needed sleep."

The sound of the angelic chimes, echoing from the exquisite grandfather clock, had them returning to the parlor. An unexpected anxiousness was now placed on all three Suttons' faces. Violet keenly concluded nine o'clock was their son's regular bedtime.

"Edward." Catherine's voice had never been sweeter, "Remember you told us, you feel safe now that Violet is here." Both mother and father were encouraging the hesitant boy.

"We will be up after Nana prepares you for bed, to tuck you in." Catherine turned to Violet to explained. "Old Nana had been Eric's nanny, and Edward loves her dearly; she'll be supervising him to ensure he prepares for bed properly. For everything else, he prefers and insist only on your company."

Edward understood they were speaking about him and gave them all a faint smile. He silently took Violet's hand, and slowly the two children walked up the stairs.

A loud cry woke and startled Violet from a deep sleep. She sat up in the middle of her huge bed, frightened, confused, and somewhat disoriented. The baffled child tried to make sense of all that had happened to her in the last few days. *I'm alone in a strange place, full of people I do not know.* Nothing made any sense.

The cry came again even louder.

"*Mio Dio!*" Violet gasped as she suddenly realized it came from Edward's adjoining room. Remembering about his nightmares, she instantly jumped out of bed and rushed to his room.

Edward was kicking and struggling with his sheets. Violet tried removing them while soothing him with comforting Italian words. Wrapping her arms around his shaking sweaty body, she kissed and rocked him.

The main door to his bedroom opened. It was the old nanny. "Violet?" she asked, confirming the girl's presence. Nodding her sleepy head at the girl's, *"si,"* the nanny retreated, closing the door.

What just happened? Violet wondered. *Why did Nanny leave? Does she believe me capable of doing this alone?*

Violet did not go looking for answers. She continued caring for the frightened little boy. *"Mio caro,"* she said, holding him tighter in her arms. Comforting a frightened child was actually familiar to Violet, from all the times she'd consoled her sisters.

Edward snuggled like a baby cub in her arms as she softly sang him a lullaby. It didn't take long for her to soothe him to sleep. As fragile as her own small body was, her inner spirit was determined to help this haunted child.

CHAPTER 12

WHAT A BEGINNING

The next morning, as promised, four women with two wardrobe racks and numerous boxes filled with apparel arrived early. Miss Kerr picked up Edward after breakfast. Catherine took Violet for her fitting. The merchandise was laid out in the large study. Young lady attire and accessories had been specifically selected. The enormous room buzzed with zealous women, fussing over their young client. Violet felt like one of her sister's rag dolls, with her limbs lifted and bent at the women's will. Catherine, sitting in a comfortable armchair, would approve or disapprove each item by merely gesturing with her head. Violet was not convinced she liked all the fuss yet was very compliant and mostly appreciative.

At ten-thirty, Esther, one of the more mature and efficient maids, served tea and freshly baked scones. During his school break, Edward joined the ladies. He entertained himself with some items of clothing, even trying on a flowery hat, which received a laugh from the ladies. Catherine didn't indulge, but a broad smile did uplift her face. Watching her son's playfulness with Violet, while calmly sipping her tea, pleased her.

When the room cleared and the assistants were gone, Mrs. Sutton asked Miss Kerr to join her and the children. She wasted no time in laying out her expectations.

"Miss Kerr, I want you to get Violet into a rigorous regiment of English lessons." She spoke in Italian for Violet's benefit. "It is crucial for Edward to be able to communicate his needs to her. It is of the utmost importance you both collaborate on how best to bridge this language barrier." After her verbal instructions to Miss Kerr, Catherine handed the instructor a schedule and dismissed her.

Violet then received her lengthy schedule, prepared in Italian. After reading her list, the girl stood in disbelief—much the same way she had with Mrs. Torantino's kind words. She believed and was prepared to be receiving her specific duties. All that was written on the schedule would benefit and enhance her. It was apparent she would not be doing physical work. The stunned child gave a grateful smiled to Mrs. Sutton as she whispered, *"Grazie per tutto."*

"Violet, my child, it is I that must thank you for being with Edward last night."

The girl had assumed, since no one had mentioned the incident, that it was in line with her duties.

Catherine spoke genuinely. "I hope all this is not too much for you. Mr. Sutton and I would never otherwise thrust this responsibility at you, at such a tender age. It was Edward's insistence that you alone care for him. He made us promise to let you care for his needs, especially with his nightmares. As Mr. Sutton explained, Edward has been distant, secluding himself from everyone, mostly other children. His attachment to you is both incredible and remarkable. You being here has brought hope to us all." The mother's honesty was emotional. She seemed to be holding back tears.

Violet was also surprised with the little boy's attachment to her. Mostly, she was grateful Edward had so much trust in her. She presumed it was because she'd rescued him from the dangerous runaway cart. Violet now needed to establish herself as capable of such personal duties and earn the parents' trust as well. She hoped they would never regret their decision in lavishing her with so much opportunity.

"I am so pleased Edward feels comfortable with me. I want to reassure you and Mr. Sutton that I am comfortable with it all. I know my age is a concern, but being the oldest of six sisters, I promise I know how to be responsible for those younger than me. Edward's needs will always be my first priority."

Mrs. Sutton, warmed by Violet's maturity, smiled. "My dear, I have no doubt. Remember, I saw your unselfishness first hand. We are grateful for your attentiveness to our son. It is important to Mr. Sutton and me that you, in turn, be happy here.

"Thomas, our stable hand, will take you and Edward for a walk through the grounds. He will acquaint you with the horses and choose a suitable one for your riding lessons." Mrs. Sutton looked down at her schedule. "I have an appointment in London and will be leaving shortly."

Violet was understandably intimidated, as well as astounded, by Catherine's generosity. She never dreamed of anyone caring for her well-being. The Suttons' kindness was so foreign to her. She feared disappointing them and making mistakes.

Sensing she had been dismissed, Violet slowly began walking away. She dreaded imposing on Mrs. Sutton in any way, yet she had no choice. Halfway out of the room, she stopped and nervously searched for the right words. "I've written a letter to my mama. May I ask you to whom I should give it?"

Catherine acknowledged the child's reluctance with a smile. "You may go to Simon for any of your needs. And Violet . . . " Catherine walked over to her. "You may always come to me. I am here for you. I am aware this must all be a big adjustment. It will take some time to get used to the many changes. We do understand you will miss your family, but please know we want to make it easy for you. Albert told us your family does not have a phone in their home. If they can arrange to use a public phone, you are welcome to call them."

"*Grazie! Grazie!*" Violet's excitement was evident by the high-pitched squeal in her voice. "I will mention it in my next letter tomorrow."

This changed everything for Violet. To be able to speak to her family and hear their voices was a miracle. For the first time since their separation, her spirits were lifting. Violet was happy.

CHAPTER 13

THE LESSON

As the months passed, the mood at the manor continued to brighten. Edward's cheerful disposition seemed to shift a dark cloud that had hovered over the manor for too long. He still had nightmares, but with Violet's help, his terror was less severe. With each episode, she had managed to calm him more rapidly. His parents were encouraged by their son's restful appearance. He was now playful and more alert. His constant laughter was contagious and brought joyous relief to his parents as well the staff.

Violet's slow grasp of the English language remained a concern. Her understanding of words was remarkable, but she was unable to connect them in a coherent sentence. Something was obviously not working. Mr. Sutton had spoken to his wife, questioning Miss Kerr's abilities as a proper instructor for the children.

Edward had overheard his parents' conversation and planned for a surprise visit to the classroom the next day. He tried to make Violet aware of this. He used specific words; mostly he waved his hands to relay the message. Violet laughed, thinking how common hand gestures were for Italians. They often used their hands to emphasize meaning and give dramatic affect to whatever they were verbally discussing.

It took some doing, but Violet finally deciphered Edward's charade. She felt a sense of contentment knowing the Suttons were not questioning her ability to learn, but rather Miss Kerr's teaching skill. Her father constantly calling her stupid had driven in her a need to prove him wrong. Consequently, Violet had always strived to achieve success in whatever she did.

Intuitively, the Suttons' perception was correct. Miss Kerr had indeed neglected her pupils. She never had lessons prepared in advance and would leave her students every chance she could for her secret rendezvous—a romance with the local veterinarian had developed when the Suttons were away. She had continued indulging secretly even after their return. A while back, Miss Kerr had confided her secret to Violet, asking for her understanding and cooperation. At the time, the young girl had sympathized with her tutor—now, not so much. After all, Mrs. Sutton had been precise in her instructions to her. Nevertheless, Violet also believed their plan to dismiss Miss Kerr was a bit harsh and nonproductive. It brought to her mind an old Italian saying: *Who leaves the old for the new knows what one leaves but not what one may find.* Both pupils felt comfortable with Miss Kerr's personality and her approach, when applied. Violet especially enjoyed being able to converse with her in Italian. What if the next tutor they hired was severe, strict, or worse, a man? No! Violet decided, with Edward's help, they had to try and save Miss Kerr's position.

The next afternoon, in Miss Kerr's usual absences, Violet copied letters on the board while Edward removed his rock collection from the instructor's desk. Putting most of the fossil rocks in his pocket, he appropriately piled English books in their place. They both pulled two tables and chairs to the front, making the classroom look more official and conducive to learning.

It was after three when Miss Kerr entered the classroom to find Mr. and Mrs. Sutton standing over the children at their desk. Luckily for the absent teacher, they had just arrived.

"Miss Kerr," said Mr. Sutton, "we want to know why Violet is not making better progress with her English lessons. We are disappointed with the results of your teaching methods. Violet is obviously a very smart young girl; therefore, the responsibility falls to you." Speaking firmly, he added, "And why were you not in the classroom just now?"

Edward went and stood directly in front of Miss Kerr. Grasping her hand, he pretended to take something from it. "Look, Father! She promised to go collect more fossils for me to study." Edward cleverly showed his parents some rocks he had been holding in his hand.

With an inner sigh of relief, Miss Kerr acknowledged her pupils' performance and gave then both a slight humbling nod. Unprepared, the flustered tutor was unable to speak and stuttered her words. "I will work harder with Violet," she anxiously tried to assure her employers. "You will soon see great results, I promise."

"Miss Kerr, my husband and I expect you to dedicate more time to this language problem—as I adamantly previously requested," said Mrs. Sutton.

"Edward's fossils are the least of our concern," William concluded, leading his wife out the door. He stopped halfway, looking back to give his son a stern look that said, "Stop wasting precious time!"

CHAPTER 14

THE LESSON'S RESULTS

From that day forward, Miss Kerr became the most diligent instructor, determined to keep her position. She had been impressed by her pupils' cleverness and loyalty, constantly praising, and thanking them both. She was grateful and humbled by the fact these two special children cared enough to help keep her position. Her dedication to their learning was soon evident. Violet and Edward were indeed bright students, both showing tremendous improvement.

Edward continued to pick up Italian phrases, while Violet made immense progress in English. Her determination continued well beyond classroom time. Her studies never ended. She constantly battled with the language barrier. Besides Miss Kerr and Edward, she practiced her English with the servants, especially Betty. Violet would engage Betty in a phrase exchange. Betty would speak in Italian, and Violet would repeat the phrase in English. They called it a "win-win," both learning to speak a new language. Violet was in total agreement with Mrs. Sutton; it was imperative she communicate fully and clearly with Edward. She wanted so much to help soothe him with comforting words in English. More importantly, she wanted Edward to explain to her in his own words what was frightening him.

The summer-like weather was tempting, and with Mrs. Suttons' approval, when permittable they took some lessons under the big field maple tree.

Miss Kerr's trust in Violet had increased exceedingly. She was comfortable confiding in her pupil some personal issues. "My veterinarian friend accepted my decision to put my pupils and employment first. He is encouraging and relieved he did not cause my dismissal."

Violet in turn was genuinely happy with the outcome. She came to believe the old Italian sayings she had heard came from real life experiences, since most proved true.

It was liberating for Violet to speak directly to Edward and be clearly understood without a translator. She asked him all kinds of questions, curious about his childhood. She wanted and needed him to retell the nightmares right after they occurred. She listened closely, trying to understand the depth of his fears. Regrettably they still sounded like a confusing mishmash of events, with a key element missing monsters.

When her sisters had nightmares, they always told of *"la Strega,"* the witch. Something was upsetting and frightened Edward, but what? Violet told herself she had to be patient. She knew it was best to go slowly. *Eventually,* Violet determined, *I will get to the bottom of all his fears.*

CHAPTER 15

THE SECRET

It was now late November. The unseasonably warm weather allowed Violet and Edward to continue enjoying their daily two-hour ride and hike. Catherine had scheduled this outing for their physical well-being.

Violet loved this time of year. The leaves on the trees had perfectly transformed from solid green to brilliant red, yellow, and rusty orange. She imagined fairies flying about at night, brushing each one with their colorful wings. She gathered different foliage to press between the pages of her books, to enjoy later in the desolate winter.

Edward collected rocks he theorized had miniature dinosaur fossils on them. He tried hard to convince Violet his theory was fact.

"More like mosquitos, at best dragonflies," she laughed, heading down the path towards a big oak tree.

"Stop Violet! Don't get any closer," Edward shouted suddenly.

"What is it? Are you alright?" she asked, alarmed, quickly turning to face him.

"There's a big viper snake behind that tree," he said, pointing at the unseen danger.

Violet looked at the tree. "You can't possibly know that." She dismissed him and took another step forward. Then she saw it. Her body froze with one leg off the ground. She stood motionless, holding her breath as the last inch of the snake's tail disappeared. Her face drained of all color combined with her stone-like stillness, Violet now resembled a Roman statue.

Edward ran and grasped her hand.

Violet tried to shake off her fear of what might have happened and stared down at Edward. "How did you know there was a snake near that tree?" Still in shock, Violet's question came out loud and angry.

Edward stepped back and shrugged his shoulders "I saw it."

"You couldn't possibly see that far! I was closer, and I didn't see it."

"I saw it when we started our walk after Thomas took the horses," he explained, looking directly into Violet's face.

"I don't understand." Violet had mastered her confused look in the last few months. The English language was still difficult at times; comprehending some expressions was not easy. Violet would have to ask for clarification. "Please explain that," she said. "Say that slowly."

Edward had his method of pausing and pronouncing each word separately. "I . . . see . . . things . . . that . . . will . . . happen . . . later, or . . . happened . . . before. I don't know why, Violet, but I do."

"Things? What things, Edward, like what?" Violet asked, a bit baffled and annoyed. She understood his individual words but not his meaning.

"Remember Mr. Mason's tractor accident when everyone believed he was getting better? I knew he was going to die."

"How did you know?" Violet did not like the game Edward had decided to play.

"I saw his funeral."

"We didn't go to the funeral, Edward." Violet was now becoming anxious, her eyes locked on Edward.

"I know, Violet; I saw it when he was waiting for Albert to drive him to the hospital."

Violet dropped with a big thump on the grass.

"Are you upset with me, Violet?"

"No, my darling, never," she reassured him. "I am just confused, I mean, I'm not sure. I don't know what I'm saying." She shook her head, then dragged her fingers through her thick hair.

Taking her hand, Edward sat down next to her. "You're the only one I have told this to. I wanted to share it all with you." Edward's voice was emotional, his small body tense, awaiting her reaction.

Violet understood the implications of being the only one he confided in. Edward trusted her to help him. She needed to push aside her shock and come up with an immediate solution.

"Edward, it is best we keep this just between us; it will be our secret together." Violet did not know what to say or do. For now, she needed time to think and hold back her emotions. She had to get Edward to promise not to tell, but how? Thinking back, she recalled making up silly rituals with her sisters. The game was meant to keep her siblings from telling their relatives things best not known. She'd gather them around telling them all to spit on the ground to "make mud." She then placed their hands in the softened dirt. Mystically, Violet circled around her sisters, mixing their mud together, while whispering, "This is our sacred pact never to tell our secret—not now, not ever."

Grabbing Edward's hand, she placed it next to hers in the mud she was making.

Edward laughed. "Violet!" He sounded excited and happy. "I saw you playing in the mud like this with your sisters, in my dreams."

Edward's casual admission jolted Violet, as though her entire body had been electrically charged. Her mind went in a million directions. Edward was a strange boy. Fear entered her mind; frightened, nervous, she felt inadequate to handle this weird phenomenon. Her head began to throb as though kicked by a mule. This little boy did not have nightmares; he was having visions.

Being thrashed into this realization, Violet felt trapped in a wind tunnel of mysterious unknowns. She had nothing to fall back on or hold on to. Her only choice was to brace herself and hope for an easy landing.

The excitable boy couldn't stop giggling.

"This is not funny!" she snapped. "You must take our pact seriously."

Edward's sad eyes made Violet understand this was not the time to panic. She would indulge later. Forcing a smile, she sweetened her tone. "We will hold hands and mix our mud together, singing these words. This is our secret, and it must never be told—not now, not ever."

Several times they repeated it, while jumping up and down.

"Ah!" Thomas' voice interrupted their ritual. "You two seem to be having lots of fun." He approached them with the horses.

"If you only knew!" Violet wanted to scream. She focused her anxiety on scraping the mud off her hands, while Edward blissfully continued jumping up and down.

CHAPTER 16

EDWARD'S VISIONS, VIOLET'S NIGHTMARE

Violet took a long, hot bubble bath, hoping to relax. She then wrote a detailed letter to her mother, mentioning all that was great. The girl mustered up as much positivity as possible; however, when finished, she began to cry.

Violet had endured her father's abuse, which made her strong. When needed, she always relied on her mother's loving and wise words. She needed some now. Violet felt so alone, missing her mother's hugs and tender encouragement. *I don't know what to do for this little boy!* she despaired. *I am afraid of doing the wrong thing and letting him down.*

That evening, dejected, she stayed in her room with a terrible headache. Mrs. Sutton went up to check on her. One look at her face, and Catherine agreed she should stay in bed.

Edward slept soundly the whole night, but Violet did not rest. She had her own terrible nightmare. It started with Edward being chased by a group of aggressive strangers. They were demanding he reveal their future to them. Desperate to escape, the frightened boy jumped into a nearby lake. The angry mob continued grabbing at him, causing him to constantly go under, almost drowning him. At the edge of the lake stood Mr. and Mrs. Sutton, mortified by their inability to control the angry mob.

Violet's presence was completely ignored by everyone. She was considered insignificant and therefore of no consequence.

This gave Violet the perfect opportunity to inadvertently save Edward. Shrewdly, the young girl dove under the water and grabbed Edward's legs. Making sure not to be seen, she tightened her grip and dragged him under with her. The two children secretly proceeded to swim away to safety.

When Violet finally awakened, her heart was pounding, and her nightgown was soaked. The exhausted child felt as if she had actually swum the lake! Discarding the wet garment, it became clear what had to be done. No one must know of Edward's extraordinary abilities. She had to protect him from everyone—including his parents.

CHAPTER 17

VIOLET'S DILEMMA

Breakfast was at eight a.m. sharp and always served in the conservatory. It was Catherine's favorite place. She had supervised every architectural feature, determined to replicate nature. To ensure survival in their new habitat, she had extensively researched ever plant, flower, bird, and butterflies. The furniture was either personally designed or chosen by her. Mr. Sutton spared no expense ensuring his wife was completely satisfied with the end results.

Three natural rock water features highlighted this spectacular landscaping. Automatic climate control maintained the colorful array of tropical plants. The manor's principal gardener was responsible for its irrigation and fertilization system. He spent at least three hours a day ensuring every system in the conservatory operated to his and the Suttons' flawless standards. Violet was in awe; she knew her mama would appreciate, and love being surrounded by nature year-round.

At eight-thirty, lessons with Miss Kerr ran until noon, with only a thirty-minute break at ten for tea. Lunch, unlike breakfast, changed location frequently. At three Edward and Violet had one hour of physical activity. The weather was unseasonably cool, but still fair for riding. Violet was anxious to speak with Edward without the fear of being overheard by anyone.

After a brisk ride, they enjoyed their walk together by the riverbank. At a discreet distance, Thomas kept careful watch while he tended to the horses.

Violet seized the opportunity to speak with Edward. "We must have a special word," she said, wanting to sound playful with him. "It will be a fun game. When you need to tell me something important—" Violet stopped abruptly. She noticed Edward was distracted and not listening to a word she had said.

"Please pay attention," she pleaded, but he continued to look around laughing. "Edward please listen to me," she insisted.

"Brutus is coming! Brutus is coming!" Edward shouted, jumping up and down in excitement.

"Your dog?" Violet asked.

"Brutus was chasing a skunk and got sprayed!" Edward said, laughing.

Sure enough, the pungent smell soon invaded her nostrils. A moment later, she heard Thomas scolding the already dysphoric golden retriever.

"Don't forget, Edward, never tell our secret," Violet managed to reinforce their pact before Thomas got nearby.

As time went on, Violet watched Edward like a cat watching a goldfish in a bowl. The more she tried to understand his strange ability, the more questions she had. Why was he like this? How had this happened to him? Would she really be able to help him?

Edward continued having his so-called "nightmares," and Violet continued to soothe and reassure him. "You are safe in my arms. What you see will not harm you, I promise."

The staff praised her attentiveness, and Catherine was especially pleased. No one seemed to notice how obsessive over Edward she really was. Violet constantly reminded him to never share their secret with anyone. She feared he would be ridiculed, branded as a freak, and exploited.

CHAPTER 18

THE PROCESSION

December was a busy time at the manor. Catherine's parents were visiting from America, which meant frequent trips to London. The staff were decorating and preparing meals for small dinner parties that happened often with little advanced notice. Miss Kerr was spending Christmas with her family in Scotland.

Extra alone time with Edward was exactly what Violet wanted. She would use their extended private time together to ask more specific questions. Hopefully she would come to understand what he actually saw and experienced.

Edward referred to his "visions" as nightmares or dreams. "That is what the grownups call them, just bad dreams." He spoke openly, totally calm, and relaxed. "I'm confused; at times I see things when I'm not in bed sleeping." Edward looked at Violet for an explanation. "I have kept those dreams to myself, but now when I see them, I can tell you. I used to dream a lot about you, Violet." He whispered low, as though letting her in on something special. "I always liked those dreams; they made me feel calm. The last vision of you I remember was about a year ago." Edward smiled with a genuine eagerness to share as he started describing some particulars about his vision. In it, there were six strong men dressed in white robes carrying a big statue of a lady in the air. Ten girls wearing white wedding dresses walked behind them. Violet was helping the girls with their veils and giving them flowers to hold. A crowd of men and women were singing and walking behind the brides. When they got to the ocean, the men put down the statue and everyone started to pray.

Edward stopped at this point and shook his head before continuing. "It was so sad, Violet, there were no boys wanting to marry the brides. The girls must have been really mad because they walked to the ocean, threw their flowers into it, and left."

Violet tried to hide how uneasy and frightened all this was making her feel. What Edward described was too real and vivid. It was a procession petitioning the Madonna to protect the fishermen. This religious festivity had been observed yearly in her mama's village for generations. The young girls dressed in their white communion attire always led the way. It was Violet's favorite day of the year—even more than her birthday and Christmas. Spending the day with her mama's family, without Ornesto, was a joyous blessing. Violet promised herself that one day she'd explain it all to Edward. For now, she wanted to learn more. Or did she? It was all too weird. Violet had vowed to care for Edward, but this was beyond her sisterly capabilities. Her mind began traveling to places that terrified her. *What if he is really possessed by an evil spirit, or even worse—the devil himself?*

With such thoughts festering in her young mind, logic soon got lost. Demonic images invaded Violet's imagination, tormenting her. *I'm no match for Lucifer,* she lamented inwardly. She recalled hearing stories of the priest having to extinguish Satan's fire with holy water while reciting hundreds of prayers. *I can get holy water at the baptismal font at church,* she reasoned. *But I only know a few prayers.* Violet shook off her doubts, believing she had to prepare herself. *I will have to repeat the same prayers again and again.* This conclusion was the extent of her preparation.

Meanwhile, Edward continued his outburst. There was no stopping him. Having a confidant to share with was apparently what the boy needed. His visions were the cause of his night terrors, and he wanted relief from them. Listening closely, Violet's tender heart could hear Edward's cry for help.

There was never any doubt the love she felt for him was greater than her fear of the unknown. Whatever demons she would have to confront, she would never abandon Edward. *I will have to find more courage. I'll look for some tomorrow.* The frightened girl's attempt at humor was a ploy to calm herself. For Edward's sake, and everyone else's, she pledged, *I must stay steadfast and be totally committed!*

CHAPTER 19

EDWARD'S OPPORTUNITY

Violet needed one thing explained. Her curiosity demanded it. "Edward, how did you find me?"

As if he'd been anticipating her question, Edward began his story. "My parents told me they were going to visit a good friend in Rome and wanted me to meet him. I knew he was really another doctor, but I pretended with them. I used to pretend a lot, which was the reason I stopped playing with other children. It was tiresome for me, so I preferred to be alone."

Hearing Edward speak of his reason not to play with other children saddened Violet. Observing his energetic and excitable character, she had no doubt Edward's loneliness was extensively difficult for the boy.

The eager boy continued, keen for Violet to know the whole story. "My parents hoped this doctor would figure out what was troubling me. On his office wall hung a big colorful map in the shape of a boot. I recognized the name of your village from my dreams and put my finger on the spot.

"I told my parents, here is where I need to go, Bontemare." I was so happy, I jumped up and down."

Violet could only imagine the fuss he must have made.

"I pleaded, please take me, please, I have to go there." The doctor friend whispered something to my parents, and they agreed to take me.

"I knew you would save my life and come live with me. I dreamed it all; I just had to come get you." Edward made it all sound simple and matter of fact.

Violet now made sense of the statement made on the train: "Edward wants you to know how happy he is that he found you." There was no discrepancy in the translation, as she had originally believed. Totally bewildered, Violet asked, "Why me?"

Edward answered with a slight shoulder shrug. The confused look on his face indicated he honestly didn't know. Violet had always been blessed with an abundance of common sense. She understood not all things in life could be explained; some just had to be accepted. Waiting for answers to your "why" could ultimately make you a bitter and angry person—like her father.

CHAPTER 20

A GIFT FROM THE HEART!

Over a century, Sutton Manor had maintained many customs. One tradition in particular was very crucial and dear to the present abidance. William and Catherine endeavored to ensure Christmas was bright and cheerful for all the villagers. Their staff worked diligently to prepare and distribute baskets of food. More importantly, every child in the village was to receive a toy. For the last few years, Edward had collected and given away some of his own toys as well. His parents wanted to teach him the importance of sharing his good fortune. This year Edward's request delighted his parents; he wanted to personally deliver some of his toys.

Catherine had scheduled Albert to be the one to escort Violet and Edward to the village. They would leave after breakfast and help distribute all the toys they had collected. Edward was anxious for morning to come and decided he would go to bed early. He explained his simple but very logical strategy to Violet: "Sleeping will speed up time and bring the new day sooner."

Sadly, that night the poor child had one of his worst nightmares. Violet's soothing words did not stop him from crying. Her own eyes were teary as she pleaded, "Please, Edward, tell me what you saw."

He could barely speak through his sobs. "The buildings were all falling on the people, even children. They were all so afraid, running to escape, but the fallen buildings buried most. There was blood everywhere, Violet." He sighed, exhausted. "I do not want to see these things. Am I bad? Is that why I see bad things? Am I a bad boy, Violet?" He continued to sob.

Violet felt inadequate and unqualified in her abilities to really help Edward. *What have I done keeping this secret from his parents?* She harshly questioned her hasty decision. Edward deserved better than what she alone could do for him.

She answered him firmly. "No! You, Edward, are the most wonderful boy in the whole world." She rocked him in her arms. Violet desperately wanted to take away his pain; she wracked her brain to come up with something—anything—to distract him from his despair. "Edward, you have magic powers," she whispered, pretending to look around for spies. "You are special."

Edward's wide-eyed showed he was intensively curious, absorbing Violet's words. "How! How am I special?"

Violet knew what she had said so far was true. Edward was special. Subsequently, putting a little twist for his benefit was needed. Keeping her voice low to suggest secrecy, she said, "You, Edward, are a superhero!"

Immediately Edward's face lit up. "Superhero!" he repeated. "Like the ones in my comic books?"

Edward's question sparked hope in Violet. She may have stumbled on an effective strategy to help him. Now she just had to be convincing and play her part well. Violet knew Edward had been sheltered in many ways. Mainly, he had never played with children his own age. He was definitely above average on so many levels but younger than his nine years in others. His excitement and growing curiosity demonstrated his willingness to accept and believe Violet's explanation.

"Am I really a superhero? Are you sure Violet?" he asked continuously.

"It makes perfect sense to me, Edward," Violet confirmed each time.

Edward's big smile showed his mind had shifted to pleasant thoughts and was now convinced.

Encouraged, Violet continued with her story. Her voice got stronger as she continued reinforcing more positivity. "Edward there are only a few heroes like you in the world. I don't know why you see these things, but I do know it's for a special reason. Remember, superheroes always keep their powers a secret. No one must ever know about them." Violet again took the opportunity to emphasize the importance of him keeping their secret.

"Now, you must promise me never again to feel bad. Heroes are the good guys, always courageous and strong." Violet was relieved she had given Edward what he most needed: acceptance. Believing her explanation would allow him to stay positive about his ability. This was a blessing, not only for Edward; it made it easier on Violet as well. "Come here, my hero, I will sing you to sleep." Kissing his forehead, she added, "Just think what fun we will have tomorrow. All the boys and girls will be so happy to receive the toys you will give them." As she soothed the little boy, Violet said a silent prayer for her superhero.

CHAPTER 21

A GIFT WITHIN A SILVER LINING

The village was a twenty-minute drive down a winding road northeast of the manor.

Entering the town, in center view, was situated the very essential Anglican church. Its steep bell tower had been a beacon of welcome to its people for centuries. At the very far rear of the cathedral lay their large cemetery.

Various small businesses lined the main street on both sides. The more predominant buildings occupied the four corners. The bank, the historical library, the post office with its own printing press, and the pharmacy soda shop.

Two schoolhouses, a big old barn, and a butcher shop took most of the east side. At the very far end of the road, recently built, was a police and government building. To the west, a few grander houses were owned by the town's professionals: doctors, lawyers, dentists, and business owners. On the south side, smaller homes bordered the town's square. In the center of the star shaped square, a memorial was erected. The monument was in honor of their dead soldiers.

Beyond the village, numerous quaint cottages were spread about. Most of their inhabitants were employed by the Suttons' estate.

The big day for delivering toys and gift baskets began on schedule. Thomas had already loaded the truck. A great portion of the gifts were directed to the church. The minister and his wife would distribute them appropriately. Thomas's task was to deliver a few larger items such as bicycles, tricycles, and wagons to designated homes.

Violet and Edward personally presented the smaller gifts. Observing the delightful smiles on the children's faces as they received their toys was most rewarding. Violet was overjoyed to have been given this opportunity. Her mama always said giving is good for the soul. Unfortunately, their own family needs had limited them. Today, Violet experienced how true her mama's words were. Giving to others in need at Christmas, she felt like she had swallowed the sun.

Picking up the last two gift boxes, Edward pointed at a small stone cottage and hurriedly walked towards it. Violet promptly rushed after him.

"I will accompany him, Albert. You may wait in the car." She spoke to him in Italian. Violet would often seek him out and indulge in pleasant conversations in Italian. She felt comfortable with him. From the very beginning, Albert had demonstrated he was considerate and trustworthy. Besides the Suttons, he was the only one who knew her circumstance. Albert had never questioned her position as a distant family relation. He was actually encouraging and did regard her as a member of the Sutton family. Violet regularly thanked him for considering her needs when he dealt with her father. "I thank you, my mama thanks you, and my sisters thank you." She would recite this litany every time she sent some extra money to them.

Albert's response had always been the same: "It was the just and right thing to do."

Approaching the small, modest cottage Violet noticed the late hour. She explained to Edward, "It is best we do not go in this time. Let's present the gift boxes to the family when they greet us at the door."

The lady opening the door had two children on either side trying timidly to hide behind her. With a big, appreciative smile, the mother immediately invited the visitors in. Edward obviously did not heed Violet's suggestion. He rushed past the woman and handed out the gifts, one to each child. He encouragement the brother and sister to open their gifts, eager to see them play with their new toys.

"I will make us all some hot chocolate," the mother offered.

"Thank you, but it's getting late, and we must head back," Violet graciously replied.

Edward was now forcefully tugging at Violet's coat. Meeting his eyes, she understood he wanted to share something important.

"Please excuse us, we need to get our driver's attention," she informed the lady. Escorting Edward out of the cottage, she closed the door. Facing him, she asked. "What is it? Tell me quick."

"Did you see the glass case with the soldier's jacket hanging in it? There is a letter inside its lining," Edward said.

"Not now, Edward! You can tell me your vision later."

"No, Violet, it's important! I saw the soldier put it there for her; it's been too long."

Violet quickly processed what was happening. Edward's latest vision needed immediate attention. She had heard stories about the war and the many men that had died. She envisioned the hopeless scenario. The soldier's last recourse was to leave his family loving words. Violet knew she had to come up with a solution.

"Come, Edward, we must not be rude. We must say goodbye."

Re-entering the cottage, Violet told the waiting mother and her children they had located their driver and thanked her again for the hospitality.

The woman smiled. "Thank you both for giving my children a nice Christmas."

Violet was frantically working her brain, trying to come up with a way to expose the letter. She was mulching on a simple but hopefully successful idea. Stepping closer to the glass display case, she pretending to be admiring it. She took a few moments before casually stating.

"I have seen many of these jackets in people's homes."

"I am sure you have, my child," the woman responded, looking wistfully at her fatherless children.

Violet gave the woman a curious look before asking, "Was there a letter in the lining like most of the other jackets?" The prudent girl hoped her question sounded as though it was a common occurrence.

The bereaved woman's eyes widened in astonishment. She instantly grabbed the jacket out of the case and with one quick motion, ripped the lining. There it was a thin, dirty envelope. The woman sat on a nearby chair, totally dazed. Her beloved husband's jacket on her lap and his last words in her hand. She did not look up as Violet and Edward left the cottage, but her loud voice did reach their ears. "God bless you. God bless you both!"

Although jubilant, Albert's passengers remained silent the whole ride back to the manor. The effect Violet felt with those words would stay with her forever. All her previous worries now seemed ridiculous. She sensed what had just happened had had an immense impact on this woman. The one wish of anyone who has lost a loved one is more time, even if it's a brief moment to share a loving goodbye. Edward had given this grieving wife an extraordinary Christmas gift.

This incident caused Violet to reassess her previous inclination. She admitted her thoughts of some kind of perverse wickedness in Edward were utterly wrong. Edward's ability was not to be feared but used for benevolence. This put a different twist to Edward's visions. To continue keeping them a secret while aiding whoever possible compounded her worries. Unsure of their future, Violet suspected life with Edward and his visions was about to get more complicated—but she was also intrigued.

CHAPTER 22

SPRING BRINGS RENEWAL

Winter at the manor had been mild, and not all was due to the weather condition. Edward's progress with Miss Violet's constant caring friendship had altered his behavior. He was no longer in a constant desolate mood. Edward now had a cheerful and uplifted disposition. Everyone agreed and were delighted, especially his parents.

Catherine was so pleased with her son's overall improvement she finally released her fears. In a private conversation with Violet, she opened up. "I've decided to accompany my husband on his business trip. Thanks to you, Violet, for the first time in years I feel confident in leaving Edward for a while. I am aware this would not have been possible if not for your dedication. The staff has been instructed to take your recommendations when it comes to Edward's desolate times. I'm assured you and Edward will receive excellent care by the entire staff."

The schedules no doubt had already been distributed by Simone. They consisted mostly of lessons and activities for the two youths. Mrs. Sutton was determined; Violet and Edward would excel in every aspect.

Her little boy complained constantly. He argued he'd rather spend his time digging for small rocks with mysterious fossil remains. He also preferred reading his comic books featuring his favorite superheroes. Arithmetic and literature were of no interest to the boy. In truth, Edward would have preferred to play and spend time outdoors, exploring his own discoveries.

Violet, on the other hand, embraced her studies. She understood the value of being educated and striving for excellence. She had three tangible reasons. Number one was of the utmost—never would she or could she disappoint, Mr. or Mrs. Sutton in anyway. Secondly, Violet, being the oldest, wanted to set the path for her sisters, thereby making her mama proud. Thirdly, she was determined to prove her father wrong. With every excellent grade she received, Violet would repeat to herself, *I am not a stupid girl!*

She appreciated the privileges the Suttons had generously given her and never took them for granted. Aside from her academics, which included five languages, she was given enrichment lessons. Twice a week, Violet was instructed on the piano and vocal strengthening. The instructor demanded an hour practice every day, which Violet enjoyed, and the staff actually looked forward to too. Catherine was convinced Violet was gifted with an amazing voice. She also ensured her charge was instructed in proper etiquette and numerous sports activities, such as fencing, tennis, and equestrian skill.

Indubitably, Saturdays were still Violet's favorite days. Her leisure time with Edward, although stimulating and appealing, was not the main reason. More significant to the young girl was the scheduled long-distance phone call. Getting to converse with her family was the highlight of her week. She promised Edward all her attention after the call to her mother and sisters ended. Mr. Sutton had made all the arrangements after Violet received the particulars from her mama. Maria's only recourse was to use the public phone located inside the town's post office.

Early every Saturday morning, Maria, accompanied by all her daughters, walked to the post office, and waited for Violet's call. Everyone in town knew at eight a.m. sharp the call from England would come. Frequently, some of Ornesto's relatives would show up, snooping about.

Waiting restlessly at her end, Violet was eager for the operator to make the connection. The calls always seemed hurried and incomplete. Since it was so public, they only spoke of pleasantries. Their personal issues were shared only in letters.

The bulk of the letters from her mother and sisters were focused on asking Violet questions about her life. Aside from Edward's visions, Violet shared just about everything. Maria had written that after giving birth to her eighth daughter, Ornesto swore, "No more children!" His vow, Maria admitted, was a blessing not only to her but the entire family.

"For this reason," Maria explained, "I've decided to name my last daughter Angelina. She is truly a little angel," the mother bragged. The letters explained the monthly supplement from her employees was promptly received. She mentioned the money did diminish some of Ornesto's harshness to them all. Unfortunately, his excessive drinking had gotten worse. Maria revealed she was not surprised he would use their money to buy more wine. His constant drunkenness, she wrote, was at least more tolerable than his verbal abuse. Maria thanked and praised Violet for her generosity and discretion. The extra concealed money was tremendously beneficial to the family. Violet suspected her mother was sharing only a fraction of how Ornesto's behaviour really was. Out of respect, she would never question or pressure her mama. Truthfully Violet was confident her mama did her best to always protect her children.

After the call, the desolated girl would retreat to her room and review the conversation with her distant family. She desperately tried to savor the sounds of their voices and all they'd discussed. Violet missed sharing, being part of her sisters' lives, and watching them grow.

Meanwhile, Edward would wait outside her door for what he considered a long time. He would then knock loudly and immediately open her door. He would not speak to Violet; he simply stood there and counted aloud. His tactics always worked. His playmate would succumb to his annoying behaviour and run after him, which signaled the start of their fun day.

Violet's unyielding love of nature had been nurtured early on by her mother. Maria had always told her daughters: "I want you girls to respect and enjoy our good earth. Open yourselves to its wondrous senses and feel our own connection with nature." Violet shared her mother's sentiments, embracing all of nature's gifts.

Spring was the season of awakening and regeneration. She marveled at how effortlessly everything unfolded precisely on time every year. She credited the conductor of this divine symphony for being flawless. From the beautiful, distinctive blossoms on the various fruit trees, to the many species of birds hatching; all was lush, harmonious, and full of life.

Today was a perfect, serene spring day. Miss Kerr began her one-hour late afternoon class outdoors. Occupying Edward by satisfying his personal niche had proven successful. His obsession with finding rocks with any kind of fossil had increased tremendously. Implementing mathematic equations with his accumulative collection resonated with him. Being asked to write descriptive compositions on his favorite subject also interested him. Edward never ran out of things to say about fossils remains. This archaeology aficionado treated his collected rocks as if they were precious gems.

The big maple tree was the preferred sitting place for Miss Kerr and her devout students. Its shade provided comfort while discussing Violet's current novel.

CHAPTER 23

SALLY AND ISABELLA

Thomas' unexpected dash towards the leisurely ladies had them startled. "The men! The men!" he said urgently. "The men, the men!" He repeated. "We are all heading for town."

He was winded, like a runner after a grueling race. His anxiousness was on overdrive, but his vocal cords were deflated. The poor man had to stop and catch his breath. He bent his exhausted body over. Putting both hands on his knees, he proceeded to take deep breaths. Still laboring to slow down his panting, Thomas valiantly continued. "Bella, the butcher's three-year-old daughter, has been missing for hours."

Both women took a few moments to absorb his message. "Isabella? Missing?" They promptly sprang to their feet.

Without hesitation, Miss Kerr declared, "We will also come, Thomas."

Approaching the small, usually bustling hamlet, it was evident something was amiss. The absence of people about was unexpected and disturbing. It felt eerie, like entering a ghost town. Thomas dropped them off, explaining he would go searching with the others. The village men with their dogs had widened their search and were now scattered across the outer fields.

Upon entering the butcher's house, the three new arrivals were hit with the somber mood. Miss Kerr walked directly to the inconsolably sobbing mother. The sympathetic women standing about merely nodded their heads as Bella's mother continuously reproached herself.

"I told Bella to play on the swing; it's my fault for leaving her. It's all my fault."

Violet stared at Edward, wondering if he sensed anything. Instinctively, he shrugged his shoulders at her in reply. He then noticed a familiar stuffed teddy bear lying on the floor. He picked it up and immediately let it fell back down. He turned and looked at Violet, who had been watching him the whole time. His expression revealed what she expected: Edward had had a vision.

Together, they left the cottage. She imagined the worst and dreaded having to ask. "What happened to Isabella, what did you see Edward?"

"I saw her falling into a hole." Edward's mouth was moving but the rest of his body was as stiff as a board.

Not wanting to hear more bad news, Violet momentarily remained silent. She envisioned a lifeless little body; yet she had to be strong and made a gesture for him to go on.

"She is crying softly."

"She's crying softly! She's crying softly!" Violet's elated repetition sounded like a chorus from a song. Her relief soon succumbed to anxiety as she realized Isabella was likely injured. "The poor child!"

Edward seemed preoccupied with his vision, moving his head left then right as if viewing a panorama—except his eyes were shut tight. "An angel! The hole is next to a blue angel."

Violet searched her memory, then recalled hearing tell of a mysterious blue angel at the cemetery behind the church. The stone angel's folded wings suggested it had landed on earth to watch over the villagers. It stood at the back entrance of the cemetery as a protective icon. Over the years, it had mysteriously turned a shade of aqua blue. Most people in town understood the color change as a miracle. Others argued the stone's mass had had a chemical reaction to the climate. Neither theory was proven or totally discredited, thereby leaving the mystery of the Blue Angel as a compelling tale for the townspeople to ponder.

Violet looked straight into Edward's eyes. "Not a word about any of this," she whispered firmly. "It's our secret. Go inside and sit with the other children; I'll come up with a plan."

Violet had no idea what to do. As usual, she started speaking to herself in Italian. Repeating phrases her mother used would encourage, comfort and balance her to focus. *Think,* she told herself and began evaluating the situation. Bella had been in the hole for five hours. The men with their dogs were searching the woods in the opposite direction. Edward's secret must be protected. *God, what am I to do.* Violet's head throbbed. She felt as though she had swallowed a piranha.

She was about to scream in defeat when she heard a dog bark. At first, she thought, *Good, the searchers are returning.* When she heard it again, she realized it came from Mrs. Miller's car. It was Sally, Mrs. Miller's daughter's French poodle.

The town children had ridiculed the dog for years. It was the way her owner had her clipped. The poodle's back end was totally shaved, making her resemble a miniature lion. The children constantly poked fun at Sally calling her "Silly Naked Butt." The men in town also dismissed the poor animal. "Whatever that is, it's not a real dog!" they spat. Violet disagreed. *A dog is a dog is a dog!*

The third time she spoke those words to herself, a solution occurred to her. Earlier she had noticed a basket full of sausages inside the butcher's house. It had brought back fond memories of Italy. Neighbors would get together and help one another when they slaughtered their pig. It was hard work made easier by their collaboration. This yearly event became a Thanksgiving feast, with singing and dancing and plenty to eat. What Violet remembered most was that the children were free to play and enjoy themselves.

As Violet entered the front door, all eyes shifted towards her. Being of no consequence, they all quickly returned to what they were doing.

She gave Edward a reassuring smile and motioned for him to stay put. Making sure no one noticed, she bent and grabbed some sausages and promptly left the house.

The streets were still deserted. Only a few outside lamps were now lit. The houses remained darkened in the absence of the owners. She ran to the car, where Sally was hanging out the window wagging her pom-pom tail. Violet opened the car door and gave Sally a taste of the sausages.

"Come, Sally," she encouraged, getting on the minister's bike that was lying on the lawn. Violet peddled away as fast as she could, waving the sausages for Sally to see. The dog must have been very hungry. Violet had to quickly gather the sausages inward or Sally would have snatched them all.

She rode the bike across the cemetery straight to the Blue Angel. *Focus on the task,* Violet warned inwardly. *No time for emotions.* She knew one word, one glance, and all her effort would be for nothing.

She placed the dangling sausages on a high pedestal, knowing the little dog would have to struggle to reach them. She then quickly raced back to the butcher's house totally out of breath. The intense pounding of her heart seemed to warn it would soon pop out of her chest. Her throat felt dry and scratchy, as if she had drunk a glass of sand. *Calm down, breathe.* She was now more empathetic towards Thomas gasping for air earlier. Time was of the essence; she entered the house not fully recovered.

With a low deep voice, she told everyone in the room, "I just saw Sally run off."

Before she had finished the last syllable, Mrs. Miller and another lady had rushed to the door. Violet was relieved she did not have to repeat the statement. They could hear the dog barking but paused to determine which direction it came from.

"It's coming from the church cemetery," one of the ladies shouted. Several women dashed out toward the church. The need to get physically involved prompted their abrupt reaction to be helpful.

Violet plopped down into the nearest chair. Her legs remained rubbery; they felt as though still peddling the bike. Her heart pounded loudly as she continued to labor with the rapid breathing. She was grateful those around her were too preoccupied to notice her panting.

What is taking so long? she wondered. *Did my plan fail?*

Edward walked over to her, relieved she was back. "I was worried for you," he said putting his hand on her shoulder. His innocent face convinced Violet she had done the right thing.

"I'm fine, Edward; we will talk later. Remember, *shhhh.*"

She was still gesturing with her index finger when the door flung open. Two women rushed in, one shouting, "We found her! We found Isabella!"

"She is safe!" the other announced joyfully, as the church bells rang to alert the men.

Isabella's mother sprung to her feet with adrenaline strength that only surfaced at times such as these. Instinctively she fell to her knees, loudly thanking God. Then in a flash, with the agility of a lioness, she was out the door.

CHAPTER 24

HEROISM SHRUGGED OFF

The headlines read: "OUR LOCAL HERO: SALLY THE WONDER DOG."

Beneath the heading was a full-page picture of Sally in all her glory. The town buzzed for weeks. At least ten versions of what had happened to Isabella circulated. The short of it was that she had chased after a kitten. Determined and careless as any three-year-old child, she was totally oblivious to her surroundings. Her only focus was on grabbing the kitten; instead, she tumbled into the newly dug grave. The fall caused her to suffer a broken leg and numerous bruises on her small body. Manifestly, the people of the small hamlet were overjoyed with the outcome and dubbed Isabella "a lucky little girl." Pictures of the child and dog were posted everywhere. Violet secretly related to one in particular. Isabella was rewarding Sally by feeding the dog a sausage.

"Edward, I want you to understand, it was your vision that actually saved Isabella." Violet was so proud. "Remember: you are the real superhero."

"I know, and you know, and that's enough for me." Edward was definite in his answer. "It's better everyone believes it was the dog. I would be annoyed if everyone fussed over me, as they are now doing to Sally. I don't want to be imposed."

"Good!" Violet responded, not intending to say it out aloud. Edward's reaction was only half-encouraging. She realized his concern was only on being fussed over—whereas her concern was on him being *ex*posed. She presumed he'd learned the word "imposed" in one of his comic books. Both words, she concluded, were accurate. It was obvious Edward's innocent mind did not totally comprehend the ramifications of his visions being exposed. He couldn't possibly imagine the frenzy and demands that would occur if people had even the slightest inkling of his gift. His strong dislike of being center of attention assured Violet he would at least be more secretive.

For now, she was relieved and grateful for the way it had all turned out. This incident strengthened her decision to keep Edward's visions from everyone. She struggled with the thoughts floating in her mind. *What about next time?* Edward's visions were unpredictable. It was inevitable he'd have more. Worrying and fretting before they happened was futile. The challenge she now put on herself, however, increased. If at all possible, Violet wanted to help resolve the crises Edward envisioned. She embraced this enormous challenge and pledged: *I will deal with whatever comes our way.*

CHAPTER 25

AN UNEXPECTED FAMILY REUNION

"I am bored!"

Edward's serious reflection on his mood made Violet laugh aloud. In his defense, it had rained continuously for weeks. The sun was still timid, not at all at its full potential. It occasionally teased everyone by playing peek-a-boo from behind dark clouds.

Breakfast had not yet been served when Edward stood, looking puckish, announcing he had important information. "Today is April thirteenth."

Everyone at the table nodded in agreement.

"Three years ago, on this very day, Violet saved my life." His smirk warned the others he was not quite done with his reflection. They waited silently, amused, to hear what he would add. Edward stared at each one for a few seconds. "I declare today a holiday. No school! No work! We should all celebrate with a family outing in London!"

Mr. Sutton smiled at his wife. Their mutual blissful reaction had everything to do with their son's outgoing confidence and personality. Edward was energetic, silly and a happy, normal eleven-year-old boy. After the years of worrying, fearing the worst, they considered his rambunctiousness a blessing.

Edward's father's unhurried response indicated he might be considering the possibility. "I suppose that's a good enough reason."

Catherine's agreeable opinion was interrupted by Betty entering the conservatory. "Sorry for the interruption, Mrs. Sutton. There is a telephone call for Miss Violet."

"For me?" Violet was surprised. "I wasn't expecting a call today."

"It's your mama, miss," said Betty.

Edward's expression gave Violet no sense of urgency. She politely excused herself and followed Betty out of the conservatory.

The phone was still in Violet's hand when the family approached a few minutes later. She looked stunned, and her body stood rigid.

"What is it my dear?" asked Mrs. Sutton.

Violet seemed confused, preoccupied, as though unaware of her immediate surroundings. She tried to regain control, but her sadness was apparent in her quivering reply. "My father died a few hours ago. My mother wants me to come as soon as possible." She rushed her words out, to keep her feelings in.

"Of course, you must go. I will make all the arrangements," William reassured her.

Catherine hugged Violet, expressing her condolences. Edward took her hand and led Violet outside to one of their favored hideaways. He was not given time to speak.

"Why Edward?" said Violet. "Why didn't you tell me? Didn't you see or feel anything?" Violet was bewildered.

Edward looked surprised. He spoke casually. "I saw your father sleeping under his usual tree and a big branch fell on him. Violet, I didn't feel sad, just calm and peaceful. I am sorry you are upset."

Violet instinctively hugged Edward. She needed to hold someone good and pure. She had no response to his honesty. Her own true feelings for her father were buried too deep. She allowed only a slight crack to appear through the cement she had poured over them. Her sadness derived from the fact that her mama and sisters had endured so very much. *How ironic,* she thought, *that his death should come from his chosen refuge. The wise, old tree must have had its fill of Ornesto.*

Violet had to stop these thoughts and focus on what was important. "Edward, my mother and sisters need me for a while; will you be okay?"

"Don't worry about me, Violet. I promise to be extra careful keeping my visions to myself. I won't tell anyone about my superpowers. Besides, I'll be kept really busy having fun." Her little man spoke assuredly, wanting to comfort her. He put his hands together in an angelic pose. "Trust me," he teased. "It will be nice for you to see your family, but please promise to come back to me."

"Absolutely! I promise." Violet confirmed without hesitation. "Edward," she asserted, confused, "you must know I will."

Mr. Sutton diligently made all the travel arrangements. The quickest way was for Violet to fly to Rome. Since the train schedules were at best unpredictable, an automobile would be waiting to drive Violet to her hometown.

By eight o'clock the next morning, Violet was in her mother's arms. It felt surreal being back in that house, yet her family surrounding her with warmth and love was familiar.

"I cannot believe how much you all have grown," she kept repeating, dismissing the fact that three years had passed since they had last seen each other. Violet could not stop kissing her youngest sister, Angelina, who was now almost three. She had only heard her voice and seen her in the few pictures her mother had sent.

The family's intimate reunion was interrupted by the overzealous in-laws' abrupt early morning visit. Barely in the door, Ornesto's siblings began bombarding Violet with personal questions. They were using their so-called "dutiful grieving time," to satisfy their curiosity, snooping in her life.

The clever young lady politely answered them all with the same reply: "All is fine, thank you for asking."

Frustrated with their niece's vague answers, they began issuing orders to the distraught widow. Ornesto's oldest sister Carmela demanded Maria and all her girls be dressed in black for the funeral and henceforth for one full year, at least. Unanimously, the relatives had all collaborated in preparing a lengthy "to-do" list for the grieving family.

"Since you're all women, I believe some things are better left to the men to settle." Uncle Francesco's statement was insistent and authoritative.

It was late evening by the time the in-laws left. They had stayed long enough to eat all the food Maria's caring neighbors had thoughtfully provided. With every dish brought in, the relatives continued repeating their well-rehearsed lament: "We have been here all day with love and support!" They wanted to convince the concerned neighbors they were a tight-knit family.

Locking the door behind them, Violet felt her exhaustion but sensed her mama needed to talk. With the other children already tucked in bed, it was the perfect time for them to have a private conversation. Maria seemed agitated beyond the obvious reasons. She kept washing the same coffee cup.

"Mama, I know something is troubling you. Please be open and tell me all." Violet spoke reassuringly. "Now more than ever I need to hear the truth."

The worried child took the cup from her mother's hand and sat her down. Maria looked drawn; her head and shoulders drooped downward. Sadness cloaked her entire being. "Life with your father was not easy." She forced the words out. "You, being the oldest, had to endure the most." Maria hesitated, still reluctant to speak.

Violet encouraged her mother to continue by squeezing both her hands.

"His drinking became considerably worse this past week. We had a disagreement, but that was not the reason. He never valued my opinion. He always did as he pleased." Maria's tone shifted and sounded resentful. "*Violeta mia.*" Her mother sighed endearingly, preparing her daughter for unpleasantries. "Your father was planning to come visit you in England." Maria hurried her revelation, watching her child's stunned reaction.

"Why, Mama? Why?"

"It's not important now."

"Mama, I need to know," Violet pleaded.

"I suppose you have the right to know, and it should come from me." Maria was conflicted but consented. "I want to prepare you; in case you hear talk around town. "Your father was determined to come and convince the Suttons to pay him more money. He believed he was entitled to it since you had been there all these years. He said you must have gotten good at your job. Therefore, he wanted his increase. After a few drinks he started boasting about receiving more money, which got him in trouble. Your cousin Renato told me what happened. His drinking buddies at the tavern got tired of him bragging about having a new suit made, for his important trip. They threw insults at him, saying a new suit does not make a man. A few even humiliated him, calling him a good for nothing, the lowest of the lowest. They exposed him by saying he had always taken advantage of his own daughter's good fortune."

Violet's whole body went cold. Hearing the word "humiliated" brought back that offensive day at the Torantinos. Not yet fifteen, she'd had to handle her humiliation with determination and strength.

Maria's afflicted voice brought Violet back to the present.

"He ranted how no one ever understood him, and he drank nonstop. His death was a bizarre accident." Maria specified this fact, wanting to reassure her daughter. "He was passed out under the ancient chestnut tree when a big, decayed branch snapped, hitting him fatally on the side of his head."

Maria showed signs of emotional fatigue and went silent. Violet respected her mother's contemplation. It was evident her mama at one time had loved her husband. "He is wearing that new suit for his last, most important trip." Maria's words came out in resigned whisper.

CHAPTER 26

LIFE CAN NOW MOVE ON

Edward had already described how Ornesto had died. Hearing about his greedy plan to grab more from the Suttons opened up old wounds. Resentment took hold of Violet, extinguishing any loving feelings she may have held for this man. She was horrified. To think he would have deliberately exposed her to all the Suttons' household, discrediting their claim she was a distant relative. This humiliation would have been devastating, not only to her, but to the people she loved. Ardently, Violet accepted Ornesto's fate without remorse.

Violet's sympathy lay with her mother and all she had endured. At this moment, at this time, what was she to say? She could not and would not heap more hardship on this torn woman. The daughter held back her disgust and refrained from further comments. Tomorrow, all aspects of this toxic part of their lives would be buried with Ornesto. It was done, finished, and courageously they would surpass it. In silence, with enormous love and respect, the loyal daughter forcefully embraced her mother. Their unspoken frustration was thrust aside and replaced with increasing relief. The two women prepared for bed, wearing serene expressions on their faces.

The tears shed at Ornesto's funeral the next morning came from his family's personal disappointments. The girls were not mourning their father's death, but rather the grief of never having a father's love. Ornesto never sought to appreciate what a priceless treasure he possessed within his own family. His blindness was self-inflicted. His obsession with wanting a son consumed him. His wife and daughters had endured his constant criticism, being told they were not enough. He demanded so much yet gave so little. Sympathy from the people in town was given to his family out of pity. Most murmured, "Ornesto was a bitter man unsatisfied with life."

After a long, grueling day with the in-laws, Maria lovingly focused on her daughters. "Come," she smiled, gathering them on the bed. "There will be big changes in our lives for us all, even our Violet." Maria's voice was strong and full of hope. "Soon we will leave this town. Uncle Francesco wants his house back, which is not a problem." Maria cheerfully added, "Your Aunt Margaret has generously given us my parents' house. She told me it was always intended for me. She wisely held on to it in fear your father would have sold it. I hope you girls are not terribly disappointed to leave this place."

"No!" Rosa was quick to answer her mother. "We are happy to get away from all of this and start a fresh life in your hometown. All the stories you have told us about your home and garden always brought us joy."

Immediately, the others, in their own anxious words, agreed. Her daughters' eagerness brought tears to Maria's eyes. "I'm sorry for the hardships you all have endured, but I promise a brighter tomorrow. I am so blessed to have such caring, loving daughters." She spread her arms, gathering them all to her.

Violet observed and appreciated her family's happiness. She was exultant knowing they would now have peace and joy in their new home. The caring girl would not impinge on their happiness and beliefs, at least not for now. Her silence had the family thinking she too would be sharing the same sense of freedom and renewal. Anticipating their financial future, Violet's sense of obligation was one reason her mother's plans could not possibly include her. The other was, of course, the major reason: Edward still needed her.

The move from one village to the next was effortless. The overzealous family packed their minimal possessions and were gone the next day. Aunt Margaret had kept their parents' family home in good condition by using money received from the seasonal rent. The house, close to the ocean, was a gem and most desirable for vacationers. It had three bedrooms, two bathrooms, and a large kitchen. The family's sitting area of the kitchen had a stone fireplace and two windows with a view of the ocean. The best view of the ocean and gathering place was of course the rooftop *terrazzo*. The family would enjoy getting use of it, every chance they could. The three balconies off the bedrooms overlooked Maria's beloved garden. It was sufficiently maintained but not to her standards. She would soon tackle the job with the pleasure and the enthusiasm of one who had longed for twenty years for the privilege.

The furnishings were sparse, old, and most unsuitable for a permanent family. Violet had anticipated her family's financial needs and relied on Mr. Sutton's assistance. He had provided Italian currency ensuring Violet had enough lira for herself and to assist her family. Unlike her husband, Maria never expected nor wanted to put this enormous burden on her daughter. Having no other recourse, she humbly accepted. It was not easy for a mother to take from one child to benefit the others. The harsh reality of their circumstances, however, made it necessary.

Violet delighted watching her sisters and cherished their time together. She noticed and appreciated their individual diversity. Having inherited their mother's caring and sweet disposition, it was all good.

Sixteen-year-old Rosa was nurturing and very mature. She had taken the big sister role very seriously after Violet left. She was firm, fair, and kind, all qualities needed to gain respect and love. Rosa had proven herself capable of directing her younger siblings. Violet believed she had what it takes to be an amazing mother one day.

Orchidea, fourteen, was a strong worker, not at all soft and delicate as her name suggested. Her stature was as solid as a tree trunk. Jobs that needed extra strength and endurance, Orchidea was the one to successfully get it done. She was also precise, organized, and kept a clean house.

Delia, thirteen, was the reader among the girls. She loved to curl up and get lost in a book. She referred to them as treasure chests: "One never knows what you'll discover until you flip through the pages." Her enthusiasm with books reminded Violet of Edward's obsession with fossils. Delia dreamed of becoming a teacher one day. With her passion to learn and share her knowledge, she would be a great instructor.

Gardinia and Giglia, twelve, were called the inseparable twins, but were actually eleven months apart. Both possessed a sense for dramatics. They created funny and intriguing stories, but always with happy endings. Gardinia, the eldest of the pair, would start a fairy-tale and Giglia would finish it. Both had vivid imaginations and loved to share. Their curious nature had them constantly asking questions. Thus, earning them the nickname "Busybodies."

Pansy was a petite but spritely nine-year-old. Dedicated, she would rigorously rehearse her singing and dancing in front of the mirror. Nightly, Pansy performed in front of the family. Her "one girl show" was enjoyed and appreciative by her audience.

Little Angelina adorably admired all her sisters. When shopping with Rosa, she would behave and only ask for one toy. Angelina always wanted to help Orchidea with her chores. She'd watch Delia read her book and pretend to be doing the same. Gardinia and Giglia story time was her favorite. Angelina listened with enthusiasm, always asking for more. When Pansy performed her singing and dancing, Angelina would jump up and down, applauding the loudest.

"Angelina has completed our garden. Her gentle presence compliments my flowers." Maria had always referred her daughters as "my perfect garden."

CHAPTER 27

REPRIMAND WITH LOVE!

Violet enjoyed spending time with her sisters, yet she felt the three older ones had raised a slight barrier. She expressed this concern to her mother. "They are acting a bit guarded and distant towards me. Not at all the way I remember them. I wonder, Mama, if they have forgotten all we shared? Maybe time has erased me from their hearts? After all,"—Violet as usual wanted to defend her sisters, even to herself—"we were all so young when I left."

"Speak openly to them," Maria encouraged. "Do not hold back. Tell them how you feel. The bond between sisters is not easily broken. Memories are stored in a compartment with a two-way door. You might have to open it from your side."

Violet respected her mother's advice. No doubt she understood her daughters better than any mother could. She had given all of them extra love and attention to compensate for their father's abuse. She had often listened and consoled them with tender patience.

Violet's time with her family was now getting shorter. She wanted to enjoy every moment with her sisters, but first, this veil floating between them had to be removed.

After supper, Violet told her three older sisters she needed to speak to them privately, in their bedroom. She was tender, but as her mother suggested, went right to the point. "It's important you know how much I've missed each of you. These past three years have been good to me, but not one day has gone by that I did not wish you were all with me. I love you all very much." She paused to give them a chance to absorb all she had said. Her next statement was in the form of a question. "Perhaps you have forgotten about me?" She was anxious but patiently waited for their answers. *Give them time to open up*, she mindfully repeated to herself.

A shy whisper finally came from Rosa. "You've changed, Violet."

"You're so glamorous," Orchidea added. "Everything about you is elegant, Violet. You look like a movie star."

An explosion of words escaped from Rosa. "Your clothes, your hair, the way you walk, your speech, it's so different. You even speak perfect Italian to us instead of our own dialect." Rosa sounded defensive.

Delia added in a grumble, "You've had the best tutors and speak four languages."

Including her perfect Italian, Violet actually spoke five languages, but was not about to correct Delia. What she had to correct was the perception they now had of her. Violet appreciated their honesty, had even excepted a bit of unwarranted jealousy. Nothing they pointed out had anything to do with how she felt towards them. She could not allow their perception to put distance between them. It was imperative to explain and show clearly her feelings and commitment to each sister.

"Time changes all of us, especially at our age; it's inevitable." Violet chose to speak in their native dialect. "I want you all to look forward to your own bright futures. I have been given great opportunities. I get to wear nice clothes, but these things are extras. What is inside me has not changed. I have always, and will always, love my sisters. The fact I could say it in different languages doesn't make it less true, but more. Please! Don't ever forget this. I am your big sister and want to be part of your lives, if you let me."

The three young girls look embarrassed and bowed their heads in shame. Tearfully, they all admitted being wrong for judging their sister solely on her outward appearance. They quickly expressed how proud they actually felt of her and her accomplishments. "We know you've worked hard and deserve it all. We're sorry, Violet! Please forgive us." Hugging their older sister tightly, they began to cry.

This was familiar, what she remembered and treasured about them. Her arms around them, always giving them comfort. Memories of the numerous times they had run to her to be consoled after a tongue lashing from their father flooded back.

Violet seized the moment, aware she had to push the slightly open door even wider. She had to convince her sisters she had not really changed that much. Releasing her embrace, she jumped on the bed and bounced around grunting like a monkey. Her silly, comical sounds bought in the younger sisters. Remembering the past, they also wanted to join in on the fun. Bursting into laughter, they would forget what made them sad and start acting silly with her. This time was no exception, as their laughter filled the room. All the sisters' inhibitions vanished. One by one they each presented their own monkey impression.

Violet began tickling Pansy, who squealed in delight. Giglia grabbed Gardinia, and together they jumped on the bed. Rosa, now holding Angelina, rolled on the crowded bed backwards. Orchidea, being the strongest, pulled Violet off Pansy and started tickling her. They all jumped in, tickling Violet.

"My cup runneth over!" Maria exclaimed as she entered the room. She tried hiding her pleasure by shaking her head. "What did I raise, a bunch of monkeys? I believe it's time we all go to sleep." She helped them off the tattered bed.

Violet moved quickly and picked up one of her suitcases. "I have a better idea." Dumping all the contents on the bed, she insisted. "Let's go through all these. I had no time to buy presents, but everything here is for you. Mrs. Sutton sent you one of her designer coats, Mama, and Edward gave all these toys for the girls to share. I have dresses, shoes, and jewelry—take it all! Even this valise." She was immensely jubilant.

Without a trace of shyness, all her sisters descended on the trove of wonders. They complimented each other on their selections.

Picking through her smaller suitcase, Violet handed Rosa one of her favorite suits. "This will look great on you," she said, holding it in front of her sister.

"Oh! Violet, I love it!" Rosa got very emotional.

"Here is the matching purse, Rosa." Orchidea happily presented it.

Maria was now wearing and admiring her gift. "I have never seen such a magnificent coat. People will surely gossip," she contemplated while stroking it.

"Tell them it was a gift from your husband." Violet was solely thinking of her mother and wanted her to have a fresh start. She quickly added, "This will stop people from pitying you, and they'll seek someone else to talk about."

Maria reflected and agreed. "I am tired of people feeling sorry for me. I never wanted that. Maybe seeing me in this luxurious coat will finally end our family's shame."

CHAPTER 28

TRUTH BE TOLD

Violet made sure to spend time alone with each of her sisters. The older ones spoke openly about their personal aspirations. They continued apologizing to her for their initial reaction. "You're still the most giving, loving, devoted big sister we remember," they affirmed.

She assured them, "I will do what I can to help you achieve your goals. Ultimately," she emphasized, "it's your own hard work that will determine your success." She smiled, then added, "Plus, a bit of friendly persuasion from me won't hurt." Violet knew earning a good recommendation from someone reputable was definitely to one's advantage. The people you chose to associate yourself with was very important in one's life and career.

Maria, without her husband's constant negativity and restraint, was able to exert her own confident character. When dealing with her in-laws, she was respectful but firm, leaving no room for arguments. "Thank you. I appreciate all your advice, but I will now handle things in my way. My daughters' well-being is very important to me. I know what is best for my family."

Violet was tremendously pleased and proud of her mama's strength and stability. The family's future, now in her capable and loving hands, would definitely thrive. It was clear to Violet the family really did not need her to stay. It was her ability to provide financial support that was essential. Maria had always been frugal; she would make sure to stretch the monthly supplement wisely. Violet prepared this argument to support her desire to return to Edward. As much as she loved her family, she missed him terribly and was anxious to get back to him.

She had to approach her mother with her decision soon and make her understand. Violet waited until Maria was in her garden, blissfully pruning roses. In her preferred environment, Violet hoped to lessen her disappointment. "I need to speak with you, Mother." Violet addressed her formally, hoping to sound mature.

"Oh, my!" Maria was surprised and reacted humorously. "You sound so serious," she giggled.

Violet realized her attempt to act mature with her mama was futile. In her presence, Violet's independence melted. Instinctively, the mother-child relationship prevailed, each accepting their given roles.

"I love you all so much," Violet said. "I am sorry, I don't want to hurt you, but I must go back."

Maria put down her pruning shears and took Violet's hand. "My dear child, you belong with your family. You must know, I would have never let you go. We will manage somehow financially, I'm sure. I appreciate you might have gotten used to your new life and all its comforts. But, Violet, your place is with us. We are your true family, and we love you."

"Yes, Mama, but Edward. I promised, I promised him!" Violet was now sobbing. Saying his name aloud remained her how he had made her promise. He knew she would need to emphasize to her mother the importance of keeping such a solemn promise.

"Stop crying, my child, you're upsetting me. Tell me what is truly troubling you."

Violet took a deep breath and wiped her tears. She considered how hard it must've been for her mama to reveal her father's greedy plan. Yet! She'd been forthright with her. Violet felt she owed her mama the same consideration. "Yes, Mama, I must tell you all."

It also occurred to the daughter that if she wanted to get back to Edward, she had no choice. Her mother was too reluctant to let her go. It was imperative her mama understood it wasn't the lifestyle she wanted so badly to return to, but the little boy. Revealing the truth of Edward's dependency, Violet hoped it might persuade her.

Starting from the beginning, Violet left nothing out. She told of the dream and explained how she interpreted its meaning. "I must protect him, Mama. I've kept the secret of his visions from his parents. I've often wondered if I made the right decision." Violet was still conflicted about her deception. "You understand, Mama, I am the only one he trusts to protect him. We've kept this secret between us all these years, and now I have shared this trust with you."

Maria's face exposed her shock and astonishment. Violet had blurted out all the details without stopping, fearing she'd lose her nerve. Her mother's rigidness made the young girl now doubt her decision. Maria's somber words were very low, as though the unsettled woman was speaking to herself. "I never imagined my own daughter in such an incredible situation."

Violet was aware her mother's instincts were to protect her, as hers was to protect Edward. She understood the struggle her mama was experiencing trying to absorb this unexpected circumstance. It took some time for Maria to compose herself. She kept fidgeting with the roses, clipping them lower and lower. Violet had done her worst and now remained silent. A few times she believed her mama was about to speak but said nothing and kept pruning. When Maria finally spoke, she took her time and was precise.

"I am proud of you, my child. I don't think—no, actually, I know—I would not have handled Edward's predicament as wisely as you did. You have always put the ones you love first and shown great sensibility. Your determination, courage, and character helped me endure my own life. You helping this little boy does not surprise me. My darling daughter, you are an impressive young lady."

"Mama!" Violet's love and admiration for her mother, at this moment, was immense. Leaping into Maria's arms, she confirmed, "I feel the same about you, Mama. You have been the source of my values and strength."

Caressing her daughter's cheeks, Maria's expressed her understanding. "This little boy needs you still. You must be there until he can cope on his own. His visions are intertwined with your life. We might never know why, but there is definitely a higher power at work here."

Maria looked pensive; directing her daughter to sit, she spoke with a mother's authority. "Before you leave, I feel it's my right to prepare my daughter for some of life's experiences." Without the slightest pause, the determined mother continued. "You are a beautiful young lady. Soon men will admire you and seek your attention. Choose wisely. Wait for your soulmate, who eventually will appear. Don't be fooled by a deceitful smooth-talker that thinks only of himself."

Maria obviously was speaking of the big mistake she had made marrying Ornesto. "Don't let your heart make all the decisions—use your sensible mind and you'll never go wrong."

Violet had not expected to be having an adult conversation and felt a bit embarrassed. She listened respectfully, realizing what this talk implied. Her mother had made a difficult decision. By giving her daughter maternal advice, Maria was preparing Violet for her future.

"I believe," Maria continued, "the base of a lasting relationship is to let the man do the pursuing. Hold back your love, don't open your big heart too soon. Allow the man to profess his love first. It's also the safest way not to get hurt.

"It's obvious the Suttons have been extremely generous and caring in every aspect. I could not be more grateful and pleased. All a mother prays for is her children's happiness. I saw your exuberance the moment I looked in your eyes. You, my daughter, should . . ." Maria stopped mid-sentence and nodded. "You should keep your promise to that little boy. You have my blessing; go back to Edward. God has put the two of you together for His own good reason."

"*Grazie! Mama cara.*" Violet appreciated how tremendously difficult this was for her mama. The task of giving her daughter the proverbial final nudge was the last thing her mama wanted to do. Maria's sensible decision to allow Violet to go back proved how totally selfless her mother was. Maria put aside her own broken heart and considered what needed to be done for everyone's good. The family undoubtedly would continue to benefit financially. Edward and Violet together would benefit from each other.

After sharing the secret with her mama about Edward's visions, Violet felt a sense of relief. For years she had questioned, wondering, if she had done the right thing for Edward. Her mother's reassurance, saying she was convinced Edward was in good hands, reinforced her commitment. This alleviated some of Violet's burden. Who better than her own mama as a trustworthy ally? As the time-honored cliché goes, confession is good for the soul.

CHAPTER 29

ORNESTO'S LAST OFFENSE

The espresso at breakfast was a real treat. It delighted Violet's "Mediterranean" taste buds. The herbal tea she had ingested for years was mostly enjoyed when accompanied with freshly baked scones smothered with creamy butter. Since the move back to her birth home and town, Maria always started her day cheerful. This morning, she appeared a bit subdued, which alarmed Violet. Was her mother rethinking her decision?

Maria gave her worried daughter an intuitive smile. "Take the frown look from your face, my child. I stand by the decision we made yesterday; it's the right one for everyone. Unfortunately, I have a problem and need your help. There is a legal matter which is upsetting me. I thought we had time to deal with it later, but since you are leaving, it needs to be addressed now. I'm sure with your intelligence, you can handle it."

"Oh, Mama," protested Violet, embarrassed.

"It's true. Don't be so modest. I sense, you do not see your own worth my child. I am so sorry for all the demeaning words you endured from your father. Please try to remember you're very special and have a lot to offer."

Violet was emotionally gratified to hear compliments from her mama; what daughter wouldn't? She also appreciated how desperately her mother wanted to erase her childhood insecurities.

"I will do my best." Violet aimed to lower her mother's expectations, adding, "Hopefully I'm able to help."

"Your father's relatives have the land deed that your Uncle Francesco claims is all under his name. I need you to read it over, word by word, in front of all of them since they are all illiterate. I believe one parcel of land legally belongs to us."

Violet was pleased her mother believed her capable of confronting the in-laws and handling this situation. She suspected her mother had a deeper motive. By showing assertiveness, determination and confidence, Maria wanted to impress on her in-laws: "No more messing with me or my daughters."

The next morning, Renato, their very dependable cousin, showed up in his Lambretta. He offered to drive Violet back to her father's hometown and wait for as long as necessary.

She conducted their meeting strategically and with professionalism. Every word was pointed out and read slowly for clarification. Reviewing the deed meticulously proved undeniably that her mother had been correct. The one acre in question was by law legally inherited by Ornesto's wife, Maria.

The four siblings considered Violet's firm and precise explanation and agreed with the document in her hands. They instructed Uncle Francesco to buy the acre from Maria. "Since it's smack between your olive trees, we insist you pay Maria a reasonable price."

Uncle Francesco grunted his displeasure but had no choice but to agree with his older siblings. He signed a bank draft for the full amount payable in a month's time. Violet wasn't sure what had motivated them to act so promptly and seal the transaction. She displayed no emotions but showed gratitude for their compliance by professionally shaking each one's hand. They, in turn, shook her hand firmly to show fairness and closure.

There was a swagger in Violet's walk that said, "I did good." She was content, mostly excited to give her mama the great news. Quickening her pace, she headed to where Renato had suggested they meet.

"Wait! Wait!" she heard a man call out. "Please, Miss Conti! I need to speak with you." Recognition jolted Violet's memory, causing her to quicken her pace.

Unfortunately, the uneven cobblestones paving the street kept catching her heels, requiring her to be cautious and slow down. She turned to see the man running towards her. He stopped just an inch from her face. Violet immediately took a big step back. He was huge, dirty, and smelled worse than their dog Brutus after he had been sprayed by the skunk.

"I am not sure if I should be telling you—maybe it's best I speak with your mother?" He sounded smug as he spat out his question.

His leering look made Violet feel violated, as if she had hundreds of creepy crawlers all over her body. "What is it?" she forced out.

"I am Pasquale, owner of the tavern."

Violet wanted to say, "I know exactly who you are," recalling the many times her mother had sent her to collect her father. Peeking through the murky window, she'd watch this dirty man pour her drunken father more wine. "Yes?" Violet's tone mirrored her unpleasant memory.

"I am sorry. I'll get to the point. Your father had some unpaid bills. I really should speak to your mother."

"No, don't bother her, I'll handle this."

"Of course, I understand." His insincere compassion sickened her.

"How much?"

"Well, I don't have them all with me. I assure you, *signorina*, they have your father's signature, as you can see."

He pulled some tattered pieces of paper from his filthy apron and showed them to her. There was no doubt. Violet recognized her father's scribbles. Ornesto, being the youngest, had the privilege of attending school for one year, and had been just learned enough to sign his name on an I.O.U.

"I'll take those." Violet wrote her address down and speedily exchanged papers. "Send me the others, and I will wire you the money at the post office." Violet wanted no more to do with this man.

"I am not sure," he snarled, waving the piece of paper while continuing to inspect her.

Handing him cash for the full amount quoted in the I.O.U.'s, Violet asked angrily, "What is it you're not sure of?"

His greedy eyes were now set on the money. "I suppose it's okay." He quickly stuffed the liras in his pocket.

"Do not mention a word of this to my mother," she ordered.

"Miss Conti, you have my word it will be between us, I assure you." His sneering whisper was as deceitful as his grin. The man had obviously gotten what he wanted, and he left quickly.

Violet could not believe this last offense. Even after his death, her father still managed to take advantage of her. *But not my family*, she furiously resolved to herself. *No more! Enough!* She was holding back tears. Filled with perseverance, Violet composed herself and made two vows that day. *My mother must never know, and I will never again set foot in this town.*

CHAPTER 30

RETURNING TO EDWARD

Violet's departure launched a wave of emotions among the family. Her sisters sobbed uncontrollably. A mention of a possible visit close to Christmas escaped from Violet. This, of course, delighted them all, extracting smiles from the younger sisters. Violet had also been diligent and requested that a phone be installed in their home soon. The convenience of a private phone was the greatest gift for them all.

Maria embraced her daughter with the depths of a mother's love as she whispered, "A part of me comes with you."

Prearranged by Mr. Sutton, a private chauffeur from Rome had arrived to take Violet back to the airport. He stood waiting patiently and dutifully for his passenger next to the automobile. A crowd of well-wishers had shown up outside their home to bid Violet a fond farewell. Maria's relatives had affectionately welcomed her and the girls back to the family's hometown.

"We want to extend our support and will help in any way needed," they had volunteered.

Violet left with a warm heart, satisfied knowing all was well and good. She slept through most of the flight back to London. It was the first time in a fortnight she'd had placidity.

Passing through the arrivals gate at Heathrow airport, Violet noticed a man holding a card with her name on it. This impersonal welcome was disappointing and surprising. Her first thought was, *Where is my Edward?* Violet almost yelled out her question.

There was no doubt in her mind that Edward would have insisted to come personally to get her. She had imagined him waiting excitedly, jumping up and down. Her little man had done it before; she smiled remembering the day. Having to focus on getting the stranger's attention, Violet masked her disappointment and waved in his direction.

The approach to the manor gave Violet a sense of déja vu. Except this time, she was not a frightened little girl facing an unknown future and feeling out of place. This time she sat with her legs crossed, poised in her designer suit, conveying, *I belong here.* Aware the driver was watching her from the rear-view mirror, she stopped her contemplation and gave him a grin.

Looking out her window, Violet witnessed a surprising scene she'd never believed possible. Thomas, although robust, was struggling to hold Brutus back. The old dog's behavior was most unusual. *Where did Brutus get his energy?* The aging hound dog, known to sleep most of his day, was now determined to get loose and run off.

This aroused Violet's curiosity. What had happened to cause Brutus to act so aggressive? In addition to Thomas wrestling with the canine, a number of servants were also gathered in front of the manor. This uncommon lingering alarmed her even further. Violet concluded something was wrong and began to feel anxious. The moment her eyes spotted Edward, Violet let out a deep exhale. Obviously, her trepidation had restricted her normal breathing.

The Suttons' Rolls Royce was now coming down the drive, slowly approaching the Mercedes she was in. Violet extended her neck like a giraffe, determined to see Albert's passenger. The unexpected acceleration from the family's chauffeur assured his passengers remained a mystery.

The second the automobile came to a stop; Violet burst open her own door and hurriedly jumped out. She dashed directly to Edward, grabbing him and giving him a big squeeze. One by one, the servants greeted her and left, some wiping their eyes. Thomas continued to struggle with the agitated canine, who was now whimpering.

"What's wrong? Where are your parents?" Violet demanded, not even trying to hide her fears from Edward.

"They are inside," he whispered, wiping off tears from his face. "Mom and Dad preferred to say goodbye to Eric in private."

"Eric? Eric, your older brother, was the one leaving? He came to visit?" By putting the few puzzle pieces together, Violet had no trouble revealing a clear picture. The timing was perfect; Eric had arrived just after she left for Italy. Violet now remembered that Edward had insinuated, while she was gone, he'd be busy having fun. "I'm sorry Eric had to leave, Edward, I know you will miss your big brother. I wish I'd arrived earlier and had the opportunity to meet him."

Edward was slowly regaining his composure and half-grinned. "I'm really glad you're home, Violet, I have loads to tell you." His welcoming words were sincere yet subdued. Eric's departure left him a bit withdrawn and melancholy.

In past years, Violet had mastered ways of distracting Edward and curbing his mood. On such occasions as this, she would reach for her bag of tricks to distract him. In an exaggerated voice, distorting her face, she'd say funny phrases in five different languages. "Edward," she started, "take your fingers out of your nose so you can hear what I have to say." The combination of her made-up phrase with her weird facial expression always extracted bursts of laughter from the somber boy. Edward rewarded Violet's effort by always asking for an encore.

After informing the Suttons of her arrival and answering a few travel-related questions, she dashed back to Edward. "I can't wait to hear all about your brother's visit." Violet's high-pitched, excitable voice sounded as though she was still performing.

Edward was just as eager and began giving her all the details of Eric's stay. He had spent the entire fortnight glued to his big brother and wanted to share everything they had done in her absence.

"Eric said I have really grown. He called me a very special young man. I told him all about you, Violet, and showed him our photos together."

Violet couldn't hold back her curiosity. "Eric must have been bored looking at all those pictures of us. Do you have any pictures of Eric?"

"No and no!" was Edward's quick reply.

Baffled, Violet lifted her lower lip "Edward, are you trying to confuse me?"

"No, Eric does not like to be in pictures. He prefers to take them, and no, Eric was not bored. He asked me a lot of questions and wanted to see even more pictures. We had tremendous fun going through them all. He particularly liked the one I took of you by the river. Eric told our parents he noticed a dramatic change in me. He kept saying it was fortunate in many ways, the day Violet came into our lives." Edward giggled, leaned closer toward her and whispered "Eric likes you, Violet, he even brought you a present. He left me important instructions to give it to you personally."

Violet was tantalized by everything Edward revealed about Eric. This was the man everyone at the manor had perpetually praised. She was thrilled and secretly kept repeating Edward's statement, over and over: "Eric likes you and bought you a present." Violet had to keep her wistful emotions in check. She needed to be sensible in front of Edward to give him a proper verbal response. "That was very thoughtful of your brother." She hoped this short acknowledgement sounded solely appreciative. She had to stay focused and be logical about Eric's feelings and motive. *How could he like me without even meeting me? Obviously, he bought the gift as a way to thank me. Yes! But why go to all the trouble?"* Violet re-examined Eric's intentions, kept leaning favorably on what she was told. It would not be smart to dispute Edward's explanation. *If Edward says Eric likes me, who am I to question it? After all, Eric is his older brother, and with Edward's insight he would know best.* This last conclusion pleased her.

"I told Eric you and I share a secret."

Edward's remark jolted Violet, causing her to stop daydreaming, capturing her full attention. She suddenly shifted from feeling blithe excitement to nervous anxiety.

"What did he say?"

"Eric told me a secret between two close friends must never be shared with anyone else. He added he was proud I did not reveal it, not even to him. Eric kept asking about my rock collection. We often spent our mornings at the river digging. He was always interested to hear all my amazing fossil theories."

Eric's response was perfect, releasing Violet from her anxiety. He was wise to reinforce, a secret pact between two friends must never be shared. Praising his little brother for being loyal ensured Edward would continue to keep it between them. Distracting Edward with questions about his fossils was genius. Violet couldn't help wondering how astute Eric actually was towards his younger brother. With all the time the two had spent together, had Edward slipped up? Eric must have sensed his younger brother was gifted, but perhaps not the full extent to which he was gifted. She continued mulching her theories in her head. Even if he became suspicious, his limited stay didn't allow him the proper time to probe. He was sensible to leave well enough alone. Violet recognized all this was speculation on her part. Nevertheless, she respected and appreciated Eric for making it easier on her.

Praising Eric was nothing new in the Sutton household. Throughout the years, all conversations about the man and his achievements were of high esteem. What made it different this time was Violet's own personal twist and connection. She had enough sense to admit her titillated feelings about him were ridiculous, but they still pleased her.

At dinner that evening, Catherine was very candid. "I'm so glad you're back with us. I was worried your mama wouldn't allow you to return."

Violet understood Catherine's concern; Catherine was a possessive mother herself.

"Mama was determined I stay with them, but I insisted and was adamant to return. I had given Edward my solemn promise I would return to him. Also, my family needs my financial assistance now more than ever." Violet's candidness left nothing more for Catherine to question.

Mr. Sutton had his own comment and readily added, "I agree, and have decided this is a good time to double your salary."

Catherine, of course, was in agreement with her husband's decision. The lady was more eager to focus on the updated schedule she held in her hand. "Violet, my dear." Mrs. Sutton wasted no time shifting the conversation. "While you were away, I was busy making some inquiries. I believe you need to learn ballroom dancing and have added it to your schedule. With the fall social season approaching, it's never too early to start."

"Ha! Ha!" Edward blurted, "Too bad for you!" As he laughed, the boy mimicked some exaggerated dance moves.

His buffoonery did not amuse his parents. His mother's stern look made Edward stop his twirling and immediately sit down.

Violet was still trying to digest Mr. Sutton wanting to double her salary. Since it had readily been dismissed, she questioned if she had heard correctly. As for dance lessons, she had zero desire to acquire dance skills. Her daily schedule was completely full. These dance lessons would obviously encroach on other activities. Riding, tennis, hiking—things she enjoyed doing would likely be cut by half. Violet had never, and would never, show displeasure, especially after Mr. Sutton's tremendous offer. She wanted to be even more compliant. There was no doubt, having observed Catherine's scheduling methods over her years at the manor, the dance lessons were a *fait comp lit*.

"I will do my best to learn, Mrs. Sutton."

Catherine's smile confirmed she expected Violet to comply. "You are a treasure! I am positive you will be amazing, as with everything you do, my dear." Catherine's compliment was sincere, but it hinted also at self-gratification. Violet believed Mrs. Sutton's aspirations were the contributing factor to her success, therefore all her achievements reflected back to Catherine.

Just before bedtime, Edward entered Violet's room with Eric's present in hand. "Open it! Open it!" he demanded.

Violet could not resist teasing him a bit. "Do you really want me to open it now? Are you sure, Edward?"

She had barely pulled the ribbon when Edward eagerly clawed at the ornate wrapping paper. He revealed a beautiful, intricately carved silver music box. Violet gasped. "It's so lovely! Thank you, Edward."

"Why thank me? I had nothing to do with it; this is the first time I have seen it. Eric picked it and bought it for you."

Violet sighed, softly caressing the box, and she repeated Eric's name. He stared at her as if she had sprouted two heads, which prompted Violet to stop acting so silly.

She had to disguise her thoughts by shifting her attention to him. "I'm sure you had something to do with it, you little monster. I absolutely adore it, come give me a hug."

CHAPTER 31

HARMLESS FANTASIES

Shortly after Edward left, Violet listened repeatedly to the melody from her exquisite music box. She was mesmerized with the tune and began swaying, imagining herself in Eric's arms.

Although alone, she felt embarrassed by her vivid imagination. Until today, Violet had never been interested or even thought about the opposite sex. This sudden awareness and interest were partly credited to her mother's cautionary forecast. Maria's adamance suggested she would soon have male admirers. Her mother's astute intuition combined perfectly with Edward's declaration: "Eric likes you." This was what had caused this unfamiliar sensation. The gift of the music box was also a tangible motivator. This tantalizing rush of new emotions were unstoppable, as flowing waters destined to cascade down a majestic waterfall. Violet was experiencing her first-ever crush. Logic, of course, had to be dismissed; she had to close the door to sensibility and open her mind to fantasy. In the privacy of her room, she gave herself permission to indulge in her own fairy-tale.

As the romance began to unfold, she faced her first obstacle. There were no recent pictures of Eric in the manor's library. How was she to envision her admirer? Her clever idea was to compose Eric's image as a sophisticated older version of Edward. She imagined the two of them dancing at a ball just like Cinderella and Prince Charming.

With every random twirl she clumsily performed, she had to admit to herself, *taking dance lessons is probably not such a bad idea after all.*

It didn't take long before her tendency to be grounded crushed Violet's romantic daydreams. She went back to asking the same obvious questions: *Did Eric buy this gift on a whim? Was he only trying to say thank you on Edward's behalf?* Her third question was the hardest to overlook. *Eric knew I was the one arriving in the automobile. Why didn't he stop to say a simple hello?* The phrase "three strikes and you're out" flashed in her head. This somber deliberation caused Violet to end her illusion of romance. *Be sensible and mature,* she lectured inwardly. This gift was a spontaneous gesture of kindness. Disillusioned, she promptly marching to her dresser and hid the music box inside the top drawer. Determined, she deliberately placed a few scarves overtop to conceal it. As it so happened, the now overstuffed drawer remained slightly open, exposing a piece of her colorful scarf.

Violet's subconscious mind wasn't completely done romanticizing and cleverly took hold. It suggested this overture was a definite sign, conveying a clear message! Eric's gift from the heart should not be dismissed. Quick to agree, she hurried to retrieve her enticing music box. Caressing and rubbing it as though it were Aladdin's lamp, she placed it prominently on top of the dresser. There it would be displayed in perfect view from her bed.

CHAPTER 32

BETTY WRONGLY ACCUSED!

For the last few months, Sutton Manor had hosted numerous festivities. They included Violet's nineteenth and Edward's twelfth birthday parties. Mr. Sutton's good friend, the local chief of police, had a retirement sendoff—a grand function. As was Miss Kerr's engagement to the village's veterinarian. Three newborn babies were also welcomed on the estate. The joint christening celebration had topped the festivities for a spell.

The staff had earned a much needed break before harvest time. Mr. and Mrs. Sutton planned a two-week getaway to the south of France. Violet and Edward were now at a threshold with their academic studies. They had both been given a reasonable timeline to consider their options. Everything was planned in detail to everyone's apparent satisfaction. Unfortunately, the best-laid plans often go awry.

Misfortune happened the first week of September. While on their morning horseback ride, Edward had another significant vision. Violet believed she had become accustomed to Edward's distressed cries. Not so! They still unsettled her. Yet for Edward's sake, she tried to be in control when these situations occurred.

"I am here, Edward. Calm down and tell me what you saw. Remember your vision cannot hurt you." Violet had used that phrase hundreds of times throughout the years.

However, this latest vision had Edward trembling and too upset to speak. Mumbled and stuttering words finally came out. "She fell! And! And! Now she is dead!"

The word "DEAD!" stunned Violet. Fear set in her heart. With her own unsettled quivering voice, she questioned. "Who fell, Edward? Who died?" She shut her eyes and held her breath preparing to hear the bad news.

Edward sped his words, like a runaway train. "Esther, our maid, it happened so fast, she was dusting and leaned too far and went over the banister, straight down." The boy then sat on the grass and went quiet.

A slight sigh of relief did escape from Violet's mouth. Her sigh was a spontaneous reaction, relieved it was not a family member. She needed to keep her composure, put her own emotions aside, and help Edward. The two fell silent. Their sadness made words unnecessary. Esther was a dear and indelible member of the Suttons' staff. She had no family of her own and had spent most of her life at Sutton Manor. Beloved by the entire household, her tragic loss would have a devastating impact on everyone.

Violet had to take charge and act responsibly. "We must head back," she said. Since riding unchaperoned for a while, Violet considered the staff would be anxious for their return. "I'm sure everyone is in shock by this terrible accident and would prefer us safely home."

Edward didn't respond, he was rigid and hesitant. His repression concerned her, as she sensed he might have more to add. She allowed Edward more time to clarify his vision. "Violet, I feel troubled," he grudgingly confessed. "There is a lot of confusion. My father is especially angry."

Of course, the Suttons would be informed of the accident as soon as possible; this would affect them all. But why would Mr. Sutton be angry? In all the years she had known the gentleman, anger was not in his character. Violet had no doubt the Suttons would shorten their vacation and return, mostly out of respect for Esther.

It suddenly occurred to her Mr. Sutton's anger could be related to a different matter. "Edward!" Violet's voice was louder than she intended.

"What?"

"I want you to be very careful in what you say."

"Not that again! I will be, I promise, don't look so worried."

"Edward, you might slip up and say the wrong thing and bring suspicion to yourself. Remember, you do not know a thing. If someone says anything about the accident you know is wrong, don't correct them."

"I won't!" Edward showed his frustration. "You can trust me to keep my mouth shut."

Violet wasn't convinced. No doubt there would be much speculation and long discussions about the accident. She decided not to let him out of her sight until this whole ordeal was over.

Esther's funeral was well attended. She had been a most beloved friend to all the staff. Her subservient character had her working harder than required. Memories shared were all of her kindness and giving nature. One by one, staff and friends voiced personal, heartfelt stories, bringing tears to everyone's eyes. They had all benefited from Esther's friendship and sincerely promised she would not be forgotten.

It was at the reception luncheon that Captain Harris confronted Mr. Sutton. "I'm here on official business," he said. "After going through all the notes, the conclusion at the station was unanimous. All our collaborating evidence indicate your maid was indeed murdered."

What had eluded Violet for many years now surfaced. Splattered on William's face was anger. He moved closer to Harris with fire in his eyes and growled. "You're pathetic. That's pure nonsense. Moreover, this is neither the time nor place for such allegations. If you need to discuss anything, come back tomorrow." William turned and walked away.

Catherine was shaking her head in disbelief. "That man infuriates me," she said.

They had first met Harris, at the retirement send-off party given for the previous captain. At the time, Harris kept making crude insinuations about Mr. Sutton.

"I will not be one of William Sutton's puppets like everyone in this town!" the newly appointed official pompously announced for all to hear.

The retiring captain was appalled. "You, sir," he rebuked, "are a disgrace to your position, and what's more, you're a distasteful human being." His reprimand of his successor had erupted a ripple of agreement among the other guests.

Violet took Edward aside. "Did you hear what the police captain said? He called Esther's accident a murder!"

"That explains all the confusion in my vision. Remember my father was especially angry?"

"You're right Edward. This is a disaster. Everything will be chaotic."

Their usual serene morning breakfast was interrupted by Simon's announcing Captain Harris' arrival. The vigilant butler hadn't fully finished his proper introduction when Harris spoke over him. "As I was saying yesterday, I'm here on official business. After considerable studies from the statements we gathered, we've come to a solid conclusion. We have agreed without doubt your maid's death was murder."

"It was a tragic accident!" Catherine rebutted. "Esther fell. She might have unfortunately become dizzy."

Edward was about to open his mouth, but Violet precluded him by adding her opinion. "She was very old, you know."

"No!" the captain answered defiantly. "We found ample discrepancies in one of your other maid's account of her whereabouts at the time of the victim's demise. Her name is Betty, and I asked the Butler to bring her to me."

"Betty?" Violet's protest had everyone's attention. She immediately reinforced her defense. "Betty is my maid and the gentlest person I or anyone could ever know." Violet held Betty in high esteem. She never regarded her as her servant but rather her equal. Throughout the years their relationship was based more on mutual friendship and cordial respect.

The captain looked sour and determined "Those women are often the most deceitful."

"Harris, you're a menace to this exceptional community." Mr. Sutton charged, grabbing his elbow, and walking him out of his conservatory. It was the last place William wanted contaminated by the likes of Harris.

"I must do my duty and take her in for questioning," Harris insisted.

"What are you basing your suspicion on?" Catherine challenged the captain, following them.

Harris displayed his professionalism by glancing at his notes. "She was the one who discovered the body, the last one to see the victim alive. Betty's whereabouts at the time of death cannot be verified by anyone. However, we do have corroborating statements from three persons on your staff about a disagreement between the victim and the accused. She—this Betty—had an argument with the victim just fifteen minutes before her death. My notes indicate the two women frequently quarreled." Harris stopped and stiffened his whole body before voicing his last conclusion. "This evidence clearly indicates there was animosity between the two servants."

"I assure you,"—William had now reached his boiling point—"there is no animosity among my staff. I would appreciate you not jumping to your idiotic conclusions. If that's all you have, your allegations of murder are bogus, and that's putting it mildly."

Simon and Betty were slowly approaching. The butler had obviously informed the young lady of the severity of the situation, as she was crying uncontrollably. She kept wiping her tears away with her apron. "I loved Esther just like my own mother," she whimpered.

"You, miss, must come to the station for questioning. I'm following procedures and no one is above the law." The arrogant captain spat back, looking directly at William.

Catherine moved closer to her husband and put her hand on his shoulder. Violet understood Mrs. Sutton believed her husband might grab the captain and physically throw him out of his home.

William's eyes shifted to the people he loved. In consideration for his family, William managed to compose himself. He spoke gently to Betty. "Don't worry! I will put a stop to these ridiculous accusations." He turned to Harris and grunted, exposing his contempt towards the man.

Violet gave Betty an affectionate hug and whispered, "The truth will come out, I promise."

Edward, standing beside Violet, kept his mouth closed but nodded in agreement.

The manor was in mourning. With the tragic death of one of their own, and another accused of her murder, everyone felt unnerved. Morale was very low. The entire staff did their tasks robotically. They spoke only of work-related matters and kept personal feelings unexpressed.

The usual passive town shared the dismay. They were outraged with the local police and began to speculate and gossip. One story spread rapidly. It was rumored the chief of police had contempt for William Sutton's wealth and influence. Harris's prejudice stemmed from the fact that his wife had taken off with a successful man a few years earlier. The betrayed husband blamed money and influence for corrupting his wife. He never acknowledged she had publicly complained for years. She admitted finally having had enough of him and his morbid character.

"What a presumptuous, pompous little man." Catherine's complaint was on Harris's character rather than his huge physical appearance. Mrs. Sutton voiced her dislike at breakfast the next morning. Her husband had just informed them that Betty had been officially charged with Esther's murder.

"Our lawyer did manage to get her released from the holding cell." Regrettably, he reported, she was put on house arrest until a judge arrived. "Harris wants to know her whereabouts at all times. He went as far as to install an officer in front of Betty's family's home." William's tone showed his disgust as he quoted what Harris was telling everybody. "'I'm personally keeping my eye on her. I'm responsible for bringing justice and I'm determined to do my duty.' The man must have a high opinion of himself. He sounds determined to continue in the direction he came up with. I believe he is hoping to further his career with this ridiculous charge of murder."

Edward nudged Violet as a reminder of what they had rehearsed the night before.

"It's incomprehensible to me," Violet began, "how easy a situation can be twisted to suit someone's theory."

"It's true." Edward's agreement came on cue. "Once a case goes to trial, anything could happen."

"It's startling how many innocent people falsely accused have ended up in jail." Violet paused before adding her last line. "All because the truth was distorted and misrepresented."

"That's terrible!" Edward animated the word "terrible."

Catherine found their exchange confusing. "*What* are you two talking about?" It was really a rhetorical question, as she quickly added, "I believe it's time for you both to be out riding?"

Violet and Edward pretend to glance at the time and promptly left the conservatory. They hid behind the plant-covered glass next to the doors, to listen in. They wanted to make sure their subtle message was not only received but also absorbed by the person targeted.

Mr. Sutton finally spoke: "I feel uneasy about all this. Harris' dislike towards me might cloud his judgment. This will fall most unfairly on Betty. I'm considering calling my dear friend, from Scotland Yard to come visit. I don't usually like to interfere, but under these circumstances I feel I must."

Catherine consented with encouraging words. "I like the way you think dear."

Violet and Edward shook hands. Their mission to get additional help by planting doubt had succeeded.

CHAPTER 33

THE PROMPT INSPECTOR

Nothing could have prepared Violet or Edward for Inspector O'Brien. He entered the conservatory the next morning and gave all at the breakfast table a military salute.

Edward was about to burst out with something exclamatory but was held down by Violet's hand yanking him to be still. It was hard even for Violet to keep a straight face. She bent her head down slightly as she had years earlier when confronted with Mrs. Torantino's moustache.

Inspector O'Brien was short and stout. His exaggerated, groomed moustache was down the full length of his face. It was perfectly twisted to a sharp point and curved inward towards his chin. He had a good-sized potato for a nose and thick round glasses. He looked as if he were wearing a plastic mask, like the ones children do at Halloween.

William's welcome was a loud, friendly laugh with a compatriot pat on the inspector's back. Edward's expression told Violet he felt cheated since his father had his spontaneous release.

Catherine seemed unaware of O'Brien's exaggerated appearance. She smiled graciously and courteously invited the inspector to sit and join them. Her demeanour did not go unnoticed by Violet. She had been tutored proper etiquette and manners on how ladies behave in company. Watching Catherine, Violet appreciated how she had been her daily example. She personified, elegance, wit, and charm—all qualities Violet aspired to achieve. Earnestly she promised herself to try and be more like Mrs. Sutton.

The conversation, after cordial inquiries about family and health, turned immediately to Betty's circumstance. Inspector O'Brien had heard of Harris and his methods. "I'm not surprised, William. Why do you think he was made to come to your small hamlet? With his crusty impertinence, he has been forced out of numerous other towns."

William was disturbed and asserted his displeasure. "We must put a stop to these allegations. The judge could be given ridiculous evidence and might be convinced to order a trial."

"Right, William," O'Brien agreed. "Once the judicial spiral begins, it speeds downwards rapidly. I will go to the station immediately and reevaluate the evidence."

Addressing Catherine with a bow, he said, "I'll be back in time for lunch."

"We will be delighted, Inspector. Please get our Betty back. This has been distressing for us all, most devastating for the unfortunate girl and her family." Catherine's words echoed all of their concern.

CHAPTER 34

OBSCURE EVIDENCE

Violet was apprehensive about her decision. Unfortunately, she had no other choice. They had nothing to substantiate Esther's death was an accident. Having Edward go through every detail of his vision was disturbing. His well-being was always her first priority. But Edward's readiness to be helpful was both permissible and reassuring. "Don't leave anything out. Even the smallest detail might be pertinent."

"Pertinent, Violet? Have you been reading mystery novels?"

"Concentrate, Edward; it's important you focus on the details." Edward was actually calm as he closed his eyes and retold the incident. He sounded as though he was retelling a movie, he had seen a few days earlier.

"Betty and Esther were arguing." He started from the very beginning. "Betty left upset. Esther continued dusting the cobwebs from the large paintings. She put a cloth on the broom handle to reach those over the banister. The cloth got hooked on the nail and was dangling over one of the paintings. She tried many times to release the rag. She finally caught the end with the broom and started to pull on it." Edward paused. "That is when it happened." With his eyes shut he proceeded recounting his vision in more detail. "The dust rag tore off as it was falling. Esther tried to grab it and leaned too far over. She lost her footing and went down." Edward opened his eyes and looked at Violet's face. She was holding both his hands as if to balance him.

"Are you okay? I am so sorry for making you do this," she said.

"I'm okay. I want to help Betty."

Violet hugged Edward. His concern was so selfless and endearing.

Still holding him by one hand, Violet dragged him running up the stairs. "Look, Edward." She emphatically pointed to the evidence. A small piece of the rag was still hung on the nail. Discouragingly, it was a tiny, horizontal, frail remnant and not easily noticed. They both agreed getting the inspector to discover it on his own would be difficult, if not impossible.

At lunch, Inspector O'Brien told William he did not get along well with Harris. "He accused me of interfering with his case. I simply suggested two heads are better than one and he should welcome my expertise. I must admit, I did remind him of my rank." O'Brien professionally acknowledged it was within his rights to do so.

"Harris, of course, resents your presence; he must be furious being forced to comply to your authority." There was a satisfied, almost humorous tinge in William's voice.

"Absolutely. I insisted to see the photographs of the body."

"And?"

"No findings, as of yet. I want to speak with your maid. What is her name?"

"Betty!" everyone at the table volunteered.

"I'll look around the area of the accident myself; maybe Harris and his men missed something."

Violet's loud cough shifted all eyes in her direction. Her own eyes were focused on a fidgety twelve-year-old boy. She'd simply meant to get Edward's attention. "Please pass me the butter." Her real coded message given in her facial expression warned: "Don't say a word."

Returning from his interview with Betty later that day, O'Brien said, "It is completely obvious this sweet young lady is innocent. She told me the reason the two constantly disagree. Betty continuously wanted to help minimize Esther's workload, which Esther stubbornly refused. Betty truly loved Esther. I will continue to search around diligently for tangible evidence."

Violet and Edward lurked nearby. They had rehearsed a small performance, hoping to lure the inspector to notice the small dangling rag remnant.

"Remember, Edward," Violet instructed him, "only say your lines, don't add more."

"We are getting good at this Violet," Edward boasted with a thumbs up.

"I can't believe you found your watch, Violet," Edward said, louder than necessary. The inspector didn't seem to notice the chatty duo. He seemed deep in thought, walking with both hands behind his back.

Violet and Edward knew they had to get even closer.

"Well, I simply retraced my steps. I returned to all the places I had recently been."

"How clever and perceptive of you to retrace your steps." Edward delivered his praise slowly.

"Yes, I would never have found my watch if I wasn't meticulous."

"Where was it?" Edward recited his line like a great actor.

"On the dresser behind my picture, it . . . was . . . hiding behind . . . the . . . picture." Violet enunciated each word deliberately, pausing as Edward used to do when she was learning the English language.

O'Brien was now upstairs. Violet and Edward joined him.

"Inspector, Violet has found her watch," Edward informed the disinterested man.

"I'm going to put it back in my jewelry box where it belongs," confirmed Violet.

"Good idea. I will wait here for you."

"Edward, you mustn't bother the inspector while he is in search for the smallest evidence."

"I know, Violet. This is where Esther was dusting." Edward's tone was serious. "It's sad," he continued. "She must have been concentrating on all those cobwebs. They're everywhere."

"Especially on the big paintings," Violet observed, pretending to play with her watch. She intensely watched the inspector, who now eyed the paintings.

"Yes!" she whispered under her breath, content his focus was now on the right place. Violet was now prepared to leave. "Come, Edward; let's leave Inspector O'Brien to do his brilliant work."

Without another word, pleased with their performance, they made their exit together. Pressed against Violet's slightly opened door, they heard the inspector's footsteps going down the stairs.

"What do you think, Violet? Did he see the cloth hanging on the nail?"

"I sure hope so. We practically pointed to it for him. We really couldn't do much more without implicating ourselves, Edward."

CHAPTER 35

THE TRUTH REVEALED

Dinner was delayed.

Earlier Mr. and Mrs. Sutton had accompanied Inspector O'Brien to the village police station and had just now returned. The instrumental duo—Violet and Edward—was eager to hear what happened but kept still. William Sutton asked Simon to gather all the staff in the drawing room.

"Please bring champagne for everyone." Catherine's happiness was transparent.

When all glasses were full, Mr. Sutton spoke. "I'm happy and grateful to announce our Betty will be reporting to work as usual in a few days. You can well imagine she is very emotional, mostly relieved this ordeal is finally over."

A gasp of contentment escaped from everyone.

Simon was the one to speak on behalf of the staff. "Mr. Sutton, we want to thank you and express our appreciation for all you have done for one of our own." Simon's words were sincere and given with utmost respect.

"Sir," Thomas spoke up, "may we know some details?"

The others also expressed their need to know. "Please, sir, tell us what actually happened?"

"Yes, of course," William obliged. "My good friend Inspector O'Brien discovered a small piece of rag stuck to a nail which held a large painting. It was the missing piece torn from the dust rag Esther used that morning. Pictures from the scene revealed the rag was actually under Esther's body. O'Brien concluded from the evidence, Esther had tried to retrieve the rag and leaned over the banister too far. She lost her balance and accidentally fell."

"To Esther, may she now rest in peace." Mr. Sutton raised his glass.

"To Esther!" everyone echoed.

The terrible ordeal now appeared to be over. Everyone hoped the household could return to normal, at least for a while.

CHAPTER 36

RETRIBUTION

Neither the Suttons nor anyone from the manor were responsible for what erupted. A petition circulated in the peaceful town, demanding Captain Harris' immediate removal as chief of police. It was successful, as the town council acted quickly. He resigned, disgruntled but unrepentant; Harris then hastened his departure from the town without a rebuttal.

Mr. Sutton, speaking to his family, summarized Harris' lack of contrition, reciting an appropriate cliché: "Leopards never change their spots."

Catherine playfully collaborated with him. "William, my dear husband, let's just be glad the beast has gone, and we have our Betty back."

Violet took pleasure in the Suttons' play with words and each other. She had nothing to add verbally and simply nodded her agreement.

Edward, on the other hand, stood with a theatrical attorney pose. This indicated to Violet he had not completely relinquished his previous acting role. With dramatic flair, hand clutching his pretend lapel, he proceeded to deliver his line: "Justice has been served."

Catherine shook her head and motioned with her hand for their son to sit down. Still shaking her head, she added, "God help the next unfortunate village Harris is appointed to next."

"Actually, my dear, O'Brien gave me good news regarding that. Harris is to leave for Boston, swearing never to return to England. My friend also predicted the cad would not last a month in the city."

CHAPTER 37

AS TIME PASSES, CHANGE IS INEVITABLE.

It was now late February. Spring was not far away.

Violet noticed a change in Edward's behavior. He acted more determined and a bit assured, like a typical adolescent. The physical changes where subtle, but his character had shifted rapidly. More and more he insisted on his independence. He would often say, "I'm in control," or, "I'm capable of doing this on my own." He would frequently remind everyone he would soon be thirteen.

It's a known fact of life: the young tend to add years to their age, while the more mature secretly subtract them. Edward liked the number thirteen.

Violet was frustrated with Edward's restrictions on her. She was jolted and surprised the day he confronted her about the ongoing superhero theory.

"I can't believe I was so naive to think it was true. You lied to me!" he charged at her.

Violet, caught unprepared for Edward's bluntness and disappointment, decided her best recourse was to tell him the truth. "I'm sorry Edward! It was just a little lie; I came up with it on a whim. Remember how upset you were back then about your nightmares? They not only frightened you, but made you feel bad about yourself. Visions of tragic world events is the unfortunate aspect of your abilities. I didn't know how to explain the connection; truthfully it was confusing for me too, Edward. I was desperately trying to help control some of your fears."

Edward listened and accepted Violet's explanation. "It worked," he admitted. "At the time, I liked associating myself with superheroes. It was easier for me to think I was one of them. It helped knowing there were others like me. I know your intention was always to protect me. You didn't want me to get hurt and be exploited or ridiculed by people."

Edward had always possessed a depth of intellect. His maturity on some matters was beyond his years. Violet believed Edward was not only gifted with visions but also an abundance of wisdom.

"The doctors my parents had examine me concluded I was mentally disturbed. When I was examined by these doctors, my fears magnified. I felt more afraid of them and what they might do to me than my nightmares. That was why I kept silent and wouldn't answer their questions. I only trusted you, Violet. I knew you would protect me. All the visions I had of you at the time calmed me."

A flashback of the one with all the young brides, put a grin on Violet's face. She was now prepared to keep her promise and explain its meaning to him.

"No need to explain, Violet," Edward halted her when she mentioned it. "I'm aware it was a procession for the Madonna. You must agree the girls' dresses made them look like brides."

Violet slightly tilted her head to one side as if contemplating. "Except there was no one to marry the little seven-year-old girls."

They both had a hearty laugh at his most significant oversight.

Violet used her laughter to hide her reluctance to give up protecting Edward's innocence. She knew as time passed, he would be less and less dependent on her for guidance. He kept insisting he was comfortable with his own aptitudes. She was prepared to give him some freedom but wasn't totally convinced.

"I know not to speak of my visions, Violet," Edward said. "Over the years you have taught me how to live with them. I do not allow them to control me; I now control them. Also, I understand some of my visions are just fragments of events I can neither help nor solve."

Violet struggled to sound positive. "Edward, I'm pleased with your level of confidence." She was sincerely happy to hear him speak so openly but felt her role in his life would diminish. Her reflection erupted a spontaneous, melodramatic remark. "I suppose I should pack and return to Italy, since I'm no longer needed here."

Edward's stunned reaction geared Violet to immediately regret her overly exaggerated comment. "You won't leave me now, will you, Violet?"

"No! Never! I was joking. You sounded so mature and in control. I wanted my little man back."

"That wasn't very nice of you, Violet. I'm not in the least amused." Edward's protest did not reflect the look on his face. He showed signs of relief, and a hint of amusement came through in his bright eyes.

Violet took this opportunity to propose an idea she had been mulching for a while. She had been tempted to suggest it a few times in the past but had dismissed it. The probability of more confusion was too risky. Now the timing felt right; they were both ready. The decision however, had to come from Edward, therefore, she presented it as a question. "Edward, what do you think about the two of us researching the phenomena of visions together? We could go to the library in town instead of using our own books."

"Not to cause suspicion!" Edward added.

"Precisely!"

Violet understood his comment meant he was all for it. He probably was as curious as she was to read about others with the same abilities.

CHAPTER 38

VISIONS PHENOMENA EXPLOITED

Choosing appropriate books for Edward to compare his experiences wasn't as easy as Violet had assumed. Most autobiographies were seriously flawed. It soon became obvious they had been embellished, written for a good read and profit. It was unconscionable to Violet to discover some people misrepresented and exploited these phenomena. Newspaper articles on the subject were even more disturbing. Self-acclaimed psychics had offered their services for a big pay out. These unscrupulous individuals would thereby coerce desperate, gullible victims into paying enormous amounts of money. She read how they had combined detective work with acting skills. Their ability lay solely on giving convincing performance and finding unsuspecting prey. Eventually, they'd slip up, exposing their fraudulent tactics. Unfortunately, the damage and skepticism caused by these events were the main reason psychics had a bad reputation. No wonder most genuine psychics chose to be secretive and cautious. Hiding their abilities from the general public had been a common practice for self-preservation.

A trilogy written by Anna Lee, dubbed a work of fiction, interested Edward. He at last was able to relate to some of the author's described events. Edward knew she was authentic and wrote from her own experiences. Anna Lee's protagonist had her first vision when she was only three years of age. Her readers were made to believe it was all fantasy. She wrote metaphorically, comparing visions to a roller-coaster ride, a journey through chaotic scenes where nothing made sense. At the start, it was all speed and sudden dips. As she becomes accustomed to the ride and all its different elements, she experienced relief. Most situations allowed the individual reader to use their own imagination. At the end of their ride, the reader's minds had traveled into a world of wondrous possibilities.

Disguising her live as fiction had proven wise. Ann Lee's books were all bestsellers. Violet and Edward came to the same conclusion: People enjoy being entertained with unexplainable phenomena they call science fiction. In reality, people were unwilling to accept visions as actual occurrences. Skepticism and fear were always on the forefront of nonbelievers. Always waiting for the one clouded vision to readily voice: "I told you so!" A psychic would only be as good as their last prediction. Unfortunately, condemnation would erupt if accuracy was not always achieved. Once exposed as a psychic, the demands would be catastrophic; the chance for a normal life would be impossible.

All this research left the two disillusioned, but not shocked. Violet's decision to hide Edward's visions had come from her own insightfulness. This in-depth reading proved, without a doubt, her persistence for secrecy was instrumental for Edward's stable future. They replaced the books back in their proper shelves and left empty-handed.

Violet worried Edward might be in some way affected by all the negativity surrounding visions. She adamantly praised her little man for all he had endured the last four years. More substantially, Edward had stopped wanting Violet's assistance for his dreadful night visions. When they occurred, he'd bravely eliminate his fears without crying out for her.

Edward explained to Violet, "I had to come up with a successful method to stop and control my own life. I remind myself all you have told me to calm down, like taking deep breaths. I realize these terrible visions cannot hurt me. I understand there is nothing I can do to help the situation anyway. Therefore, I distract my thoughts in whatever way I can, and eventually they fade away."

"Edward, I am so very proud of your determination! With your new perspective on your visions, you'll have some peace. Please remember you have used your gift for so much good and will continue to—but always in secret."

"I am so thankful you thought of what was best for me all these years. Having your trust and being able to share with you made all the difference."

Violet was grateful and pleased to hear Edward acknowledge his appreciation for her protectiveness over the past years. *However.* A prickly voice in her head kept nagging. *Violet!* it said, *that was for the past; you're no longer needed. It will never be the same.* Ashamed of her thoughts, she scolded inwardly. *How pitiful I've become, wanting things to stay the same for my sake.*

Edward had to nudge Violet to get her attention. With a broad smile plastered on his face, he said, "I have a plan! Since you're no longer my protector, we can now be partners." His wide-eyed expression indicated how genuinely pleased he was with his offer.

"Thank you for the promotion—it is a promotion, right?" she teased, happy she could still find some humor in all of this.

"You must take me seriously." Edward's words had an anxious edge to them. "I'm not ready to impose this responsibility on my parents. I feel it's not yet time. I want things to remain as they are for a while longer. It will be different, but I believe it will be better. You won't have to worry or watch over me like a hawk."

Violet listened attentively, focusing on the fact her little man wanted to continue keeping his visions between the two of them. Elated, she involuntarily let out an exclamatory sigh. The soon-to-be partner was slightly embarrassed, showing outwardly her relief. She felt more time was needed to reinforce not only Edward's future but hers as well.

Violet had to put her own emotions aside, to reassure him. "I'll do what makes you happy; your needs will always come first. I've cared and loved you as my little brother." Violet hugged Edward tightly as she had thousands of times before.

Edward wiggled his way out of her arms and gave her a look of annoyance. "I also feel sisterly towards you, *but* I believe I'm getting too old for all this hugging." He stepped back at least a foot and showed his stubbornness by standing stiff like a toy soldier.

Edward's serious proclamation gave Violet a rude awakening. Another hurdle she'd have to prepare for and overcome. This glimpse of an older Edward would soon replace her sweet little boy. "Do you really believe my sisterly hugs and kisses will actually shock anyone?"

Her question and challenge were both ignored.

Violet realized their future now consisted of many difficult changes, and *she* not *he* would have to adjust. Edward entering his adolescence would affect parts of the relationship. She must face the inevitable truth. Teenage boys get embarrassed with shows of affection and try to hold back their emotions.

CHAPTER 39

PAST MISTAKES AND PRESENT EMBARRASSMENT

Violet didn't have to open the letter to know its contents. She hid it in her pocket with shame. It was the fifth from Pasquale, that dishonest, dirty tavern owner from Ornesto's hometown. He continued to produce I.O.U. notes allegedly signed by her dead father. "How did I allow this disgusting man to get the better of me?" Her intent at the time had been to protect her mama. She had never imagined the extent of this man's deceit and greed.

After the second letter, she suspected he was actually forging her father's signature. He had been clever and always asked for an amount she could easily pay. He also would insinuate that if she would rather, he take the matter up with her mother. Violet feared this extortion would continue until Pasquale died.

The phone rang just in time to get Violet out of her miserable mood. *"Ciao Mama!"* she answered, trying to sound cheerful.

"I have been called many things but never 'mama'," the deep, masculine voice protested with a gentle chuckle.

Violet, instantly embarrassed, promptly corrected herself. "I'm sorry, sir. This is the Sutton Residence. May I help you?'"

"Violet! It's Eric."

She almost dropped the phone. "Eric? Our Eric, I'm so glad." Violet had to hold back her excitement. His name had sent electric waves through her entire body. "I mean, I'm glad to finally speak with you." She stiffened her body to regain composure. "How are you, sir?"

"Fine, you sweet thing, just fine. I heard you didn't like my gift much."

"Of course, I did! I do! I love the music box." Again, Violet tried to remain calm. "I mean, it was very thoughtful of you to buy me such a lovely gift."

"Edward told me you tossed it in the trash."

Violet was so flustered she didn't hear the teasing in Eric's voice. "I'd never! He couldn't have."

"Edward actually told me you play it day and night."

Violet was mortified. "I just like the melody, that's all."

"I'm glad; I hoped you would enjoy it."

Violet listened attentively, captivated with the sound of his deep voice. She wanted to hear more and asked, "Did you choose it especially for me?"

"Absolutely! I put a lot of thought in what to buy such a caring young lady. It was my way of thanking you for all you have done to help my brother. You obviously have an extraordinarily positive influence on him."

Violet was ecstatic. She wanted to express her appreciation to him for reinforcing her secret pact with Edward but felt it was inappropriate to bring it up. She simply responded, "Thank you, sir, for thinking of me."

Edward entered her room with a handful of rocks. "I would also like to speak with Eric when you are done." He gave Violet a shifty grin as he placed his daily collection on her desk.

"Sir! Edward is back and requesting to speak with you."

"Thank you, Violet, we'll connect again soon. It was my pleasure speaking with you."

"Yes, it was." Violet bit her bottom lip, "I mean, it was nice speaking with you as well." She immediately handed the phone to Edward and walked to her balcony.

Maria's call came an hour later. "The operator couldn't get through," her mama complained.

"Edward was speaking with his brother Eric." Violet decided not to upset her mother by mentioning her own conversation with the man and how silly she had behaved.

Violet was sulking, totally convinced her conversation with Eric had gone all wrong. She dissected it a hundred times and always became more mortified. *He must think I'm a dunce—even worse, a silly child!* She quivered at that thought. A creative "do-over" was her way of feeling better and calming herself. Promptly, she rehearsed an intimate two-way dialogue in front of the mirror. This refined and mature conversation ended with Eric expressing his desire to continue their intellectual talk soon face-to-face. Still unsettled, her only solution was to question the younger brother.

"Edward, really! What did Eric say about me?"

"For the millionth time, he said you sounded sweet. That's it!"

"He must've said something else. You're just protecting my feelings."

"Yes, Violet," Edward answered sarcastically, "Eric thinks you are very silly, and terribly bossy and you wouldn't stop talking."

"You are a monster!"

"Now, will you stop asking me any more questions about Eric?"

"You are incorrigible! And I thought we were partners." Violet raised her head and left Edward's room with her nose in the air.

CHAPTER 40

BE CAREFUL WHAT YOU WISH FOR

Edward was true to his word and did not run to Violet with all his visions. She continued to question his determination.

"Why make it hard on yourself, Edward! I'm always here for you."

"No, Violet! Let's be logical. You can't always be around to help me. Ultimately, I have to take hold of them. The sooner I depend on my own control, the better. If a vision comes on suddenly, I must learn to be rational and stay calm. I need you to stop worrying and trust me. Truthfully, my visions don't frighten me anymore."

Great! Violet thought, *At last the fear factor has been conquered.*

"Some still disturb me, but most of them are just annoying."

His last statement told Violet Edward needed to share. She remained quiet, encouraging him to talk.

"Sometimes . . ." he paused, lingering with his thoughts before continuing. "The hardest part of my visions is how unpredictable and intrusive they are to my life. I might go days with nothing; then suddenly a vision just pops up. Most have no purpose except to annoy me. I'd like to have a control switch to turn them off. A few days ago, Mom and I were speaking with the minister when I was hit with a vision of his wife. She was kissing a man at their house. I was surprised. Why was she kissing a man when she already had a husband? I of course kept my mouth shut used my self-control and simply listened to the conversation. The minister was informing Mom he was in a hurry to get home. His wife's brother, whom they hadn't seen for two years, was arriving for a visit. That man I saw in my vision kissing his wife was her brother. I know kissing your own brother is okay. So why did I get that particular vision?" Edward question was rhetorical, he didn't want Violet to answer. He had his own conclusion ready. "I suppose at times I will simply pick up on an individual's emotions or event in their lives for no real purpose."

Edward's admission of frustration, and his perspective about his visions, did not ease Violet's mind. On the contrary, she was convinced Edward, on his own, might slip up. The threat of public exposure was even more imminent.

"Edward, you must be diligent; never give the slightest hint of what you see or know. People will wonder, become suspicious and question your knowledge. Remember, all the books we researched mention visions are puzzling. They are not always consistent and accurate. You may only get partial messages. Best to ignore them altogether."

As usual, Violet worked her brain, trying hard to come up with a tangible solution. Edward needed to distract himself from his visions. A method to blur them out, push them aside. Anything to make it easier on him. "Whistling! I believe you should start whistling when you get a vision; focus on whistling." The suggestion sounded so ridiculous they both laughed aloud. However, Violet still needed to make her point. "It's best for people not to know what the future holds for them." This philosophical statement opened a subject the two had not yet discussed.

Edward looked surprised. "Is that how you really feel; you'd rather not know things?"

She realized his question had numerous implications, but her mission was to put him on a smoother, less risky path. "I have been tempted many times to ask you about myself," she confessed, "but thought best not to."

"Because it's not fair to me?"

"Yes, but mostly I'm apprehensive about what your vision might mean for me. As we know, they do not tell the whole story. Therefore, I might be tempted to allow myself to be motivated by them and react accordingly. It's best to leave fate to reveal itself." Violet hoped Edward would take in her message and put the visions aside—or at least give them less importance.

"I appreciate what you're saying. Thanks for your honesty; it allows me to see another point of view. I often have mixed feelings about what to tell you or not to tell you. I promise to remember what you just said and respect your wishes."

The outcome of this conversation now had Violet frustrated. She compared it with the half-witted one she'd had with his older brother. Disillusioned, she questioned herself: *Why do I speak before thinking it all the way through? Edward is probably even more confused. I want him to ignore most or all of his visions, not just the ones about me.* Saying her plan aloud, Violet admitted how unrealistic she was. Edward ignoring his gift, even if that was possible, would not be her Edward. Their life together was based solely on the fact that he'd acted on a vision. *I probably achieved putting more distance between us.*

In her dismay, Violet held tight to one important fact. *I possess my own ability: My method to get Edward to open up and talk has been highly successful.* This was not a boast—on the contrary. Violet had patiently cultivated her persuasive skills over many years. It had been detrimental in giving him the help needed. *When necessity presents itself, I will use it to get Edward to reveal what he knows about me.*

CHAPTER 41

THE FOUR SUTTONS

Betty knocked lightly on Violet's slightly open door and peeked in. "Miss Violet, you and Master Edward are needed in the library. Mr. and Mrs. Sutton asked me to come get you both." It was apparent by Betty's enthusiasm she knew what was coming.

"What is it, Betty?"

"Oh no, Miss! I heard by chance and will not repeat it."

"Of course not, Betty, sorry! I should not have asked."

"We'll go down promptly." Betty nodded and left, still wearing her now permanent bright smile. She was eternally grateful for having been spared the disgrace of a demoralizing trial. The humbled woman had acquired a constant state of bliss.

Betty had confessed to Violet, "I never imagined I was loved and cared for by so many people."

Violet interpreted what Betty had experienced. Being told you are loved feels and sounds wonderful; receiving the benefits of being loved, when most needed, is life changing.

"The suspense is killing me; I can't wait to see their reaction!" Catherine's words reached their ears as they entered the library. Mr. Sutton was sitting at his desk while Catherine hovered over him reading a brochure.

William waved for the summoned duo to approach. "I hope we haven't inconvenienced you both by taking you away from something important?" He, of course, was sarcastically teasing the pair.

The two exchanged glances; both were lost for words, surprised with Mr. Sutton's uncharacteristic behaviour. Violet watched as Mrs. Sutton strategically separated dozens of schedule sheets.

Waiting patiently to be told the reason they'd been called down, Violet dubiously wondered if Edward already knew. If so, she was in trouble. His face revealed nothing to her. He seemed oblivious, as clueless as she most definitely was.

"William, tell them," Catherine commanded. "I want to see their reaction."

Mr. Sutton took time to stand, acting somewhat ceremonial, as though preparing to give an important speech. He cleared his throat and put one hand on Catherine's shoulder. "This June," he announced, "we are all, *all*, taking an ocean voyage. We are leaving for a month's holiday to New York City, U. S. A."

Violet was in disbelief; did the word "all" mean her as well? She stood motionless, not knowing how to react.

Edward, on the other hand, had no problem demonstrating his excitement. To his personal *modus operandi*, jumping up and down, he added shouts of "Hurrah! Hurrah!"

Violet remained bewildered, wondering why they would consider taking her on such a trip.

"Well, my dear, aren't you happy?" Catherine questioned Violet's subdued reaction.

"I'm speechless! I don't have words to express my appreciation. Thank you so very much Mr. and Mrs. Sutton, for including me."

Catherine's was quick to finish shuffling her papers to address her traveling companions. "We have much to prepare before we leave."

Mr. Sutton sounded resigned and shook his head in agreement. "I'm sure, my dear wife, these preparations include shopping trips to London and Paris."

"Yes, husband darling, we ladies must look our very best. Mustn't we, Violet?"

The word "ladies" flashed like a neon sign in Violet's head. She felt humbled and a bit awkward. Did Mrs. Sutton just refer to her as a "lady"?

Respectfully, Violet answered, "I will put myself in your capable hands, Mrs. Sutton. This is all overwhelming and delightful." Violet continued holding back. Deep down, she wanted to jump up and down but decided to voice it instead. "I might join Edward in his victory dance."

"Oh yes, dance," Catherine said. "Your lessons were also part of this plan. I wanted to fully prepare you to be the belle of the ball in New York."

Catherine's boast indicated to Violet this had not been a spontaneous venture; more importantly, Violet had been included from the very beginning. Thinking back, Violet remembered wondering why Catherine insisted she learn ballroom dancing. She had attended very few seasonal parties. She marvelled at Mrs. Sutton's foresight in giving her ample time to perfect her various dance steps.

"They won't know what hit them when the four Suttons invade New York," Catherine announced in delight.

"Is Edward's older brother joining us there?" Violet asked, attempting to sound nonchalant. In truth her entire body tingled at the very thought of Eric.

"Not this time," Eric's father responded. "He is presently in the core of finalizing an important business merger."

The significance of Mrs. Sutton's statement resonated in Violet's heart: "The four Suttons." Including Violet. This meant she would be introduced as an important part of the family. "Mrs. Sutton, I'm honored." Violet's response was understandably meek.

"What is the matter, Violet?" Edward looked at her, confused. "Why are you so quiet? Aren't you happy?"

"I'm more than happy. I'm humbled. Thank you, Mr. and Mrs. Sutton!"

"My dear." Mr. Sutton wanted to confirm their decision. "Remember, we all agreed from the very being, you were to be treated as a member of this family. Well! you've proven you certainly belong with us. You have been nothing but a pleasant addition for us all. We could never repay you for the remarkable change your attentiveness to Edward has made. He is now well adjusted, sensible, and—" William stopped and shook his head. "I was about to add 'mature,' but looking at him now I'll save that pronouncement for a later time."

Edward was still performing his wild dance, resembling a chief medicine man calling for rain.

That evening Violet wrote a lengthy letter to her mother filling her in on everything. She included having spoken with Eric a few times and receiving his gift. Violet had thus far avoided speaking about him to her mama. Knowing how perceptive her mother was when it came to her daughter's feelings, Violet feared her mama might pick up on her ridiculous fantasy of the man. It was fine for her to secretly dream of Eric, as long as no one suspected her absurdity. No. It was easier to write things in her letter. There she could control what to divulge without probing questions.

Her heart felt as light as a feather tickling in her chest. She reviewed the delightful letters she had also written to her sisters. She wrote informally as if she was verbally conversing with them. She promised loads of pictures, assuring them she would write all about her experiences. Violet lay in bed, wanting to savor her happiness.

Her rapture did not last long, as her subconscious mind echoed voices from her past. Her insecurities took hold, overflowing her thoughts. *I might disappoint them all. What if their friends in New York dislike me? They might focus on the obvious, that I'm not really one of them. What if they shun me and want nothing to do with me?* All these hard questions made Violet become apprehensive about this trip. She made up her mind to be reserved, to hold back and not draw attention to herself. In other words, she wanted to become virtually invisible.

Foreseen

When in distress, Violet always reached for the one constant consolation: Eric's gift. Its soothing melody helped her return to pleasant thoughts. Smiling, she remembered the day Betty had gifted her with a record of the song "Fascination." Betty had silenced Violet's gratitude and many thanks. The maid reminded her mistress of all she had given and done for her throughout the years. Humming and swaying along to the popular waltz, she finally relaxed—until her thoughts shifted to Edward. *No doubt,* she concluded, *it won't all be smooth sailing.*

Ironically, this time Violet had a spark of excitement anticipating their next undertaking. She admitted Edward had always given her what she needed most: a purpose in life.

CHAPTER 42

PREPARING FOR THE VOYAGE

As Mr. Sutton predicted, Albert was kept busy driving Catherine and Violet into London. They also went to Paris for a few arranged shopping days. The two ladies visited exclusive establishments such as Dior and Chanel, commissioning, "one-of-a-kind" designs.

Catherine's impeccable fashion sense received countless praises. The coordinators and designers listened to her suggestions and complimented her choices. Between fittings and excessive shopping, the weeks flew by. *However*, this extreme purchasing was all new and enduring for Violet. She appreciated Catherine's patience and efforts to always include her. Often Catherine would insist Violet give her opinion on fabrics, colors, and design choices. Violet minimized her contribution when Catherine continued to compliment her selection. At times, Catherine actually modified some of her own previous ideas to include Violet's. Modestly, Violet acknowledged Catherine's compliments with a grateful smile. She had no doubt Mrs. Sutton was set on building her confidence.

Their purchases overloaded the Rolls Royce's boot with packages, resulting in their chauffeur having to share the front seat with oversized boxes.

When needed, the fatigued ladies would break from shopping to frequent "quaint" cafés. Catherine preferred petite hideaways well regarded for their discrete service to high-profile patrons. Their mandate was to protect their clients' privacy.

The final day of shopping was done; everything was now completed. Catherine was beaming and seemed eager to speak to her charge. The delectable tea and scones remained un-sampled. "I'm especially impressed with your choices today, my dear." Catherine's voice sounded operatic. "You're very meticulous, even with the smallest details. Nothing escapes you, Violet. For example, it did not occur to me to replace the rhinestones with delicate pearl beads or to incorporate tiny pleats to the silk fabric instead of the usual gathering."

Mrs. Sutton's compliments today were specific and overly generous. Violet felt compelled to give Catherine more than her usual grateful smile in reply. "I would never have known the difference between silk and polyester if not for you," she said. "Thanks to you and Mr. Sutton, I have had the very best instructors. How could I not do well?" Violet returned the compliments back to where she truly believed they belonged.

Catherine reached over to pat Violet's gloved hand. "My dear young lady," she began, giving Violet a curious grin. "I don't know why you have always underestimated your own abilities."

Violet had heard those words before from her mother and readily dismissed them. Hearing them from Mrs. Sutton, she was beholden but confused. Catherine of all people was aware of her initial ignorance.

"Violet, my dear." Catherine was determined. "I'm not done with you yet. Don't presume just because one has opportunities they automatically excel in life. I have witnessed more failures in others than I care to mention. Whereas you possess a sense of pride and determination. Please understand, your success manifested from your desire and willingness to learn. I recognized those qualities in you from the very beginning, and I am never wrong!" Catherine laughed at her humorous boast.

Violet remained reluctant to join in and only let out a throat sound.

She was stunned by what Catherine suggested and felt undeserving. "Mrs. Sutton, your attentiveness and commitment to my betterment has been overly generous. I don't know how to express my gratitude."

Catherine leaned close and shook her head. "Violet," she whispered, "it took me years to get over that almost-tragic day." As she retold the terrible cart incident, her entire body shivered. Obviously, it affected her still. "I looked up and saw my precious son about to be crushed. It's impossible to explain the horror a mother feels when she sees her child in danger, and she is unable to help."

Violet's own sisterly love for Edward made it easy to relate to Mrs. Sutton's anguish.

"Then an angel jumped over him saving his life, with no thought to her own welfare." Catherine's tearing eyes revealed her ongoing gratitude. "That scene is imprinted in my mind forever."

Violet had always minimized her heroic deed. "I reacted as any human would. Really, it was just instinct."

Catherine would never agree. "Yes, Violet it was instinct—within you!" Her rephrasing of those words reinforced Catherine's esteem for her. "Above all, Violet, your devotion, and loving care over the years helped Edward tremendously. When you came to live at the manor, you being a child yourself, we had no expectations. Our only hope was you would be a friendly companion to our secluded son. Edward so desperately wanted you; we couldn't refuse his deep wish." Catherine had more to say. "Violet, you have been his earthly angel. He has become a mature, stable young man with a bright future. William and I are aware more than you know of your commitment to his well-being. Your worth to our family is immeasurable. If there is any debt owed or thanks due, it is from us to you. This trip will show everyone how indispensable you are to our family." Catherine finalized everything she had said, by adding, "Please don't ever forget this."

Violet was elated. She had always known the Suttons were grateful, but now she knew the full extent of it. They were also proud of her.

The trunks packed, schedules distributed, goodbyes said, the four Suttons were off. Albert would drive them to Southampton where the *Queen Mary* was ready to set sail on another trans-Atlantic voyage.

CHAPTER 43

THE VOYAGE

The dock was deserted; the usual bustle of strolling passengers had not yet commenced. Only the longshoremen loading the ship with cargo and luggage were noticeably at work. The captain had arranged a discrete pre-boarding for William Sutton and his family, to embark at 5:00 a.m. This precaution had been implemented to avoid the mad rush of people—mainly nosey reporters always lurking about. They aggressively pounced on the wealthy and influential people, trying to scoop stories and photos for their newspapers and broadcast media.

Captain Lynwood welcomed the opportunity to repay some of Mr. Sutton's generosity. William had recommended him for this prestigious position and also had most of Lynwood's extended family working on his cargo fleet. It was not in William's character to ask for privileges. However, Catherine persistently reminded him of a few unpleasant incidents with assertive reporters. "I don't intend to be harassed by them as on previous trips. Violet and Edward must be protected from being bombarded with personal questions."

Violet marveled at how a powerful self-assured man like Mr. Sutton always considered and listened to his wife's requests. The men in her hometown would never think of doing so. They demanded respect even when they were wrong. The decision to do or not to do something was solely theirs. Her father epitomized that selfish behaviour.

He would do what he wanted, and when he failed, he would blame everyone but himself.

Inadvertently, Violet's mind wandered back to her lost childhood. The last time she'd risen at 5:00 a.m. was to clean the pigpen. Almost choking with emotion, Violet said aloud, "How different my life is now."

"Are you okay, Violet?" Edward questioned her statement.

"I'm more than okay, Edward, my mind just traveled back to years long past."

"Why do that now? I need your help to carry this heavy case." Edward pointed to the black, rectangular suitcase he was struggling with. He had a good grip on the top handle but was still dragging the bottom end.

Violet lifting the other end unleashed her complaints. "I can't believe how heavy this small case is! What's in it, rocks? Why didn't you let them take it with the other trunks?"

"Hush," Edward whispered. "I want this case with me! They would have damaged it." His tone and look told her he knew this for a fact. "I'll show you my collection later."

Violet shook her head. "I don't like this one bit. I don't need to know or see anything," she scolded all the while helping him.

Violet's and Edward's staterooms were identical, and of course, next to each other. Both had a spacious sitting area with a walk-out balcony. Their sleeping quarters included a large bed with a separate change room and a five-piece ensuite. Mr. and Mrs. Sutton's double quarters were elaborate and one deck higher to accommodate their extended circular balcony.

This transatlantic crossing would take less than one week, with no ports of call.

Mr. and Mrs. Sutton wisely recommend they all needed a few hours of rest. The diligent parents also suggested they comfortably stay in their staterooms until the great ship was well at sea.

Edward expressed his disappointed to the one person he knew would agree with him. "I'm thirteen, very inquisitive, and compelled to nurture my curiosity. I want to explore the whole ship from bow to stern. I agree to rest for a few hours, *but* not to stay in our cabin until the ship is well at sea. I want to experience all aspects of this voyage, starting from '*bon voyage.*'"

Violet agreed with Edward's eloquent speech, but wouldn't dare say it aloud, having read all she could on this grand ship. She found it hard to contain her own infinite curiosity. The *Queen Mary* had recently been restored to her former grandeur. Her artisanship was skillful and particularly impressive. Violet knew there would be well over fifteen hundred passengers plus the crew on board. This trip was unimaginable, a dream come true. She secretly decided to encroach on Edward's unrestrained character. He would find a way to explore the ship and ultimately be her excuse to fulfill her own wonder.

Bursting through their adjoining stateroom door, Edward yelled out, "Are you still sleeping?"

"Edward, really! If I were, I wouldn't be now. You must learn to knock before entering a lady's quarters." This was the first time Violet had referred to herself as a "lady." It made no impact on Edward. Violet also readily dismissed it. "I could have been undressing," she insisted, trying to look annoyed.

"I know your habits so well. If you were undressing, you would not only lock but bolt your doors."

Violet ignored his response, not wanting to acknowledge how right he was.

"I'm going on deck! Come with me and see the commotion."

Edward was not one to be contained. It took less time than she had anticipated. It impressed on Violet how much they really understood one another. Although his suggestion pleased her, she made a slight verbal protest.

"We mustn't! We were told." As she muttered her unconvincing rebuttal, they both rushed out the door.

Never could they have imagined such a hullabaloo. It instantly rewarded the rambunctious duo's curiosity. Violet's moment of apprehension disappeared; her doubts and guilt were immediately replaced with stimulation. Edward's defiance was exactly what she wanted, expected, and needed. Observing hundreds of overzealous passengers on deck was not only exhilarating but a unique experience.

"Violet, stick with me." Edward sounded pleased and determined. "I promise we are going to have an adventurous voyage."

"You better stick with me," Violet insisted, giving him her big sister look. "I don't want us to get separated and be forced to scream out your name." She was half teasing.

The diligent crew were patiently directing passengers who demanded service and attention. Most of the voyagers hovered at the ship's rails, waving hankies, and throwing streamers at people on the docks.

Violet embraced the heightened atmosphere. She attentively took in the scene, not wanting to miss a thing. On her far left, she noticed a group of women wearing silk saris. Their bright colours and glimmering attire were extraordinary. Violet was astonished by the contrast between the brightness of the colours they wore and their subdued demeanour. They were detached, almost oblivious to the chaotic surroundings. She wondered if it was within their culture, this control and restraint.

Edward interrupted her pondering by tugging at her arm. "Look at those two." He pointed at a couple kissing passionately. "Yuck! *Why* would anyone want to kiss someone's open mouth? It's disgusting." Edward's boyish horror was clear; he meant every word.

Violet tilted her head to get a better view. Her conclusion was definite. "They are newlyweds." She believed only a new married couple would be so passionate and dare to show affection in public.

She sighed, wondering what it would feel like to be kissed by a man. A giggle escaped her lips as that thought lingered. She was nearly twenty, and the only kissing of a male she had done was the sisterly kind. Even the physical affection she usually showed Edward was non-existent lately. "Don't stare," she reprimanded, but then realized Edward was gawking at her. Immediately, Violet looked elsewhere. "How about them?" She pointed at two girls wearing matching middy blouses. "They must be sisters, and close to your age. You'll have playmates," she teased loudly, hoping to get the girls' attention.

The two identical faces turned their way, gave them a quick stare, and simultaneously stuck their tongues out. This was obviously not the first time they had performed their act. It was flawless.

Violet and Edward both shrugged their shoulders and walked away, laughing.

The *Queen Mary's* triple horns blasted, drowning out their laughter; "Her Majesty" was ready to depart. The crowd's cheers immediately intensified. The chief steward bellowed repeatedly, "All ashore, going ashore."

Violet observed most passengers were excited, anticipating a luxurious voyage ahead. Some wept, probably aware they would soon miss loved ones not joining them.

Reluctantly, Violet suggested to her enthused and still-eager partner that they return to their stateroom.

Disappointed, Edward protested. "Don't you want to go see the immigrants? I read they have decided to make America their new home. I think that's the ultimate adventure, having to start a new life in a different country." Edward certainly was enthused and believed all he had read to be true.

Violet had her own view on that subject and firmly replied, "No!" She gave a disapproving grunt and quickly pulled him toward the stairs.

CHAPTER 44

VIOLET'S METAMORPHOSIS

The atmosphere in the grand dining hall was electrifying; glitz and glamour were definitely on the evening's menu. Ladies paraded like peacocks in their elaborate gowns. Violet wore a soft, coral chiffon strapless gown. The peach colour complimented her light, creamy complexion. Her long, black, wavy hair added to her dramatic, unique beauty.

Catherine wore midnight blue. Her gown had literally hundreds of crystals sewn everywhere. She looked mesmerizing, as though the brilliant star-lit sky had draped her body.

"My dear, you look stunning," William voiced his admiration for his wife. With the same sincerity, he turned to Violet. "You, young lady, have a natural and rare beauty. You look enchanting in your new gown."

Violet realized Mr. Sutton had never seen her dressed so maturely, and he was being gracious. Unprepared for his compliments, a rosy glow suddenly appeared on her porcelain cheeks.

Catherine moved closer to Violet, helping to adjust her shawl. "William! You have embarrassed our modest young lady."

"I have only stated the obvious," he protested.

Catherine's serious expression towards her husband had Violet hastening her composure.

"Thank you, Mr. Sutton, for the compliment," she quickly expressed, "and Mrs. Sutton, thank you for choosing this exceptional gown."

With the atmosphere once again tranquil, they now all shared a memorable moment.

"Edward!" William playfully assumed a pompous persona, undoubtedly to coincide with their surroundings. "My son!" he instructed. "You have the privilege of escorting Violet, as I have the privilege of escorting your mother."

Edward was most agreeable and played along without the slightest protest. Violet was naturally prepared for her little man's performance. Earlier, a very enthusiastic adolescent had burst into her stateroom to inform her of his successful negotiating strategy. "When Mom presented me with her demands on what duties I'm expected to carry out, I took my opportunity. Timing is everything," Edward pointed out.

Violet gave him a suspicious grin as she wondered how many times Edward's insight had worked to his advantage. His expression before continuing confirmed to Violet he knew her thoughts. "My request was minimal," he defended. "In exchange for my gentlemanly performance, I asked Mother for free time during our days at sea to do things I enjoy. Mom paused a moment to consider and agreed to my simple proposal."

The captain's table was positioned on a dais to the right of the huge dining hall. A three-tier candelabrum highlighted the elaborate centerpiece. The glow from a dozen candles danced among the large pink roses. Protocol invited only distinguished influential passengers to join the captain's table.

The *maitre'd* personally escorted the Suttons to their table. Mr. Sutton sat at the right of Captain Lynwood, Mrs. Sutton at his left. Edward sat next to his mother, and Violet sat next to Mr. Sutton.

An elderly couple, also guests of the captain's, were acquaintances of the Suttons. Conversation started comfortably and pleasantly.

Nothing discussed interested Violet; indubitably, she politely listened and respectfully answered any questions addressed to her.

After dinner, Edward's parents excused him from the table. They had arranged for him to go watch a movie. It was obvious Violet would accompany them to the ballroom. Catherine had constantly alluded to their fun evenings of socializing and dancing.

As they entered the great ballroom, all eyes shifted towards the trio.

"This is a prelude to your evenings in New York," Catherine whispered into Violet's ear.

William proudly escorted the ladies, one on each arm. With a cordial nod, he acknowledged the many people who politely greeted them.

Violet's first mature encounter with "high society" ended successfully.

CHAPTER 45

FIRST ENCOUNTER WITH THE OPPOSITE SEX

After a grueling evening, Violet retired to her quarters exhausted. Sleep was quickly defeated by her somber mood. She laid in bed, taunted by her skeptical questions. *If dancing with all those men was supposed to be enjoyable,* why *did it feel like punishment?* All the unnecessary whirling about with the many partners left her dizzy and confused. Some of the "gentlemen" were not so gentle, repeatedly tossing and bouncing her like a rag doll.

Admitting she was naïve and clueless when it came to the opposite sex, she continuously tried to be gracious and courteous. Unfortunately, most of the men seemed arrogant, some silly, others misinformed.

Steven amused her, but for the wrong reasons. He insisted on speaking French, which proved to be comical. His incoherent statements and ridiculous references had her struggling to restrain her laughter. She was tempted to correct him but held back, remembering Catherine's earlier advice: "Just dance, smile, and agree with whatever your partner says. Be modest, don't expose your intellect. Show your sweet disposition, and you'll enjoy the evening more."

Violet felt hypocritical with it all. She was especially unsettled by the constant encouraging smiles coming from Mrs. and Mr. Sutton. What had happened? What were they trying to convey? *Only a few weeks ago I was playing with Edward.* She was neither ready for men nor wanted any part of dating. Her playful fantasies with Eric were just that—fantasies. It had nothing to do with reality.

Restless and sleep deprived, a horrifying thought burst into her mind. *Maybe the reason the Suttons included me on this trip was to find me a husband. Of course! Edward is getting older and soon will no longer need me.*

The vacation she had dreamed off would be her demise. She tried to calm herself and analyze the situation logically. To evaluate further, Violet had to resort back to her two-way conversation. This practice was developed at a young age, out of necessity. Being the oldest child had its disadvantages. She'd never go burden her younger sisters with her problems.

Her mother was understanding and loving but also overwhelmed with all her daughters' needs. With six younger siblings there was always one in dire need, therefore she had to be strong for them. Her two-way argument always started with questions. This back-and-forth exchange with herself was her way to rationalize, thereby put any situations in perspective.

So what is wrong with them wanting me to find a nice man? I am old enough. It's bound to happen sooner or later.

But I am not ready! she almost screamed out her rebuttal.

Her head was full of more questions and unconvincing answers but ultimately a smidgen of acceptance. *When I do marry, he won't be a self-serving, selfish man like my father was. I'll wait for my soulmate, just as my mama told me to do.*

Violet was inconsolable and missed the one key element: Eric's music box. Unfortunately, tonight, the thought of her precious comforter filled her with more anxiety. Facing reality was always difficult.

Violet Conti, you are shameful. Enough of this ridiculous fantasy. You've never met the man and only spoken to him a few times on the phone.

Her practical side now seemed back in control. When it came to Eric, she had learned to ignore logic, but not tonight. Tonight, actual men, not phantoms, had held her. Reality was so different from fantasy. It opened her eyes. Youthful longing over Eric had shut them out. *Besides, he might have someone in his life.*

Violet didn't like that last statement and immediately countered. *Not likely*, she challenged. *Mrs. Sutton would have mentioned it.* The string holding together her illusion of Eric was getting thinner, but it had not completely snapped. She held on, tucking it gently in the cavity between her heart and her emotion. *Just in case,* she proclaimed, biting her bottom lip.

CHAPTER 46

TIME TO MINGLE

Violet made an executive decision! The week on board the *Queen Mary* would not be dampened by her suspicions. This whole trip had been a dream come true. *I would be crazy not to enjoy it all to the fullest,* she told herself. *It is time I experience new and different things. After all*—Violet now resorted to a well-known cliché—*experience is the best form of education.* Her first mandate was to stop being critical of her overzealous admirers. She would keep an open mind towards men and welcome the many changes.

William insisted breakfast, which he considered family time, be set on their balcony. It allowed them privacy to relax and discuss the day's agenda. It had not been possible for Catherine to draft a complete pre-voyage schedule, nevertheless, she specified certain times they all had to be together. Besides their breakfast ritual at 8:00 a.m., lunch was at 12:30, 3:45 sharp for high tea, and 6:00 p.m. return to their cabins for a brief rest and ample time to dress for dinner.

The hours in between were for fun and games. Catherine voiced her indifference to Violet's choices: "Stay with us and play board games or accompany Edward."

"More like boring games," said Edward.

"I believe it's best Violet accompany Edward, dear. One never knows what the boy might get into." William gave his son a suspicious look.

Catherine's repeating of her schedule was not appreciated but respectfully obeyed. Both harmonized their agreeable response from ten feet away: "Absolutely!"

Edward's excitement was irrepressible, his curiosity at its peak. "I can't wait to go below and mingle with these interesting people."

Violet understood Edward was again referring to the immigrants he had read about.

"They chose to leave their native countries to make America their new home."

Edward acted as enthusiastic as an archaeologist discovering a new-ancient find. He obviously didn't grasp this particular discovery was of raw emotions, not dead bones. Their decision to immigrate, Violet believed, was most difficult and full of apprehension, not adventurousness.

Again she delivered a definite "No!" which left Edward stunned. He stopped talking, but his gloominess needed consoling.

Violet toned down her crusty approach. She had to explain her reason for not wanting to go below. It was important she made him understand why. "I know you are genuinely excited to meet these diverse people, but I'm not sure they want us nosing about." Violet recalled how her own sisters had reacted to her demeanor and outer appearance on her first visit back home. "We will stand out in our expensive clothes. These poor people want to be left alone. I believe most didn't have a choice about resettling in America. The decision to leave their own country was probably made out of necessity." Violet's voice sounded nostalgic as she struggled with her words.

Edward didn't seem convinced; obviously he had no idea what she was trying to say.

Violet had to explain further and be more specific. "My definition of immigration is separation, loneliness, and heartbreak. Imagine the anguish having to leave your loved ones, not knowing if you will ever see them again. Then you arrive in a strange land with completely different customs and language." Violet paused and stared at the vast ocean. "One feels displaced, destitute, and even frightened." Her sad words were genuinely expressed from a place of deep inner experience.

Edward listened with compassion to everything Violet was revealing to him. "Those were your emotions when you came to England with me." His voice had a measure of guilt and unmeasurable appreciation.

Violet felt ashamed and ungrateful; exposing only the negative emotions was unfair. "All those feelings were a lifetime ago and just a little at first," she relayed honestly. "Edward, remember, I had you to constantly bother me. Your timing was impeccable. You would burst into my room at the most opportune time with your hilarious clown face and make me laugh away my tears." Violet suddenly shut her mouth, but a slight upward curvature remained on her lips. Her wide-open eyes had a glare of understanding. This light-bulb moment had her resembling The Mona Lisa. "Edward! All those times . . . you sensed my feelings." She spoke her words softly, wanting to share her sudden awareness.

Edward's confident expression confirmed her revelation was spot on.

"Precisely!" He added, "Just as I know we must mingle with these immigrants."

Violet took a deep breath inward. "Why am I surprised by the depth of your perception?" Sighing outwardly, she asked, "What now, Edward?"

CHAPTER 47

SHARING DIVERSITY AND SIMILARITIES

Violet was still apprehensive as they took the last step to the lower deck. She mumbled something about wearing casual clothes then tugged on Edward's shirt. Without any warning, she tugged his neatly tucked shirt from his belted trousers.

"What are you doing?" he protested, removing her hands and re-tucking his shirttails. "Are you suggesting we strip naked?"

"No, silly, I though loosening our clothes and acting less prim and proper, we might just blend in."

Edward retorted with his own definite "No!" He said, "No hovering over me, either. Remember, I am British and nearly thirteen."

He sounded so serious; Violet had trouble holding back her laughter. "All right, sir, as long as I can see you at all times, you are on your own."

Violet was expecting a "thanks"; instead, she got Edward's "grown-up" look. Her sarcastic approval didn't escape him.

"Your trust is liberating; you make me feel like a two-year-old child." Edward gave his own back.

His sarcastic rebound had no effect on her. She actually enjoyed their tête-à-tête, especially when they conversed in Italian. Although Edward's pronunciation was accurate, he lacked the native passion

Italians inject when they speak. Violet, of course, had inherited the dramatic flair, bringing it forth at will.

The atmosphere among the passengers on the lower decks was not at all what Violet had predicted. No doom and gloom or despairing cries—in fact, the opposite. The people they saw were friendly and positive and displayed a camaraderie between each other. There were no outward shows of sadness, loneliness, or loss. No evidence of negativity at all, not here, not now. These courageous people had seemingly embraced their choices. On this ship, at this time, differences were not obstacles. The passengers came together as one group, sharing the same hopes for a new beginning.

After glancing at Violet with his "I told you so" expression, Edward dashed toward a group of boys playing marbles. Throughout the years, Violet and Edward had learned to communicate with their personalized expressions and body language. This had been essential in keeping their secret while getting their message across.

Violet's body would stiffen, except one foot would tap. Or she would rub one of her temples; sometimes she coughed loudly. All were signals to Edward: "DON'T SAY A WORD."

Edward's silent responses were usually facial: one lip over the other said, "I need you now." Rubbing his eyes was an alert: "I just had a vision." Casually looking at his feet told her "Don't worry."

His latest was her favorite. He would squint his eyes, tighten his upper lip, and raise his nose. Combining these three gestures was supposed to convey, "I am in control! I know what I am doing! Leave me be." Violet affectionately saw a resemblance to a defiant toddler, determined to get his way.

She was finding it difficult to loosen her protective grip over him. The emotional glue binding them together had hardened, holding her heart completely.

As the late morning sun intensified, a sporadic gush of wind was welcoming. However! The wind did played havoc on Violet's long, loose hair.

Her numerous attempts to gather it all were unsuccessful. At times her hair was blown so forcefully it mimicked a raised waving flag.

A young lady with a broad smile approached, offering her a piece of yellow ribbon. "For your hair, miss." She spoke with a deep Italian accent.

Violet thanked her, speaking in her native tongue. "*Il mio nome è Violetta*," she introduced herself while making good use of the ribbon.

"*Me lo immaginavo*. I thought you were Italian with your gorgeous black hair. My name is Lucia," she introduced herself, kissing Violet on both cheeks.

Lucia was a slender, pretty young lady, in her early twenties. She had also inherited thick, lustrous hair. Her loose, auburn braid decorating her left shoulder complimented her deep, dark brown eyes.

There was an instant camaraderie between the two ladies as they conversed for a while about Italy and their hometowns. Eagerly, Lucia introduced Violet to a few slightly older women chatting while knitting and crocheting. They were so confident in their craft, these ladies continued working without a need to glance down at their work. Their hands seemed programmed like precise machines. The spirited conversation was amusing, full of family stories. Husbands' and childrens' constant wants and needs were compared and laughed about. All the women came to the same conclusion: "Our men would be lost without our strength and support."

Time had literally sailed by; Violet was so charmed by the ladies she hated to leave. Edward annoyingly pointed at his watch, indicating it was getting late. Promising their newfound friends they'd visit the next morning, the two hurried off.

"We don't want to get in trouble on our first day." Edward couldn't help teasing Violet.

"Look who is the responsible one." Violet smirked while messing with his already wind-tossed hair.

Their new companions had made a positive impact on them both. Edward seemed to have benefitted from this experience. He was relaxed and definitely playful. Stepping in front of Violet to ensure her full attention, he added to his warning. "We mustn't rock the boat."

Violet gave him a poke on the arm. "Good one!" She was relieved their time apart was gratifying for them both.

"I'm going to bring my marble collection tomorrow. Wait till they see my rainbow allies, all my agates, and get a load of my red vampires."

Violet had no idea what he was saying but was delighted hearing his plans for tomorrow. Spending time apart and around others was all new, yet Violet was not as anxious for Edward as she had first anticipated.

"It felt so familiar speaking with the Italian ladies." Violet shared her experience with Edward. "We exchanged amusing stories, chatted about family dynamics; it was light-hearted and fun. I enjoyed myself tremendously. Edward, I owe you an apology for the way I carried on earlier."

The boy looked annoyed. "What?" he questioned, giving her his serious expressions. "You're overly prudish, Violet. Lighten up. You're allowed to have your views, even if they are wrong at times. Making mistakes is not that big of a deal; we all eventually make some."

Violet stared at her little man, trying to evaluate his peculiar statement. One thing she knew for sure: Edward's comments were rooted from deep insight. Her concern now was when and how she would falter.

CHAPTER 48

REACTING THE RIGHT WAY

Spending time on the lower decks became a daily routine and a helpful distraction.

Edward told Violet he was following her advice to dismiss some of his visions. "With each day, it's getting easier to achieve. Actually," he admitted, "I've become comfortable with some aspects of my visions; they entertain me."

Violet noticed an expression of tranquility and calmness reflected on Edward's face. They both understood this implied an enormous shift in his future. No more would his visions torment him! Violet quietly thanked God for this gift, and Edward smiled and voluntarily hugged his partner. It was a symbolic hug, his tight embraced was his way of letting go, releasing Violet from years of worrying over him.

To reinforce and further convince his partner of his accomplishment, Edward started a game of "Who's who?"

"As you know, Violet," he began, "visions appear to me randomly; most people give out nothing. With a few, I pick up bits and pieces. Others, I receive their vibes and clear visions." Edward's speech was a casual introduction, as if he was talking about the weather. "See that man standing in the corner wearing the large hat?" Edward discreetly pointed at him. "In a few months, he will be arrested for stealing and sent back to his country. This man"—he gestured to his right—"is going to become a famous singer." Looking at a young woman dressed in bright red, he laughed. "She will have lots and lots of boyfriends."

Violet pretended to be disinterested, telling him to stop. This was a part of Edwards' visions she never considered. She was embarrassed to admitted it was intriguing, getting glimpses of strangers' lives. Her curiosity took over, excusing it all as harmless play. She had to know more.

"How about that lady?" she blurted out.

Unfortunately, their whispers and giggles did not go unnoticed. A husky, miserly-looking man approached the laughing duo, demanding, "What's so funny?"

Shocked by the unexpected abruptness, Violet failed to offer the crude man a quick and suitable reply.

However, Edward was ready with his answer. "It's the children, sir. They keep playing pranks on the grown-ups. They hide the men's hats and undo the women's knitting and tie knots in their yarn."

"Ugh! Children. It's in their nature." The big man softened as he gave his own understanding. With a sad expression, he simply sauntered away.

Edward explained to a puzzled Violet, "He is agonizing over leaving his wife and three children behind. I knew by bringing up children's antics he would mellow."

Edward's explanation eliminated Violet's immediate concern while intensifying a lingering, more personal one. His intuitive and creative response to the man's rudeness rectified the problem—but without her help.

The mallet had fallen. For years, Edward's visions had brought on many predicaments. Secretly solving these unusual dilemmas had always been Violet's fortitude. Until now. Edward's new outlook on his visions not only allowed him to accept them but manage them on his own. Violet agonized over this admission. *Truly I'm no longer needed. Obviously, my input is no longer essential.* Her little man had solely and successfully controlled all aspects of his visions. He had done it all without her inventive solving skills. Violet was dejected. A painful throb invaded her head. This tremendous headache felt as if the mallet had come down, smacking her straight on the head.

Even Lucia's bubbly personality didn't diminish her melancholy mood.

"You look like you lost your best friend—or maybe a man friend?" Lucia teased, playfully poking Violet's ribs.

The unexpected contact made Violet react defensively. Her backhand hit Lucia's arm causing her friend's sewing basket to spill all its contents on the deck's floor. People nearby stopped what they were doing to collect the runaway items. Bolts of thread, needles, buttons, and other belongings scattered everywhere.

Embarrassed, Violet apologized profusely to her friend. Lucia waved it off, hysterically laughing like a hyena. She curled over, hitting her knee, enjoying all the commotion it caused.

Edward had joined the many retrievers of Lucia's contents. He returned with a handful of items and a grave expression. There was no mistake. Violet knew before he asked to speak with her; he had experienced a disturbing vision. "Lucia needs our help," he said without hesitation.

"Lucia?" She was the last person Violet expected would need anyone's help. She was so carefree and exuded confidence. Violet glanced over at Lucia, still laughing loudly with legs crossed and arms holding her tummy. Her laughter was contagious, arousing other passengers to join in her fun.

Edward became agitated as he spoke. "I picked up a photograph of a man with her other items and immediately I got a jolt. The vision was clear. He is a bad, dirty person who lives in a cellar." Edward shook in disgust. "He is devious, cruel, and enjoys abusing people. I saw him slapping the face of an old woman."

"Lucia did mention she was going to America to marry someone she'd never met. He claimed in the correspondence to be very wealthy and supposedly paid her passage."

"It is all lies. This man is poor and a horrible human being. Violet, what are we going to do?"

Edward's question motivated Violet as never before. She felt reinstated to the "solving" position, a position she had assumed was no longer hers. Putting emphasis on the word "we," Violet's reply sounded more like a declaration. "We will take up the challenge and succeed as we have done in the past."

CHAPTER 49

LUCIA'S ADMISSION

Lucia was not suspicious when Violet bombarded her with a multitude of questions. On the contrary, the young lady was excited her new friend was interested in her life and was eager to share all the details. "My aunt arranged everything. I went to live with her in Essex after my uncle passed away two years ago. Things were good for a while. I practiced my English and sewed many pretty dresses for my aunt. It all changed after she met another man. She did not want me around, and I did not want to go back home. Her man told her about his great friend in New York City. He wanted a wife and would pay for her passage to America. My aunt decided this was the perfect solution for everyone. She explained this man designed buildings, earned lots of money, and lived in a big house. She told me his family was respectable and he would take very good care of me."

Violet wanted to scream out, "You have been fed a bunch of lies." It was inconceivable her aunt would deliberately misguide her own niece. Violet held to the probability her aunt's new man was telling the lies. Thinking back to her father's behavior, her hopes were dimmed; Ornesto's arrangement had been even worse. At the very least, this woman was not Lucia's blood relation.

"Lucia, why would you marry without love? Don't you think this man sounds too good to be true?"

Violet's bold questions stunned the future bride. Her face paled. "What do you mean? Have I foolish been?"

Violet was not about to correct her grammar, nor could she continue with the bold approach. "I am sorry." Violet believed an apology was needed. "I suppose you could be one of the lucky ones."

Lucia was not satisfied with the last part of her friend's apology. "Violet, you are holding back. *Di mi*—tell me."

Violet had no intention of holding back. Her pause was to find a way to come up with a clever story, a disastrous tale, one that would make Lucia question her decision.

"My mother's second cousin's sister-in-law had an arranged marriage. It turned out to be a nightmare. The man she married just wanted a maid, and if she complained he would beat her."

Lucia let out a slight gasp. Violet sensed the story was not dramatic enough, so added, "She didn't have to put up with it too long—she died the next year."

"*Mio Dio,*" Lucia gasped, this time in complete horror. "That might happen to me!"

Lucia's frantic reaction assured Violet she had planted her healthy seed of doubt. Returning to her innocent, unpretentious voice, Violet again apologized. "I'm sorry, Lucia, that was a terrible example. Your life will hopefully have a better ending."

Lucia didn't speak, but her face flushed with embarrassment. The frazzled girl reached into her basket, pulled out a picture and gave it to Violet. Her head now hung low demonstrating she was ashamed.

Looking at the photo, Violet struggled to hide her disgust, partially because of what Edward had revealed about this man Lucia was to marry. In her opinion, his outer appearance reflected his inner blackish soul. The man looked like a weasel with a hat on. Lucia's face mirrored Violet. For a few moments, neither spoke.

Lucia finally blared, "*E bruto.* Ugly! I just wanted to go to America." Her honest confession didn't surprise Violet.

She would not shame her with the obvious questions. The two young ladies stared at the picture in silence, then exploded into a juvenile laughter. Lucia's laugher immediately became uncontrollable sobs.

"I don't want to marry him! I don't want to marry him!" she cried out, wrapping her arms tightly around Violet in despair. "My life is ruined, there is no way out. I took his money." Lucia let out all the sordid details. "He paid for me; he owns me."

This admission chilled Violet through her entire body. "Lucia, I can't breathe." Her words were said in jest, hoping to calm this stressful moment.

"I am frightened; what am I going to do?" Lucia whimpered.

Violet took a deep breath; she wanted to give Lucia a glimpse of hope. "Let me think about it. Edward and I will come up with a plan, I promise."

Lucia's eyes pleaded for help, and she squeezed Violet even tighter as if relinquishing her life to her.

When Edward finally returned, he was too excited to let Violet speak. "I am the champion!" He almost sang his words. "Look at all these." He was shaking a big pouch full of marbles. "I won them all, I was brilliant!" Edward's immodest shout was uncharacteristic. He never boasted about his achievements. Violet suspected this particular accomplishment was elevated by Edward's lost childhood and the many emotions never experienced. Being able to play and compete with other boys caused him to manifest his win to a high level of importance.

Yet she had to be stern. "Give them back, Edward! You know you must."

"Violet, I won fairly!"

"I have no doubt you did, but those marbles are all these boys have, you, *caro,* don't need them."

Edward gave Violet an entire speech about the code of playing a betting game. Unequivocally, he pointed out, one must always honor one's losses. Finishing his detailed explanation, her little man predictably agreed with his partner.

Edward's unexpected gesture stunned the jubilant group of boys. Eagerly, all but one accepted their treasured marbles back. The one reluctant boy, in his late teens, hesitated, shook his head, and began to walk away. Edward stopped him and put the marbles in his hand; the young man nodded in appreciation. He then removed the largest red marble he had and offered it back to Edward. No verbal words were spoken by either competitor; they simply allowed their actions to speak for them.

Violet was gratified and pleased to witness this gesture of respect from them both. Edward, finally receiving a personal token for his selflessness, was not only deserving but warranted. The young man's thoughtfulness was impressive. By stopping to do the right thing, he verified his own true mature character.

CHAPTER 50

BEING ABLE TO HELP IS REWARD ENOUGH

The solution for Lucia's predicament came to Violet while dressing for dinner. It was complicated and required her to do something she'd never done before. For the scheme to work, she would need to involve a third participant. The thought made her uneasy. Asking Mrs. Sutton for a personal favor after all her generosity was unconscionable. Unfortunately, there was no other way to help Lucia. Catherine's input was critical for their plan to succeed. When she presented her idea to Edward, he eagerly agreed.

"It's perfect! That will work."

Getting Mrs. Sutton alone that evening, however, proved difficult. She was the Queen Bee, and acquaintances on board constantly swarmed around her. Violet had always admired Catherine's courteous and gracious repertoire and was not surprised it allured others. Mr. Sutton had always appreciated his wife's popularity. He also knew his duty was to rescue her on the rare occasion it became overwhelming for her. He'd approach, imposing the husband's privilege to dash his wife away. William's boast he had impeccable timing was questionable, since it coincided with Catherine's rehearsed "come get me" signal. It was a simple gesture; her left hand would touch her right earring, and William would come. He'd then request his wife's company for a private stroll around the deck.

Edward had his set time to excuse himself for the evening and would not allow an extra minute to elapse. Tonight, before rushing off, he did make time to approach his mother and whisper something in her ear. He walked over and nudged his partner, giving her an encouraging smile.

Catherine immediately focused her attention on Violet. Taking her arm, Mrs. Sutton escorted the young lady to a private corner. "What is it, my dear?"

Violet felt uncomfortable but knew Catherine well enough not to dally and promptly get to the point. "I am sorry, Mrs. Sutton, for bothering you, but I need your help."

Catherine's expression revealed she was eager to hear more. "Go on," she insisted.

"It's about a woman I've befriended, and her circumstance," Violet muttered, in a rush to get it out before changing her mind.

Catherine looked into Violet's eyes, took both her hands, and spoke reassuringly. "My dear, I am more than happy to help; tell me what it is you need."

Mrs. Sutton's readiness to commit encouraged Violet to calm down and relate Lucia's story. She made sure to put emphasis on the most disturbing elements. Lucia was enroute to marry someone she had never met or spoken to. Her aunt had made the arrangements so rapidly, not allowing her time to think it all though. "He paid for her passage, but now she is afraid and regrets following her aunt's advice. She fears by accepting his money, she is now obliged to marry him. Lucia has nowhere to go and sees no way out." Besides the obvious omission of Edward's vision, Violet shared every detail.

Catherine listened intensely to all Violet divulged, then promptly responded, "I understand your directive; Lucia's problem will be solved if she has U.S. sponsorship, resident address—and a place of employment would be an added plus. You, my dear, are very clever to suggest my parents."

Mrs. Sutton's candidness surprised yet pleased Violet. She had not dare to mention the Johnsons, but it was obviously implied.

Foreseen

How considerate of Mrs. Sutton, Violet thought, *to spare me from having to solicit.*

"I'm in total agreement my parents' involvement will be the perfect solution for a new immigrant." Catherine's statement was given with confidence; this problem had now been solved. "I am seriously appalled by this story of manipulation. Tomorrow, after breakfast, I want to meet this unfortunate girl in your stateroom. Violet, I commend you for wanting to help this young lady. I give you my word that we shall. Now, stop fretting and enjoy your evening."

With Catherine's promise, nothing more was needed. Any trace of doubt faded; Violet had total confidence their plan would succeed. Lucia would be spared a horrible fate and be given a chance to have a good life. Saving Lucia from a bad marriage and giving her a bright future had great significance for Violet. She could hardly wait to see her friend's relief. Reflecting on the absolute misery Lucia would've surely endured, she herself was thankful and intensely grateful.

The next morning, Lucia arrived at Violet's stateroom wearing the suit she had designed and sewn for her upcoming nuptials. Cordially greeting Mrs. Sutton in English instantly gave a positive impression on her host. Catherine was pleased the young lady spoke adequate English.

When Lucia's showed her couture skills, Catherine was impressed and praised her impeccable talent. "I have no doubt your skills will be a great asset to you, young lady."

Their meeting lasted less than thirty minutes, as Mrs. Sutton had come prepared. She spoke directly to Lucia, reinforcing her parents' commitment to help her get established in America. Catherine gave the new immigrant an introductory letter that included her father's influential name and her now high-society place of residence and employment. "If needed, this letter will prove legal and unquestionable sponsorship for your immigration officer."

Catherine prepared a separate envelope containing American money and her parents' address. She then shook Lucia's hand, smiled at the two young friends, and left.

The door to Violet's stateroom was barely closed when Lucia screamed with joy.

Their celebration was brief; Violet was vigilant, and seriously announced, "Now, phase two." She picked up the phone, and seconds later Edward walked in with an armful of his clothes.

"I have written a letter to—what is his full name, Lucia?" Violet didn't get an answer. Her friend was unsure to what or whom Violet was referring. "His full name, your . . . sweetheart." Violet laughed.

"Ha! Him. Sabestiano Mallazani." Lucia pronounced his name as if to say, "what was I thinking?"

"What a vile mouthful," Edward blurted out, unable to stifle his obvious dislike for the man.

Violet suspected her partner held back on how disturbing his vision of this man truly was. This thought intensified her eagerness to lay out their escape plan. "The Italian letter is on your behalf. You are informing him that your chronic skin condition flared again; therefore, you have been too ill and unable to make this voyage. For the present time, you have decided to return to your hometown. In good faith, you are returning all his money." Violet squinted her eyes. "We are sure after getting his money back he will forget the whole arrangement. Also, he will have no way of getting in touch with you."

Lucia looked impressed. "What a clever idea. You two make a great team. He definitely will not want a sickly woman for a wife."

"Exactly!" Edward confirmed as he finally plopped all the clothes on the armchair.

Lucia was curious and seemed confused. "What's all this laundry?" she joked. The young lady was oozing with happiness, anticipating her freedom, living in America and working for amazing people.

"Insurance," Violet said. "In case the disgruntled lover hangs around when we dock in New York. After going through customs, before getting off the ship, you will disguise yourself as a boy. Added precaution doesn't hurt," Violet informed her friend with exuberance; helping someone as deserving as Lucia was tremendously gratifying.

Lucia inspected the trousers, shirt, and baseball cap Edward generously donated. She immediately smacked a big kiss on his cheeks, squeezed his young face in her hands, and murmured, *"Grazie, tesoro."*

Edward understood calling him "treasure" was to show endearment. Violet had called him that thousands of times over the years. He now had no need for all this "mushy talk," as he called it. Freeing himself from Lucia's hold, he gave Violet an envelope, grunted his discomfort, and retreated to his own cabin. The two compatriots were now alone to finalize more specific details.

Thanks to Mrs. Sutton's monetary generosity, the exact amount of Lucia's passage was counted and put in the envelope. The letter of regret was added and promptly sealed tight. On the front, in bold letters, Lucia wrote: *PER: SABESTIANO MALLAZANI.* Immediately after *Queen Mary* docked, their plan would be set in motion. A ship steward would be commissioned to ensure the envelope was properly hand-delivered to the man.

"How can I ever repay everyone's kindness?" Lucia cried, holding Violet. "You saved my life," she whimpered.

Fortunately, she would never know how accurate that statement was. Preventing Lucia from a miserable existence full of abuse was gratifying. Violet couldn't stop think of her own circumstance years earlier. She felt by helping Lucia, everything had come full circle. All thanks to her little man. Lucia would now have the life she had dreamed of, full of possibility and happiness. Edward's gift and compassion had benefitted so many, and yet he himself had not received the proper, personal "thank you" he deserved. His reaction to Lucia's simple grateful gesture demonstrated he neither wanted nor expected gratitude. This was nothing new; through the years, Violet had tried to praise and thank him, but he would just wave it off. Edward's reply was always the same: "Being able to help is reward enough." His added statement always tacked on Violet's emotions: "I wish I could do more."

CHAPTER 51

ADMIRATION OF CHARACTER

Lucia had a peculiar trait: simultaneously she'd cry and laugh. Not because she was indecisive. On the contrary, she was comfortable showing her raw emotions. If sad, she would cry, but if a solution suddenly presented itself—snap! She instantly cheered up.

Such display of inner feelings was uncommon for Violet. This verified how different she was from Lucia. At an early age, Violet had disciplined herself to conceal her own fears and needs. She wouldn't dare show her father how hurtful and demoralizing his verbal abuse was. The deep love and appreciation for her mama and sisters would not permit her to burden them with more sadness.

As for Mr. And Mrs. Sutton, Violet convinced herself it was inappropriate to show them anything but respect. They were so giving and thoughtful; they deserved better than dealing with her in any melancholy mood.

As she'd recently discovered, her efforts to hide her deep feelings from Edward were not only futile but absurd. Nevertheless, she had tried. Examining the restraint, she had put on her emotions, Violet unveiled a serious consequence: by suppressing her sadness she had also held back other parts of her true character.

Lucia's demonstrative character had been a source of inspiration. Her constant disbursement of emotions had inspired Violet. She considered adapting a bit of Lucia's openness. Violet had conquered many challenges in the past, but this particular one would be difficult. With all the restrictions she had embodied over the years, revamping herself was not an easy task. An inner battle with her own concrete beliefs would be hard to break though.

Lucia's squeal grabbed Violet's full attention. "Of course! I know the perfect gift." She cheered up while mopping her tears with Edward's trousers. "I will thank you by creating and designing the most amazing wedding dress for you."

"Lucia! What are you saying?" Violet was unprepared for her friends far-fetched offer and readily protested. "Please don't mention anything to do with marriage. Remember, we're still trying to prevent yours from happening."

Lucia quickly checked herself. "You're right, of course you're right. No talk of marriage. It is just my way of giving back. It makes me feel good."

Violet understood; Lucia's giving nature was evident right at the start of their friendship. Her honesty and unguarded remarks were the qualities that had attracted Violet to her even more.

CHAPTER 52

U.S. PORT

What makes a large group of diverse people with obvious differences unite? A single denominator, the proverbial "common thread." This was their last night at sea, the voyage's end. All passengers from the lower decks, as well as the upper circle, plus the entire crew, were in a festive mood.

The captain's black-and-white gala, celebrating their final farewell, was highly anticipated and well attended. Catherine's black lace strapless gown, with a sweeping train, was incomparable to the hundreds of other women in black. She radiated a unique elegance all her own.

Our young lady was equally stunning, in a cloudy-white empire Chanel gown. A hint of black velvet leaves adorned the wide, rounded neckline. The slightly protruding pointed tips created the illusion of a necklace. The fitted silk skirt had a second layer of sheer overlay floating openly as Violet moved.

Admirers uttered a harmonized chorus of "aww" as the two ladies entered the ship's grand dining room.

Later, in the Imperial Ball Room, Violet danced all night, displaying no discomfort. Her mandate was to convey and convince the Suttons she was enjoying the evening. Her heart was full of sincere gratitude and appreciation, not only for all they had done for her, but for giving Lucia a new life.

She struggled slightly with the one persistent nagging question: *Are they determined to find me a husband?* Every time she danced by them, in the arms of a handsome partner, they nodded in approval. Based on the encouraging smiles they flashed her way, it seemed probable.

Yet Catherine had been sympathetic to Lucia's hasty arrangement. She had shown outrage that anyone could be forced into a loveless marriage. Clinging to this fact made it easier for Violet to keep her suspicions hidden and her big smile exposed.

The Suttons' balcony was perfect to view the approach to the New York Harbor. As the Statue of Liberty came into view, loud cheers erupted from the emotional crowd on deck. The chaos among the excited passengers mirrored their behavior when the ship departed Southampton, except two notable attributes were absent: anxiety and sad tears. They had been replaced by excitement and jubilation.

Edward and Violet had to be content observing the escape plan for Lucia through binoculars. They nudged one another as, step by step, the scheme unfolded.

A rough-looking man marched towards the steward holding the poster. The commissioned steward stood on a high platform. The bold, embellished letters spelling the name "Sabestiano Mallazani" were hard to miss. The man marched towards him. Aggressively and rudely, he grabbed the envelope from the young steward's hand and ripped it open. The money was quickly shoved in his pants pocket. He scarcely glanced at the letter and crumpled it in his hand. He then crumpled what seemed to be a photograph. He angrily tossed both papers on the pavement. The two now unessential pieces of crumbled paper were quickly kicked around by the crowd. The unaware participants continued kicking the discarded papers until they disappeared into one of the gutters.

The brute shoved a few people from his path, gave one swift look about and strutted off, counting his money. His rapid flight was a welcoming sight for the two partners. They had been correct in assuming his concern was on retrieving back his money.

The concrete dock was soon emptied as automobiles and taxis paraded away full of happy people. The passenger in one of the taxis appeared to be a teenage boy wearing a bulging baseball cap. Lucia was on her way to her safe haven.

Violet and Edward nudged each other one last time, quietly acknowledging, "Mission accomplished."

CHAPTER 53

SETTLING IN NEW YORK CITY

Violet had never been shy; her hesitation came from always considering others first. She would evaluate a situation and behave accordingly with what she believed was appropriate. When they arrived at the Johnsons' home, Violet chose to remain a few feet back. She didn't want to intrude on what she considered an intimate family reunion.

Abigail Johnson's pleasant and charming personality matched her appearance. Her warmth radiated from her generous smile. Her short, silver, finger-waved hair complimented her rosy complexion. She was an imposing woman, slender and tall, the same six-foot height as her husband, Harry James Johnson.

Harry considered himself a "no-nonsense" man. He followed his own rules, never restricted by others. He aggressively rushed to greet his family, grabbing, pulling, and hugging each in no particular order.

Violet was not allowed her thoughtful courtesy of staying back. Mr. Johnson instinctively grabbed her as he did the others.

"What an enchanting little Snow White we have here!" Harry proclaimed, lifting Violet practically two feet off the ground. "We'll have no problem finding her a Prince Charming!"

His loud announcement was the last thing Violet wanted to hear. It confirmed her suspicions of a conspiracy, to marry her off! They were all in on it. She regretted allowing those thoughts back in and reprimanded herself. *Stop fretting! This is not the time.*

Mr. Johnson's clumsy embrace was actually a welcoming distraction. Swinging from Harry's arms like a pendulum, Violet was forced to focus on her awkward situation. The physical yet comical imbalance between her and the large man replaced some of her mental worries.

"Father, please, let us at least get through the door before you start running our lives." Catherine's reproach was never meant to nick at her obvious affection she held for her father. It was delivered with a humorous, endearing tone.

Abigail simply smiled at her daughter's futile request, before adding, "By the way dear, your gift arrived safely. Not a problem; she will be well taken care of."

Catherine nodded, acknowledging her mother's acceptance, which ended their quick exchange on that matter. Violet intuitively knew they spoke of Lucia, just as she knew it best not to intrude or question.

Patting Violet's hand, Abigail closely observed her. "You have indeed blossomed since our last visit my dear. You are a lovely young lady. Harry means well but can be a bit rough around the edges. We still love him, right?"

Violet agreed with her own smile and a quick nod. Abigail's calming observation was meant for Violet's benefit. She promptly gave a disapproving glance at her husband. However, Harry was irreproachable and remained amused by everyone's reaction.

"Don't worry, Violet; I won't let them marry you off just yet." Edward's rescuing comment aroused a hearty laugh from everyone, eliminating any discomfort Harry's words had caused.

Mrs. Johnson's strategic plan to get everyone settled comfortably was enacted. Abigail had drilled her staff and issued written orders. It was quite clear to Violet where Catherine had inherited her impeccable organizational skills.

A soft-spoken Norwegian girl with slightly protruding front teeth and thick golden braids crowning her head was assigned to care for

Violet's needs. She was barely a few years older than her charge, but very serious about her duties. She had Violet's trunks opened, gowns immediately hung, and a bath running all in the time Violet took to undress. Her mind was preoccupied thinking of Lucia. She wasn't worried, just curious on how her friend was settling in. Violet had no doubt Lucia was given immediate attention from the Johnsons. After all, she had been sent and highly recommended by their own daughter. This alone was enough for the Johnsons to do their utmost to ensure Lucia's treatment was the very best. Eventually the topic of Lucia would come up; she would have to be patient. The Johnsons would deal with Lucia's situation efficiently and successfully.

Over the years, Violet had observed how enterprising households handled employment status. It had been a frequent occurrence at Sutton Manor, most probably the same would occur at the Johnsons' estate. Violet recalled on any given day a family member of a current employee would show up also seeking a position. They would then be evaluated on their qualifications and placed in one of the numerous locations. Violet was convinced Lucia's talents as an exquisite seamstress would be thoroughly reviewed by the person authorized, and that she would be hired on her merits.

Dinner was promptly at seven. The table was impeccably set, and all seated looked grand in formal attire. In total contrast was the very casual conversation from the hosting couple. Although English was spoken, it was evident they were in a different part of the world.

"Cathy, dear, your father and I considered you might all be well-worn after your long voyage, which is why we agreed not to invite guests." Abigail sounded as if she had made a huge sacrifice.

"Yeah, tonight is for family to catch up, but tomorrow night is a whole new ball game. Right, Eddie, my boy?" Mr. Johnson blasted across the large dining room at his grandson. "There might even be a nice American gal for you, Eddie, my man."

"Father, please, I don't appreciate my son being called Eddie. His name is Edward," Catherine asserted firmly. Abbreviating names had always been a pet peeve of hers. She had often debated the question "what is in a name?" She'd argued that without proper names, the world would be in chaos.

Harry, always an instigator, was determined to continue. "Right-ho! But in America—"

"Grandpa!" Edward shrewdly interrupted him. "You are most thoughtful, but I believe since Violet is so much older, we should all concentrate on her."

Everyone hummed in agreement. Violet was on the other side of the spectrum and not amused with her little monster's comment. She threw him a phony smile, knowing her message was clearly received: "I'll get you later." Being the center of attention was unbearable and a personal nightmare for the unpretentious young lady.

"Father, will you try to keep this event tomorrow moderately simple?" Catherine asked hopefully.

"My dear," assured Mr. Johnson. "Only a few friends with grandchildren Violet's age— and of course camels and elephants." He chuckled, pleased with himself.

"Don't pay attention to your father, Cathy; our main purpose is to introduce Violet to a few young people."

Violet swallowed her food before she intended to. Her best-laid plan of being invisible on this trip had just flown out the window.

"How considerate of you, Abigail," William voiced his appreciation for his in-laws' thoughtfulness. "I'm sure Violet will enjoy spending time with her own age group."

Violet was silent but quick to widen her smile to all at the table.

CHAPTER 54

A DAY IN THE PARK

The hazy morning weather was ahead of schedule. It was uncomfortably hot and humid, more conducive to late July than early June. Abigail's meticulous, well-set schedule was presented at breakfast. Among its "to-do's," William was to accompany Edward and Violet to Central Park. Mother and daughter would be preoccupied finalizing last-minute details for the evening event.

"We want you out of our way, but back precisely at three." Catherine was insistent on the importance of being punctual. "Violet needs time to rest, then prepare for a fun-filled evening with the younger guests."

"Yes, dear, I promise to be back no later than 2:55." William's obedient words, combined with a playful, reverent bow, received a hearty giggle from Abigail.

Taking the car for what would be a brisk fifteen-minute walk would never be considered by the trio. Nevertheless, it was promptly ready and waiting for them. Sam, the Johnsons' chauffeur, had hitched two bicycles at the rear of the automobile for the two youths to venture out further and enjoy more of the view. A huge picnic basket sat on the front seat opposite him.

William briefed the two eager tourists on the time and place they would all meet for lunch. Violet and Edward were both enthralled to explore as much of the world-famous park their biking legs would permit.

The suggestion to stop and rest came from the older of the two bikers. "This is a great spot to relax and take in the scenery. I love watching the swans gliding gracefully through the waters. Their delicate beauty gives me a sense of calmness. They seem oblivious to our presence; yet we are captivated and compelled to keep watching, as though they are gifting us with a great performance."

"Violet, you're so poetic. You should consider writing poetry. I predict," Edward teased, pretending to look into a crystal ball, "you would be smashing at it."

"My mind is always on what you're going to come up with next. There's no room for anything else."

Their fun-filled exchange ended, as Edward's expression became serious. At times like this, when their lives appeared "normal," Violet would retract her wish for Edward to somehow stop having visions. She wanted him to enjoy life as a carefree thirteen-year-old boy. Although he kept reassuring her he now had control, she could not stop worrying for him.

"Violet, I am going to visit my cousin Bernard on Tuesday. I'll be gone for a week."

"That's fine, Edward. Now, what is it you're not telling me?" She had her own intuition when it came to Edward's eccentricities. Violet knew his every twitch and tone had meaning and this tone had "caution" written all over it. Edward hesitated to say more which heightened Violet's persistence. "Eddddwaaaarrrdddd."

"Tonight, you're going to meet some nice people but also some not that nice," he cautioned.

"Edward, please be more specific."

"I can't be more specific. I am just not sure. Remember my vision with the preacher's wife kissing a man? It was so vague; the fact that he was her brother escaped me. I promised myself when I have unclear visions never to assume what they mean."

"Are you saying I'm going to be kissing a man?"

Edward shrugged his shoulders. "Your feelings are confusing; besides, you don't want to know certain things, right?"

"Well!" Violet was defensive. "I assure you, Mr. Edward James Sutton, I am not going to be kissing anyone."

From his laughter, it was obvious Edward was enjoying rattling her. "As I was saying, I'll be back in a week. You'll be fine. Besides you should lighten up on this trip and have fun."

With that said, Edward was done with the conversation. Violet, on the other hand, had a lot to think over. Edward had insinuated her need to lighten up and make mistakes before. Was he suggesting she was in danger of doing something stupid? She was prepared to put her guard up and be extra cautious.

They were hungry after their extensive bike riding and happy the picnic lunch was laid out. In less than twenty minutes, what remained had been repacked.

William was eager to follow up on the results of a chess game he had been observing. "I will be back soon, and then we'll be off." His intentions were sincere.

As most people know, *time* and *a game of chess* are not mates. Once the challenge commences, the game's duration is unpredictable. The opponents in the match William was observing, were both masters. Their moves demanded intense strategy, consuming time from both sides. Each player analyzed what their next move would extract from their opponent. At this high level of chess, time was of no consequence.

William's explanation to justify his tardiness was in theory indisputable, but lame.

"We are going to be an hour late! Mom won't be happy," Edward warned.

"She is going to kill me!" William kept repeating as he urged the chauffeur to drive faster.

"Father, why not say you wandered off and got lost? The police officers took an hour to find and return you safely to us." Edward tried to sound serious giving the pretentious suggestion to his father.

William was not pleased with his son's attempt to be humorous at his cost. "Cheeky, isn't he, Violet?"

"You'll not get an argument from me, Mr. Sutton; I'm not very fond of him myself right now." Violet meant every word. She had tried for hours to get Edward to reveal more about his earlier warnings. He had cleverly managed to answer her questions without giving her any tangible info.

William's punishment for their tardiness was not the unforgivable guillotine, although, in response to Catherine's sharp scolding, he feigned protecting his neck. Lucky for him, his wife's own time restraint limited further rebukes to his theatrics.

Taking Violet's hand, Catherine said sharply, "We will speak of it later."

"I am full of anticipation, dear, and will prepare a proper defensive speech." William's attempt to reduce tension with his humor fall flat.

"Like father, like son," Violet observed, their respective attempts at comic relief failed miserably. She attributed this fact to their poor timing. Never try to be funny when the recipient of your humor is obviously agitated and definitely not in the mood for comedy. The comments received will tip the scale towards sarcasm rather than humor.

CHAPTER 55

PARTY CITY

Mr. and Mrs. Johnson's small gathering turned out to be close to one hundred friends. It was an elaborate affair. Nothing had been overlooked.

As the guests arrived, a seven-piece orchestra played Vivaldi's "Spring." This was to coincide with and compliment the Johnson's party theme. The decor had transformed the great room into a spring garden. A multitude of various blossoming potted trees encircled the perimeter of the room. Strategically placed between ivy-covered lattices were hundreds of blue forget-me-nots infused with white crocuses. Huge urns displayed hundreds of tulips and daffodils. This overflow of greenery gave the illusion of walking into a garden.

There were ice sculptures, chilled shrimp, oysters, platters of caviar. Fountains of floating liquid chocolate surrounded with trays of tropical fruits invited tasty dipping. Numerous servers made sure guests enjoyed frequent flowing champagne and *hors d'oeuvres*.

Violet's curiosity got the better of her. She slipped out of her room to peak at the crowd below.

Olga, her assistant, anxiously pleaded, "Miss Violet., allow me to finish helping you dress, you would not want to be tardy for your special evening!"

All eyes were on Violet as she appeared at the top of the staircase. She wore her Dior off-the-shoulder, emerald chiffon gown. Its tiny crystals shimmered through the pleats of the basque top. The floating skirt, slightly elongated at the back, swayed as she walked. Her lustrous, wavy, black hair fell loosely over her lightly tanned shoulders. The glow of the emerald earrings paled in comparison to her own sparkling green eyes. Her full, soft, pink lips turned up, creating a warm and generous smile.

William offered his hand as she reached the bottom step. "Everyone!" he announced. "I am proud to introduce Violet, our guardian and an established member of the Sutton family." His authoritative voice confirmed what the crowd perceived: Violet was important to this family.

The guests themselves had an air of self-importance. It was understood that the Johnsons would not invite just anyone to their family soiree.

An immediate rush toward Violet was imminent. Most had to feed their curiosity. The more mature guests simply wanted the introductions done, to continue socializing with William and Catherine Sutton.

The younger group of guests were genuinely eager to speak with her, especially the young men. They commented on her appearance with words she was not familiar with. Violet was not sure if they were at all flattering. Some uttered phrases like "Hubba hubba!" and "What a mama!" They seemed to describe her as a fat, old woman. Nevertheless, their accents certainly entertained and amused her.

Violet struggled to remember all the names as they blurred out. She wondered if this ritual of multiple introductions was ever successful. With names flying about in a rushed manner, Violet conceded, it was impossible for her to keep them straight.

She gave a look toward Edward that cried, "Save me!" However, the prompt rescue came from Mr. Sutton. He offered his arm, leading her to the dance floor. Violet would have enjoyed the opening dance if not for the inescapable feeling of hundreds of eyes judging her every move.

With the dance floor now officially open, eager young men stormed towards the honored guest. She graciously accepted every dance invitation.

"Oh no, my dear!" Mrs. Johnson interrupted, practically snatching Violet's hand from another excitable dance partner. "You look flushed and fatigued. I insist you take a break from dancing to enjoy some refreshment."

Violet was definitely exhausted and grateful for Mrs. Johnson's insistence. Her throbbing feet had swollen at least two sizes larger than her shoes. She wouldn't dare remove them in fear she'd never get them back on. Besides, proper etiquette must always be observed, no matter the sacrifice. Violet had a flashback of the many times she was made to walk barefoot and immediately shrugged off her pain.

At evening's end, Mr. Johnson's voice echoed in the large, now-empty room. "Compliments are in order!" he boasted. "My hat's off to my daughter and my lovely wife for managing a most successful party. You are the only two ladies I know who could successfully pull such an elaborate event in a day."

"Harry Johnson!" Abigail's voice was stern. "You know I've been planning this for over a month."

Harry laughed. "It was all she talked about. Still, I am proud of its success and my two gals." He embraced both in his arms.

Harry was not done with his speeches. Turning to Violet, he asked, "Any prospects, dear, from all those young bucks? Did you find one you prefer?" He grinned.

Violet wanted to give him a definite no, but softly answered, "I didn't really get a chance to speak to anyone for more than a few minutes."

"Harry Johnson, stop your teasing! You're such an instigator." Abigail cast a disapproving look, hoping to stop her husband from asking more questions.

Harry's son-in-law provided a response, releasing Violet from more embarrassment. "Our young lady has always been sensible. She will make a wise decision at the right time."

Abigail let out a slight yawn; her sleepy gesture reminded everyone of their own fatigue. The consensus to promptly retreat upstairs to their comfortable beds was unanimous.

Every bone in Violet's body ached, especially her feet. Worse, her thoughts munched away any peace for her. They were the same nagging questions she had had on the ship: *Why do they always ask if I'm interested in any particular man? Why is it so important* now? Violet dared not admit it aloud, but deep down she knew the answer. It was age appropriate. Twenty-year-old women back in her hometown were already mothers, or at least married. Edward no longer needing a companion was also imminent. The number-one mandate for her future was to get the old maid married off.

Reflecting on the evening, Violet remained disillusioned. She was disappointed in the lack of maturity the men she danced with demonstrated. Sadly, she concluded they were even less interesting than the men she had met on board the *Queen Mary*.

As usual, Violet questioned herself. She began to wonder if her expectations were too high. Edward's intellect was not to be compared. He was a walking encyclopaedia. In the last few years, he'd absorbed knowledge like a sponge. He would express his views on any given subject: politics, human rights, history, and of course, his passion, fossils. The few conversations she'd had with Eric were interesting and informative. His comments on world events always left her wanting to hear more. The young men tonight were only interested in bragging about their American cars. Most of the conversation focused on the model, performance, and speed of the vehicle. Conversing with the young ladies was pleasant, friendly, but also limited. Their passionate topics discussed were dating, fashion, and the next party event.

Foreseen

Violet resolved that since she had very little in common with her new acquaintances, her best course of action was to keep her mind open, and her mouth shut.

CHAPTER 56

DIFFERENCES AND CHALLENGES

Early the next morning, our young lady received an unexpected invitation. The group of friends she'd met at the party had arranged a sightseeing excursion with her. The eager voice on the phone pleaded, "Violet please say yes. It will be a blast showing you around our great city. We'll be your tour guides for the day!"

Violet hesitated; she was a bit apprehensive about spending a whole day with people she had just met. Her solution, of course, was to take Edward along.

At breakfast, everyone at the table listened as she proposed her outing should include Edward. It was a unanimous "No!" With Edward's voice being the strongest. Everyone agreed the invite had not been extended to include him.

Harry's off-kilter comment—"Edward won't fit in, he's too tall!"—momentarily confused Violet. Her problem-solving skills were always challenged around him. She had to stop to consider what he meant to say, instead of the words he'd spoken; it was like deciphering a riddle.

However, this particular riddle wasn't much of a challenge for our witty young lady. Mr. Johnson didn't want to say Edward's age for this particular group was the issue. So, the clever grandfather replaced height for age, making it complimentary to his grandson.

Violet realized she too was being vague. Including Edward in the outing wasn't at all for his enjoyment but for her benefit. Secretly, she believed having him along would prevent her from making mistakes. When had their roles changed?

Admitting her true motive was alarming; disappointed she began chastising herself aloud. "I know my own capabilities and can take care of myself."

Her determined outburst grabbed everyone's attention and had Edward laughing. Embarrassed by her blunder, she nervously excused herself.

As the day progressed, Violet felt rather foolish about her lack of confidence earlier that morning. Her new American friends were attentive and fun to be with. She was actually having a marvelous time.

Sue was the outspoken one and obviously the group's leader. She was petite, with a slim body and pretty face. "I have the day all planned," she announced, tossing her long, blonde hair and batting her thick eyelashes.

All seemed impressed! Sue had spent so much time preparing a detailed schedule. Violet was the only one who recognized her itinerary was written on Mrs. Sutton's stationary. Naturally, Catherine would readily assemble a precise route, ensuring they would not miss any popular attractions: The Empire State Building, Statue of Liberty, and the Metropolitan Museum of Art, to mention a few. Catherine wouldn't allow the group to simply "wing it."

After the sight-seeing on the itinerary was completed, the group was famished. They all unanimously agreed to head directly for their favorite hangout, for food and drinks. The quaint diner was packed with vibrating youthful energy. The group marched in and passed a few empty tables, straight to a large circular corner booth. They stood, arms folded, causing the three already-seated occupants to hurriedly relinquish their seats.

Sue took one menu from the young server and waved off the others. "We only need one," she instructed and began ordering. "We will have—"

The list of food was practically every item on the menu. After the befuddled waitress had gone, Sue giggled in contentment. Seeing Violet's perplexed expression, she giggled even louder. "I love doing this, it confuses her, but it also makes it easy for her to remember, right? Let me explain my logic to you, Violet. I order all the different meals so we can share and have a bit of everything. Isn't that marvelous?" Sue delighted in her own brilliantly rational system.

Violet simply nodded in agreement with whatever Sue had said. She had agreed with everything all day to mask her confusion. It had become apparent to Violet that things were done differently in America.

The group's confidence and carefree spirit was exhilarating but intimidating. Inwardly, Violet wished she could be more like them. Until recently, she had never questioned her behavior, believing that being meek and respectful was what was expected. Her new friends' expectations had no boundaries. Violet enjoyed all their diversities; she found them pleasantly amusing.

CHAPTER 57

YOUNG ADULTS UNRESTRAINED

"Robert, darling! If you don't stop taking random pictures instead of properly posed ones, I *will* take your camera away!" Lorna threatened her boyfriend. They had been dating for a few months now.

By their physical appearance, Violet had assumed they were related. Both were tall and slender with auburn, wavy hair, and hazel eyes. She concluded brother and sister but had ventured wrong. Observing their different personalities, Robert's flamboyant and laid-back attitude clashed with Lorna's meticulous, precise approach. Violet ascertained they made the perfect "odd couple."

Freddie in his oversized glasses was the intellect. He reminded Violet of her sister Dahlia, and she considered him interesting and informative. His friends not so much; they found him overbearing and boring, demanding he keep his "useless information" to himself.

Ted was the charmer, displaying Cary Grant elegance. He opened doors, pulled chairs for the ladies, and generously complimented them. Their appreciative smile seemed his ultimate reward. Today he lavished his attention on Violet, embarrassing the newcomer—thereby amusing the others and himself.

With the car radio on full blast, their loud discussions sounded more like a heated political argument. However, world affairs, were not a priority for this young group. Their passionate exchanges and opinions focused solely on the popularity of songs and celebrities. Violet soon understood their disagreements really had no consequence; it was all in fun. Why turn down the radio? Shouting out loud who the coolest or dreamiest singers and movie stars were seemed more energizing.

Violet's lack of familiarity on the subject of American celebrities aroused the determined aficionados to solicit her support even more. Each screamed out their favorite, trying to sway the hesitant rookie to his or her side.

Violet used diplomacy. "I couldn't possibly choose one; your suggestions are all so smashing."

Their carefree and nonchalant approach to life was intoxicating. Violet tried hard to blend in to this most colorful tapestry, but the grey patch she had to add lacked lustre. She hoped her enthusiasm would make up for her obvious inexperience.

Sue embodied leadership and loved to control any situation. A few hours earlier she had received praise and admiration from her peers. A police car with flashing lights and sirens blazing had pulled alongside them. The officer demanded she stop the car. He accused Sue of driving through a red light. She was in total control and didn't even flinch. The confident young lady, calmly explained to the policeman her grandfather, Judge McClure, would believe her explanation.

"I swear the stop light was still amber when I drove through."

The officer pensively re-evaluated the situation, and then waved them off with a stern warning: "Drive carefully."

When the police car drove off, Sue's friends applauded her for a job well done. Without losing momentum, they all returned to their loud discussion as though nothing had happened. Witnessing this level of confidence astounded the newcomer.

Sue stopped the car in front of the Johnsons' mansion five minutes before the scheduled return time. Ted jumped out and gallantly helped Violet by taking her hand. His attentiveness received mocking comments and laughter from the others.

"Eight. Movie. See ya!" This was Sue's summary of their evening engagement. Condensing phrases was how the group talked to each other. It was their own code. Rushed dynamics fed their energetic spirit. Why waste time enunciating every word? Violet knew she had better clue in, catch on, or be left out. She kept reminded herself she was in a different country.

Truthfully, Violet had to admit to herself, *I don't have a clue what young people in London find popular either.* Living at the manor these past five years had sheltered her from outside influences.

With Lucia, her Italian friend, Violet had analyzed that she had suppressed her true emotions most of her life. Spending time with this group of young Americans, she recognized another flaw. Unlike them, she had never demanded anything or ever expressed her personal preferences. She never disagreed with the choices made for her. All the Suttons had lavished on her was humbly accepted but never expected. Edward was the only person who knew her completely. No revelation there—after all, they shared everything, even her unspoken feelings. Violet's alarming contemplation forced her to focus on the truth. Most of her time had been spent with Edward and studies. She had not allowed herself to be passionate about her own life and definitely lacked worldly experiences.

Her new American friends' zest for life was exciting. They nurtured self-confidence and self-importance. How did Sue put it? "When I am with older people, I never listen to what they say or mean what I say."

Violet was not aware there was such a disconnect between generations. Was it more dominant in America or was it global? She decided her loyalty must balance more toward her peers. After all, she was one of them. Thanks to Mr. and Mrs. Johnson for taking the initiative, she now was part of this great connection. Harry intuitively suggested young people will do what they know best: have fun. He was always pleased and eager to give others his personal knowledge and insight. Experiencing this new way of life with her own age group had opened this self-diagnosed recluse's eyes.

Fun and leisurely activities had always been carefully scheduled for her. Riding her horse, exploring nature, and singing were all she had indulged in. All great and good but limited, she now thought. Sharing activities with vibrant people her age felt different and more exciting. Their outspokenness and temerity to do what they wanted, whenever they pleased, was, in Violet's view, strength of character.

CHAPTER 58

LIFE'S LITTLE CHANGES

Having to sit though dinner that evening was tedious and painfully slow for at least two at the table. Edward wanted to spend his time triple wrapping his most delicate fossils for his trip in the morning. Violet had to change into attire more appropriate for a night at the movies. Savoring every bit, the four adults showed no concern for time. They seemed amused watching the fidgety duo waiting to be excused.

Our Edward's patience, as we know, has always been limited; time had run out. Abruptly, he stood and announced, "Violet and I have commitments elsewhere and need to be excused."

With a hint of playfulness, the adults individually voiced their consent.

"Of course!"

"Don't let us detain you."

"By all means!"

"Enjoy your evening!"

On their way up the stairs, Violet thanked Edward for speaking up. "I didn't want to be rude".

"Violet, my dear, sometimes you have to take matters into your own hands and do what you gotta do."

"Wow, Edward! You sound like a real American."

"Yep, I'm trying to fit in, just like you."

"Maybe I am trying to fit in, but I believe my new friends genuinely like me," she defended, adding, "When in Rome . . . "

"In my vision—" Edward voiced before Violet interrupted him.

"I know I've been nagging you to reveal some details, but I'm glad you remained firm. I need to let life unfold as it should. I am determined to have a great time, and you should too."

Violet felt good about her little speech. "Remember: don't let your visions control your day. Try to push them aside and have fun."

Edward shook his head affirmatively.

"Right you are, Violet. Let us make a pact not to worry about each other, come what may. I'll be back in a few days." He smiled, patting her shoulder.

This gesture of patting each other's backs was Edward's way of replacing their once frequent and affectionate hugs. Violet had agreed to less hugging and kissing but disapproved of this exchange. A pat on the back, she protested, was too impersonal. Too detached and masculine. To demonstrate her disapproval, she intentionally replaced the pat on his shoulder with a hard smack.

CHAPTER 59

MOVIE NIGHT

"We called a few other friends," Sue told Violet as she squeezed into the crowded car. "The 'more the merrier' is my motto!" Lorna managed to say before an elbow hit her in the mouth.

At the theater, the group lingered under its marquee. The young ladies were more interested in showcasing and commenting on each other's new purchases. The sprouting men admired the different models of cars that drove by, pointing out some new-and-improved features. Not one seemed interested in entering the theater to enjoy the movie. Even inside they spent ample time at the vending bar, choosing their snacks. They eventually trickled in, heading straight to the back seats.

"It's all an excuse to get out and be together," Sue explained to the puzzled Violet. "We've already seen this movie. For some," she smirked, "it's our third time."

As the lights went down, the dark theater became a juvenile playground. Popcorn flew aimlessly, seats were kicked, and sporadic whistling echoed everywhere. The frazzled usher's patience was tested to the max. He darted from row to rowdy row flashing his light in faces, warning, "Be seated and quiet or be escorted out."

Each time, the guilty party pleaded innocence, assuring him they were there only to enjoy the movie. Frustrated, the employee would stomp away.

How strange all this behavior was for Violet. Why go to the theater if you're not going to watch the movie? It was like wearing earplugs to a concert.

It became obvious. This group actually made their own rules. Not at all the conduct she was used to. These young adults fought against restrictions to whatever they considered fun. Violet let loose a bit of the rebel she had hidden deep in her; impulsively she threw back popcorn that had landed on her lap. She didn't want to seem rigid over simple hijinks and joined in. *Why not have fun and let loose?* She gave herself permission. *I want to embrace this feeling of liberation. No restrictions, just enjoy, at least for this summer vacation.*

A few hours later, sipping on milkshakes, the group spoke of their upcoming plan. Violet was unsettled and reluctant to participate. Her newfound "freedom" was fading sooner than she'd anticipated. She could never consider being part of what they were proposing. Instinctively, she retreated back into her protective shell.

Edward's vision about her making some kind of mistake began to fester in her mind. In truth, the thought of asking the Suttons for permission to join them held her back.

"You must come, Vi! Two nights in Niagara Falls, doing whatever we please, will be a blast. Also, you will complete our circle. We'll all be coupled up," Sue said, giving a knowing smile at Ted.

Rehearsing a few different reasons and scenarios to convince Mr. and Mrs. Sutton into letting her go was exhausting. The one thing Violet managed to achieve out of the exercise was a throbbing headache. Requesting permission to go on an unsupervised trip at the age of twenty should have been easy. For Violet, asking for anything personal for herself had always been difficult.

She considered suggesting she'd use her own money, but immediately dismissed that idea. Violet could not insult them. Throughout the years they had been adamant, all her needs and care came from them. Besides, Violet knew this was not about money. They had always lavished her with the best. It was Violet's own sense of unworthiness that held her back. She had never dared exert her own desires.

Exposure to this self-indulgent attitude of her new American friends somehow made Violet feel even less equal. Why couldn't she have a bit of Lorna's spirit, or Sue's confidence, or a bit of the entitlement they all seemed to have?

Violet knew the answer was fear. Fear it could all be taken away. She could not forget her responsibility to her family and, of course, who she really was. Her life had always been focused on pleasing others. *I was not born privileged. All I have is because of the Suttons' generosity.* Violet's worst fear was failure and disappointing her family. It had always consumed her. Imagine being sent back because of her insubordination. All these negative thoughts were exhausting. She sighed dejectedly, telling herself, *Violet Conti, you're unequivocally dull, insignificant, and full of flaws.*

CHAPTER 60

BALANCING CHANCES

Morning light has a way of diminishing the dark feelings from the previous night. Violet's mood was dramatically better when she joined Catherine at breakfast. "I'll be spending most of the day at the tennis court," the young lady informed.

"Apparently!" Catherine smiled, observing Violet in her tennis attire. "You look very professional," she complimented.

"This adds to the outfit, don't you think?" Violet proudly waved her hand side to side as the Queen did when passing through a crowd. Twisting her wrist was the tennis bracelet Edward had given her on her twentieth birthday. Its prisms bounced about, flooding the room with a rainbow of colours, delighting both ladies.

"I've just spoken to Edward. He asked me to remind you he'll be back soon. Sorry, I cannot remember what else, he wasn't specific. He jumped from one thing to another, mostly talked about his cousin Bernard and fossils. I tried to listen, but I'm not really interested in hearing about animal remains." Catherine had never understood Edward's fascination with fossils. Like most good parents, the Suttons never discouraged or encouraged but always supported their son.

Violet didn't have a chance to reply. Mrs. Sutton was not finished. "Early next week when he returns, we will plan another party. Of course, your new friends are all invited. We believe you will enjoy having them come."

"I'm not sure they will be able to make it."

"Why not? I was told they live to party."

Violet had decided not to ask the Suttons' permission to join the group's getaway plans. This conversation, however, made it possible for her to sneak it in. "They are planning a trip to Niagara Falls for a few days and have asked me to join them." Violet rushed through the last part, hoping Mrs. Sutton would not comprehend what it all entailed.

Catherine's response was prompt. "My dear, Mr. Sutton and I would not feel right in letting you go. Your mother would worry. Traveling with us is perfectly acceptable, but strangers? I am sure your mama would object. Sorry, dear."

How peculiar to bring up my mother, Violet thought. In all the years with the Suttons, Catherine had only mentioned her mama in times of illness. *Why such concern? Does she not trust my friends? Or worse, me?* Violet felt hurt and somewhat defensive.

"If your heart is set on going to Niagara Falls," Catherine continued, "I will make arrangements for us all to visit."

Violet, still festering, allowed her disappointment to erupt in a sharp, "Whatever!"

Instantly, she softened her tone. "I would like that very much." Lowering her head, Violet was ashamed she had uttered that most condescending phrase. Never before had she been so rude and abrasive. Holding her breath, Violet waited for Catherine's reaction, wondering if Mrs. Sutton was as disappointed in her as she now was in herself.

"I believe it will be a fun few days," said Catherine, indicating she had dismissed or chosen to ignore Violet's abruptness. "I'm sure Edward would be excited to visit the Canadian side and look for new fossils. He has found an ally in Bernard who also loves to dig and catalogue fossils."

Violet was relieved the conversation had shifted back to fossils but still felt uneasy. The appearance of the Mr. and Mrs. Johnson ended their conversation. After everyone exchanged cordial wishes for a good morning, Violet discretely made her exit.

She still had half an hour before her scheduled picked up to go play doubles tennis. This would be ample time to enjoy a visit with Lucia. Between commitments with her new friends and Lucia's dedication to her new position, they had not seen much of each other.

In their few earlier conversations, Lucia had enthusiastically shared how kindly everyone treated her, especially Mrs. Johnson. "I will prove I am worthy of all their trust."

Violet had never doubted Lucia's gratitude and determination to do her very best. She had mirrored the same resolution for years towards Mr. and Mrs. Sutton.

"It's Lucia's day off, Miss Violet," Olga informed her. "She now lives with the cook. It is a perfect arrangement." Olga was pleased to reassure her, "Mrs. Teresa's home has been a refuge for many new immigrants over the years. Lucia will be comfortable there."

Violet was pleased; she thanked Olga for her sincerity and promptly agreed. "Absolutely! I understand Lucia will enjoy being able to speak in her native tongue." With Lucia's outgoing and very giving character, she undoubtedly would attract many new friends. Violet believed Lucia had the fortitude to stand on her own and make her new life in America a great success.

The tennis match lasted an intense two-and-a-half hours. The competitors played like professionals competing in the Wimbledon finals. At the end of the game of doubles, Ted and Violet won the privilege to order their very own lunch.

"I am positive Violet is a champion in everything she does." Ted's overly generous declaration again erupted mocking sounds from the others. The intended target was most uncomfortable and tremendously embarrassed with the whole scene. She directly excused herself to go freshen up.

CHAPTER 61

FACED WITH REALITY

It was in the ladies' changing room that Violet's day suddenly turned disastrous. She opened her purse to retrieve her bracelet, and it was gone. Panicked, Violet emptied the entire contents on the vanity. She picked up each item individually, shaking and rubbing it, as if by magic the item would turn into her bracelet. Nothing! No bracelet. Frantic, she ran to her friends, pleading for their help.

Their total careless attitude and disregard stunned and demoralized her. Sue suggested she simply replace it. Lorna waved it off, reminding everyone of the many things they all had lost recently. The men dismissed it all together. Their only concern was to fill their stomachs with food. If not for her years of self-control, Violet would have burst into tears.

"The bracelet was a precious gift from Edward; it means the world to me!" She needed to make them understand how devastated she felt.

"Ask him to buy you another one. He has lots of money. Besides, Vi, you probably left it at home." Ted's comment made her question the possibility. She remembered grabbing a cardigan at the last minute.

"I might have taken it off then." Violet held steadfast to that possibility.

Back in her room, Olga helped Violet search every inch of the space; nothing was overlooked—still no bracelet. Olga urged her to get dressed for dinner, promising she would continue searching.

Violet's distress and exhaustion showed on her face. All at the table were genuinely concerned and questioned her. William's fatherly tone made Violet's spirit sink even lower. She told them of the missing bracelet. With every heart-wrenching word she shared, relief seemed to appear on all the others' faces. Convinced her audience didn't understand, Violet repeated her heartache. "It was the bracelet Edward bought me for my twentieth birthday."

"The tennis bracelet you showed me this morning?" Catherine said. "I'll go back to that jeweller and ask him to get one exactly the same," she assured Violet, pleased with her solution.

Harry's booming voice vibrated as always. "Tomorrow, I will buy you ten bracelets if it will put a smile back on your pretty face."

The family's responses were in total contrast from those she heard earlier from her friends. Their obvious concern and generous offers were heartfelt and appreciated "Thank you all for offering, but I cannot accept. I loved the bracelet because it was a gift from Edward. I was careless. I lost it. It's gone and irreplaceable." Violet's sadness increased with every admission, but she dared not shed a tear.

She sobbed uncontrollably that night. The lost bracelet was only part of her devastation. She felt let down by her new friends. Until now it had been all fun and games. Surely that could not be all one might expect from friends. "What about loyalty, helpfulness, understanding, and genuine caring?" she asked aloud. These qualities were the essence of Violet's character, what she believed to be the base of true friendship. She was disillusioned with every one of them, including herself. With their level of self-absorption, compassion had somehow been lost. *To think I wanted to be more like them and fit in their lifestyle! When tested just a little, they proved to be superficial and without substance.*

Gone was her praise from the previous nights. Not only did the group not offer to help her, they showed little interest in her distress. Violet could not understand or forget their lack of empathy. If this was the kind of friendship this group had to offer, Violet wanted no part of it.

CHAPTER 62

SADNESS! SUPPORT! SOLUTION!

All was not lost. Violet knew where to get her loving, caring, and most reliable support. She could not wait to speak with Edward the next morning. Catherine was neither surprised nor curious when Violet anxiously asked to speak with Edward. She handed her the phone when she was finished talking with her son and walked away.

At first, Violet made idle chitchat with him until Catherine was out of earshot, then she bluntly asked, "Edward, what happened to my bracelet? Please tell me!"

Edward hesitated and stubbornly reminded her of their agreement not to use his gift frivolously. Violet was overjoyed; his comment meant he knew.

"Not now, Edward," she persisted.

Her anxious and tearful plea undid the boy. Reluctantly he began telling her of his insight. Violet stayed completely quiet, knowing from experience to respect Edward's focus and not interrupt. Besides, what Edward was revealing was a total shock.

Taking a deep breath as if she had done all the talking, Violet composed herself and demanded the name of the pawnshop.

"No!" This time Edward was adamant. "I left that out purposely. Violet, you must wait for me to come home. We will handle this together."

He tried to change the subject, but Violet would not stop her pleading. She then brought out a weapon never used. Violet cried! Edward caved and told her all he knew.

It was inconceivable of Ted, the "charmer," to be so cruel and conniving. He had gotten away with it for years, stealing from his old aunt. Lately, he focused on wealthy prospects. He would befriend them just to steal their valuables. Edward said others in the group were innocent victims as well. Violet remembered Lorna mentioning how many items she and the others had lost.

In her anger, Violet's body squirmed in disgust. *Ugh! What a deceitful, terrible person! And I thought him charming!* She shook her head, disappointed in her recent lack of judgement. She wanted to rid herself of all traces of Ted. *But first he should be taught a good lesson, and I must be the one to do it. But how?*

For a moment, she considered including Lucia in the plan, but realized that was out of the question. She would have to explain how she came to know these facts, compromising Edward. Violet considered the pros and cons and concluded. *Time is the crucial enemy. If I wait for Edward's return, my bracelet might be gone forever.* The more Violet thought it through, the more she convinced herself to go solo.

CHAPTER 63

TIME FOR ACTION

The very next morning, Violet started her pursuit of justice. Getting the job done had been her forte for years. After breakfast, she asked if she could spend time at The New York Society Library. The chauffeur dropped her off at the front of the historical building, on 53 East 79th St. Thanking Sam, she assured him she'd call when she was ready to be picked up.

As the sleuth entered the front door of the library, she immediately slipped out the building's side door. Hailing a taxi, she gave the driver the name and approximate location of the pawnshop.

The cab driver shook his head. "I'm familiar with that particular sordid pawnshop; it's in a very sleazy part of Brooklyn. Are you sure, miss, you want to go there?"

Violet definitely did *not* want to go. Her apprehensiveness must have been obvious to the driver. She forced a broad smile and gave the man a firm nod. Seeing Edward's birthday gift back on her wrist gave her the incentive to boldly steer ahead. The thought of her bracelet being worn by anyone else was unbearable and not an option.

"I will not be long," she informed the cab driver, encouraging him to stay close. As an added incentive, Violet instructed. "You may keep the meter running while you wait for me." This was also to ensure her a quick getaway.

The shop was worse than a dump. Layers of dust and cobwebs covered the cluttered, perhaps once-significant items. Violet could never have imagined any business establishment so dingy and filthy. The crammed decrepit furniture was now inhabited by dozens of well-fed cats. The horrendous smell was unendurable and quickly turned Violet's stomach. She rushed to place a handkerchief to her nose for relief. Determined, she took hold and swiftly maneuvered through a narrow aisle towards the back.

Like a jack-in-the-box, a ragged old man sprang up from behind a high, wooden counter. Before speaking, he rudely eyed her up and down while simultaneously running his dirty fingers through thinning, greasy hair. He aimed a smirk at her, exposing a mouth of decayed green teeth.

"What can I do you for?" He leered with a sense of power, which was understood by Violet. His cocky look said, "Hey, this is my domain; you chose to come in here, so you need something from *me*."

Violet played her own arrogant card by forcefully slamming the picture of her bracelet on the counter. Bringing forth her Italian heritage, she confidently shouted. "I've come to buy back this item." The man's eyes widened curiously as she spoke with her Italian accent. Violet was a master at languages and speech; she thought this was the perfect time to use her skill and sound aggressive. The proprietor quickly examined the photograph. The spasmic nodding of his head indicated he knew the item, and, of course, the circumstances behind it.

He didn't open his mouth but turned and removed a brown envelope from one of twenty or so small drawers mounted on the wall behind him. With a quick shake, he emptied the contents on the counter next to the picture.

There it was! Violet stiffened her legs to keep her composure.

The entire time, the man seemed to be enjoying himself, shifting his eyes from the bracelet to the lady. No trace of guilt for his part in this transaction.

"How much?"

"Well, missy, since you are a pretty little thing, I'll take only what—" he stopped mid-sentence, then said, "Well, let's see . . . "

Violet assumed he was figuring out the most he could get from her.

"One hundred smackers," he announced firmly.

Violet didn't understand his choice of words, but common sense suggested he meant one hundred *dollars*. The amount was totally insignificant to her. She never intended to bargain with an obviously dishonest person and had made sure to have sufficient cash in her purse. Cleverly, she had divided the money into small amounts in separate bundles. Intuitively, she knew it was best not to expose a large amount of cash in front of anyone. She had actually brought with her a few individual packs of hundreds. Violet was prepared to make the exchange promptly. Her goal was to get Edward's bracelet back, no matter the cost, and return home safely.

Robotically, she took out one of the pre-packaged money rolls from her purse and counted aloud: "Twenty, forty, sixty, eighty, one hundred dollars!"

The cash was spread out on the grimy counter, leaving the man's extended hand empty. As the man greedily grabbed the money, she in-turn scooped up her bracelet. In a flash, like one of Edward's superheroes, she dashed out. Heart pounding, she practically leaped into the waiting cab.

Back in the safety of her bedroom, Violet could not stop shaking. The emotional strain of what she had just done played havoc on her stomach. Anger, disgust, and fear blended together with the putrid smell of mould and cat litter.

Her stomach felt twisted in knots; the release of its contents was inevitable. She lay on the bed with a wet face cloth over her forehead, trying to recoup.

As she twirled her rescued bracelet, the sparkles seemed more brilliant than ever before. Successfully retrieving her beloved bracelet had made Violet feel a strong sense of pride in herself. Never before had Violet patted her own back. Not once, after solving the many incidents that occurred after Edward's visions, did she allow self-pride to take hold. The lack of experience with this overpowering emotion prompted the now overly confident young lady to make a decision she would later regret.

CHAPTER 64

TIME FOR JUSTICE

"Ted must be stopped, and I have to be the one to do it." Violet convinced herself a coward such as Ted would crumble once confronted. He would be shocked and humiliated knowing she would be the one to expose him. Believing she could shame Ted into repenting was naïve and presumptuous, yet Violet was determined.

The perfect antidote for a hot, muggy summer afternoon was Lorna's weekly pool party. She encouraged her guests to invite more friends. Ten invited guests ensured a crowd of thirty or forty lounging around the well-landscaped backyard. The young bathers coped with the intensity of the mid-afternoon sun by frequently dipping in the huge, rectangular pool. Unruly splashing encouraged aggressive games of defence and offence.

The reflecting sparkles dancing off Violet's wrist caused Ted's eyes to blink. He was so distracted; the cad clumsily spilled his beer. With the back of his hand, he quickly wiped the trickling suds from his chin and bare chest. "You look terrific, Vi, in your summer dress! I really love your new bracelet." Ted was quick to take her hand to get a closer look.

Violet was repulsed by Ted's charming act. He definitely had perfected the whole charismatic, irresistible performance. Violet had to work hard to control her anger and focus on her answer. Without hesitating, she gave the sharp, confident response. "Actually, Ted, this is the original; I reclaimed my beloved bracelet." Boldly, she went on. "I discovered your pawnshop. You are now officially out of business! I suggest you get out of here fast and never show your face around us again; or—" her pride burst through, crusting her tone—"I *will* expose you for the lousy thief you are."

Violet's last word was barely a gasp. Ted had twisted her wrist so hard she felt a sharp pain running up her shoulder.

"If you open your big mouth, I'll kill you!" Ted enunciated, his threat an inch from her face. His eyes bulged as he went on threatening and intimidating her. "You're the one who has to get the hell out and go back to wherever the hell you came from."

"Stop it, Ted!"

Sue's command surprised and stupefied Ted. He reacted by immediately releasing Violet's wrist. "I have been watching you two lovebirds," she playfully confessed, swaying her bikini-clad body towards them. "It seems you guys are getting pretty serious, right?" she tilted her head, questioning.

Realizing Sue was clueless as to what was really happening, Ted laughed in feigned innocence. Violet rapidly pulled away and ran towards the pool area. The crowded patio had turned into an obstacle course. She had to zigzag around scattered lawn chairs and tanning bodies. Focused on escaping though this maze, Violet didn't notice Sue following her.

"Violet, are you okay? I didn't mean to upset you."

"I am not upset, really; I am just not feeling well and need to get home."

"Oh good! I thought you were disappointed I intruded on your time with Ted. You do look very flushed; your eyes are watery," Sue observed.

Violet's anxiety had her heart racing rapidly; she wanted and needed to get as far away from Ted as possible. Concerned, Sue escorted her friend to a shady corner. "Sit here and wait, I'll tell Lorna I'm driving you straight home." In a mad dash, Sue rushed in search of Lorna. She returned promptly, wearing a muumuu dress over her bikini, and was insistent on helping Violet into her sporty automobile.

CHAPTER 65

EDWARD RETURNS

The dejected young lady sat in silence while Sue drove, rambling on about something or someone. Violet took time to politely thank Sue but swiftly closed the car door and dashed straight to her room. For the second time in a week, she emptied out her agitated stomach. Feeling like such a fool, she now questioned her decision. Perhaps confronting Ted with feeble threats wouldn't be a good idea. *Why would my words have any impact on a ruthless con artist?* His continuous crime spree proved he had no morals. The only other unscrupulous individual she'd dealt with was Pasquale, the tavern owner back in Italy. Violet cringed to think that he was still taking advantage of her.

Why? Why? she repeated, punching the innocent satin pillow. *Why didn't I heed Edward's warning about making mistakes?* Violet felt demoralized, she was angry and frustrated with her own irrational behaviour. She admitted acting arrogant instead of intelligently. *I have allowed an inflated ego to override my sensibility and judgement. Retrieving my bracelet should have been enough.*

Over the years, Violet had never disregarded Edward's advice, always respecting its source. She had always analyzed a situation logically all the way to completion. This time she'd acted on impulse and a dash of pride.

The hours she spent on *mia colpa, mia colpa* was not self-pity but for disappointing the one person she never intended to. Violet feared

Edward's opinion of her noetic character would surely be tainted. *He might never again put his full trust in me.*

She accepted full responsibility. Her overzealous action had resulted in her life being threatened. *Why didn't I stopped after I had retrieved my bracelet? I took a bad situation and made it worse.* Violet was totally exhausted, asking the same questions over and over. Her berating caused the victimized lady to fall back on her bed, admitting defeat.

By 2:00 p.m. the next afternoon, she was humbly reviewing her botched-up case in front of her "judge"—the highest magistrate.

Edward kept shaking his head repeating, "My main concern was your safety, I didn't want you to get hurt."

She in turn kept trying to assure Edward, "Ted was only bluffing."

"No, Violet! This is serious; you could have gotten injured."

"My arm is slightly tender, but my ego is deeply bruised. I promise not to let it loose again."

"You did nothing wrong except believing Ted had some decency. He obviously has none. Don't worry, I will handle this; I know what must be done." Edward's words excused Violet's reckless behaviour, but his determination disconcerted her.

His last statement was not what she wanted to hear; it was also not a good time to oppose him. After dinner, they would rationally review it and come up with a solution. This time they would do it together.

Various topics were discussed at dinner that evening. Violet contributed as much to the conversation as possible, her goal being to mask her own unsettled emotions. She was agitated, eager to have the evening over so she could speak with Edward alone.

Abigail's request could not have come at a worst time! "I prefer dessert be served in the parlor tonight. Violet, will you delight us with your extraordinary musical talent?"

Refusal was never considered. A cordial nod with an agreeable smile was Violet's answer.

Flipping through the music sheets, Violet's subconscious mind ruled her choice. She began singing the melancholy aria from *La*

Bohème. Unfortunately, her usual perfect pitch suddenly lowered into a faded whisper.

Four anxious voices exploded with the same question as Violet was unable to control her tears. "What is wrong? I knew it!" Catherine exclaimed, handing Violet her monogrammed handkerchief.

"We all knew something has been troubling our princess," Harry boomed. "Did someone hurt you?"

Violet was dismayed with her inability to control her emotions a bit longer. This shift in character was shameful and embarrassing. Frustrated, she questioned, *Where did myself-preservation divert to? Why and when did this change in me occur?*

Edward shrewdly hurried to Violet's side, encouraging her to tell everyone about the incident. Standing literally in center stage with all the attention focused on her, she felt vulnerable and totally exposed. It was futile to hold back now. Obviously, she had no choice but to tell them a version of her story.

"This man . . ." Violet's two words aroused gasps from all four adults.

William demanded his name.

"Father, let her continue," Edward insisted.

Violet took those few minutes to rethink her approach and start her story again. "I accidentally bumped into Ted at Lorna's pool party yesterday."

"He is one of the people in the group she has been going out with," Edward jumped in, giving her the anchor she needed to calm down.

"Our encounter caused him to drop a black pouch, spilling its contents on the pavement. Pieces of jewelry scattered everywhere, and my bracelet was among them. I grabbed my bracelet, and without thinking I threatened to expose him." She hurried through her modified version of how she had retrieved her bracelet, hoping they believed her agitation was caused mainly by strained nerves. Admitting she'd acted rashly, threatening the man with exposure, was Violet's way of excepting responsibility.

"He stole your bracelet?" Harry sounded surprised and relieved, as were the others.

Frustrated he didn't get the intended reaction, Edward's spoke up, adding, "It gets worse."

Violet felt like a mouse with its tail caught in a trap; she was doomed. There was no way of stopping Edward. "Ted twisted her wrist and threatened to kill her if she opened her mouth." His emphasis on the word "kill" caused the effect Edward wanted. For a moment there was dead silence.

The anger on William's face looked as fierce as it had when he had confronted Harris, back in England. He turned to his father-in-law, outraged. "This is very serious, Harry, and will not be tolerated."

"Yes, I agree." Harry's uncharacteristically quiet voice unsettled everyone. "We must handle it in just the right way." Harry's intensity and fierce contemplation had him resembling a military commander.

Catherine had been standing just a foot from Violet during the entire revelation. She stepped closer, put her arm around her charge, and declared, "I don't want you out of my sight."

Abigail responded by voicing her recommendation. "We'll go shopping tomorrow while the men decide how to handle this dreadful boy."

The very next day, talk of an elaborate scheme being set up by the men had the whole staff excited.

Harry decided the ladies should be spared the particulars. He justified his gallant decision, saying, "This secret mission is easier to execute than it is to explain." He did reiterate his first order of business had been to contact the boy's aunt. "She had nothing good to say about her nephew. Apparently, he has been taking advantage of her for years. She spoke of his extensive greedy demands and not having the means to support them. The poor woman sounded desperate in her plea for help." Harry showed signs of being genuinely concerned for the aunt. "She said, 'My wish is for the boy to go back to my brother's farm in Ohio. I'd appreciate any assistance making that happen.'

This meek lady deserves to be burden-free. I've decided to be her fairy godfather and grant her wish." Harry was being his usual ambiguous self. He looked calculating and full of mischief. He turned to his wife and asked, "Dearest, would it be possible to arrange a party in just a few days?"

"Is Saturday at eight what you have in mind, dearest?" Abigail's was quick in responding, letting him know she was up for his challenge. "I'll prove to you, Harry James Johnson, how totally resourceful we ladies can be." Abigail squinted her eyes to exert women's help is always essential.

Harry, as usual, was enjoying getting his wife riled up. He knew it was payback for his false compliment a few weeks prior.

Arranging this hurried "Entrapment Party," Harry had asked his wife to curate in only a few days had more than its usual challenges. It had the whole household stimulated and hopping about. With two strong women designing and directing separate itineraries, even the most efficient staff might succumb to chaos. Mother and daughter had to stop and agree to share their "to-do" lists. Their consensus was to each focus on specific tasks to avoid contradictions and duplications, thereby confusing the staff and causing unnecessary work.

Making sure Grandfather was kept somewhat restrained was Edward's chore. He mindfully collaborated with the adult males to ensure all went according to plan. He, of course, had been tight lipped, and wouldn't include Violet in this caper. She had no choice but to respect her little man after her previous disregard.

Catherine assured Violet her help with the actual party preparations was not needed. "Mother and I have it all under control."

Dispirited about the whole ordeal, Violet kept mostly to herself. Her heart was full of guilt for causing everyone in the Johnson household extra work. Her only relief came from Lucia, who had a wonderful way of putting things in perspective. "You saved me from my brute. They save you from your brute and will have fun doing it."

Violet suspected Lucia had overheard specific plans but knew she would never reveal a word. There is a code of ethics among the respectful staff, which is long and detailed; however, the one-phrase version often recited simply says, "What goes in your ears must never come out of your mouth."

CHAPTER 66

COME PARTY AND GET YOUR COMEUPPANCE

Saturday evening at 7:33, the first guest arrived. By 7:50, all but one were present. Violet braced herself. "Stay calm," she muttered under her breath as she spotted Ted boldly entering the foyer.

Her agitation was short-lived as Edward promptly approached the unsuspecting victim. He welcomed Ted with a friendly gracious pat on the shoulder and conversed with him for a while.

Ted seemed interested in what Edward was proposing and followed him, wearing a smirk on his face. Violet's first impulse was to go slap that smirk from his face. There was no doubt in Violet's mind this man's arrogance had no boundary. Ted definitely deserved whatever was about to happen to him.

Her total faith in her little man's insight gave her the assurance Ted had no chance. In the end, Edward would effortlessly prevail over the likes of him. She was right. That was the last Violet saw of Ted that night or ever again.

Early the next morning, hoping to find Edward alone, Violet rushed to breakfast. She was surprised to find half the staff mingling with the family, Lucia among them.

"Come join us." Mr. Johnson waved at her.

Violet walked in, confused, a bit apprehensive, but mostly curious.

Mr. Johnson was more capricious than ever. With his loudest voice he cheerfully thanked his staff as they complacently returned to their duties.

Lucia stopped to give Violet a little wink before following the others out of the breakfast room.

Edward could not contain his excitement; his body bounced rhythmically. "Grandpa, you must start from the beginning. Violet needs to hear everything."

She reacted by giving them all an outward smile. Inwardly, she wished this whole mess with Ted had not been so publicized.

"Well, my dear," Harry started, but his irksome pause was immediately filled by his eager grandson.

"It was brilliant, Violet. We all played our parts perfectly. You of all people would have been impressed."

Violet understood what Edward was insinuating. She had been the master of manipulation for years on his behalf. While taking on the role of protector she had to be creative but also sneaky. Helping unsuspecting people while protecting the source had somewhat challenged Violet's morals. In her defense, she believed the outcome justified the means used to get the job done.

With dramatic flair Edward continued. "I lured Ted into the billiards room by wagering a good sum of money for a game of snooker. I made sure to mention I had been playing for a whole month, allowing Ted to believe I was an easy target."

Violet had no doubt her little man knew exactly what bait to use on Ted.

"Once in the room, I made the excuse we needed more chalk and left him."

Edward now gave his grandfather a nod.

Harry took over recounting the events that followed. "I had two of my muscular men, Sam, our chauffeur, and Klaus, our horse trainer, ambush that wimpy kid from behind."

Violet's interest peaked. Totally engrossed, she swallowed her bit of croissant and waited to hear more.

"They shoved a gun in his back and warned, 'Don't turn around or make a sound.' Immediately they draped the black hood Lucia had sewn over his head and dragged him out the back door. My men bound his hands and feet before tossing him into the trunk of the Lincoln town car." Harry's grin expressed he approved of his men's executive decision to aggressively induce maximum discomfort and fear on Ted. The men had driven upstate to Harry's horse farm, he explained. There, they untied and shoved him into one of the stables. Two other men pretending to be prisoners were placed in the next stable. They were actually his stable hands wanting in on the fun. The men had their own lines prepared and immediately went into their performance.

One asked the other, "What did you do to get the big boss so mad?"

"I spilled some red wine on the boss's blue suede shoes. It was an accident! I was nervous being in his presence, got me all shook up."

The other confessed his sin against the boss. "I lost his favorite white silk scarf. I checked it at the nightclub with his hat, but someone must have pinched it. That wasn't my fault!"

Harry was on his preferred platform; he loved retelling the story word by word and adding his own flair. "The one guy asked, 'Do you think they will beat us up just to teach us a lesson?'

"'Well, they certainly won't *kill* us,' answered the other, making sure he used Ted's own ultimate word: KILL.

"Both then turned their attention on him. 'What did you do to get the boss angry?' they asked?'

"'Who, me?' said Ted.

"My men said Ted was in a state of shock, terrified, trembling uncontrollably.

"He replied, stuttering every word: 'They obviously got the wrong guy. I have never met your boss. I don't even know your boss!'"

Harry paused allowing everyone, especially Violet, to enjoy the mental picture of a frantic and terrorized Ted. Eagerly, Harry continued.

At that point, he had the chauffeur and butcher reappear. They grabbed the two fake prisoners, asked a few more questions, then mercilessly shot them both with blanks. The two victims dramatically staged an impressive death scene.

Then Sam immediately ordered Ted to stand. The poor boy had turned white, with his eyes bulging out. He started whimpering and pleading, "Please don't kill me! You have the wrong man. You've got the wrong man!" he repeated over and over.

"This is where it got real for the rascal," snickered Harry.

The butcher roared out, "Are you Ted Russell?

"Yes, but—"

"But! But nothing you worthless piece of trash. YOU threatened Violet Conti's life. She is the boss's niece."

Harry allowed that revelation to linger for a few seconds, then let out a satisfying laugh. "That was my idea," he bragged, before continuing.

His men were determined to frightened Ted to the max. Sam wanted to demonstrate how worthless criminals are and shouted out his order: "Just shoot him!"

"Oh, please! I beg you. Don't kill me. I'm sorry, I'm sorry! I'm just a stupid kid, I didn't know who Violet was related to. Please, have mercy! I will do anything! I will leave New York and never return. I'll go back to my parents' farm in Ohio. They are old and need my help to keep the farm. I promise I will leave as soon as you let me, and never return."

"Well," said Harry, pausing just a beat. "The men succeeded in getting what they wanted and decided to stop their torment, before the pathetic guy had a heart attack. Klaus pretended to be sympathetic."

"Ah! The kid has an old ma and pa. Maybe we should let him go back to Ohio to help them out. Besides, I've killed my quota for this week."

Sam nodded in agreement. "I've actually exceeded my quota. Why not send the stupid kid back to his mommy. He might turn his life around and stop being a piece of trash."

"Thank you! Thank you! I promise! I promise to leave tonight."

Harry went silent, allowing his expression to show how pleased he was. Then he said, "My men ensured Ted's ride back was as comfortable as his previous one. They dropped him off in front of his aunt's house with a warning: 'We know everything and have eyes everywhere. You better be on the next train to Ohio . . . or else.' Before leaving, Sam added an assurance: 'Be grateful and good to your parents, after all, they gave you life. Twice.'"

A triumphant smile lingered on Harry's face, his detailed account now over. He seemed most gratified with his performance, as his audience, especially Violet, was impressed. She believed Mr. Johnson was about to take a bow. She was wrong; the proud man demonstrated his triumph by raising both arms straight up, resembling a "V" for victory; he then sat back in his chair.

"Grandpa," Edward protested, "you forgot the best part."

"Oh yes. His aunt called this morning to thank me. Ted did pack, and he left immediately for Ohio, promising never to return."

"Grandpa!"

"And yes, there was an added little incident." Harry obviously enjoyed teasing the boy.

All knew of Edward's limited restraint; they were not surprised when he blurted out, "Ted peed himself, Violet." The adolescent comically pointed to the front of his trousers and the floor.

Everyone roared a hearty laugh at Edward's explicit gesture.

CHAPTER 67

FRIENDS IN NEED

Violet soon ended her celebration. She had been so impressed with the elaborate scheme and its result she had forgotten one crucial detail. All this would not have been unnecessary if not for her stubbornness. Standing with her head down, she began apologizing. "I am so sorry for putting you all through this ordeal."

Mr. Sutton sharply interrupted her. "No, Violet! We are the ones to say sorry. We threw a lamb into a lion's den."

"Yes, precisely." Catherine quickly supported her husband. "I should've prepared you better."

"All is well that ends well." Abigail quoted Shakespeare to confirm the happy conclusion.

Everyone nodded in agreement. Abigail waved her arms, pleased the quote got their attention, and announced, "Tonight we are going to the Ritz to celebrate a job well done."

Violet still wanted to exert her deep appreciation to everyone. "At the very least allow me to thank the staff personally for the time and effort given for my sake." Violet hurried her request, hoping once said it would be considered.

"Believe me, all involved enjoyed every minute," Mr. Johnson said.

Abigail shook her head. "Imagine that scoundrel getting away with his deceitful ways for so long."

Harry said, "I spoke to his aunt this morning. The sweet, delicate woman sounded very relieved the boy had finally gone. She wanted no particulars and asked no questions, was just genuinely pleased for our help. She confessed suspecting he was up to no good and would eventually ruin his life."

"You know, Grandpa!" Edward sounded determined to get everyone's attention. "If not for Violet's courage to confront Ted, he would never have been exposed. Violet is tougher than she looks." He demonstrated by giving his partner a hard pat on the shoulder, causing Violet to stiffen her upper body.

"Very true, a point well made, my boy," the grandfather acknowledged.

"You are absolutely right, Edward," the others were now quick to agree.

"That cowardly thief would have continued stealing from more unsuspecting victims." Abigail sounded appalled.

Harry slowly walked around Violet, inspecting her as a general would a soldier. "Looks can be deceiving. You might look like a lamb but you're more of a ram. You, young lady, have real gumption!" Harry honored Violet with a solid military salute.

And just like that, Edward had managed to shine the spotlight back on Violet. She was now the one in the starring role of this, "good-triumphs-over-evil" story.

Our young lady was very relieved this ordeal was finally over and glad to admit her assumption had been wrong. She not only judged herself harshly, but also her little man. His views and respect for her had not diminished in the least. All was good, even better, between them. Edward repeatedly and candidly had said, "Making mistakes is not always a bad thing."

There was no mistake this time, Violet was sure; Edward had foreseen her misadventures with Ted.

CHAPTER 68

TOURING... TOURISTS

"I feel we all need a break, a little getaway." William's desultory comment was quickly snatched up by his wife.

"I know the perfect place," she eagerly responded, winking directly at Violet.

William began rubbing the center of his forehead with his two fingers. "I suspect, wife dearest, you probably have the itinerary already planned out!"

It was on the trip to Niagara Falls that the family decided to continue visiting other cities. They ventured into Canada and spent a few nights at the Royal York Hotel in Toronto while exploring the city's many attractions. They returned to New York City a few days before their departure to London. This only left enough time for quick goodbyes and packing.

Abigail's usual cheerfulness was diminishing daily as the family's vacation time was coming to an end. It had all been fulfilling, remarkably intriguing, and of course brief. Whenever Abigail mentioned them leaving, Catherine reassured her parents they would soon return. Overhearing a conversation between mother and daughter about Edward's future had Violet's listening more intensely.

"Plans are nearly finalized, Mom. You know our son's needs and happiness have always been our number one priority."

Catherine's comments sparked Violet's curiosity. She had to know more and would probe Edward for details on their flight home.

Her last thought of Ted was positive. Hopefully his experience with men he believed ruthless criminals would detour him from a life of crime. Perhaps being faced with death and given a second chance had taught him to appreciate a quieter life.

Edward and Violet were delighted to see Lucia adjusting so well to her new environment.

"I am overjoyed, living in America surrounded by wonderful people, but mostly I am thrilled I'm single." Lucia expressed her gratitude in her own distinctive fashion: by aggressively hugging and kisses them both continuously. She did not forget her promise and handed her friend the note for a one-of-a-kind, custom wedding dress, upon request.

As time was definitely limited for individual goodbyes, Catherine thoughtfully organized an afternoon luncheon for the young group. The food would be prepared to specifically appeal to their taste buds. Included with hot dogs, hamburgers, and French fries, a complete soda stand, and an ice cream sundae bar were set up.

Violet stood before her friends. "I have prepared a short speech," she announced, shuffling a stack of long sheets of paper. The grudging expressions on her guests' faces, followed by groans, influenced the host to abort her humorous jest sooner than she anticipated. Amused but a bit begrudgingly, Violet put down her blank pieces of paper on the table.

"Thank you all for graciously including me in your group. Sincerely, I've had the most fun and take with me extraordinary memories. I shall never forget you and my summer in New York."

The robust cheers signaled her abbreviated, genuine speech was perfect.

Later, Violet personally thanked Sue and Lorna in private. They spoke of their desire to visit Europe the following summer. "We will come to England and get you first. Then we'll backpack across

Europe" Sue's voice cracked with hint of emotions. The three girls hugged, aware this most likely was an elusive dream.

"Violet," Sue addressed her friend, almost apologetic. "We haven't a clue what happened to Ted; he seems to have disappeared!"

"Even the guys are puzzled." Lorna also sounded confused.

Violet thought it was time to end the mystery. "Ted's aunt informed Mr. Johnson he left in a hurry for Ohio. His parents desperately needed his back on the farm."

"Wow! That will be a change. Instead of partying like an animal, Ted will be cleaning after the animals." Sue seemed to enjoy visualizing that scenario.

As the last guest waved goodbye from their moving vehicle, Violet released a bittersweet sigh. A slight pout set on her face as she thought back at all she had experienced in just one month. Getting to share her time with vibrant people had opened her mind to various possibilities.

She had certainly lightened up on this trip and was better for it. Her exposure to young members of the opposite sex, although not what she hoped, did have some enjoyable moments. Her own uninhibited indulgence with the group had also made a slight impact.

Edward was right; mistakes are not detrimental, the end of all, but part of life. Striving always to do what others expected had been her creed since childhood. Her feelings of unworthiness had diminished but were not completely discarded. As she ran up the stairs, she embraced all her experiences. They were part of her and would ultimately affect some changes in her. For now, Violet was happy to get back to her unpredictable days with her little man. Questioning Edward about the conversation she had overheard about his future plans was upmost in her mind.

CHAPTER 69

BIG CHANGES COMING

The flight from New York back to London turned into a personal nightmare for Violet. She never dreamed the answer to her simple question would cause her so much anguish and turmoil. "Are you sure, Edward? Are you sure that is what you really want?" she pleaded, holding back tears.

"Yes, Violet, it has already been arranged."

Edward's decisiveness stabbed her heart.

"I am shocked, this is so unexpected. Why didn't you confide in me?" Violet's voice cracked with sorrow.

"I did mention Bernard's school a few times, but you weren't interested. Besides, I really didn't want to ruin your vacation."

Violet thought back on how self-absorbed she had behaved on this trip. Now she was losing her Edward.

"It has the best facilities for studying geology and archaeology," he explained. "It truly is the right choice for my future," he tried to assure and make her understand.

"So, the main purpose of this trip to America was for you to register at this school with your, what, third cousin Bernard? You're going to make America you new home? Now I understand why you were so impressed with the new immigrants on the ship!" Violet's injured heart made her words bitter.

"Not necessarily. I decided after meeting with some of the counselors and inspected the school's facilities; it's absolutely perfect for me."

Edward's last statement made Violet stop her attack. *Consider the source,* she kept telling herself. Edward had never before spoken so confidently and bluntly about his future; she had to listen and respect his decision.

"Violetta." Edward was obviously trying to lighten her mood by calling her Italian name. "All this time you believed the trip was to find you a husband. Aren't you glad that was not my parents' intention?"

"Glad" was not even close to what Violet was feeling. It was closer to panic. All kinds of thoughts buzzed in her head. Mainly, there would be no reason for her to stay at the manor.

"I suppose I must leave when you do." Violet did not mean to say those words aloud; they sounded pitiful. Try as she might to hide her devastation, her eyes puddled with tears. Violet was an emotional wreck. Where had her restraint and self-control disappeared to? All those years she had been the master of hiding her true feelings from everyone.

"Be patient, Violet. Take your time. You might want to stay right where you are." Edward spoke slowly, his precise and positive words prompting Violet to be suspicious. This time she promised to listen more closely. This time she would not act impulsively. Wiping her eyes, she gave him an agreeable smile.

Violet's perception of her little man gave her the anchor of hope she needed for now. *I will bide my time,* she reconciled. *Even if I do not understand fully the depths of Edward's insight, I do know he cares and loves me and would never steer me wrong.*

A week later, plans were finalized. In just a few months, Edward would leave Sutton Manor to attend the prestigious school in America.

The following week, an opportunity was suggested, detouring Violet from also leaving the manor. The local school offered her a position teaching languages for the new scholastic year. This part-time employment gave her a small sense of accomplishment, being reinstated in a prominent role. Truthfully, Violet viewed it a temporary steppingstone; giving her more time to consider other possibilities. Lately, her constant daily challenge was trying to mask her devastation about Edward's pending departure. The lingering sadness left little room for planning her future and none for happiness.

Part of Edward's new school curriculum was a pre-planned geological excavation trip to Egypt. Bernard arrived in London with his father, who would accompany the young men. He would also remain with the boys in Egypt since he was an aficionado of such sites.

Edward's excitement on the morning of their departure undid Violet's fragile emotional state. She was wallowing in self-pity.

"Violet, please do not be so sad, I will be back in a fortnight. You need to take a walk, go to your favorite spot by the river," Edward insisted.

Violet felt guilty for dampening her little man's excitement. She was behaving like a child losing her playmate. Evidently, it was much more than that. For the past five years, Edward had been her entire life. Violet could not imagine being without him. She battled to keep herself in check. *How selfish I have become. I should be happy for Edward. He deserves the best school. All I ever wanted was his happiness; I will not spoil this important life experience for him.*

On Edward's own initiative, the two hugged and kissed each other goodbye. Violet held on a bit too long, then she forced a broad smile and marched bravely out the back door.

CHAPTER 70

RUDE ENCOUNTER

Her 'pity party' was over. A brisk walk had always been the perfect remedy to alter her mood. Gliding through the meadow, enjoying the high grass tickling her ankles, Violet felt connected with nature. The trees still full of foliage, brimming with chirping songbirds, was her favorite kind of music.

She sat on her usual large rock by the river. The rhythm of the rapid waters hitting the rocks was fierce and yet exhilarating, as though she was listening to one of Beethoven's symphonies. She dangled her feet in the river, playfully splashing about, hoping to let go of her sadness. Violet closed her eyes and recalled her strange, unimaginable life with Edward. Every moment she had shared with her little man was full of intrigue, adventure, and lots of love. She would always be grateful to Edward and their mysterious, intertwined lives.

Having to let go was difficult, yet deep down she knew it was inevitable. They'd eventually have to pursue individual lives. Although Violet kept disagreeing with Edward when he continuously repeated "This was as good a time as any." She understood exactly what he meant. More time would not lessen the sadness of having to separate. They both had to be strong and work harder to let go. Violet promised herself, *I must stop being selfish and make it easier on him.*

A crunching sound from the other side of the river interrupted her reminiscing. Today the sun's rays were extremely intense, blinding Violet's vision, making it impossible for her to focus. Crossing the river to investigate was tricky, but she had achieved it a few times in the pass. Spotting a herd of deer and their fawns feeding made the challenge rewarding. *I might get lucky and see those delicate creatures again.*

On this most dejected of days, Violet needed to be uplifted. Excitement took hold of our young lady, thereby the careless decision was made. Removing her sandals, she gathered her dress in hand and once again took the challenge of crossing the river. The zigzag pattern of the random rocks made it impossible for the adventurer to keep her balance. Stepping from one slippery rock to the next proved more difficult than she recalled just a few years ago.

Down she went, legs up in the air and arms waving wildly over her head. Sitting in the cool water, she experienced no pain from the flip; it actually felt refreshing. She had a childish impulse to start playfully splashing the cold water about. A horrible familiar sound, however, halted her movement, destroying the moment. She immediately recalled when and where she had heard it before. It was unmistakably the same mocking, hearty, male laughter she'd received from the Torantino brothers. Violet was thrust back, vividly recalling that humiliating day years ago in Italy. With the same determined pride, she sprang to her feet in defiance. "How dare you laugh!" she yelled towards a man's silhouette. Her squinted eyes could barely see his frame.

He stood, hands on hips, rocking back and forth, still laughing. With a loud, deep voice, he replied, "I could not stop myself. It was hilarious the way you—"

"Sir, you are no gentleman!" Violet forcefully interrupted. The frazzled lady was determined to prevent this rude man from speaking and giving a play-by-play of what *he* considered comical. He had to be stopped from embarrassing her even further. "You show no concern for my well-being. Why! You should have asked if I was hurt!"

"The way you sprang to your feet assured me you were fine."

His confidence and direct response irritated her even more. "Still, a proper gentleman would not laugh at someone else's misfortune." Violet mumbled her words while squeezing water from her dress. She carefully made her way back to the riverbank she had left. Finding her sandals, she fastened them and started back toward the manor, purposefully ignoring her intruder.

"May I offer my services?" he asked.

"Don't you think it's a little late for gallantry?"

"Not from what I'm observing." The man's answer was unclear to Violet. "Don't misunderstand," he continued. I'm definitely enjoying looking at your shapely body through your wet, clinging dress. I just thought you might want to cover up?"

Violet's embarrassment flared; arms and hands frantically tried to cover her most intimate parts. Mortified, she noticed the silhouette had begun descending from his side and coming towards her.

"You stay where you are! Don't you dare get any closer!" Violet shouted, vainly trying to intimidate him.

He laughed briefly while moulding something into a ball, and then yelled, "Catch!"

With the bright sun still obstructing her view, Violet was unsure what he was doing. Luckily, the item he tossed fell onto the bush a few feet from her, nesting in its branches.

The intensity of the blinding sun continued to irritate Violet's eyes, causing her to keep them half-closed. She kept peering in its direction, wanting to be ready, in case the figure made an aggressive move toward her. She deftly walked sideways to the retrieving bush where the object had fallen. The item had spread open, revealing it was a man's cardigan. With a swift yank, she loosened it, wrapped it around herself, and without looking back promptly ran towards home. The agitated lady had miraculously gained the speed of one of her agile fawns.

By the time Violet entered the manor's gates, she had calmed down considerably. She reasoned the chances of ever meeting that rude man again were nil. The fact she had his cashmere cardigan was of no consequence. *After all, he aggressively chose to throw it to me.* Her reasonable thoughts justified the ownership. Her concern was on her gruesome appearance. The sun today was in high form; it now used its energy to dry the drenched young lady. Unfortunately, her dress was stiffened and creased like an accordion. Her hair resembled a wig only a circus clown would wear. Desperate not to be seen, she slipped through the same back door she had used earlier to make her exit.

This was obviously not Violet's finest day. A few steps inside the door, she literally bumped into Catherine.

"Great! There you are!" Mrs. Sutton sounded eager, most uncharacteristic for our demure lady. "I have been wondering where you disappeared to. Come, I have a surprise."

Violet was astonished with Catherine's level of excitement; moreover, she had dismissed her disheveled appearance. "I fell in the river," Violet volunteered on her own. "I'll go up immediately and change."

Catherine was too focused and enthused with her own purpose; her eyes did not shift to inspect. "Nonsense! You look fine! Come, come." Taking Violet's hand, she practically dragged her to the library without stopping until they were in the center of the room. "Violet, meet our Eric!"

CHAPTER 71

REALITY STINGS

There, standing beside the trophy cabinet, was a tall, muscular, and devilishly handsome man. "Ah! But I have already had the pleasure," he said, extending his hand. "Our meeting was most fascinating," he added, shaking her hand firmly.

Violet was dumbfounded! With the speed of lightning her blood rushed through her body, aiming for her head, its explosion setting a chilly, red blush on her face.

This could not be happening. It was not at all how she imagined her first meeting with Eric! She had fantasized their first encounter a thousand times. In all of them, one thing was certain: she always looked her very best.

This was hopeless, a total disaster! Not only did she look a mess, but that rude exhibition at the river had sealed her fate. Gone forever was her opportunity to make a lasting first impression. This realization tortured her.

It took all her restraint not to run from the room. Violet had to take hold of herself and act appropriately. The last thing she wanted was to confuse Catherine; she also had to show Eric some maturity. "Yes of course." Violet glanced at his cardigan dangling over her left arm. She paused to consider what to say next. "You must be the *gentleman* who graciously offered his help at the river." Her courteous words were chosen wisely, but a hint of indifference in her voice was difficult to disguise.

Eric's smirk revealed to her he was amused.

Catherine of course accepted Violet's complimentary words with pleasure. "Our Eric has always been the proper gentleman."

It was no revelation whatsoever; the entire household, including Violet, held Eric in high esteem.

"I try, I do try," he teased.

His flamboyant response and confidence left Violet unbalanced. She felt it was time to leave before her body or mouth would react regrettably. "Please excuse me. I really must attend to myself." Her right-hand waved acknowledgment to her tousled appearance. Violet's quick exit, had her finishing her last statement from the door. "I'll be down for dinner!"

In the sanctuary of her room, Violet bemoaned, *Eric, finally here, finally here! And I was crude and spoke abruptly to him. He's had worldly experiences and acquired a great sense of humor. The incident he witnessed at the river was actual funny. Eric knew I wasn't hurt, so his teasing and laughter was justifiable.*

Violet chastised herself for reacting immaturely and allowing her pride to get the better of her. *In my defence, I didn't know it was him. I believed I was speaking to a rude intruder. Why didn't I recognize his deep voice? I should have known it was Eric. Edward!* Violet charged him as if he were standing in the room. *Why didn't you tell me Eric was coming home? You little monster!* Violet kept reprimanding. *Insisting I go to the river, you knew Eric would be there.* There was no doubt in Violet's mind; Edward was enjoying himself. *The harsh blinding sun obstructing my vision, making it impossible to see his face.* Violet stopped internally ranting to take a deep sigh. *He is just as I imagined, except his eyes are a deeper, darker blue.* Once again, she was lost in her fantasy of Eric.

To amend the day's blunder, Violet instituted a perfect plan. *I will ensure an exceptional evening demonstrating my intellect, maturity, and courteous charm.*

Full of anticipation she gave herself a quick glance in the mirror. Taking the neatly folded cardigan in hand, she took a deep breath and started for the stairs.

She hadn't reached the stairs when Eric approached, calling her name. "Violet, you look stunning, dressed up so beautifully."

Violet wasn't given time to graciously respond to Eric's compliment, as he swiftly added while grinning.

"Yet I still prefer your wet look."

"Sir," she addressed him respectfully, "I'd appreciate you never mentioning that incident. Actually, I prefer you erase it from your mind completely."

Looking grim and confused, Eric stepped closer and whispered, "Why? Why? would I want to do that? On the contrary, that's a scene I never want to forget."

Moving a step back, Violet tossed away her predetermined plan and asserted, "You, sir, are crude. You obviously take pleasure in my embarrassment. I shall not give you the satisfaction."

With graceful agility, Eric moved his towering six-foot-four frame within an inch from her face. Ignoring her discomfort, he instructed "Call me Eric." The warmth of his breath, the smell of his aftershave and his deep, sexy voice made Violet feel lightheaded.

Violet leaned back against the banister for support. Her left hand grabbed the wooden rail, while her right held his cardigan next to her chest as a shield.

Mr. Sutton's timely appearance was welcome. "I see you two have met and are obviously getting along." He directed his eyes towards his son. Shifting between them, William quickly put his arms on both their shoulders in a fatherly embrace. "You will have plenty of time to get to know one another. For now, I believe Catherine is waiting on us."

Unsure how to react or respond to Mr. Sutton's subtlety, Violet smiled but said nothing. She immediately questioned her behavior and how their exchange might've appeared. Violet reminded herself Eric was his son, and she should be more respectful when speaking to him.

CHAPTER 72

LIFE! BETTER THAN FANTASY!

At the dinner table, Violet kept meticulously studying the dinnerware and contributed very little to the conversation. The family took turns reminiscing and catching up. At times, William and Eric shifted to business concerns. Catherine would interrupt, adamant no business be discussed at dinner. Her main focus was to speak of Eric's personal adventures and encourage Violet to give an opinion. An agreeable nod was all she had dared to add. Relieved dinner was nearly over, our young lady planned to skip dessert and ask to be excused for the evening.

Before she had the chance to voice her request, Eric's most unusual question stopped her. "Violet." He sounded perplexed, but his eyes looked mischievous. "Do you intend to return my cardigan, or have you decided to keep it?"

Eric's unexpected and very direct inquiry about his cardigan surprised Mr. and Mrs. Sutton. They looked confused and curiously awaited her response.

Violet not only had to halt her retreat but was forced to do the one thing she had avoiding all evening: give a verbal answer.

Eric's most-unwarranted, blunt question reminded Violet of her little monster's assertiveness. Cheekiness was certainly a Sutton trait. Earlier at the stairs, Eric's comments had rattled her. She was so preoccupied trying to calm herself, the cardigan had been the last thing on your mind. At dinner she had tucked it on her lap, dismissing it the entire evening.

The silence in the room was in anticipation of Violet's answer. She desperately wanted to roll the sweater into a ball and toss it at him. *How appropriately justifiable,* she thought, smiling inwardly. Outwardly, she chose to act appropriate.

Standing on her toes in the pose of a ballerina, she deliberately sweetened her voice, before giving her reply. "Sir, my intention was invariably to return your cardigan." Extending her arms, with the cardigan in both hands, she gently placed the item in his hands. "I have been waiting for the opportune moment to do so, thank you." Violet, maintaining her prima persona, added, "I must ask to be excused. I am very fatigued this evening."

Eric let out a hearty laugh. "It must've been the unplanned dip in the river that tired you out!"

Violet had been proud of her self-control but was unsure how long she could keep it up. Biting her bottom lip for restraint, she began to move away from the table.

It was Catherine's comment that halted her retreat this time. "I suppose we could discuss the details of Eric's party tomorrow?"

Three sets of eyes questioned Catherine's casual announcement.

Undeterred by their surprised stares, she continued. "A welcome home party for Eric is a must. Everyone must know our Eric is home to stay. We will have it in two weeks when Edward returns." Mrs. Sutton's explicit plans were said with decisiveness, leaving no room for disagreement or discussion from her audience.

The numerous events of this most unpredictable day disrupted Violet's nightly routine. She was fermenting in a wave of emotions. First, it was Edward's sad send-off, then her embarrassing encounter, and now the shock of Eric being home to stay. Her mind was overstimulated with all that had happened. The music box and its fantasies remained closed. The events of the day were tossed back and forth for hours. As much as she wished Eric did not mention the incident at the river, she admitted not feeling as offended as she alluded. She was more concern as to *why* Eric continued teasing her. *Maybe he's playful because he views me as a child!* That had always been Violet's worst fear. The few times they spoke on the phone she wondered if she came across a bit childish. *Tomorrow*, she resolved, *Around Eric I will be sophisticated and demure.*

The next morning, Violet had a quick breakfast in the kitchen with Betty. She wanted to avoid Eric, at least until evening. She left for the stables via the rear delivery door for her usual much-anticipated morning ride.

There he was, mouth grinning and eyes piercing. He looked as stout as the two stallions he stood between. His sandy blond hair flopping ever so gently in the breeze caused Violet's heart to race.

"I see you prefer to sleep in!" Eric exclaimed.

"It's only eight, besides, what I do prefer is to ride *alone*."

"Strange, I was under the impression Edward always accompanied you." Eric was definitely toying with her. "I'm sorry; I would never impose on your solitude; except I need a guide. I confess these woods are unfamiliar and a bit confusing to me."

"What you are is incorrigible," Violet half-whispered, grabbing the reins from his hand.

She mounted her horse with a quick pull of the reins and galloped away. In an instant, Eric was riding alongside. Their brisk ride was exhilarating, filling their lungs with fresh air. Neither said a word; their shared enjoyment spoke volumes. It was evident they both had a passion for a long ride. When they eventually slowed their pace, Eric skillfully maneuvered his horse in front of Violet, forcing her horse to stop.

"I believe we need to rest," he said.

"I am not tired," she assured him, panting out her words.

"Are you afraid to be alone with me?" he questioned while dismounting.

"I'm most certainly not in the least afraid of—"

Violet was interrupted by Eric's hands around her tiny waist. Lifting her effortlessly off the horse, he glided her ever-so-slowly close to his body. Looking in her eyes, he warned, "Maybe you should be."

Violet stared defiantly at him. "Sir," she huffed. "Do you know who I am?" She immediately regretted her arrogant tone.

"I know exactly who you are, you sweet thing. You not only saved my brother's life, but your continued devotion to Edward brought serenity to my entire family. I can never thank you enough."

His sincerity touched her, but she felt embarrassed forcing him to say these things. "I love Edward; I don't need or want thanks for any of it."

Eric nodded while leading the way.

"Sir!" Violet pronounced authoritatively. "As your guide, I must insist you follow me. These woods are deceiving and treacherous." Violet warned Eric, fully aware his sense of direction was flawless.

"My apologies! After you, my lady." Eric gallantly stepped to the side, exaggerating a low bow.

Violet performed her part on cue; she strutted ahead of him with a pompous Victorian flair. Their combined performance was too much for her to hold back a slight giggle, which of course erupted into an uncontrollable burst of hearty laughter.

Eric stood watching Violet's hysteria with a puzzled look. He seemed like he was trying to solve a riddle. "I'm baffled," he admitted, while sweeping his fingers through his hair. "Just when I thought you could not possibly be more enticing, you prove me wrong. I love your defensive energy, but your laughter intoxicates me. I cannot choose which I prefer. Don't ask it of me!" He put up his hand, mimicking a stop sign.

Eric's compliments vibrated in Violet's ears, then volcanically erupted. Its sentiment traveled, searing through her entire body like hot lava. His message was clearly received. Eric viewed her as a woman. The attraction was mutual. She struggled to contain herself, afraid her excitement would lead to a juvenile display of delight.

They sat silently by a slow-moving brook, allowing nature's sounds to entertain them. Violet felt she was living one of her dreams; but this was real, and time was her enemy. Reluctant, she suggested they head back.

Eric stood and extended his hand to assist the young lady to her feet. Savoring every moment, Violet graciously accepted.

She looked directly into his eyes, smiled, and spoke softly. "I'm glad we spent this time together."

Eric's eyes turned a stormy blue. He pulled her to him and whispered, "Me too, love, me too."

Their bodies were so close their hearts had but one rapid beat.

Violet pulled her head back. "Please, sir. Let me go."

Immediately, Eric obliged. "You are such an innocent little thing. I have been bold indeed."

Violet was insulted. She wanted Eric to see a sophisticated woman, not an inexperienced child. "I assure you, sir, I have been in the arms of many men."

"Many men?" he questioned with a hint of incredulity.

"Yes!" she answered with determination. "In New York I was considered a social butterfly."

To prove her point, Violet compulsively squeezed closer to him, shut her eyes, and puckered her lips.

Eric's laughter was devastating; it was the ultimate insult he could have given her.

"I hate you!" she hissed and tried to escape his circular embrace.

"Violet, my sweet little thing." Eric's voice was low and seductive. He swept her into his arms and kissed her passionately.

Violet was breathless; her body and mind were floating in a mystical trance. Tears trickled slowly down her face, eloquently revealing her innocence. The softness of Eric's fingers tenderly brushing them away felt as sensuous as his kiss.

This was more than Violet had ever fantasized. Her first kiss. Eric had awakened an unexpected physical need that was not unwelcome.

CHAPTER 73

AND SO IT BEGINS

After dinner that evening, Catherine asked Violet to please entertain them with a few songs.

"If you're not too fatigued," Mr. Sutton was thoughtful to add.

"Nonsense! Edward is not here to tire her out."

"I'd love to." Violet readily agreed, wanting to spend as much time in Eric's company as possible. His presence inspired her. Her voice was pitch perfect. Her fingers feathered through the piano's keys as Eric's had done earlier, wiping the tears from her face. His piercing, admiring gaze as she played and sang made Violet feel esteemed, appreciated and, most importantly—dare she hope—loved.

Her angelic voice touched the appreciative staff, bringing tears to their eyes. Cheers of "Bravo! Bravo!" and vigorous applause filled the room.

At the evening's end, Eric eagerly insisted he accompany Violet up the stairs.

"I shall have the horses ready for our ride in the morning." He smiled, kissing her hand.

Violet wanted to tell Eric this had been the most unforgettable day, but she held back her words, hoping her intense, lingering look would convey her thoughts.

Foreseen

With her lips pressed on the spot Eric had just kissed, Violet laid in bed listening to their song. For years, she had fantasized being in Eric's arms, but reality surpassed her dreams. She infused her day's experience in her heart and envisioned for the first time walking down the aisle. Violet was in love. This overload of emotions pulled her in many directions. As always, she longed to share her joy with her mama and sisters. Her tears had the combined taste of longing and joy. The drops on her satin pillow quickly spread, exposing a heart shape. Romanticizing, our young lady interpreted it all to signify true love.

The next morning, she rushed through her breakfast and dashed for the stables, but Eric was not there. Thomas had already saddled her horse. He greeted her in his usual friendly manner. He then handed her the mare's reins and a folded note. She wanted to question him but realized Eric had been discrete. Thanking Thomas, she waited until he was off a good distance before opening to read the note.

Sorry, sweet thing! Had to go to London on an important personal matter. Will be back tonight.

Violet read his words over and over, each time admiring his penmanship more and more. Although the note was merely a few informative sentences, she viewed it as her first love note. Gently, she folded the paper in four and tucked the note in her bosom. Violet's mind was too anxious to enjoy her morning ride. Returning home, she hoped to occupy her thoughts by preparing work for her soon-to-be students.

Mr. and Mrs. Sutton were away visiting friends and not expected back until dinner. Still feeling unexpired, Violet finished a light lunch and opted to take a stroll in the gardens. The vibrant late-August gardens possessed Violet's thoughts, taking her on a journey. The destination was always the same: her sisters' and mama's rose garden. *Most likely they were all preparing for the next school year.* Wistfully, her mind was musing over a few likely scenarios. Vividly she imagined her sisters scurrying around their cluttered two bedrooms, pulling out items they needed to inspect. Dahlia, the bookworm would be especially excited, categorizing all the books she'd read over the summer months. Their indecisiveness in choosing what clothes to wear would simultaneously cause disagreement. *Until Mama steps in to calm things and solve their dilemma.* Violet enjoyed envisioning all their theatrics.

Immensely absorbed with her vivid imagination, Eric's sudden appearance startled the lady. She sprung up at least a foot from the garden bench.

"I'm so sorry! I didn't mean to frighten you." He inadvertently let out his hearty laugh.

Violet, composing herself, gave him a questioning squint. "I'm not convinced, sir, if your words are given sincerely."

She was so glad to see him, she wanted to jump right into his arms. "I wasn't expecting you until tonight."

"I hurried back. I could not stay away. See what you've done to me?"

"Me, sir? I'm totally innocent." She inched closer to him.

"You sweet thing." Eric wrapped her in his arms and tenderly brushed his lips on hers. Violet's sigh stirred Eric's appetite. He devoured her with hungry kisses, and she surrendered eagerly. "You're so tasty," he moaned.

"I'll have Simon prepare you a food tray. I'm sure you'll enjoyed that more."

Violet waited for his refusal of nourishment.

Eric responded quickly, "You are so perceptive. That's exactly what I need."

"You're doing it again," she scolded. "Why do you tease me so?"

"Simple," he volunteered. "Your reaction. I love igniting that spark hidden deep within you. You are fascinating in so many ways, yet I sense some restraint. You were always so proper on our phone conversations. I want to get to know the real you." As he beamed his piercing sky-blue eyes down into her meadow-green eyes, creating the perfect scenery, he appealed, "Open up to me, Violet."

Violet was ecstatic. She understood his meaning. Eric was committed to their relationship. "Are you saying you are a bit fascinated by me?" Violet purposely used Eric's word to let him know she was aware of his many references to the song on their music box.

Their combined smiles acknowledged their cohesiveness without words.

Wanting to sound demure, in perfect French, Violet asked for confirmation *"Juste un peu?"*

"Absolument, ma douce," Eric answered, his French as fluent as hers. "My little flirt," he added, kissing her passionately.

"Only with you, sir. Only with you," she managed to say breathlessly.

"I know, I do know." Eric's words confirmed he never doubted her morals or honesty.

"What was so urgent in London?" Violet asked.

Immediately wondering if this was too personal, and if she might've been too presumptuous, she said, "Sir, only if I'm not being too inquisitive!"

Eric was speaking before she had enunciated her last word. "A good friend of mine asked to meet with me. He went through a bad spell a few years ago. His family rallied around him and helped get him back on his feet."

"Was he ill?" Violet's concern was genuine.

"His heart was broken by a ruthless, conniving woman. She promised to marry him just to make an old boyfriend jealous. When her plot succeeded, she carelessly dumped him. Patrick took her betrayal worse than we all believed. We kept reassuring him, saying he deserved more and was better off without her. A week later, his family called from the hospital. He was fighting for his life in intensive care. In his despair, Patrick did something regrettable. Fortunately, his roommate found him in time."

"It's tragic when one loses all hope." Violet's compassion and sympathy came from her own experience with separation and loss.

"Patrick's family wanted to get justice and sue, but the vixen's parents settled." Eric's bitter words retelling the incident showed Violet how repulsed he felt. "They agreed to pay his hospital and therapy bills. In the end, the heartless vixen escaped smelling like a rose."

"She smells more like a pile of manure to me." Violet spoke while twitching her nose, demonstrating the foul smell the Jezebel's behavior had undeniably discharged.

"Do that again," Eric insisted, looking very amused.

"You, sir, must stop being so greedy, always wanting more and more."

"What are you referring to, Violet? Are you trying to get me to kiss you again and again?" Eric murmured as he randomly continued kissing her face. "A lady should be restrained and hold back her admiration."

Eric's words were whimsical. However, Violet became self-conscious, remembering her own mama had warned her to hold back. She replaced her usual witty comeback with a timid apology. "I am sorry if my behavior is not like other ladies'."

Eric became rigid and replied with a serious undertone. "Violet, you must know I jest. I love how genuine you are; you do not play games. Your transparency and innocence are refreshing. Please, sweet thing, don't ever change."

The sincere plea in Eric's dim voice persuaded Violet to continue being demonstrative. She quickly consented, snuggling her head on his chest, infusing an internal calmness in them both.

CHAPTER 74

AT LAST A WEDDING

"I'm curious to know, how is Patrick now?"

"I'm glad to say his story has a very happy ending. He found a lovely lady and they are getting married on Saturday." Eric paused to give Violet a smile. "Patrick asked if I would be his best man."

"That is a great honor for you, sir."

Eric looked serious and squinted his eyes for effect. He placed both hands on Violet's arms before speaking. "If you do not stop calling me 'sir,' I will have to bite your nose."

Over the years, Violet had said his name thousands of times. Her reluctance to openly call him by his first name came from a sense of respect, not only to him, but to Mr. and Mrs. Sutton. She understood how absurd her formality might seem to Eric. It was preposterous, considering her intimate behavior, to refrain from calling him by his first name but not from his lips. His direct order was all she needed and wanted. With a timid whisper, she confessed "I do like your name; it's perfectly suited to you."

"Thank you! Now let me hear you say it." He nudged her chin with his index finger.

"Eric," she whispered, then instantly wanting to make light of it all, she repeated with a serious robust voice, "Sir Eric."

"Now that wasn't so hard, was it? I'm Eric and you are 'sweet thing.'"

Eric was enjoying himself. Their light-hearted exchange was fun for Violet as well. She was rapidly learning to take part in his enticing sense of humor.

"I suppose," she retorted," I should call my mama and make her aware of my name change. I'm sure she'll get used to it."

Eric's smile indicated he was pleased with her quick comeback, yet he shook his head as though judging her. "I was about to ask you to be my guest at Patrick's wedding, but you're too cheeky."

Before Eric finished his latest tease, Violet shouted "Oh! Yes! Sir! I mean, Eric!" She embraced him, burying her face in his chest and mumbled. "I'd love to go."

Pleased with Violet's enthusiasm, Eric leaned in to kiss her, except this time she abruptly pulled away.

"I really must call my mama and sisters and tell them this great news."

Eric showed his disappointment, waving his empty arms he questioned her. "Is there a reason they need to know you're invited to a wedding, right now at this moment?"

"Absolutely! They will want to be included in my excitement." Violet's real reason for calling was her own need to share. All day she had been thinking about and missing her family. This was just an excuse to hear their exciting voices and add to her joy. She playfully curtsied and ran off.

Saturday, the morning of the wedding in London, Eric found Violet waiting for him.

"I've already had breakfast," she informed him, rising from the foyer armchair.

"Good," he replied and turned towards the conservatory. As an afterthought, he stopped, turned around, and most cordially yet naughtily asked, "Violet, may I please go help myself to some also?"

Just as saucy, she wanted to say no, but restrained herself. She hoped her facial expression revealed what she thought of his requesting permission to eat. Silently, the young lady directly sat back in the armchair, crossed her legs, and adjusted her hat.

From a few feet away, Eric paused again; this time he stood perfectly still and smiled. He let his eyes wander appreciatively from Violet's head to her toes. *"Mademoiselle!"* he called out, *"jue garte manifique."*

To compliment the autumn season, Violet had chosen to wear a burnt-orange linen suit by Chanel. She included an ivory silk scarf for contrast. Her matching shoes and purse were burnt orange with a hint of ivory brushed in in a wave pattern. She tucked her hair loosely under the floppy hat that matched her suit. Tied around its perimeter was a similar ivory silk ribbon. Her only makeup was a light touch of Rommel mascara and new autumn-shade lipstick.

The ceremony was simple and private. Not at all what a young Italian woman expected. The weddings Violet had witnessed as a child were anything but private. Everyone in the small town would in some way take part in the day's event. The church was always packed to capacity. Those unable to squeeze inside stood outside the half-open door. The enthused crowd was content to get even the slightest glimpse, as though the couple were famous celebrities, and they were the emphatic fans. Happily, they waited outside, wanting to be the first to shower the newlyweds with rice, *cumpete,* or flower petals. Violet had thrown her handful of rice countless times; it represented a blessing for the couple's new life together. The bride and groom's reception always included the invited guests' extended families. If aunts and uncles were invited, the invitation included their children and their children's children. To leave any member of a family out, no matter how far removed, would've been disrespectful. Therefore, the number of guests was determined based on the members of each family.

The love shared by Patrick and his lovely bride Victoria was evident. Their eyes were locked on each other through the entire ceremony. The bride and groom slowly repeated their vows, emphasizing every word. After the brief ceremony, the few friends and family most genuinely congratulated the happy couple.

At the back of the small church, on the lawn, a tasty celebratory luncheon was laid out for the guests to enjoy. As time was limited, immediately after the meal the families of the bride and groom accompanied the newlyweds to their send-off. Their honeymoon would be spent crossing the Atlantic. The couple had everything arranged to start their new life in Canada. Eric had generously gifted the couple with passage and an upgraded stateroom. Also awaiting the happy couple was chilled champagne and a feast of goodies. Eric had given the chief steward specific instructions to ensure Patrick and Victoria were treated royally for the entire voyage to Halifax.

The groom took his best man aside and spoke from his heart. Patrick's emotional speech was intended for Eric's ears only. However, Violet innocently and most unintentionally overheard.

"Thank you, Eric, for all your support and care throughout the years. Your words of encouragement when I needed them most were invaluable. I'm here today in most part because of you. I am grateful for your presence in my life and especially for today." Warmly, Patrick shook his friend's hand and embraced him with a heartfelt hug. "I would not be here today without your help!"

From what Eric had told her about Patrick's turbulent past, his best man warranted Patrick's gratitude. Violet had never witnessed men exposing sincere admiration before. She marvelled and appreciated the emotional openness and level of respect the two men shared.

After the newlyweds waved their final farewells, Eric's suggestion delighted Violet. "Our day in London is only half over. Let's leave the automobile parked and take a stroll. It will give us the opportunity to enjoy this great autumn weather we have been having."

Violet squeezed his hand in agreement. She was so exhilarated spending all this time with Eric, she didn't trust her voice to speak sensibly.

Her silence, however, encouraged Eric to divulge. "In my travels, I have been impressed by marvelous architectural structures and different cultures, yet I always felt detached. Today . . . " He paused to focus on their surroundings. "Today I sense a connection. London feels hospitable, inviting, and tantalizingly. Do you hear it? It's whispering to us, 'Welcome, Violet and Eric.'" He inhaled deeply before filling their silence. "What I'm trying to say has been expressed more eloquently in poems and love songs. They suggest how your surroundings take on new meaning when shared with someone special. I plead guilty to dismissing those songs as ridiculous and a bit exaggerated. I now admit their sentiments have merit." Eric took Violet in his arms. "I've seen London countless times, but today, being here with you, it feels more grandeur. I'm appreciating our historical city like never before."

Softly, Violet added her few words. "My thoughts exactly." She would not say more. Eric's expression of their time together was in accord with hers. She understood that walking hand-in-hand though the city was indeed the essential part of how they now viewed London.

As they continued their leisurely stroll, the aroma from a bakery shop nearby enticed Violet. She led Eric in its direction with a slight nudge.

He playfully protested by swaying his upper body against hers, mimicking the famous Leaning Tower of Pisa. Her child-like facial expression invited Eric to kiss the tip of her nose. They chose a cozy corner table for privacy. Lingering over steeped tea and freshly baked scones, they spoke mostly about Eric's travels. Violet asked him a multitude of questions, which he patiently answered. As they sauntered through Trafalgar Square, they both agreed to extend their London sightseeing. Carefree as genuine, enthusiastic tourists, they reviewed all the historical sites. They headed to the north end of the palace, to Westminster Abbey Cathedral. There, the young couple wanted to make a most personal memory by standing under Big Ben to kiss while the bells rang. They meant it as an inside joke, asking one another if they heard a bell ring when they kissed.

They issued not a thought to the distance accumulated from their parked automobiles until it was time for their return. Most thoughtful and adamant, Eric insisted on hailing a taxi back.

"You must be terribly uncomfortable in those shoes," he sympathized.

"Not really," she assured him. "I learned at a young age to endure discomfort." Violet wished she had not been so blunt.

"Your childhood must've been difficult indeed." Eric's empathy implied he had some knowledge of her life prior to living at the manor.

Violet felt this was not the time or place to talk about the unpleasantries from her past. Eventually she would share it all with Eric, but today she was too happy.

"Yes. I won't deny it but look at me now!" Smiling widely, she almost sang her words. "I am with the most handsome, intellectual, caring man in the world." She had wanted to say those words for a long time.

"Violet." Eric's voice was low, his eyes narrowed. "I am most uncomfortable being placed upon a pedestal."

Undeterred, Violet returned his look. "You have done the same with me."

"Yes, but you belong on an even higher pedestal; you are a sweet thing."

Again, Violet was too full of joy to be serious. "The argument stops here; I believe in a peaceful surrender." Dramatically, she waved her ivory scarf.

Their loud laughter caused people to stop and stare at the silly couple.

The drive home with the top down was invigorating. Violet began singing "Santa Lucia," one of her most-beloved Italian songs. To her amazement, Eric joined in with a strong voice and Italian lyrics! Violet beamed with delight. The man she loved spoke her native language. She stroked his windblown hair and caressed his cheek to show her pleasure. They continued their drive home, chatting fluently in Italian.

CHAPTER 75

THE WORD

With the party a few days away, Catherine gave Violet her list of things to oversee.

"I depend on your meticulous eye for detail. Please make sure all is done perfectly."

Violet was happy to be kept busy. With the teaching position date not yet finalized and Eric discussing business for hours with his father, her leisure time had tripled. Eric would meet with Violet on her afternoon walk through the gardens. They would discreetly seek a private corner for their much-anticipated hugs, followed by lengthy conversations, mostly in Italian.

Today he was over twenty minutes late. Anxious to be with him, Violet returned to the manor to look for him. She heard voices coming from the library. Closer, Violet recognized the three distinctive voices: Mr. and Mrs. Suttons', and of course Eric. They sounded engaged in a deep discussion.

She paused to smooth her hair and then heard her own name being mentioned.

"Well, son, what do you think of our Violet?" said Mr. Sutton.

"She is a sweet child," Eric responded noncommittally.

Catherine challenged him "You would never convince the men in New York she is a child. She is a sensible, mature young lady of twenty."

"As I recall," William noted, "she wasn't interested in any of those eager men. Maybe at this party one of your friends will be interested. Of course—" William made a quick pause as if reflecting, then added, "—if they don't object and are keen to marry a foreigner."

The implication of that word had Violet stumbling back as though stabbed in the heart. She had just experienced the meaning of the ancient adage: "The pen is mightier than the sword." That one word, "foreigner," wounded her as sharply as if it were a dagger. *If they do not object to marrying a foreigner.* The phrase pounded repeatedly in her head, as she ran from the house to the stables. Impulsively, she saddled her horse and urged her mount to speed away. Her objective was to escape her demoralizing pain.

Her dark mood increased as the afternoon turned to evening. The skin on her face was stiff from her unwiped tears. The pit of her stomach convulsed as she swallowed the truth. She could never marry Eric; she was not good enough. *I am a foreigner.*

The persistent drizzle drenching her hair reminded Violet of the day she first met Edward. Her anguish faded momentarily as she recalled that tormented child and felt proud on the strides they both had made together.

As the downpour intensified, Violet knew she had to get back to the manor. Scoping her surroundings, she realized in her haste to get away she had adventured deep in the woods.

Don't you dare get lost! she scolded herself while aimlessly riding in circles. The woods were so dense with tall trees, their canopy hid any guiding natural light. Violet had lost all sense of direction; she was confused and totally disoriented.

Cold and drenched, she began to shiver and started to feel light-headed. "Stupid, worthless girl." She kept repeating her father's words. Her devastation was so great the poor girl now agreed Ornesto had been right. *I am stupid.* The feelings of unworthiness had spread rapidly like an irritated skin rash. There was no fight left in her dimmed spirt. Leaning forward on her horse, she surrendered her faith. Her eyes were about to close when a galloping noise startled her.

It was Eric, yet Violet showed no trace of gladness; she was not even relieved to see him. She had hoped it was Thomas, her good friend the stablehand instead.

"Violet! Thank God. We have been sick with worry." Eric spoke breathlessly, apparently consumed with fatigue.

"I am fine!" Violet insisted, almost falling off her horse from exhaustion. "Sorry for the inconvenience."

"Inconvenience! What is wrong with you? Father and Catherine are overcome with worry."

"I'm sorry for being so stupid, but what do you expect from a foreigner?"

"Foreigner!" Eric repeated the word and intuitively understood. "You overheard our conversation! Is that what all this is about?"

"Yes, lately I have forgotten my place."

"Your place? Now you're being silly," he protested.

"Silly! Childish! Are there other names you'd like to call me?"

"Sweet thing." Eric's voice was tender.

"I supposed you would like to kiss me and have your way with the servant girl."

"Stop it! Stop demeaning yourself. Don't you know how much you're loved by everyone?" Eric, obviously frustrated, took her in his arms to prevent her from falling.

"Maybe Edward loves me," she mumbled, biting her bottom lip.

"Maybe?" Eric repeated, evidently shocked.

Violet covered her face in shame. "I know he loves me. I love him too," she sobbed.

Eric tied her horse to his, grateful the rain had stopped. "You'll ride back with me," he told her.

Stripped of all her strength and dignity, Violet surrendered. Her immense exhaustion found comfort in his body heat. She cradled in his arms and swooned to sleep.

Eric carried her into the house. William waved the staff away and prepared the couch himself. He put all the cushions to one side and Catherine grabbed a blanket. The endearing looks on their relieved faces told Violet what she already knew.

"Oh, my dear, dear child you gave us such a fright. We don't know what we'd do if anything happened to you." William's voice was shaky. Catherine had traces of tears on her face.

From her collapsing, weak body, Violet's conjured up enough strength to voice her sincere apology. "I'm truly sorry I ventured out too deep into the woods and got lost."

"You're home and safe now, you'll take a hot bath, have some hot broth, and rest with a hot water bottle."

"Dearest," William interrupted his wife's uncontrollable rambling. "It's well said but best done, don't you agree?"

With a deep sense of relief, they both let out a nervous laugh and began to relax. At one point—perhaps just for a moment—they had lost hope. The dread of the unmentionable had perhaps briefly entered their minds, but they had not dared spoken.

After her hot bath, Violet snuggled in her warm bed. Catherine sat next to her while the young lady obediently sipped the hot soup.

"I will have a breakfast tray sent up in the morning. I want you to sleep in these next two days and get well rested for the party."

Eric entered Violet's room as Catherine was leaving. "Don't stay long," she ordered. "Violet is exhausted and needs to rest."

Eric nodded his consent to Catherine; he then closed the door and walked to her bedside. They locked eyes. The guilty lady knew she was about to be interrogated. His single word was to the point. "Confess," he demanded.

Violet was not about to make excuses for her behavior. "I admit I made a terrible mistake and leaped to the wrong conclusion. It's obvious the word 'foreigner' was meant as a factual description, not a discriminatory put-down by your father."

"There! Are you happy now?"

Eric's determined look did not subside. "Admitting you're wrong about a misused word means nothing. I want to know what's in your heart."

Violet could not tell Eric her irrational behaviour resulted from her acknowledging she might lose him. The word "foreigner" brought her back to reality and her heritage.

"I cannot explain my behavior," she managed to reply honestly. "As for my heart, it's full of love. Mr. and Mrs. Sutton have always treated me as an equal to Edward. I have felt their loving parenting all these years." Admitting this fact aloud was easier than Violet thought; the truth often is.

Eric, lifting her face with both his hands, bent close and whispered softly. "Never ever forget this, sweet thing." He then kissed her forehead gently. As he was leaving, Eric noticed his music box on the dresser, gave Violet a smile, and opened it. She smiled back at him, trying to mask her sadness.

With Eric gone, she sank deep under the covers and let out an anguished sigh. *How dare I aim so high? Eric deserves someone of his own social standing. He definitely deserves someone better than me. I have been selfish thinking how perfect he is for me, never considering if I'm perfect for him. My deep love for him blinded me, but the 'word' opened my eyes to what is just.* Facing reality, Violet remained awake for hours trying to reconcile to the fact she could never be Eric's wife.

CHAPTER 76

THE PARTY'S UPS AND DOWNS

The morning of the party, Violet's mood elevated considerably. She was cheerful and full of anticipation. The contributing factor was not the big evening event, but the afternoon. Edward was coming home. She roamed the manor, asking the staff if they needed her last minutes suggestions or input. They discreetly made it clear everything was all under control, and dismissed her by saying, "Thank you, miss."

At 2:35 p.m., Violet's eagerness caused another rare moment not soon forgotten and retold for years. Her aggressive dash towards Edward caught him totally unprepared. His body slammed to the ground with Violet on top. Stunned but amused with the result, they both laughed aloud.

It was definitely déjà vu, bringing them both back to their first encounter in Italy. Her continuous motherly patting to reassure he was not hurt was also innate.

"I'm okay, Violet," he reassured her. "I wanted to come home a few days earlier, but the itinerary could not be changed." Edward's apology was sincere.

Violet shook her head. "I'm the one to say sorry and ask your forgiveness; I've been a real nuisance." She was ashamed to admit she had not considered the effect her moods had on Edward. For the last two weeks, both her mind and heart were obsessed with Eric. "Why didn't you tell me about Eric's return?" She demonstrated her displeasure with heavier than necessary strokes while continuing to dust him off.

Edward looked a little befuddled. "You, Violet, are complicated and confusing. You said it's best to let life unfold itself. Now you say you want to know what's next? I'm not the mister know-it-all you think I am."

The look of skepticism on her face said she knew he knew, enough. What she did not know was who Edward was really protecting. Her concern for her little man prevented her from stressing him further. She affectionately reminded him, "You are still my little monster! I'm so happy you are home."

"I know that for sure. But please no more crying. You exhaust me."

Edward had a way of making her feel at least three emotions at the same time. She was about to point that out when his family appeared.

Eric gave Edward a firm handshake, then a bear hug.

"Look everyone I'm almost as tall as Eric." Edward's measuring skills tended to lean towards his benefit.

"Almost," Eric repeated the operative word, laughing over the obvious one-foot difference.

While sandwich-hugging their son, his parents agreed that Edward had definitely grown a few inches in his absence. "Egypt agreed with you," they complimented, admiring his tanned complexion.

"Edward, we will have to wait till tomorrow to hear all about your excavating adventure," said Catherine. "Tonight is all about Eric and his party."

"I'm all for that," Edward responded, immediately giving Eric a rigorous nod.

Violet took in the scene. It was her first time witnessing the two brothers together. She noticed Edward's persona was different with Eric. There was of course the obvious sibling love and respect, but she sensed much more. Edward looked at his older brother with reverence. Analyzing as she always did, Violet concluded Edward's insightfulness was in play. No doubt Eric had earned that level of admiration.

It was obvious even in just a few weeks of knowing him that Eric was a man of integrity.

The staff, as usual, had been extremely diligent ensuring all preparations met Catherine's and Violet's standards. They also shared in the joy of finally having the entire Sutton family together. This party was a celebration for them as well. and none begrudged the extra work. Simon always had leeway to do what was best for the staff. For large functions that happened numerous times every year, he had the authority to hire additional help, usually from the staff's own households.

Preparing for Eric's party, Violet struggled with her thoughts and emotions. Rationally, she accepted Eric was a Sutton, and she was a Conti, but her heart wouldn't listen to reason. Try as she might to heed her mother's advice, she could not push away her love for him. That stubborn heart of hers had embraced him for so long; it would not let go. She feared there was no escaping the fact that Eric was permanently etched inside. Violet quickly dismissed any rational thoughts and threw caution to the wind. Her objective was to just focus on the here and now. Our young lady was secretly wishing to have a memorable evening. Unfortunately, just like the famous cliché, she had to be careful what she wished for.

An abrupt knock on the door, followed by a quick burst into her room, was of course Edward's M.O. "Wow! Violet, you look awesome!" He had always given her compliments, but tonight he seemed overly generous.

"Awesome! Isn't that the word you use to describe your fossils?" she teased.

"Yep!" Edward's verbal answer was short, to the point, and sincere.

"Well, then, I'm flattered." Violet was just as sincere. "Thank you, Edward."

As they left her room, Edward encouraged Violet to take his arm, as they had on the *Queen Mary*.

Approaching the center of the elaborate circular staircase, Edward stopped and stepped back. "After you," he insisted.

Violet understood and smiled at her little admirer. She appreciated his thoughtful gesture, giving her a grand entrance.

Descending the spiral stairs, Violet's eyes found Eric waiting for her. Inwardly, she reinforced and justified her earlier decision. *I will allow myself to enjoy Eric's company. My role tonight is to assure he has a great time. After all, it is his welcome home party. Tomorrow, I will be sensible tomorrow,* she half promised.

Tonight, Violet had taken extra care in her looks. She chose to wear her favorite exquisite, haute couture, Christian Dior strapless gown. The delicate chiffon infused various shades of violet, perfectly boasting her name. The colors went from light on top to dark purple waving the floor. Her hair was loosely woven to the back, revealing her slender shoulders. She adorned her neck with a fine silver chain, highlighting a single amethyst teardrop. The prisms from her matching earrings danced with the multi-shades of the gown.

At the bottom step, Eric's eyes were focused, and his hand extended. "Violet," he said, "You look breathtaking."

All for you! she wanted to shout, *All for you!* She refrained from voicing.

"Violet, I need to speak with you now." Eric was insistent as he took her hand.

Her agreeable smile indicated she was eager to hear what was so urgent.

"Not so fast!" a loud male voice roared out the commanded as four men rushed towards him. "You sly fox, no wonder we haven't heard a peep from you since your return."

Eric's mannerism changed and his voice deepened. "Violet," he said. "These so-called gentlemen used to be my friends."

One by one, while dramatically kissing her hand, they introduced themselves. Michael, John, Matthew—and Greg, the outspoken one.

They were all handsome, charming, and witty. Violet imagined the mischief and chaos they caused whenever they were together. As though the men had just been instructed by Shakespeare, they each eloquently lavished the maiden with their own dramatic, divine sonnet, emphasizing her beauty and virtues.

As the music started, Eric reached out and took Violet's hand. "This is our dance," he affirmed, aiming his assertion at his friends.

Unaffected, they rebutted with their own faux protests.

Violet's heart danced before her feet moved as she recognized the familiar tune. It was, "Fascination," their song, the song that started her hopes, her dreams, and her secret fantasies. Being in Eric's arms, although the grand room was full of people, Violet imagined they were alone dancing under the stars. She recalled the first time she fantasized over him and her clumsy twirls. Not tonight. Tonight, Violet was gliding in his arms.

"I have something important to ask you later." His warm breath was so inviting she extended her delicate neck like a graceful swan.

Later, Violet thought, seemed decades away.

Eric's friends were perfect gentlemen, and Violet did not mind dancing with all of them. They all shared the same interest, talking about Eric. Their stories reinforced how dependable, considerate, and giving he was. They all complimented his ability to be a great judge of character. He always knew who to trust and who to avoid. This unique proficiency had assisted Eric in achieving great success in his global enterprise conglomerate. Violet never doubted his character and knew it all to be true. His longtime friends' praises were simply a delight to hear.

Over the course of the fun-filled evening, Eric and Violet mingled with the enthused guests, but never lost sight of each other for long. Wherever they stood, their eyes would meet.

When her eyes glanced toward him this time, he was eagerly coming for her. The anticipation of being in his arms again had her a little flushed and in need of a fan. Unfortunately, his father rerouted his advance, calling Eric to join him. He was speaking with a tardy couple who had just arrived and immediately wanted his attention.

The four exchanged greetings and chatted awhile. A few seconds later, Eric took the woman's arm and escorted her to the terrace. Violet's entire body went cold. She suddenly felt emotions all new to her. This, she soon realized, was her first experience with jealousy. She had not felt this sickened earlier in the evening when Eric danced with other women. Was it because this particular woman oozed glamor?

She had stylish short, blonde hair and flawless doll-like features. The ivory, skin-tight gown shaped her perfect body and exposed her entire back. Violet had seen revealing gowns as this only on models and movie stars. She admitted her appearance was elaborate but definitely inappropriate for this particular gathering. What Violet really found unacceptable was how this woman squeezed her body next to Eric as they walked together toward the terrace.

A conversation two men were having close by distracted her contemplation.

"I was told you were unable to join us." Eric's friend John questioned the man who had just arrived.

"Yes, I had to postpone my trip until the morning. Penelope called and demanded I escort her to Eric's party. She wanted to see Eric again."

Again? repeated Violet to herself. *So, he knows her. Of course, he knows her; they all come from the same social circle.* A particular circle Violet believed could not be penetrated by the likes of her. Admitting being the inferior one was obviously painful but truthful.

Greg, Eric's demonstrative friend, approached her with a glass of Champagne. "My lady," he addressed with a smiling, "Edward has retired for the evening but asked me to bring you a refreshment."

"Thank you, Greg." She graciously accepted.

Sipping her Champagne, Violet casually asked him a question that was consuming her insides. "Greg, do you know Penelope?"

"Who! The imposing goddess?" he spat, apparently not intending it as a compliment. "I assure you, she's definitely not my type. I like the dark-haired beauties." Greg gave the young lady a genuine smile.

The next time Violet saw Eric was on the dance floor. They accidentally bumped into each other. Penelope, with her perfect smile, giggled unapologetically. "We weren't paying attention," she said, adding, "Eric stop making me laugh."

"Penelope, this is Violet, my brother Edward's adopted sister." Eric introduction was a bit askew.

"So, you're a member of the Sutton family! Pleased to meet you."

Violet's need to find a flaw in Penelope had manifested in her piercing, childlike voice. It was squeaky and most irritating. Violet quickly returned her smile while wondering about Eric's strange introduction. *Why introduce me as his brother's adopted sister? Was it to show strictly a family bond?* Violet was confused but would not in any way contradict him. Instead, she reminded him about his earlier request to speak with her.

"That will have to wait," was his abrupt answer to her. He then added a short speech Violet found even more baffling than his introduction. "Time does not always erase certain feelings. When the opportunity arises to retrieve them, one must do so fully. Violet," Eric enunciated her name looking directly into her eyes. "I must keep a promise I made myself years ago."

With a double twirl, Eric led Penelope off the dance floor, leaving Violet to decipher yet another strange message. What was he trying to convey to her? She reviewed every word he said over and over, but to no avail.

The party was winding down. Violet was glad to see the guests leaving, especially one, until Eric offered to drive her home.

"You are a gentleman, unlike my vanishing escort." Penelope's words came out in a squeal. "I am exhausted. You won't take advantage of me, will you Eric?"

"Penelope, my dear, I will not make promises I might not be able to keep." With her hyena-like laughter and flirtatious looks, Eric's saucy answer was obviously what she'd hoped to hear.

Violet held tight to her emotions, but her legs were starting to betray her. The climb up the stairs was a struggle; her feet felt as if stuck in deep mud. With sheer determination, she reached her room, closed the door, and slowly slid to the floor. She sat on her beautiful violet gown that was now spread out like a dust rag. The emotional roller coaster she had been on all evening had drained her. Violet wept.

Eventually she got to bed but found no peace. Her mind would not stop tormenting her. Once Eric saw Penelope, he'd become a different man. *Had he been in love with her for years? Did their reunion spark old feelings? Was that what he tried to tell me?* All she could do was ask herself more questions, but she found no answers.

Violet believed no woman could ever love Eric as deeply as she did, but Penelope was more his social equal. She was born privileged into high society. With his global enterprise, Eric needed a worldly woman by his side. A woman with a respected name like his. A poor "foreigner" such as herself had nothing to offer a man like Eric.

It was after 3:00 a.m. when Violet heard Eric's car approach the manor. She opened the music box, listened to "Fascination" one last time, and said goodbye to her dreams.

CHAPTER 77

PENELOPE

The two brothers had gone fishing by the time Violet came down for breakfast. Traces of enduring sadness cast shadows under her eyes and over her pale face.

"Violet, my dear, you need to get more sleep, your eyes look strained," Catherine observed. After a successful party, Mrs. Sutton was in her glory and in a harmonious, relaxed mood. "Eric and Edward will return . . . " Catherine's statement was left incomplete as Violet turned even paler. "As I said, it's best you go back to bed, my dear. You had an exhausting evening."

By mid-afternoon, after some needed sleep, Violet felt much better. She was enjoying a cup of tea with Catherine when the two fishermen walked in with the catch of the day: Penelope.

"Look who just arrived," Edward pointed out, sitting next to Violet.

"Mrs. Sutton, Eric told me to come by at any time for a game of tennis. I hope it's not too inconvenient." Penelope politely sought confirmation, which seemed to please Eric.

"My dear, friends of Eric's are always welcome. Come, have some tea."

Penelope appeared to anticipate Catherine's agreeable reply. She had dragged Eric by the arm and was practically sitting on his lap.

Her sporadic bursts of unwarranted laughter annoyed Violet. Even Catherine and Edward rolled their eyes a few times at the phony display.

The expression on Edward's face had alerted Violet before he asked, "Violet, would you please come take a walk with me in the garden?"

Asking aloud was for the others' benefit. Violet had already made a move, immediately accepted, and was pleased with Edward's aptitude. She presumed he wanted to share some insights about Penelope.

Knowing, of course, about her feelings toward Eric, he was sympathetic. "I'm so sorry, Violet. I don't want you to be so upset. Eric is confused right now. Just be patient."

The fact that Edward was caught in the middle, showing his concern, demoralized Violet. All she ever wanted was to protect him, and now she was the cause of his worry. Violet knew she had to stop her ridiculous shenanigans, not only for her sake but for Edward's.

"Eric is an intelligent man; he knows what he wants, and obviously it's not me. I was just deluding myself. Edward, you must promise to dismiss my silly behavior from your thoughts. Please don't blame Eric for any of this." Aware of Edward's insightfulness into her feelings, Violet had no choice but to be straightforward and honest. "I have been pretending for years that Eric was the man for me." Admitting this was extremely difficult for Violet. It was the first time she felt embarrassed talking with Edward. She wanted to make light of her romanticizing and tried putting a humorous twist on it. "Girls, you know, are different than boys. We have vivid imaginations. Sometimes we like to pretend about love and marriage; it's all childish games. However, I am an adult now and must face reality. I will accept Eric's decision, and you must too. He deserves to marry whomever he chooses. Edward, I promise to stop feeling heartbroken. I'll start dating, maybe go to a movie with someone."

Violet could not have been more open and sincere. She spoke from her heart. She desperately needed Edward to believe her and not worry. Eric was his brother, and she was determined to keep their relationship friendly and loving. She would never tarnish Edward's admiration for his older brother.

After speaking with Edward, Violet turned to Albert. Albert's friendship had always been based on trust, respect, and loyalty. From the very beginning, he'd presented these qualities by caring for Violet's needs. He dealt shrewdly with her greedy father, assuring her own financial income. He had thoughtfully taken time to reassure a frightened fifteen-year-old girl with encouraging words. Throughout the years, his sincerity and helpful advice were always for her benefit. He had never revealed to a single person Violet's dismal background. He respected and treated her as a member of the Sutton family. Without a doubt, she was convinced Albert was the reliable choice to confide in. *He is perceptive and will understand my predicament.*

Albert listened and simply nodded, making it easy for Violet to explain what she needed. The mature and gracious man did not wait for the distressed lady to ask.

"Miss Violet, it will be my honor and privilege to take you out this evening and whenever you wish. I do understand and promise to keep you occupied for as long as I'm needed." Albert added, "I must confess, I do not like Master Eric's new lady friend. She is rude, demanding, and above all, phony."

"Albert!" Violet pretended to scold him. "You must tell me how you really feel. Truthfully Albert, I agree she is all that, but she is also very beautiful and sophisticated and comes from an influential family."

"Miss Violet, I understand by pointing out these facts you are trying to be logical." Albert shook his head. "I also believe that when a woman flaunts her beauty but lacks sustainable qualities, she eventually loses her appeal. In my opinion, a self-absorbed woman is distorted and confusing, like a Picasso painting. You, young lady, are one of a kind, exquisitely flawless. You're beautiful, yet modest, very generous, and continuingly putting other first. That is what I've always loved about you."

As Albert spoke those words, Eric walked by, "What's going on?" he demanded.

Violet immediately responded, "I don't feel we need to explain ourselves, but if you must know, sir,"—she emphasized the "sir"—"Albert and I are good friends, just like you and Penelope."

"Penelope?" he said. "We were never friends. You, of course, are correct Violet, I do apologize. I have no right to interfere in your plans, as you don't in mine."

"May I be of assistance, sir?" Albert instinctively asked, putting on his chauffeur hat.

"I'll be taking my own car. You both obviously have things to discuss." Eric's tone had a razor-sharp edge to it. His body was rigid as he rushed off.

"What was that all about?" Albert was curious.

"I am also confused, Albert," she admitted. "I believed Eric and Penelope had been past friends. I suppose their relationship was more intimate. He was very specific that I stay out of his plans." Violet's voice was a mere whisper.

Albert tried to cheer Violet by putting on a playful expression. "I wish I had a detective's hat, he joked, waving his chauffeur cap about. "I'll keep working on some theories as to why Master Eric behaved so oddly and let you know my conclusion."

"Please do, Albert." Violet played along, trying to sound indifferent. In truth, Eric's obsession with Penelope was the toughest thing she would ever have to overcome.

CHAPTER 78

PENELOPE'S BLUNTNESS

Saturday mornings, Violet's priority was her designated extended phone visit with her family. She closed the door to her room for privacy and so as not to disturb others. Their phone conversations tended to get dramatic, personal, and hilariously loud.

As Violet picked up the phone to dial the operator, she heard Penelope's voice yelling on the extension. "Father, I demand you do this. Just call William Sutton, tell him you and mother are going away for a week and would appreciate if they allow me to stay here."

Her father calmly responded from the other end. "Dear," he pleaded, "we don't know the Suttons that well. It would be extremely presumptuous, don't you see?"

"I don't care if it's a bit embarrassing for you, Father, just do it! I want to get my hands on Eric, and I need a week. Now give the phone to my maid, I need her to start packing."

Slowly, Violet put down the receiver and sat on her bed. *I must tell Eric, no Catherine, maybe Edward, and say . . . what? Penelope wants Eric to fall in love with her. He seems mesmerized by her already. I would come across as a jealous, meddling fool.* Violet evaluated her options. *Maybe my best course of action is to keep silent.* Her contemplation was interrupted by an aggressive knock on the door.

"Violet, it's Penelope, may I come in?"

She was the last person Violet wanted to see, and she seriously considered not opening the door. The second knock was even more persistent. Reluctantly Violet made herself slowly turn the knob.

The door was barely open an inch when Penelope boldly shoved her way in. "I thought you might be in here." There was an air of arrogance in her tone. "I want to speak with you. Since you're Edward's adopted sister or whatever . . . " Penelope looked at Violet, revealing she was unimpressed. "I want you to know, I intend to marry Eric." Her candidness shocked Violet. "I know you overheard the conversation with my father. I've come to warn you to stay out of my plans."

Violet was determined not to show weakness in front of Penelope. "It's not my place to interfere in Eric's life," she said coolly.

"I'm glad you know your proper place—after all, you're just a paid employee."

"Penelope, I'd advise you never question the Suttons' affection and support for me."

"My! My! Aren't we full of ourselves? Just stay out of my way or you'll be sorry." Penelope's threat was not only confident but showed an air of predominance over Violet.

Violet had had enough of Penelope's rudeness. "Not everyone is as accommodating as your father." Holding her door open, Violet ordered, "Get out of my room!"

Penelope's infuriated look was Violet's reward. Her swift comeback had clipped a bit of the intrusive moth's wings. Penelope's face became distorted, like a spoiled child not getting her way, and she quickly left without rebuttal.

Once her lengthy, fun-filled conversation with her family was done, Violet questioned the intense conversation she'd had with Penelope. *What did I do? I was abrupt and crude, yet I don't regret it a bit. I simply gave back some of her own.* Violet felt pleased she had spoken directly and with authority.

Handling this situation with such control strengthened her self-worth. *Where did all my confidence come from?* she asked, smiling at the image in the mirror. The most antagonizing but beguiling person came to mind. "Eric!" His constant teasing had unleashed her swift, unguarded responses. He had continuously complimented her tenacity, saying he admired her spunk. Ultimately, his encouragement had ripped away her restraint. She was grateful to Eric for insisting she be forthright and not hold back. With him, she had become outspoken. Assertiveness was the missing key she needed to open her restraint, her personal door. Finally, she could unlock the chains and remove the shackles her father had put on her. Subsequently, over the years, Violet confessed having tightened them even more herself. Ignoring her scars had allowed them to multiply and ultimately oppress her. It was hard to erase the aftermath of abuse. It clung to one's inner consciousness. Her determination and strength had sustained her, yet she continued to allow the feeling of unworthiness to plague her life. It had not been enough to simply push aside her fears. They had aggressively surfaced at her most vulnerable time. This new revelation struck her like a lightning bolt. *I most face my childhood insecurities openly and honestly. Only by exposing my vulnerabilities will I be able to overpower and destroy them. I was humiliated and verbally abused as a child, but I'm not a child anymore. Winning small battles is not enough; I must completely demolish this falsehood from its foundation. Never again will I allow my father's cruel words to have power over me. I have worked hard and succeeded in making my life better.* Understanding this important difference, Violet vowed never to feel inferior to anyone ever again!

With all this soul-searching, she re-examined her subconscious and gripped firmly to her self-worth. After all the positive encouragement over the years from her mother, Catherine, Edward, and Eric, she at long last was ready to embrace her strengths and accomplishments. The reflection she now viewed in her mirror was that of a confident young lady.

"I'm no longer that tiny, timid, insignificant fifteen-year-old. I am perceptive, educated, and have an abundance of opportunities." With this healthy attitude, Violet now believed and professed, *I do have a lot to offer! I stand on an equal field with anyone!*

Having this new outlook, Violet made herself evaluate more justly Eric and Penelope's relationship. She admitted her prejudice towards Penelope was her social status; she was Eric's equal and more suited to him. She now realized Penelope's wealth and origin had nothing to do with Eric's choice. Eric had praised and admired her, Violet, from the very start. He had never treated her as inferior in any way. She was the one reflecting her insecurities and sense of unworthiness on others. Eric was known for his fairness and great sense of equality. All his friends complimented his great judge of character. By choosing Penelope, Eric was simply following his heart. As devastating as this was to admit, Violet had no choice but to reconcile with the truth. *I should not be so quick to judge Penelope's motives. She might have hidden qualities that I'm not aware of. I am just as guilty of flirting and wanting Eric to marry me.* She recalled how he had laughed when she boldly made the first move. *My own belligerent flirtation was sinful. I started things, puckering my lips and squeezing closer to him. It was shameful. I acted like a Jezebel.*

Violet's lack of experience with matters of the heart had her wishing for a confidant, someone she could trust to give her helpful advice. Edward and Catherine were of course out of the question. Then who? No doubt her mother, definitely her sisters, would have plenty to say. After their initial awkwardness years ago on her first visit back, they had never again shown signs of restraint. Violet's sisters loved being straightforward and giving their opinions. Their advice at times was impractical, but always given with love and support. Geographic distance from her family had always been extremely difficult, at times even unbearable for her. This could definitely be categorized as one of those unbearable times. When it came to the opposite sex, Violet had no one to discuss do's or don'ts. Her mother's earlier advice was not forgotten but didn't give her all the answers. She had already made the number one mistake her mother had warned her against doing: falling in love too deeply. To know you are part of a large, loving family yet unable to derive its rewards was disheartening. Her family was like refreshing water down a deep well—without a fetching bucket, it was unobtainable.

She considered her options and wondered if she should leave England. "Not just yet," her mouth quickly spoke out the words her heart dictated. Violet convinced herself she had two concrete reasons, and both had to do with Edward. Firstly, she had to stay and see her little man off to school. Secondly, and more importantly, Edward's precise statement on the flight home: "Violet! You might want to stay right where you are." *My presence here might still be needed. I must stay!* For the moment, Violet was content with her definite decision. Realistically, she knew she had to revisit it at a later time.

In keeping with their generous characters, Mr. and Mrs. Sutton instinctively welcomed Penelope into their home. "While your parents are away, we are pleased to accommodate you," Mr. Sutton offered.

Penelope's manners and response were especially charming. "I'm so grateful. I really didn't want to stay with my aunt. She is always introducing me to men she believes would be suitable husbands." Penelope paused to gaze directly at Eric. "I want to pick my own husband."

Eric responded with a broad, agreeable smile.

William reacted to their exchange with fatherly advice. "Young people today should take time and get to know one another." His message was reinforced by the serious tone in his voice.

His cautionary statement, however, did not deter Penelope. Immediately, she asserted, "True love happens quickly and unexpectedly."

Eric added his sentiments on cue. "Most definitely." Then he elaborated, making a compelling speech. "Love is a spiritual awakening affecting your whole being. It ignites the flame that is deep within one's soul. The mind and body must respond or be consumed!"

A giggling response came from Penelope. "Eric that was beautiful, you almost made me cry."

Edward pretended to be physically sick.

Violet listened intensely, absorbing his every word, as she had done the day they had spent in London. Eric had described precisely the feelings she was experiencing for him.

CHAPTER 79

TRUE CHARACTER EXPOSED

The following week, Eric and Penelope were inseparable. They spent their mornings playing tennis and taking long rides. Violet noticed they never went in the direction of the river, probably to avoid running into her and Edward. *Fine with me,* she thought, determined to keep her own distance. Not for Penelope's sake but watching them together was still too painful. Penelope's body was always stuck on Eric, as though he was a large magnet, and she was a piece of raw iron.

Every evening Penelope would insist they go out, and Eric eagerly obliged her every suggestion.

Saturday morning at breakfast, William outlined the evening plans. "Catherine, Edward, and I are invited to the Taylors. Violet must not be left alone; Eric, I recommend she accompany you and Penelope for the evening."

Penelope tried to sound agreeable. "Yes, of course Violet may join us. We are meeting some friends at eight in London."

Eric grunted his agreement "Fine with me."

Violet beamed with pleasure. "Thank you all very much for your consideration." She gave them a gracious smile before relating, "I also have a personal commitment tonight." The young lady was relieved; she had accepted Albert's invite to join him for dinner.

Edward was delighted and gave Violet his look of approval. Catherine and William were also pleased she had plans. A big grin was plastered on Penelope's face. Eric's face was passive, but he still asked, "With whom?"

Violet was eager to share her evening engagement with them all. "Albert's sister is visiting from Germany and would like to meet me."

"Albert?" Penelope repeated condescendingly. "The chauffeur?" She smirked "I suppose he is better suited to your class."

And that's when Penelope put that proverbial foot in her mouth. Everyone at the table gasped at her attempt to humiliate Violet. Eric's face was set, without expression. This time Violet knew she did not have to defend herself. She simply leaned back in her chair, anticipating what was about to happen. She had tried to warn Penelope, but arrogance never listens.

"My dear Penelope." William stood, for impact, making sure his point would be clearly understood. "Violet's class and position is the highest of anyone at this table."

A look of disbelief flared on Penelope's face. "I assure you I didn't mean to offend." Her words were careless and sharp-edged, entirely unrepentant.

Edward stared right through her and snapped back with the truth: "Of course you did."

Catherine's emphatic expression revealed her dismay. "I'm appalled with your insinuations!" she reproached her unpleasant house guest. "You obviously have no idea how much Violet is esteemed and loved. She is invaluable to our family."

Catherine's words were meant to puncture through Penelope's prejudice. Unfortunately, she remained rigid, the sentiments barely nicking her pretentiousness.

It was Violet's heart that leapt. Listening to the family declare their respect and love for her to Penelope was an extraordinary gift. With humble appreciation, Violet spoke. "Thank you, Mr. Sutton for being the father figure I always wanted. My respect for you is immense. Mrs.

Sutton, I accredit my development to your attentiveness and commitment." Violet stepped closer to Catherine and hugged her. "Only a devoted mother would have done as much."

Both women tightened their embrace.

William, still standing, immediately enclosed them both in his protective arms.

Penelope was fuming and unwilling to listen to more. She rejected their outburst and disregarded their reprimand. Annoyed with the show of affection, she spoke out forcefully "Eric, it's late, we must go."

"Yes, I agree, it's time we leave." Eric's lack of expression and cold demeanor had him resembling a robot.

For a brief moment, Violet met his eyes. They were dark set in anger. Not at all the reaction she'd hoped for from him. He possessively took Penelope's arm, demonstrating his absolute commitment to his lady.

CHAPTER 80

GONE BUT NOT FORGOTTEN

"The conservatory is exceptionally bright and full of life this morning," Catherine cheerfully stated. "Come, Violet, we will enjoy a pleasant breakfast, now that Eric has taken Penelope back home." She sounded especially pleased giving out that information. "Something about that pushy girl irritated me. Having her around made me appreciate you even more."

"Thank you." Violet laughed, realizing it felt good to let go of sadness, even briefly. She strolled in looking striking as usual in her riding attire. "Edward and I are going for a short ride after breakfast; will you be joining us, Mrs. Sutton?"

"Not today, my dear. I will be accompanying William to London and be back late. I suspect it will only be Edward and yourself for dinner."

Violet concluded she was insinuating Eric might be staying with Penelope. Naturally, Mrs. Sutton's genteel character would restrain any further comments. Clearly, Penelope was not one of her favorite people. Nevertheless, Catherine would never permit herself to question Eric's choice.

Violet welcomed spending time alone with Edward. She planned to bombard him with a million questions, hoping to get one or two answered. He had become excessively secretive, determined not to share his visions or insights with her.

Violet blamed herself. Edward was simply abiding by her own request and staying steadfast to her convictions. They had shared everything for years; their pending separation was difficult for them both. Recently, Edward had been the one showing stability and maturity—Violet not so much. She struggled with her indecisiveness and occasionally had tried bending the rules to suit her needs. Honestly, deep down she was proud of Edward. It was her own human weakness that needed work. Not knowing Eric's future tormented her. She justified her behavior, promising it would be the last time she would plead for Edward's insightfulness. After dismounting while on their leisurely walk, she'd take the opportunity to interrogate her little man.

Edward rode his horse alongside Violet, slowing her pace. "Violet," he said seriously, getting her full attention; evidently, he had his own game plan. "Please don't be so unhappy."

"What is it, Edward?" she asked tenderly, encouraging him to speak.

"Arrangements for my departure for school have progressed. My parents will be accompanying me and reside in America for a few years as well."

"That doesn't surprise me, Edward. I thought as much. It makes sense." Violet totally expected Mr. and Mrs. Sutton would accompany their son and want to live near him. It also gave Catherine the opportunity to spend more time with her parents.

"I would ask you to come with us, Violet, but truthfully I don't see you taking up residence in America."

This admission from him gave Violet her incentive to start her inquiry. "Edward, you infuriate me. Why is it okay to reveal what you don't see me doing?" Violet hurriedly seized her opportunity. "I want to know about Eric's future." Her need was so intense, she looked ready to cry.

Edward's expression suggested he was willing to comply. "What do you want to know, Violet? I will be brief and direct."

Without hesitation, she asked, "Is Eric getting married?"

"Yes."

"Soon, Edward, soon?"

"Yes."

"Why? He seems so unhappy. Penelope is so demanding." Violet regretted saying those words aloud.

"Stop worrying about Eric!" Edward scolded. "He is going to take care of everything. Eric is in control, especially with Penelope."

"Do you see him happy, Edward? Is that what you're trying to tell me?" Violet had to know.

"Yes, he is."

Those three words were bittersweet.

"Yes, he is!" Violet repeated. She loved Eric so much she wanted him happy. The bitter pill she had to swallow was that he would be happy without her.

A sudden anguish in Violet's heart overwhelmed her. Her stomach felt like a small ship tossed about by twenty-foot waves, destined to capsize. There was no denying it; she had lost control of her heart, her body, and her mind. Loving Eric had consumed her whole being. Losing all hope crushed her. Life without Eric would be empty, a meaningless existence. Violet knew she could never love another man so deeply, so completely, ever again.

Edward's eyes were drained of color; he looked miserable and gloomy. His whole body sagged low on his horse. Violet realized the sorrow festering in her was consuming him as well. She could not do this to him. Edward had always been her number-one priority. This little man had given her so much. His feelings and needs had always come first. For his sake, she must end this destructive self-pity.

Violet's caring and giving nature was her strength. Her ability to consider others first was embedded in her character. Her thoughtfulness would now be her own saving grace. Once the mind shifts to the well-being of others, instinctively the focus is no long on your own devastation. Pausing to consider others ultimately gives back purpose and meaning to one's own life. This fundamental truth is the difference between people who lose all hope and those who find a reason to live and fight through their despair.

Time spend with Edward was now short and precious. All they had achieved together in the last five years could not be devalued by her sadness. This was not the way she wanted Edward to remember her. Back in New York he had boasted to his family that she was resilient; this was her opportunity to prove him right.

Yanking the reins of her horse, she attempted to turn back time. "I know a perfect spot by the river, where we can dig for new fossils." For the love of her little man, Violet had transformed herself into an excitable teenager. With a squeal and high pitch voice, she yelled out, "I'll race you!"

CHAPTER 81

ERIC'S QUICK DEPARTURE

Eric was just walking in as Violet shoved another letter in her pocket. He looked refreshed. "I must speak with you," he said forcefully, yet his voice was calm, and his tone had a hint of relief.

Violet wanted to scream, "No! I do not want to hear you declare love for another woman." Pasquale's letter demanding more money was enough bad news for one day. Her response, however, was contained. "We'll have to speak later, sir. I have a scheduled call with my mama."

Not waiting for his reaction, she raced up the stairs to her room.

Purposely, Violet avoided Eric for the rest of the day. From the library window, she noticed him in the lavender garden speaking with Edward. He seemed agitated, almost furious. She wondered if Edward had expressed his dislike for Penelope, for her sake. Violet could not bear if her heartache brought ill feelings between the two brothers. She vowed to fix things by amending a friendly relationship with Eric. Aware Edward and his parents were again dining out, she'd take the opportunity to speak openly with Eric before dinner.

Her reconciliation was not meant to be. Simon informed her that Master Eric would also be absent at dinner that evening. Of course, he would be dining with Penelope. Violet was a trifle disappointed but welcomed the much-needed time to prepare a more convincing and gracious speech.

The next morning, after a night of rehearsing her congratulatory speech, she went looking for Eric. She was resigned and determined that if she could not have his love, at least she would keep his respect.

Inhaling the aroma of freshly baked scones, she made a U-turn in the direction of the conservatory for breakfast. She reasoned it would be better to confront Eric on a full stomach. Subconsciously, she was stalling.

"Violet, come," Catherine called out in a cheerful voice. "William has been commissioned as Eric's secretary this morning. We all must hear," she went on, half joking, "he asked his father to convey—what was it, dear?" At times, she enjoyed playfully teasing her husband.

William was amused with his wife and enjoyed her light-hearted humor. He played along by giving a most serious response to contrast Catherine's sense of humor.

"Eric had an urgent matter to attend to and left quite abruptly yesterday afternoon. He requested I let you all know he'll be back in a few days with a big announcement." William's delivery of the message was indeed professional; however, his facial expression relayed his own confusion. Obviously, the details of his son's message were as vague and puzzling to him as they were to the other three.

Catherine, now more subdued, voiced her concern to her husband. "I do wish he'd slow down. Eric seems like a man on an intense mission."

Reflecting on what Catherine might be insinuating, Violet's half-eaten scone had lost its taste.

The ability for us to live in the present is not easily achieved. Thoughts of our past or future come to disturb us. Life would have been much easier for Violet if only her focus was on today. She tried hard to embrace the "here and now" and enjoy every moment with Edward. Unfortunately, she couldn't quite hold on for long. Her thoughts kept flashing to a bleak future without her Edward and Eric.

This devastating storm in Violet's life could not be ignored much longer. Her heart was being relentlessly smashed against the rocks by the raging waves of reality. Her only recourse was to find shelter for her beaten heart; admittedly, the only refuge was to go back to Italy. With Eric's pending marriage and Edward and his parents leaving for America, she had to make a decision. Her life had come full circle; it was time to go back where she belonged. The love from her mama and sisters would sustain her. Violet had more than enough means and credentials to continue supporting her family. She would teach languages, mainly English to the Italian children, thereby enhancing their future possibilities.

As satisfying as these plans were, life without her Edward would be doleful. He kept insisting the timing was right for them to move on, but never actually agreed or encouraged her to return to Italy. She was confused; her mind was clouded and unable to read what Edward was not saying. One thing was certain: she disagreed about the timing. It did not feel right for her; she was not ready to let him go. Violet had always known one day they would separate; it was inevitable. *But not now. Not yet.*

CHAPTER 82

SECOND ENCOUNTER

Violet's greatest pleasure was her daily rigorous horseback ride with Edward, but today he stubbornly declined.

"Today you'll be better off without me, go on your own," he insisted repeatedly.

She suspected Edward was protecting himself from more of her probing and lamenting. All her persistence didn't change the stubborn adolescent's mind.

"You'll enjoy your day more without me," he kept saying.

"No! I will not," she wanted to scream before her horse galloped away.

No matter which route she took, Violet always found herself by the river. It had always been her sanctuary. Even Savannah, her beloved mare, intuitively knew where to go. Today her gloom was so intense she barely noticed what nature was offering. She rushed her dismount, desperately trying to shout off her mind and heart, both consumed with Eric. Sitting at the riverbank proved to be the wrong place for tranquility. The rapid flow of memories and her first kiss were again brutally beating at her. Her turbulent mind was relentless; it started to play tricks on her. She could swear she heard Eric's voice!

"I knew I'd find you here."

He sounded as though he was just behind her.

"You look so sad," the voice continued.

Violet stood and turned around.

Eric was so close their bodies brushed together.

"You're back," Violet whispered, stunned he was standing so near.

"I have to start making plans for my wedding." His words were precise.

She sat back down, not trusting her legs.

"What's wrong, sweet thing?" he asked. "Don't you believe two people who love each other deeply should get married?"

"Yes, sir. *Si*, you should marry the woman you love . . . if you're absolutely sure?" Violet hated that she questioned him.

"Yes, I'm sure," he confidently answered her; he reached out his hand, offering to help her stand. As he pulled her up, their faces were barely an inch apart, but neither moved. Eric seemed determined to say something and spoke hurriedly. "From the first moment my eyes set on her dripping wet body, standing right there." He pointed to the riverbank. "At that moment, I knew I wanted her to be my wife."

Eric tightened his grip to support Violet as the impact of his words sank in. "Eric!" was all she had time to say before his mouth covered hers.

Their passionate kiss was so intense they fell onto the grass. The fall did not separate them or stop their kissing. Violet didn't want her dream to end, and Eric rallied in his need for her. He kissed her with the hunger of a man who had been deprived nourishment for too long. He trembled as his lips sought every part of Violet's face.

"My whole being shivers with love for you, Violet. My heart and my soul need your nearness."

She felt a sense of rebirth as his words exploded inside her. With tears of joy streaming down her face, she gasped, "Eric!" Then whispered, "I love you more than life itself."

"You have shown me the depth of your love, my sweet thing. I am so sorry for all I put you through. Thank you for not leaving."

"I was convinced you were in love with Penelope, but my heart wouldn't let you go." Violet confessed.

"That was the plan. I had to make it seem sincere. I wanted her to fall deeply in love with me."

"Why, Eric! Why?"

"I understand your dilemma and want to explain it all in detail." He motioned for her to sit, indicating it would take a while. However, Eric's first statement was straightforward and revealed at once the climax. "Penelope is the manure-smelling woman."

The stunned look on Violet's face was infinite. She stared at Eric with her mouth open but speechless.

CHAPTER 83

THE REVEAL

Eric's eagerness to divulge all the sordid details had words rushing out. "When my good friend, her date, introduced us, I realized she was the ruthless woman who had ill-used Patrick. I was shocked she had the impudence to show up at my party. Later, her escort confided Penelope demanded he leave without her. She falsely told him I had insisted I be the one to drive her back home. Her ambiguous behaviour indicated this woman was still playing hurtful games. As you know, Patrick is fine now, and happily married, but what about her next victim? I worried Penelope could still manipulate and damage some of my other friends. I could not allow that to happen again to any of them. I assured my friend, the man she was now evidently using for her own gain, that I would take care of Penelope in just the right way."

Before continuing, Eric took Violet's hands as a gesture of apology. "I wanted and actually tried briefly to explain it to you, but realized it wasn't right. I could not include you in my scheme to discredit her. Besides, I knew as in all things, to succeed it had to be all or nothing. It nearly broke me to see you so sad. It was my faith in your love that kept me going."

Violet was delighted to have the man she loved grasp her inner character so profoundly. Eric's positive and unquestionable view of her love sealed their union ever so tight.

"When Penelope declared her love for me," Eric continued, "I literally laughed in her face. My words were harsh but nothing she didn't deserve. Determined she not misunderstand, I rudely spat my words out at her. I asked her directly, "Do you really believe I could love a manipulating, conniving, self-serving, deceitful woman like you?" The shock on her face was rewarding.

"Her rage was out of control; she tried to slap my face. I anticipated her attack and blocked her hand. Screaming, she threatened, 'My father will destroy you!'

"I remained calm, reminded her I am not to be trifled with. I said, "Remember, I have not laid a hand on you, not so much as a kiss. You are the one claiming to love me. I'm simply rejecting you." Then I thrust the key question at her: "How does it feel, Penelope, to be used? To have your feelings crushed, perhaps to the point you don't want to live?"

"'So that's what this is all about,' she said. She'd finally clued in, returning the attack. "Your stupid, weak friend!'"

"'No.' I exalted in informing her of Patrick's status. "My good friend is happily married. This lesson in life and relationships is all for your benefit. I hope now that you've had a taste of your own medicine, you'll end your deceitful, manipulative behavior."

"Regretfully, she continued her attack by trying to mock me. 'I'm not in love with you,' she said, 'never have been, just your money.'

"Her insincere defense made it all too clear; her arrogance was beyond redemption. I'd had enough of Penelope, and with no other option, I gave her a firm warning: "Your scheming days are over. Word gets around. Stay away from my friends. Everyone saw how you threw yourself at me. That was the reason I agreed to take you out every night. I wanted all your friends to see that Penelope doesn't always get her way. I'm sure you have lost most of your influence. If you continue, I will expose your conniving ways."

"With that said, I was done with her, I turned my back and left her standing outside her parent's front door."

Violet was ecstatic with all Eric had revealed. She didn't question his tactics but had to confirm one thing. "Really, Eric? Really, you never even kissed her?"

Eric laughed, shaking his head. "I thought you might catch that. How could I ever kiss her when I had tasted your sweet lips? Violet, you have my loyalty and my faithfulness."

As he was saying these words, Eric went down on one knee. "My sweet, fascinating lady, will you marry me?" Eric's proposal was given with deep longing in his voice.

Violet knelt beside him, tears of relief and joy parading down her cheeks. "*Si, Si, Si!*" She accepted with confidence that grew stronger with each "Yes." "I will be your wife!"

At that very moment, a gush of wind blew through the trees, freeing some brightly-colored foliage. As the leaves cascaded down, slowly they twirled around and around the couple; Eric and Violet seemed intertwined in a symbolic, heavenly blessing.

"Violet, my love, I have something I must confess." Eric's intensity to speak had Violet's full attention.

"Years ago, when I bought the music box for you, I had a hidden agenda. I hoped by listening to its melody you would think of me."

Violet was a bit embarrassed to admit her own fantasies. In time, she promised to reveal his plan had not only worked but had sustained her throughout the years. For now, she needed to hear more from him. "Why?" she asked.

"The time I spent with Edward, all he talked about was you. He raved about your wittiness, your caring, and your determination. He showed me pictures of all the fun times you shared together. I was captivated; how can one person have all those amazing qualities? You fascinated me."

Using their word, Eric revealed the first time he had thought of her in that way. "I had an enigmatic need to connect with you." He then showed her a picture he had tucked in his wallet. It was of her sitting by the river. "I've carried this with me for all these years."

Violet felt confused, thinking of all the chances he could have taken especially the day they literally crossed paths. "Why didn't you stop the day I arrived at the manor? We could've at least met face to face, even for a brief moment."

"You were so young, barely seventeen, and I had commitments in different countries. I believed once my eyes set on yours, I would not want to leave. I told Albert to accelerate, so I wouldn't have time to change my mind."

Violet felt a warm sensation tingling within her entire body. This revelation truly was fascinating; two people who never physically met sustained themselves for years with thoughts of the other. She supposed it wasn't totally uncommon. There were the pen pals and oversea relationships which ended in everlasting love. The obvious difference was that this couple had shared a mutual admiration. Eric and Violet had kept their feelings secret. This explained to her why their love had exploded so rapidly once they were alone together.

"I have missed you these past few days."

Eric's words had Violet cuddling next to him whispering, "Why did you leave, where did you go?"

"That, my love, was my gift to you. I noticed some frustration as you tried to conceal a letter, and instinctively I knew something was wrong. I saw Edward in the lavender garden and asked if he knew anything about it. He told me about the tavern owner in your hometown extorting money from you for years."

Again, she was impacted. "I never tol—" She stopped mid-word, not wanting to cast suspicion on Edward.

"Once Edward gave me all the details, I decided it was time I paid him a little visit. I asked two of my more intimidating friends to join me. The three of us showed up at his tavern and gave that crook eight hours to come up with all the money he extorted from you over the years."

Listening to Eric speak of that deplorable human being, Violet impulsively tightened her hands into double fists. Anxious, she wanted to know more. "Did you threaten him with the authorities?"

"Not exactly; just his miserable life."

"That works too." She laughed, envisioning the scene, and remembering what had happened to Ted, her other tormentor.

"Pasquale was shadowed so closely by the two rough-looking men; he managed to hand over the money in less than an hour."

"My friends left immediately after their job was done; I extended my stay, taking a small detour to another town." Eric's words were said incidentally, yet his mannerism was mischievous and energized, like an excitable toddler in a toy store. A broad smile indicated how pleased he was with the next piece of news. Casually, as though he was referring to the weather, he informed. "Your mother and sisters were most hospitable." He was staring into Violet's eyes, anticipating her reaction. He was not disappointed; instantly her face lit up like a night sky bursting with fireworks. All Eric had released was so spectacular, it left her temporarily speechless.

CHAPTER 84

DOING IT RIGHT

Violet's astonishment had restricted her vocal cords. She was unable to voice her appreciation.

Eric had no trouble speaking and was prepared to answer her unspoken question. "I wanted to do the proper thing, by ask your mother's permission for us to marry."

Violet wanted desperately to express her gratitude and forced herself to speak. Her words were again trapped by her overpowering emotions. "I . . . I . . . " was all she was able to get out. Her tears trickling down her face voiced her happiness.

Eric tenderly held her close. "Don't cry, my love. I had an extraordinary and enjoyable experience. Each of your sisters possess their own unique and special character. The one common quality they all share is your sweet disposition. Your mother impressed me with her remarkable stability. She nurtures an open mind and yet she is very decisive in her beliefs. I gave her your gift."

"Gift?" Violet's low, quivering voice barely made its way out. Her confused and curious stare was priceless.

Eric was not quite done astonishing her. He had become her personal magician, performing all these extraordinary acts. One by one, he continuously exposed unexpected gifts. Each reveal was more exceptional and thrilling than the previous, rendering Violet in a daze.

"Think about it my love. All the money you had 'saved' with Pasquale's 'help'?"

Eric embraced Violet and kissed the top of her head.

She held on to him possessively and let out a sigh.

"One last thing," he murmured over her head, allowing his voice to travel in the open air. "I've invited your family to our wedding next month." Tilting her chin up, looking into her eyes, he repeated, "Next month. I cannot wait much longer to make you my wife. Hopefully all this makes up for some of what I've put you through with Penelope?"

For years, Violet had masterfully fanaticized her life with Eric. This man she loved had not only met her expectations but surpassed them all. Exhilarated by Eric's love, the young lady couldn't hold back her emotions any longer. She embraced Eric's neck, bending his head towards her, and began aggressively kissing him.

"My lady, you must try to control yourself," he teased, holding her tighter.

"Never!" She responded with authority. "I am Italian! It's in my nature."

Violet's growing confidence was now hers to expose at will. For the first time, she was proud of every aspect of her life. Everything she had endured and accomplished had brought her to this moment. She would never again feel inferior to anyone. She told herself her personal needs and desires are as important as anyone else's.

Eric's broad smile confirmed he was pleased she'd finally exposed her true character. Embracing Violet in his arms, he exclaimed, "Excellent answer! I've always known you are a spirited young lady. I am so very proud of you, my love. You're resilient and determined yet sweet and modest, the perfect blend. Remember, sweet thing, never hide your emotions, your highs, or lows, don't hold back, especially with me."

CHAPTER 85

OFFICIALLY EDWARD'S SISTER

Back in her room, Violet's jubilant mind would not be contained. It kept reviewing every word Eric had revealed. The horrible, nightmarish life tormenting her was over. This new awakening had her overwhelmed and in total bliss. Her body began to dance about, and she giggled like a giddy child. It brought to mind Scrooge, Charles Dickens' character in *A Christmas Carol,* when he awoke to find he had not missed Christmas. This was a feeling of rebirth. To be given hope of great possibilities when all seemed to have been lost was pure joy!

The door adjoining Violet and Edward's room had bursts open hundreds of times in the last five years but never with such vigor. Her little man's anticipation was proudly unconfined as he walked in.

"Are you happy, sister?" Edward asked, obviously knowing the answer.

"I am ecstatic!" she sang out. "Too happy to even reprimand you."

"I'm sorry I couldn't make it easier for you. I didn't know how to explain what Eric was doing with Penelope. It really was confusing but knowing the outcome did make it easy for me." He gave his confession with a squeaky giggle.

Violet could not resist pouncing on him. She knew the worst punishment to inflict. Her torturous tickling had always been effective and enjoyable for her. Abruptly, Violet stopped their playful wrestling as a hypnotic look had set on her face. Opening her mouth, she enunciated his name slowly, as if spelling it out.

"Eddddwwwaaarrrd!" She hurriedly shook herself to reveal her lightbulb moment. "I will officially be your sister! How did I get to be so blessed?"

"You saved my life, remember?"

"No Edward, you saved my miserable life."

The young man let out his usual giggle. "We could argue who did what to who all night, or would you rather go see . . . Eric!" It was Edward's turn to tease Violet. He mimicked her voice while saying his brother's name amorously, revealing he had full knowledge of her fantasies. This was a climactic moment for our two protagonists; all they had shared had brought them to this place in time. Edward's face exposed a serenity Violet longed to see.

"I am relieved the charade is now all revealed." Edward's words told Violet it had not been easy for her little man to be so secretive. She took his hand, wanting to reassure him all was good between them.

Violet spoke openly, wanting to eliminate any guilt Edward might be feeling. "I not only understand your brotherly bond but encourage it."

She was about to include more but noticed Edward's mannerism and expression had suddenly changed. It was unmistakeable; she had seen him in this state hundreds of times. His body was still, his eyes glared in nothingness; for a few seconds he was lost in a total trance.

Violet was annoyed. What a convenient moment for him to be having a vision.

Blinking his eyes twice, as if refocusing, Edward looked directly at her and spoke in a mere whisper.

"Violet! Perhaps . . . just maybe . . . everything might all have been for Eric's benefit? If so . . . " Edward now took a strange pause, smiled, then added, "Eric should be the one thanking us both, don't you agree?" He had slyly switched to a more comical tone, concluding his observation with a casual, dismissive laugh. However, Edward's light-hearted delivery did not fool Violet. His insinuation lingered on in her intuitive mind. She pondered over his short summary, mostly his unusual question. Was their encounter, coming to live in England, all so she would marry Eric? Edward's visions were more intertwined than she could ever scrutinize.

Throughout the years, Violet had tried making sense of Edward's gift. Admittedly, all she really had done was accept his strange ability and help keep his secret. She had also believed Edward's decision not to share personal visions had originated from her request not to know, to allow life to unfold. Violet was now suspicious of Edward's true motive not to share. Recently, he had excluded her completely, revealing nothing. It seemed logical Eric had been his number one concern. Violet had no trouble with that theory; on the contrary, she resolved to stop questioning and further putting pressure on her little man. Regrettably, her mind didn't communicate her last decision fast enough, for the very next question Violet asked was a direct contradiction. "Edward, will your parents accept and be happy about Eric and me?"

Edward let out a sigh, showing his exasperation. "You cannot help yourself, can you? Haven't I proven I'm committed and determined not to speak of my visions?"

"Yes, Edward, you have, and I truly respect that. But—"

"No, Violet, no buts. Butts are to sit on." Edward always enjoyed laughing at his own jokes.

Having dealt with so much inner turmoil, Violet had generated a very serious persona. Her sense of playfulness had been suppressed for so long, she wasn't usually amused and simply shook her head. Today, of course, was different; a slight giggle managed to escape. She'd found her elusive happy button. Violet was now experiencing a bit of Lucia's character. Sad? Be sad! Happy? Embrace a good laugh. She was definitely happy and wanted the whole world to know of her happiness. Eagerly, she joined Edward in his hearty laugh, affirming she consented to his decision.

"I promise to stop forcing you to compromise for my benefit. Edward, your determination and perseverance have my complete support. I believe what you're trying to achieve is remarkable."

"Violet, you were my protector and teacher. Your encouragement and insistence to keep pushing my visions aside was instrumental. It allowed me to take control of my life." Edward's words constantly had double meaning; he'd answer questions she hadn't asked but thought about. He had consistently shone the light back on her, except Violet knew better. Giving him the advice was the easy part. Edward had undoubtedly worked tirelessly and endured much to accomplish this difficult feat.

"Let us both agree we helped and learned from each other. One thing I will demand of my little brother..." Violet's happiness radiated from her face. Extending her arms, she sang out, *"Un grande abracio."*

CHAPTER 86

FINALLY

Violet anticipated Eric's announcement at dinner would initially come as a surprise to both Mr. and Mrs. Sutton. Understandably so, she justified since she herself was still in a state of disbelief. However, her hopes were by evening's end they all would be in a celebratory mood. Not for one moment did the bride-to-be suspect the entire family would be thrown a curveball.

The dining table was already occupied when Edward, Violet, and Eric walked in the room. Catherine and William raised their eyebrows, not for the trio's tardiness, but rather questioning Eric's choice to sit parallel to Violet. According to proper etiquette, the chair was designated for Edward, yet the tolerant couple gave no verbal protest.

Violet desperately wanted to sit even closer to Eric and secretly hold his hand under the tablet. Edward's look related his decisive message: "Behave." It reminded the anxious young lady of all the stern looks she had given him over the years. Violet was fretting, anticipating Eric making their life-altering announcement. Her eyes constantly shifted towards him, in case of any advance signal from him to prepare herself.

Nothing out of the ordinary was discussed during the family's four-course meal. Eric's casual statement, "Violet has consented to be my wife," came as the family was savoring their crème brûlée. His announcement not only surprised the parents but got a gasp from the blushing bride-to-be.

William's face showed a hint of confusion as he whimsically asked his son, "Did I miss something? What about that bossy thing?" His simple but straight-to-the-point questions were meant to steer Eric on.

"Seriously, Father, never!" the son assured, indicating he was not playing his game. Eric's expression mirrored his displeasure at the svelte suggestion, even if his father meant it in jest.

Catherine's face beamed in delight as she proudly exclaimed, "My intuition was spot on. I sensed chemistry between you two from my first introduction in the library. I saw something in Eric's eyes I had never seen before."

William and Catherine's placidness indicated they were delighted with this astonishing news. Eric's declaration had them all now sharing smiles. However, Edward's casual comment not only removed their smiles but stunned the four at the table into complete dismay.

"I've known about them for a long while and even had glimpse of their wedding ceremony in my vision."

Dead silence filled the room as everyone exchanged stares. As though a door had flung open, they all inhaled deeply taking in the fresh air.

William stood and walked to his wife's side; he put both hands on her shoulders before saying slowly, "Finally."

A calming sense of relief radiated from everyone's faces, including Edward's. William's direct focus was on his young son as he added, "We have been aware of your gift for some time, Edward."

Catherine's gentle nod confirmed her own awareness to the boy.

There was an urgency in William now; he eagerly continued to explain in detail. "Comments from my good friend Inspector O'Brien caused us to question certain things. O'Brien related he hadn't a clue how to prove Betty's innocence. He confessed that it was the two children that literally led him to the evidence." He was impressed, mostly bewildered, by your keen perception. Perhaps, O'Brien spoke in jest, but he suggested the children possessed supernatural powers. We of course dismissed the humorous conversation with a good laugh. It wasn't until much later, as your mother and I discussed the whole ordeal, we began to question other events. All the nightmares, all the baffled doctors; it was all there, right in front of us and misunderstood for years.

"Edward, your mother and I believed getting you professional help was the right thing to do. We were afraid of making mistakes and handling it all wrong, which we obviously did."

"Your father and I struggled with it for a while." Catherine sounded just as apologetic as her husband. "We wanted to question you but felt it best to leave things as they were for a while longer. Our fear was of making an even worse error by confronting you, thereby forcing you to explain when you evidently were not ready."

William focused his eyes on Violet. "You both handled it so well; we didn't want to ruin all your hard work, Violet."

This was now her opportunity to confess. Lowering her head in guilt for deceiving them, she spoke sincerely. "I don't know what to say except that I am very sorry."

A firm "No" came from both Mr. and Mrs. Sutton, stopping her from saying more.

"Please do not apologize to us my dear, we totally understand," said William. "At the time you were a mere child yourself and believed Edward needed protection from everyone. Your decisions and actions were based on your commitment to our son's safety and well-being. We commend your selflessness and appreciate how difficult it all had to have been. Especially the remarkable way you secretly handled unexpected situations."

Eric had been holding Violet's hand the whole time. He squeezed it even tighter to confirm his own awareness and agreement with his father.

Edward had remained silent, patiently waiting for it all to be said. He then stood, walked over, and hugged his parents.

The first words from their young son were a heartfelt, "Thank you." Edward then continued with his gratitude by acknowledging all they had given him. "Your deep love and concern for me is the reason we're all here today. You listened to my request and arranged for Violet to come live with us. That was the most essential decision made in my life. Your need to make me happy and give me serenity brought home the secret cure."

The praise Edward gave his parents was not only deeply appreciated by them, but also Violet. She wanted Edward to relate that without Mr. and Mrs. Suttons' support and trust, none of it would have been possible.

"I know it was especially difficult giving me the privilege to tell you in my own time. Thank you again for putting me first." Edward walked back to his chair, before continuing. "What I need now is for everyone to believe I'm completely capable of handling my visions on my own. With Violet's help I've achieved control over them, and I've been on my own for some time now. Violet, you have taught me well, and I'm so grateful." Edward paused before saying his final thought. "Now! The rest is up to me."

"Son," William addressed him with pride and respect. "Your mother and I will support your decisions. We want to help in any way possible. Please let us make up for our ignorant past. Your well-being is all we have ever wanted. If ever you want or need help, don't hesitate to come to us."

With that said, William, buzzed for Simon. "Tonight, our family has a lot to celebrate, bring out Champagne. Make sure to bring up enough for the staff. We want to share and celebrate our happiness with all the household."

The Champagne was served in the drawing room.

"What an unexpected perfect evening this turned out to be!" William generated an aura of bliss as he raised his glass to give a heartfelt toast. "To our Violet, the sweet child I have always loved as my own precious daughter. It is with great joy and satisfaction to know you will soon officially be a Sutton. To my son Eric, for choosing the perfect woman for his wife. We are proud of the man you have become and all you have achieved. And our special Edward, for his courage to handle what his extraordinary talent brings his way."

Filled with bubbly Champagne, the crystal flutes clinked, echoing everyone's happiness. Ensuring the evening continued blissfully, the wedding was the only topic discussed. Never before had the Suttons' conversations been more lax yet excitable with anticipation.

Catherine whispered into Violet's ear, "I am happy for you, my dear; mostly for Eric for all the love you will bring into his life."

Violet was so touched by Catherine's words she was rendered speechless. She demonstrated her appreciation by affectionately hugging Catherine and kissing her on both cheeks.

Sinking into her soft bed that evening, Violet pressed her lips on the ring adorning her finger. Eric had slipped it on just before they kissed good night.

"This was my mother's," he whispered. "I know she would want you to have it." He sealed the moment by tenderly caressing and kissing the palms of both her hands.

Violet felt as though a divine force had lifted a huge boulder from her chest. Penelope was gone, Pasquale was no more, Eric's and her love had been declared to both families, and the burden of Edward's secret had been shared.

"Edward, my precious Edward," she repeated. There was no doubt in her mind he had not slipped up but rather chosen that particular moment to reveal his secret. She marveled how impeccable his timing truly was. With the family soon venturing in separate directions, the secret had to be exposed. Edward's boast of having control was for his parents' benefit. It was his way of giving them all peace of mind. He wanted to reassure and release them from any burden. Before falling into a sound sleep, Violet listened to her music box, whispering to herself, "Mrs. Eric Sutton."

CHAPTER 87

THE WEDDING GUESTS

With the wedding just a month away, Catherine briefed her staff with detailed schedules. Simon hired more than his usual help to handle the extra duties to support the manor's regular staff. This time he added five expert seamstresses to come assist the American designer. Lucia, while speaking with Violet on the phone, had confessed her request was unexpected, then immediately screamed for joy, adding, "I'm up for the challenge and thrilled to be doing it."

Everyone would be kept busy getting things done within the short timeline and specifications. Eric and Violet, the "lovebirds," as Edward had dubbed them, had their own "to-do" list. Sending out invitations, speaking with the caterers, and choosing their wedding cake were but a few requiring urgent attention.

Edward's biggest chore was to stay out of everyone's way. He admitted watching all this unfold was much more exciting than his own sneak preview. Starting school, a month late was of no consequence; he'd simply unearth more fossils. He seemed calm, enjoying everyone in their mad rush to get everything ready in only one month.

The arrival of the special guests weeks prior to the wedding had Sutton Manor bursting with youthful energy. Violet's mama and her seven daughters flew in from Italy, accompanied by Rosa's fiancé

Giuseppe, and old Padre Giovanni. The Johnsons of course brought Lucia and also included Sue and Lorna in their entourage.

The dinner table was anything but formal. Everyone was too happy to care what he or she should wear or which fork to use.

Raising his glass, Harry Johnson toasted four deserving individuals. "Here's to Violet's good sense to hold out for Eric. By far the best man, and to my Catherine for choosing William." He then added in his most precocious voice, "Here's to all you lovely young ladies. I am overwhelmed by your beauty and vitality."

Abigail was always ready to shake her head when her husband spoke. She had a consistent look, her eyes scolding, yet in total contrast, her mouth was in a constant smile. Her expression was a perfect example of an oxymoron. The young ladies' giggles gave Harry exactly what he aimed for.

Sleeping arrangements were made simple for the staff. Violet's sisters were astounded by the size of the rooms and insisted they all share two adjoining rooms. Maria would share Violet's quarters to avoid being the girls' disciplinarian. This would allow them to have fun and Maria her rest. Sue, Lorna, and Lucia resided in the north wing of the manor. They shared a large sitting area with three adjoining but private bedrooms. The three had become well acquainted with each other on the flight. Sue and Lorna were very much impressed with Lucia's fashion designs and quickly became friends. They admired her talent and seriously discussed interest in opening a business together. The guest cottage off the lavender garden was reserved for Giuseppe and Padre Giovanni.

"Exhilarating," "exciting," "chaotic": three words that definitely described the ladies' shopping days. The men clearly expressed they'd rather do anything *but* go shopping.

"It's bad enough shopping with one female; a dozen would be capital punishment." Harry's tone was serious; he didn't even attempt to be humorous when he added, "I'm speaking for all men."

William was less dramatic. "I've made arrangements for us to enjoy the great outdoors with some hunting and fishing."

In truth, the female group had no need nor desire to be accompanied by any male. They all agreed serious shopping was an art form, best accomplished by females only. It required stamina, creativity, and concentration, all which are lost if worrying about a whining, bored man. They simply wanted leverage to use later and therefore allowed the men to believe they had gotten away with something.

Everyone had an opinion; there was over a dozen suggestion on colors and accessories for the bridal party. Ultimately, all but one agreed with the choices made by the soon-to-be bride. Little Angelina, her flower girl, was determined and couldn't be persuaded. She had fallen in love with a bright red, puffy tutu and held it tightly in her arms to affirm her decision. Big sister offered to buy it only if little sister promised to wear it the night before the wedding. A toothless smile signaled Angelina's joy and ultimate agreement.

Watching her families' excitement was a dream come true for Violet. She thought back to her very first day at the manor, twirling in delight in her magnificent room. She had desperately wished to share it all with them. Being able to now give them what money could buy was beyond her wishes, but admittedly not as essential as she once believed. Violet understood her mama's happiness and worry-free expression had nothing to do with any monetary gifts; it was attributed to the one gift granted from her soon-to-be son-in-law.

Eric had shown respect; he'd agreed to give Maria what she most desired for her daughter's wedding. Padre Giovanni would be officiating the marriage ceremony in Italian. Besides the fact that Padre was Maria's first cousin, he had also baptized Violet and all her sisters. This consideration meant everything to Maria. She could now relax and treasure every moment of Eric and Violet's wedding.

The only other request Maria did make was in relation to her other passion: gardening. She suggested Violet's and her sisters' flower bouquets coincide with their names. As for Angelina's basket, it would be filled with petals from all the various flowers. Everyone loved what Maria proposed, especially Catherine. She complimented Maria on how uniquely appropriate her creative idea was. The humble woman was not used to praise. She quickly responded to Mrs. Sutton, expressing what a fine and extraordinary lady she was. Maria also took the opportunity to personally thank Mrs. Sutton for *everything*. The mutual appreciation and admiration both women shared stemmed from their maternal bond to Violet. Still, communicating their gratitude for one another proved difficult. Instinctively, the two mothers chose not to make the other uncomfortable. They demonstrated their union by supporting Violet, making sure the focus was totally on their daughter and her special day.

Lucia's design for Rosa, the matron of honor, and the five bridesmaid dresses, thrilled Violet's sister. A deep purple velvet was chosen for the top of the gowns. A 'V' cut neckline was perfect to showcase the pearl necklace with a drop diamond pendant. The extravagant necklaces with the matching earrings were the bride's gift to her sisters.

Lucia had cleverly taken the young girls' individual personalities into consideration, thereby modifying each dress design to suit their particular preference. The intricate placement of either pearls, sequins, or ribbons on the fitted three-quarter-length sleeves had each dress stand out. A full-length light purple, shimmery taffeta bell skirt would also be adorned differently at the waist. Each young lady would have their own choice on a specific belt.

Abigail marveled and praised Lucia's talent. She expressed to Catherine and Maria how elegant, and age appropriate the designs were for the young bridal party. The sisters were thrilled; never had they imaged owning such a magnificent gown.

When Violet entered the library wearing her gown for the final fitting, all the ladies reacted with raw emotions. The bride-to-be looked majestic! As though a freeze button had been pushed, movement from her admirers suddenly stopped. Their stillness had them resembling mannequins in a display window. Tears continuously trickling from their eyes magically boosted them back to life. Their silence was broken as they reached for handkerchiefs. An abundance of genuinely flattering words flew out from everyone's mouths. Violet began waltzing around the room, deliberately accentuating Lucia's breathtaking, one-of-a-kind wedding gown.

The wide bateau neckline exposed Violet's shoulders to emphasized her long delicate neck. A fitted, elongated, soft smile-shaped satin basque complimented her small waist. It was completely embellished with tiny pearls sewed around leaf-shaped crystals. The full shantung raw silk ballgown flowed, spreading its cathedral-length train halfway across the room. The scalloped-lace bottom was meticulously decorated with crystals and pearls.

Violet opened her arms wide, inviting Lucia to come to her embrace. "You are brilliant!" Violet proclaimed loudly. "The dress is spectacular, more than I could ever dream!"

Her praise humbled Lucia into silence, but only for a moment. That was all the time her ebullient character would permit. She cheerfully shouted, "The best for the best. I produced what you most definitely deserved."

Then she added softly for Violet's ears only, "I also give you my lifetime of gratitude and friendship."

CHAPTER 88

THE PAST AND THE FUTURE

News of the upcoming wedding spread happiness through the village. The residents were delighted and blessed the happy couple. They were relieved to hear the sweet little girl they had grown to love would be the next generation's Mistress of Sutton Manor.

In keeping with the mode to support their local businesses, most of the wedding supplies were purchased from the local merchants. A few specialty items need from London were ordered by the merchants themselves. This practice encouraged the rest of the villagers to do the same. "Buy local" was a time-honored mantra. It helped the small hamlet flourish.

Eric and Violet expressed their desire to the villagers who so wished to be included in celebrating their wedding day. To accommodate the festivities, a big tent would be set up in the town's main square. Eric generously financed the merchants to ensure an abundance of food and drink. The couple wanted to ensure their wedding day be fun and memorable for all.

Two days before their nuptials, Violet noticed a hint of sadness in Eric's eyes. One thing she was certain of was that Eric was not having second thoughts about marrying her. In truth, she had never imagined devotion such as his. She considered asking Edward for clarity but stopped herself. The privileges she wanted were unfair to both brothers. Besides, she had promised Edward she would stop. His own behavior had also demonstrated he had perpetually sealed his lips. "I know nothing," was now his favorite phrase. Violet knew deep down Edward's decision was for everyone's benefit. She would have to rely on her own abilities and be straight and open with the man she loved.

Eric gave Violet a questioning smile when she voiced her concern. "I didn't think it showed," he responded.

"Just to me, my love, just to me." Violet caressed him gently.

Eric's eyes held Violet's gaze, "I have been thinking about my mother," he explained. "I'd like us to visit her grave together tomorrow."

In silence, she eloquently and symbolically kissed him gently on his cheek. "I have the perfect flowers to bring her. I want to thank her for having such a wonderful son and also make her a solemn promise."

The understanding between them didn't need words to explain what promise Violet intended to make.

After dinner that evening, family and guests scattered in several directions, all having their own agenda. Violet noticed William and Eric standing by the dining room window having a quiet conversation that ended in a warm embrace. Eric then left his father and immediately walked over to her. He didn't say a word, simply took her hand, gesturing he wanted his future bride to accompany him. The eager young lady was most curious, wondering where and why she was being lead, but decided to play along. She'd hold back from asking any questions, patiently waiting for Eric's readiness. Neither spoke, as they walked hand in hand through a narrow corridor on the east side of the manor. Eric stopped as they reached a steep staircase. It led to one of the lower attics of the mansion.

"Come, sweet thing," Eric released the soft voice from within his chest. "I need to show you this special room. No," he corrected, sounding melancholy, "I *want* to show you."

Violet recognized this distinctive tone in Eric's voice; it sounded nostalgic! She had experienced it herself many times at Christmases, birthdays, and special celebrations. Nostalgia, the intense feeling of longing for absent loved ones in times of joy. Violet genuinely wanted to help Eric with this personal reveal. She hoped her reaction would be appropriate and relieve some of his sadness. With the key still in the lock, Eric paused before opening the door. He lifted Violet's lowered chin and brushed a gentle kiss on her lips, filling the somber moment with love. "It's all good," he reassured.

They entered a massive room bursting with furniture and ornamental treasures. In reverence, Eric kept his voice low, as one would entering a church. "These were all my mother's personal belongings. She did not have a daughter to pass them down to, but now she does. Violet, I am giving everything to you to do with as you wish." Eric spoke as his eyes traveled through the entire space.

Still holding her hand, he guided towards a wooden chest-of-drawers. Opening the first drawer, he exposed a sliver chest full of jewelry. His eyes watered as he opened a blue velvet box displaying a pearl necklace. "I would like you to wear these on our wedding day."

"Oh, Eric! I am overwhelmed." Violet's voice quivered. "They are exquisite." She buried her face deep in his chest and murmured, "I have nothing to give you."

He lifted her face with the tip of his fingers and shook his head. There was something in Eric's expression Violet had not seen before: vulnerability. "You, Violet, you are my gift. You giving yourself to me is more then I dared dream. You are the essence of love, purity, and sweetness. You are my rare gem." Eric took Violet's hand and sat with her on an empty divan. "Violet, I want to reveal a side of me I've never shared. For years, I have shielded my heart so it would not be broken. My fear of losing hindered any kind of loving relationship; therefore, I chose to keep my distance. It obviously arose from the loss of my mother. I am sure Edward suffered from my detachment. The barrier I had built around my heart lost its resistance the day I met you. Thinking of you from a distance was conveniently safe. Having your love was so powerful it broke through, awakening my senses. I now have relinquished my fears. I realized how terribly wrong I had been. To push love out of one's life for fear of losing it is by far the greater loss. Sharing my life, my love, with you fulfills me. Thank you, sweet thing, for restoring my heart and soul."

Eric's sincere proclamation gave Violet what she in turn hoped for: her constant desire to be needed.

CHAPTER 89

A NIGHT OF ANTICIPATION

The honored guest participating in the rehearsal dinner the night before the wedding enjoyed an abundance of camaraderie and laughter. Eric's friends escorted and pampered Lorna, Sue, and Lucia. The ladies were immediately charmed by the men and vice versa. Promises were made, or at least implied. Violet playfully winked at her friends, hinting she approved.

Later that evening, the bridegroom left with his friends to spend the night in London. Catherine had made arrangement for a few local beauticians to come and pamper the young ladies with various services. As night turned into the next day, the overly-stimulated young ladies' shenanigans had transformed the place into a carnival. Maria finally had to pull the "mother card," sweetly but firmly sending everyone to bed.

After taking a leisurely bath, Violet entered her chamber to finding her mama waiting. Flipping her bed covers to one side, Maria smiled and invited her child to lay beside her.

"Come here, my little one" she said, making room for Violet in her bed. Neither felt awkward; even after years of separation, mother and daughter were serene in each other's arms. Maria let out a sigh, kissing her firstborn's forehead. *"Violetta mia."* Maria spoke in her dialect. "You have been an inspiration, not only to your sisters, but also to me. Your courage and generosity have sustained us. Your support gave us the strength and ability to succeed in our own lives. I am sure you will be a devoted wife and loving, caring mother. I see Eric deeply loves you; more importantly, he respects you. He is a gentle and giving man. I know you will share an amazing life together. I could not be happier. You are my pride and my joy. God blessed me the day you were born. *Grazie figlia mia* . . . thank you, my daughter."

These words of praise from her mother were the same that kept her going all her life. Knowing she was loved unconditionally had strengthened her character. This had been her mama's most precious gift to her.

Fearing her reply would probably get drowned by tears, the child simply cuddled closer. This show of affection was comforting, familiar to both mother and child.

CHAPTER 90

JOYOUS CEREMONY

The bridal procession was definitely unique. One by one, six sisters walked in with confidence and poise. Held perfectly in place, their personalized flower bouquets boasted each of the young ladies' names. Combs decorated with purple violets held back their lustrous, long, black hair.

The energetic seventh sister, little Angelina, in a white princess dress, resembled a mini bride. Her basket, dangling from her arm, overflowed with the petals from the various flowers. She giggled timidly as she grabbed her first handful of petals. She then proceeded to spread them generously over the carpet, as rehearsed.

The congregation stood when the organ music announced the bride's entrance. All eyes were on the bride. The enthusiastic guests did not hold back their delight. Violet looked radiant; her left arm tucked under Mr. Sutton's right arm. Her right hand held firmly her elaborate bouquet. The deep purple orchids cascading down the front of her white gown were striking in contrast. Anchoring her twenty-foot veil was a royal tiara. Catherine and William had been bold enough to make their humble request to their longtime friend. It was to represent the traditional "something borrowed."

Today, Violet was determined to focus and master being in the moment. She wanted to cherish every second and tuck it away in her memory box.

William smiled at her and affectionately squeezed her arm with his own. Speaking softly for Violet's ears only, he said "Thank you for giving me the privilege of escorting you down the aisle. I feel honored and proud."

Violet took a deep breath before using a word she'd never said before. "Thank you, Dad," She affectionately gave him the most intimate, beloved title possible.

As they took their first step forward, William complimented her in Italian. *"Violetta! Sei splendente!"*

The bride stared straight ahead. What she saw on Eric's face would remain imprinted in her heart and mind forever. Love beaming from his eyes ignited her soul.

At the altar, William lifted Violet's *vizo*, veil. He gently placed a kiss on her forehead as a sign of his blessing. Edward stood beside them to take part in the next symbolic exchange. Together with his father, they placed Violet's hand into Eric's open palm. Edward then took his official post as his older brother's best man.

The ceremony was entirely in Italian and when the priest announced, "I now present Mr. and Mrs. Eric Sutton!" the overcrowded church erupted with applause and cheers. The newlyweds were showered with rice, Italian *cumpete,* and money before getting into their automobile.

CHAPTER 91

MEMORABLE SENDOFF!

Their ride back to the manor had the new husband and wife amazed and humbled. Both sides of the road were lined with hundreds of people cheering and throwing flowers. This unexpectedly boisterous show of unity, support, and loyalty by the villagers was heartfelt and greatly valued by the young couple.

The elaborate reception party exceeded even Catherine's expectations. Everyone who contributed had done so with the utmost care and diligence. The guests swarmed the couple with warm hugs, congratulations, and best wishes.

Violet's three American friends rushed toward her, screaming how beautiful she looked. They complimented on how extraordinary everything was, especially Eric's friends. Sue admired the brilliance of the diamonds on the princess-style tiara. Lorna raved how Violet's snow-white wedding gown accentuated the deep purple color of the bridesmaids' dresses. Lucia gushed how Violet's beautiful figure gave prominence to her one-of-a-kind design.

The Johnsons gave their heartfelt blessings. Harry, of course, did not stop there. He reminded them all about his original observation.

"I was correct calling you Snow White. You reign over your seven sisters. And! You enchanted your Prince Charming."

Harry's boastful laughter alerted Catherine and William to rescue the speechless but amused bride. "Violet, your husband," Catherine smiled, embellishing the word "husband," "is looking for you." She then gave her father an endearingly look and led the bride away.

She seized the moment to give Violet a little send-off speech. "Throughout the years, you have brought me so much joy. Thank you for the privilege of being your adopted mother. Violet, you have always been exceptional. I couldn't imagine a better daughter."

Violet treasured Catherine's words, knowing they were sincere and came from her heart.

As they hugged, Catherine whispered, "Don't wait too long to give me precious grandchildren. I am overjoyed to think Sutton Manor will once again hear the sound of little feet."

It was almost time for the couple to take their leave. Violet's sisters surrounded her, asking questions, kissing her, not wanting to let her go.

Maria, firm but tender, had to step in. "Let Violet go to her husband." As she spoke, Maria had trouble containing her own emotions and burst into tears of joy.

Edward took pictures of the family embracing. He then grabbed Violet's hand and pulled her away. He led her to one of the many secret places they used to hide in as children.

"My head and heart are full of your joy." Edward's words sounded like song lyrics. "I'm so happy for you."

Violet smiled, remembering how much they had shared together.

Edward shook his head. "Did you really believe I would leave you before it was all completed? I kept telling you the timing was right," he smiled. "You now will have a different kind of partner. One you will love and care for like you did me."

Violet marveled at her little man with his enormous abilities and insights.

"I saw all this unfold and, as hard as it was, I never told you. I respected your beliefs, Violet, to let life unfold on its own. I hope this proves I really am in control, and you must not worry about me any longer. We have a unique bond between us. Our lives connected for a multitude of reasons. You will always be a big influence in my life. The fact you married my brother just adds another layer to the depth of our union."

Violet interpreted several meanings to Edward's profound message. However, she had to express what she knew was true, along with her thanks. "You brought me here and gave me this amazing life. Edward, you did save me from a life of misery."

Shaking his head, Edward answered. "Violet, I believe you are where you're meant to be. No one, including me, controls destiny. Our actions may alter how we get there. The choices we make may cause our journey to go rocky or smooth. Ultimately, it's all been mapped out by a higher power."

Violet had another epiphany. She was in awe as never before with her brother. "Your visions, Edward, are only part of your uniqueness. To have such knowledge and wisdom at your age is an astonishing gift. Your sense of what is good and just is also another one of your great abilities."

Edward's eyes peered into Violet's. "That," he said, "I learned from your example. You taught me goodness."

Neither said more. They hugged, knowing their past, their present, and their future would always be intertwined.

CHAPTER 92

THEIR STORY BEGINS

It was Albert honking the Rolls Royce's horn that alerted Violet and Edward to return.

Eric extended his arms as his bride approached him. "Come, my sweet, you must go change and throw your bouquet."

Shamelessly, a bevy of squealing young women reached for the symbolic bouquet. Lucia was the lucky lady, jumping up and down with the beautiful orchids. She kissed Violet on both cheeks and squeezed her hard, saying, *"Grazie, grazie per tutto."*

Violet whispered Edward's words: "Lucia, you are where you were meant to be."

Everyone waved enthusiastically as the Rolls Royce pulled away, horn honking. This was the same automobile that had driven that runty little girl to her new destiny.

Albert met Violet's eyes in the rear mirror and smiled. Earlier he had conveyed his best wishes and happiness. "I've always known you were a resilient little girl and a very special young lady. Thank you for proving me right."

"I am very honored to be part of your life. You deserve your happy ending." Violet respectfully hugged and assured him, "You are my friend for life."

FORESEEN

In the bridal suite of the Ritz hotel in Paris, Eric uncorked a bottle of French Champagne. He poured some of the bubbly in a wide, crystal glass for his bride and toasted to their happiness.

"Our lives together will be an adventure," he promised. "We will travel the world and live life to its fullest. Mostly we will respect and support each other. Violet, you are my everything, and from this day on, my love, for you it will be even more transparent. I will not say 'I love you.' Instead, I will ask, 'Violet did you feel my love today'?"

Violet, with the poise of an elegant lady but the glow of a sweet child, answered, "Yes, Eric, my husband."

Our ending. Their beginning!

Printed in the USA
CPSIA information can be obtained
at www.ICGtesting.com
JSHW022024100923
48064JS00001B/3